The Guardian

JUL 1 5 1997

Joan Wolf

The Guardian

WHEELER
PUBLISHING, INC.
ROCKLAND, MA

★ AN AMERICAN COMPANY ★

Published in Large Print by arrangement with
Warner Books, Inc.
in the United States and Canada.

Wheeler Large Print Book Series.

Set in 16 pt. Plantin.

Library of Congress Cataloging-in-Publication Data

Wolf, Joan
    The guardian / Joan Wolf.
        p. (large print) cm.(Wheeler large print book series)
    ISBN 1-56895-454-9 (large print)
    1. Large type books. I. Title. II. Series
[PS3573.O486G82 1997]
813'.54—dc21   97-16195
                                                   CIP

For Patty, Eileen and Peggy: we band of sisters

The Guardian

CHAPTER
one

My God, my God, my God, he's reading Gerald's will.

It was as if someone had just dealt me a sudden and stunning blow to the head.

I stared at the lawyer standing in front of the closely clustered family group, and my fingers closed convulsively around each other in my lap.

I thought again, with shocked comprehension, He's reading Gerald's will.

I think it was the first time I truly understood that my husband was dead.

A deep voice from the chair next to mine murmured, "Are you all right, my dear?"

I pressed my lips firmly together and nodded. Uncle Adam reached over to pat my clenched hands gently, and then he returned his attention to Mr. MacAllister. The dry, dispassionate, legal voice droned on:

"In the event any part of my estate becomes payable to my son, Giles Marcus Edward Francis Grandville, before he attains the age of twenty-one, a separate trust shall be established for him, to be held by a Guardian, hereinafter named, upon the following terms, conditions, and for the following purposes."

As Giles was only four years of age, it came as no surprise to me that the estate would be tied up for him in a trust.

Giles was the earl of Weston now. Gerald was

dead. I drew a long, unsteady breath and stared fixedly at the splendid green and white marble chimney piece that rose behind Mr. MacAllister's long, narrow head.

I had not been prepared for this kind of emotional reaction to the reading of the will. Perhaps that was why it had happened, I thought. It had caught me unaware.

The last few days I had felt as if I were living through an unreal nightmare.

After Gerald's death, the servants had shrouded the house in black, and for twenty-four hours his body had lain in state in the Great Hall. All day long neighbors and tenants had filed past his coffin. Then, yesterday, hundreds of black-robed mourners had formed a great funeral cortege from the house to the church. Giles had been beside me all during the church service, and his small hand had held tightly to mine when the vicar had said the prayers over the casket before it was lowered into the vault that already held six earls of Weston.

Giles had helped me. I had needed to be calm for him.

But Giles was not here today. Nor were there hundreds of eyes watching me. And Mr. MacAllister was reading Gerald's will. I breathed deeply, moved my eyes to the lawyer's face, and struggled to focus my attention.

Mr. MacAllister was still on the topic of the trust: "The Guardian herein named shall have the power to manage, sell at public or private sale, lease for any terms, or otherwise convey without the order of any Court, and to invest and reinvest the trust property..."

It seemed unbelievable to me that my little son was now the earl of Weston.

The atmosphere in the room changed subtly. I sensed a faint rustle, as of people coming to stricter attention. I brought my own attention back to Mr. MacAllister and realized that he was coming to the naming of Giles's Guardian.

Mr. MacAllister sensed the drama of the occasion and paused. He glanced up from the long, legal document he was holding and let his eyes run consideringly around the semicircle of faces assembled before him in the library of Weston Hall.

There were not many of us. I sat in the middle with Uncle Adam and his wife, Fanny, on one side of me and my mother on the other side. On the far side of Mama was Gerald's uncle Francis Putnam, and next to him was Gerald's cousin, Jack Grandville. The rest of the Grandville family had returned home directly after the funeral.

Mr. MacAllister returned his gaze to Gerald's will and began to read slowly and clearly: "I hereby name, constitute, and appoint my brother, Stephen Anthony Francis Grandville, as Trustee and Guardian for my son, Giles Marcus Edward Francis, and Executor of this my Last Will and Testament..."

There was more, but we didn't hear it.

"*Stephen!*" Jack's voice completely drowned out Mr. MacAllister's nasal drone. "Gerald can't have named Stephen!"

Mr. MacAllister lowered his document and looked at Jack over the rims of his spectacles. "I assure you, Mr. Grandville, the earl did most

3

certainly name his brother, Stephen. I was the one who made the will for him, so I should know."

Mama's clear, cool voice made itself heard next. "Stephen is in Jamaica," she said. "He has been in Jamaica these last five years. He cannot possibly act as Giles's guardian from halfway around the world. You will have to name someone else, Mr. MacAllister. I cannot imagine what Gerald was thinking when he named Stephen."

Mr. MacAllister said calmly, as if he were totally unaware that he was dropping a keg of lighted gunpowder into our midst, "Mr. Stephen Grandville will have to be called home to assume his responsibilities. In fact, I have taken it upon myself to write and apprise him of the contents of Lord Weston's will."

"Well, that was damn cheeky of you, MacAllister," Jack said furiously. His handsome face was flushed with anger.

"One of the family should inform Stephen of his brother's death." For once my mother agreed with Jack; she had always been a stickler for form. "Such news should not come from an attorney."

"I also wrote to Stephen about Gerald's death," Uncle Francis said quietly. "Both letters will doubtless arrive in Jamaica on the same boat."

"Suppose he refuses to come back?" Jack said. "After all, he could still be arrested for that escapade of five years ago, couldn't he?"

"There was never any question of an arrest," Mr. MacAllister said coldly. "The authorities were fully satisfied by his father's promise to have him leave the country."

"No charges were preferred," Uncle Adam agreed. "Stephen is perfectly free to return to England should he choose to do so."

My mother turned to me and demanded, "Did you know Gerald had named Stephen, Annabelle?"

"No, I did not." I looked at the family attorney. "When was this will executed, Mr. MacAllister?"

"Shortly after Giles was born, Lady Weston," he replied gently.

I pressed my lips together and tried to keep my face blank.

Mr. MacAllister attempted to reassure me. "Mr. Stephen Grandville is to be Giles's guardian, Lady Weston, but I can assure you it was always Lord Weston's intention that the care of your son should remain with you."

I nodded.

"I cannot understand why Gerald did not name Adam," Mama said.

I stood up. "This discussion is pointless. Gerald named Stephen. I am quite certain, however, that when Gerald made this will he had every expectation of living well beyond Giles's majority." My voice shook treacherously. "I am going upstairs," I said.

"Mr. MacAllister has not finished with the will, Annabelle," my mother said.

I didn't answer. I simply walked out the door.

The dogs were waiting for me in the hall passageway, and as usual they trailed close behind me as I went up the stairs to the nursery, which was situated on the third floor of the house. I looked first into the schoolroom and

5

found it empty. The dogs and I went along the corridor, past the governess's room, and into the playroom. There I found my son and his governess, Miss Eugenia Stedham, sitting at a table, putting together a puzzle of a map. I had allowed Giles to resume his regular daily schedule today, hoping that after five days of mourning, the familiarity would help him cope with his grief.

Giles pushed back his chair the moment he saw me. "Mama!" he cried, and came running to throw himself against me. The dogs went to curl up on the blue hearth rug in front of the unlit fire.

I caressed the back of my son's head, rejoicing in the feel of his strong, sturdy body pressed against my legs, his face buried in my stomach. I looked at his governess and said, "I think that Giles and I will go for a walk this afternoon, Miss Stedham."

Giles pulled away from me and clapped his hands. "A walk! Just what I would like to do, Mama."

"Have you eaten your luncheon?" I asked him.

He nodded, his gray-green eyes bright with anticipation. "I ate it all," he said.

Miss Stedham had gotten to her feet. "It is rarely a problem to get Giles to finish his meals," she said.

I smiled for the first time that day.

"Let Miss Stedham dress you warmly, Giles," I said to my son. "It may be sunny, but it's still rather cold."

Miss Stedham said, "When shall I have him ready, Lady Weston?"

"Right away." I ruffled my son's sleekly

6

brushed hair. "Come along to my dressing room when you're ready, Giles. I have to change my clothes, too."

"All right, Mama." He turned to Miss Stedham. "Come on, Genie. Let's go!"

I turned to leave, and the dogs got up and followed me.

Outside, the March day was sunny but blowy and chill. Giles skipped along beside me, delighted to be outdoors after a morning spent in the schoolroom learning his letters and his numbers. We set out from the south entrance of the house, the dogs racing before us, leaping wildly, circling back to us again, then racing on ahead once more. The path we took led us through the formal gardens, where the blue and pink hyacinths were coming out and a few early trees were showing promise of the blossoms to come.

A small stream marked the end of the formal gardens, and we leaned over the wooden bridge and admired the marsh marigolds and violets and lady's-smock, whose brightness colored the grass along its banks. We continued on, following the path between two fenced paddocks where some of my Thoroughbred hunters were turned out on grass that was beginning to green up nicely. We stopped to say hello to the horses and to pat their necks before we continued on our way to the wooded hillside that was our destination.

Spring was showing herself in the woods also. The birds were singing, and we saw daffodils and periwinkles, primroses and the blue speedwell whose color I loved. The pussy willows were out, and Giles and I picked some to bring home to Miss Stedham.

Like my son, I was very glad to be outdoors. I had spent a seemingly endless week sitting beside Gerald's sickbed, holding his hand and listening helplessly as his breathing became progressively more difficult. And then there had been the funeral.

I drew the crisp, cold air deep into my healthy lungs and felt life course through me. I looked up at the intensely blue sky, with high white clouds scudding along it like sailboats, and thought, Stephen *is* coming home.

"Mama," Giles said, "where is Papa now?"

I looked at my son. His cheeks were ruddy, and the knees of his breeches were caked with dirt. I sat down on a fallen log, heedless of my skirt dragging in the mud. "Papa is in heaven, darling," I said gently.

"But we putted him in the floor of the church yesterday," Giles said. "How can he be in heaven if he is in the church?"

"Papa's spirit is in heaven," I said. "When we die our spirits leave our bodies and go home to God. Papa doesn't need his body any longer, Giles, so he left it behind in the church."

Giles scowled. "I didn't *want* Papa to die, Mama."

I reached out and drew him close. He had always been a cuddly child, and now he pressed his face against my breast. "I don't *like* him being in the church floor," he said.

Tears flooded my eyes, and I shut them tightly, forbidding them to fall. "I don't like it either, Giles," I said. "But Papa got very sick. There wasn't anything we could do to keep him with us."

He said, his voice muffled by my breast, "You're not going to die, are you, Mama?"

"No, darling. I am not going to die." I managed to say the words very clearly and firmly.

He lifted his face from my breast and looked up at me. "Never?"

His cheeks were flushed with healthy color, but his light gray-green eyes were filled with apprehension. "Everyone has to die someday, Giles, but I am not going to die for a long time." The apprehension still clouded his gaze, and I added, "Not until you are a grown man with children of your own."

The idea of himself as a grown man with children of his own was sufficiently impossible to him that he was reassured, and his eyes cleared. He began to turn away, but I put my hands on his shoulders and made him look back at me. "Papa left a will, Giles. Mr. MacAllister read it to us this morning."

He was intrigued. "What is a will?"

"It's a... a list... of things that Papa wanted to have done in case he died. One of the things he wanted was for his brother, your uncle Stephen, to come home to look after Weston for you."

"Uncle Stephen?" Giles said. "I don't know my uncle Stephen. He lives somewhere else."

"He has lived in Jamaica for the last five years, so you have never met him, but Papa has said he must come home to look after Weston for you until you are big enough to do it yourself. You are the earl now, darling. I know it is hard to understand, but you have taken Papa's place."

Giles gazed solemnly back at me. "I know," he said. "Genie said I was Lord Weston now."

9

"You are Lord Weston," I agreed, "but Uncle Stephen will take care of running Weston Hall and the farms until you are twenty-one. People will call you 'my lord,' but none of the responsibilities for Weston will be yours for many years."

Giles frowned. "But Uncle Adam takes care of Weston Hall and the farms."

I nodded. "I imagine he will continue to do that."

"Then why do we need Uncle Stephen?" my son asked.

"Papa named him to be your guardian," I said.

Giles, who was as sensitive to my moods as a tuning fork to a note, shot me an alert look. "Don't you like Uncle Stephen, Mama?"

I laughed. I stood up. I gave my son a hug. "Of course I like Uncle Stephen. You will like him, too. He is fun."

We began to walk back toward the house. "Does he like to play?" Giles asked eagerly.

I drew in a deep breath of air. I could feel a headache coming on. "Yes," I said. "He likes to play." Something flashed by the edge of my vision. "Oh look, Giles," I said enthusiastically. "I think I just saw a bunny."

"Where?" he demanded, his attention, as I had hoped, neatly diverted from the subject of Uncle Stephen.

When I walked into my dressing room some forty minutes later, my mother was waiting for me. The dressing room, which opened off the bedroom I had shared with Gerald, was supposed to be my private domain, but I could not seem to make my mother understand that. Of course, the room had belonged to Mama during all the years that she had been married to Gerald's father, and I suppose she still felt a proprietary right to it.

She was seated in a chintz-covered chair in front of the fire, sipping tea, when I entered.

"I cannot understand why you did this room over," she said, as she said every single time she came in here. "It was perfectly elegant when I had it. You have made it look so common, Annabelle." Her exquisitely straight nose wrinkled as if it had been assailed by an unpleasant odor. "Flowered chintz," she said in disgust.

When Mama had used the room it had been done in straw-colored silk. It had indeed been extremely elegant, but I had always been afraid I would dirty the upholstery when I sat down, and the dogs had rubbed mud on the silk draperies. For my purposes, the cheerful chintz was much better.

Mama's green eyes moved to regard my person. "Really, Annabelle," she said, her disgust deepening, "how can you allow yourself to be seen in such disgraceful garments?"

"I took Giles for a walk," I said. I sat down on the chintz sofa that faced Mama's chair, stretched out my legs, and contemplated my muddy boots. "We both needed to get outside. It has been a difficult time."

In respect for my grief, my mother forbore to comment on (a) the mud, (b) my posture, and (c) the dogs, who had curled up in the pool of sunlight in front of the window. "Poor Gerald," she said. "How could so young and healthy a man get an inflammation of the lungs severe enough to kill him?"

She made it sound as if it were Gerald's fault that he had died.

"I don't know, Mama," I said wearily. The headache was now lodged securely behind my eyes. "The doctor said that these things happen."

"Well, they shouldn't," she said.

I had no answer to that.

She took another sip of tea. The silence lengthened. I looked at my mother, and for the first time I noticed a few strands of silver in the pale gold perfection of her hair. "I cannot understand why Gerald would name Stephen to be Giles's guardian," she said.

I went back to looking at my boots and kept my voice carefully neutral. "Stephen was his only brother. I should think it was a natural choice."

"Nonsense. Gerald and Stephen were never close."

I shrugged and said something about blood relationships.

Finally Mama got to the point. "Did you have anything to do with this decision of Gerald's, Annabelle?"

I looked up from my boots. I met her eyes. "No, Mama, I did not."

After a moment she looked away. "Gerald must have been insane," she said. "What does Stephen know about running an estate like Weston?"

"He has been running the Jamaica sugar plantation for five years now," I pointed out. "He is not without experience, Mama."

12

My mother gave me a pitying look. "His father sent him to Jamaica because the plantation was in such bad financial condition that even Stephen couldn't do it any more damage."

"I understood from Gerald that Stephen has actually done a good job, Mama. At any event, the plantation has not gone bankrupt, like so many others in Jamaica."

I heard what I was saying and scowled as fiercely as Giles. Why was I defending Stephen?

"At any rate," I went on coldly, "I am quite certain that Stephen will want Uncle Adam to continue to look after Weston as he has always done."

"I certainly hope so," my mother said. "Stephen has always been sadly unsteady. He couldn't even stay in school; he was always fighting."

I opened my mouth, then shut it again. I was not going to fall into the trap of defending Stephen to my mother.

"If Stephen does come home, he cannot live in this house with you," my mother said.

I stared at her in bewilderment.

"Do not play the innocent with me, Annabelle," she snapped. "You cannot live here unchaperoned with Stephen."

My bewilderment turned abruptly to disgust. I said, "Mama, Gerald is not yet cold in his grave."

My mother lifted her chin. She is an incredibly beautiful woman, but the beauty is all on the outside. I have never liked her.

"I am only thinking of your reputation," she said.

I do not think I have ever been so angry with

her. I stood up. "Mama," I said, "please leave."

She looked at my face and wisely decided it was time to retreat. She swept to the door and paused for a moment, looking back at me, clearly intent on having the last word. "You should be wearing black, Annabelle," she said.

She closed the door firmly behind her, leaving me alone with my headache.

CHAPTER
two

Normally, in March I would be finishing up the hunting season and getting ready to remove to London for the social season, but Gerald was dead and nothing was normal anymore. The resulting empty feeling of being alone and adrift was all too achingly familiar, and I spent a great deal of time with Giles. I told myself that he needed me, but in truth I think I needed him more.

A welcome touch of normalcy returned to my life with the visit of Sir Matthew Stanhope, our local squire and master of the Sussex Hunt, who came to see me on March 29, two days after the hunt season officially closed. We met in the small room behind the staircase that some years ago I had turned into an unofficial office for myself. I offered him some refreshment. He had wine; I had tea.

"Fenton's shrubbery got trampled the other day," he said as he settled back into the old velvet-covered armchair and drained off half his hock. "Some damn fool cousin of Watson's got run away with."

Keeping the local farmers placated was usually my job. "Oh dear," I said. Fenton was one of the Weston tenants, and I knew how proud he was of his new shrubbery. "Has someone told him that the hunt will replace the shrubbery?" I asked.

"Went to see him myself," Sir Matthew informed me. "He ain't happy, though. His wife says, what if the baby was out in the shrubbery? The baby would have been trampled, she says."

Unfortunately, Mrs. Fenton was right. I put down my cup in irritation. "How the devil did that fellow get into Fenton's *shrubbery*, Sir Matthew? The hunt had to have been at least three fields away!"

"We were, Annabelle, we were. But the damn fool was riding a borrowed horse—a nervy Thoroughbred—and he couldn't hold him. Horse took him right into the shrubbery."

We regarded each other with shared disgust. Sir Matthew had the ascetic face of a medieval scholar, but he was a countryman and a horseman and the best damn master of foxhounds any hunt could hope for. He had known me since I was eight years old.

I said, "It won't benefit the hunt if the local farmers begin to feel that they are not safe in their own gardens."

"I know, I know." Sir Matthew finished his hock, poured himself another glass, and got to the point of his visit. "Do you think you might go to see the Fentons, Annabelle? Get them to see that this was an accident, that it won't happen again?" He cleared his throat. "Hate to ask it of you right now, my dear. I know you're in mourning." Sir Matthew's thin, austere face

15

looked appropriately grave. "But the Fentons are Weston tenants, and if Mrs. Fenton stirs up the other farmers' wives…"

"The Sussex Hunt will be in trouble," I finished.

We looked at each other in silence.

The Sussex Hunt was our mutual passion. As I mentioned earlier, Sir Matthew was the master, and our pack of very expensive foxhounds was quartered at his home, Stanhope Manor. The cost of hunting a pack of foxhounds was enormous, however, and Sir Matthew could not be expected to bear the whole of it. That was why our hunt, like so many others, ran on subscriptions.

To be a member of the Sussex Hunt, you had to pay a certain amount of money per year. Members were allowed to bring guests, and the guests, of course, also had to pay. We needed the money to run the hunt, but it was absolutely infuriating when people introduced riders who couldn't be trusted to control their mounts. We had had another such disaster at the beginning of the hunt season in November, when a visitor's horse had kicked a hound. I had thought Sir Matthew was going to have an apoplexy right on the field.

"I will speak to the Fentons, of course," I said.

"Thank you, my dear. I can assure you that I have spoken quite sternly to Watson. Told him if he pulled such a damn fool trick again, he wouldn't be welcome to ride out with us."

I nodded agreement.

Silence fell. The sun chose that moment to come out from behind the layers of gray clouds that had filled the sky all morning, and the room brightened as if all the lamps had suddenly been lit. The office had always been the one room in the house that belonged solely to me, and I usually spent a part of each day working at the big library desk that was the room's centerpiece. It was here that I kept the records of the household expenses as well as the expense records of my own hunter operation.

My eyes lifted now, as they so often did, to the oil painting by George Stubbs that hung upon the wall facing the desk. It was a picture of Thoroughbreds exercising on Newmarket Heath. Gerald had given it to me for my twenty-first birthday, and I loved it. Unaccountably, my eyes began to sting.

"How are you managing, Annabelle?" Sir Matthew said. "How is young Giles going on?"

I tried to smile. "We are doing as well as can be expected, Sir Matthew. It was such a shock. I don't believe I have really comprehended yet that Gerald is gone."

He shook his head. "A young man like that, so full of life. What was he... twenty-nine?"

"He was twenty-eight," I said.

"How many times has he hunted all day in the rain, got soaking wet, and never even come down with a sniffle?" Sir Matthew demanded. "How could he have contracted an inflammation of the lungs in *London*?"

I rubbed my eyes tiredly. "I don't know, Sir Matthew. He just did."

"I'm sorry, my dear," he said. "I'm a blundering old man to be prosing on at you like this. But you know that if you need anything from me—anything at all—you have only to ask."

17

I gave him a real smile. "I do know that, and I am grateful. At times like this, one needs one's friends."

He gave me a shrewd look and asked, "Is the duchess still here?"

By "the duchess" he meant the Duchess of Saye, who also happened to be my mother. Two years after the death of the sixth Earl of Weston, Gerald's father, Mama had snared the duke of Saye for husband number three. She adored being addressed as "Your Grace."

"She's leaving this afternoon," I said.

"Good."

We smiled at each other with perfect comprehension.

"I heard from Adam that Weston's will named Stephen as Giles's guardian," Sir Matthew remarked next.

"Yes."

He nodded with approval. Stephen had once saved one of Sir Matthew's prize bitches from being gored by a bull, and in Sir Matthew's book Stephen would always be a hero. "Good thinking on Weston's part," he said now. "Adam is a great gun, but he's too old to have charge of a young 'un like Giles." Sir Matthew ran his fingers through his short, graying black hair and said loyally, "You know, Annabelle, I always thought there was more to that story of Stephen being caught smuggling than ever came out."

"Perhaps there was," I returned indifferently. "But it all happened five years ago, Sir Matthew, and I don't think it much matters anymore."

"I suppose not."

I changed the subject. "Is it true that Durham is selling his pack?" I asked.

His whole body snapped to attention. "They're sold," he said, and paused dramatically before adding, "For two thousand guineas, Annabelle."

"What!"

Sir Matthew nodded solemnly, poured himself another glass of wine, and settled in to tell me all about it.

The following morning I went to visit the Fentons. Their farm lay near the village of Weston, so I took one of the wide, grassy rides that crisscrossed Weston Park and eventually I reached the village road. It had rained before dawn, and the woods on either side of the ride were still wet and dripping. The world smelled fresh and new, the arched neck of my chestnut Thoroughbred mare was glossy with good grooming, and the springiness in her steps testified to her energy and her health. It was the kind of morning that makes one feel glad to be alive. I simply couldn't bear to think of Gerald, so I touched Elf lightly with my heel and we galloped all the way to the Weston Road.

The Fentons' farm was prosperous looking, with two large barns, a cart house, a granary, and a piggery. It would have looked even more prosperous if the small square of boxwood shrubbery that jutted out from the right side of the house had not looked as if it were the victim of a demented gardener. I surveyed it from Elf's back, picturing in my mind what must have happened: the horse had come crashing in on one side and its momentum had carried it across the small square of grass and out through the shrubs on the other side.

The thought of a child playing in that small enclosed space, in the way of those murderous iron-shod hooves, turned my blood cold.

"My lady!" Mrs. Fenton was at the farmhouse door, wiping her hands on her apron. I smiled at her, dismounted, tied Elf to the front gate, and went inside.

Susan Fenton was a few years older than I, the daughter of one Weston tenant farmer and the wife of another. She took me into the kitchen to brew tea, and her expressed sorrow about Gerald's death was undoubtedly sincere. I thanked her and we took our tea into the small, chilly sitting room that was used only for "company." Susan Fenton placed the teapot on a gateleg table and gestured me to an oak chair whose seat was softened by a blue-and-white embroidered cushion.

I arranged the full skirt of my gray riding habit. "I've come to apologize about the shrubbery," I said.

Her pretty face, with its fresh apple-blossom skin, was very sober. "I know you'll make good on the shrubbery, my lady, that isn't my concern. But my Robby often plays out there by himself. It's protected, see." She sipped her tea. "Leastways, I thought it was."

"I was looking at it from the road. The horse came right through it?"

"Aye. Fair scared the heart out of me."

I could see how it would have. "It wasn't one of the hunt members, Susan," I assured her. "It was some fool of a visitor on a horse he couldn't handle."

"It don't matter to me who it was, my lady," Susan said very firmly. "I know this is Weston land, but Fenton has a lease on it, and I don't want no hunt coming near my house again."

The grandfather clock in the room chimed the hour, and I waited until it was finished before saying, "They aren't supposed to come near the houses, Susan. Sir Matthew says that the rest of the field was a mile away."

"Small comfort it would have been to Robby's grieving mama and papa that the horse wasn't supposed to come near the house," Susan retorted swiftly. "He was near the house, my lady, and he could have killed my baby."

Perhaps I should explain here that Susan and I do not have the sort of relationship that usually prevails between a countess and the wife of one of her tenants. She had known me since first I came to Weston Hall as a lonely and unhappy child. She had taken me to pick blueberries and had taught me to plant a vegetable garden. It was Susan who had first told me about a woman's monthly flow.

"You're right, of course," I said with resignation. The delicious aroma of baking bread wafted into the room from the direction of the kitchen, and I sniffed blissfully. "That bread isn't finished by any chance, is it, Susan?"

Susan knew how much I loved her bread. "It will be finished in a few minutes, my lady, if you can wait."

"For your bread, Susan, I would wait an eternity," I said.

She looked pleased, and reluctantly I returned to the business that had brought me. "You have never had any problem with our own hunt members, have you?"

Susan frowned thoughtfully at the row of

21

pewter plates arranged decoratively on her oak sideboard. "No," she finally admitted.

"Suppose I recommend that in the future no one will be allowed to hunt with us except members?"

She looked uncertain.

"You know all our members, Susan," I said reasonably. "There is no one among us who can't be trusted to stay away from houses."

The Sussex Hunt was remarkably democratic, and Susan did indeed know all our members. Several of the more prosperous tenant farmers hunted with us, as well as the owner of the King's Arms in the village. It was the disapproval of this last personage, Harry Blackstone, that probably weighed the most with Susan. If Harry's hunting was spoiled by Bob Fenton's wife, Bob would find himself unwelcome in the taproom of the King's Arms. This would not sit well with Bob.

"There will be a great deal of ill feeling toward you and Bob if you refuse to allow the hunt to cross your fields," I said, ruthlessly exploiting this advantage.

Susan gave me one of her "That's one point for you" looks. I smiled guilelessly.

"Would the rest of the hunt members agree to eliminate guests, my lady?" she asked.

"They won't be pleased," I said frankly. "It will probably mean that their subscriptions will have to be raised. But I think you have a valid concern. Either we will have to hunt solely on the Downs, or we will have to be more careful about whom we allow to come out with us. Your Robby could indeed have been seriously hurt if he had been playing in the shrubbery when that horse came crashing through."

Over a second cup of tea and a few slices of Susan's bread, I promised to send men over from the hall with fresh boxwood plants to replace her ruined shrubs. I had finished my refreshment and was getting ready to reclaim Elf when Susan said, "Did you know that Jem Washburn was back, my lady?"

I subsided back into my chair. "No, I did not know that Jem was back." My surprise sounded in my voice.

One of Susan's cats, seeing that my lap was empty, jumped up to make herself comfortable. I began to stroke her soft gray fur.

"Washburn is dying, but I don't think Jem has come back to say good-bye to his dear old pa," Susan said ironically.

"Washburn is a pig," I said. "Everyone always knew that he beat Jem, but no one would ever do anything to stop it."

"Mr. Stephen tried to stop it," Susan said.

My hand stopped its stroking motion, and the cat turned her head, fixed a commanding stare on me, and gave a sharp, indignant meow. I began to pet her again.

"Bob says Jem has come home to take over his father's lease on the farm," Susan told me, "but he's afraid Mr. Grandville won't give it to him. Jem was wild as a boy, but I hear he's steadied now that he's older."

I scratched the cat beneath her chin, and her purr got louder. I said, "It is not Mr. Grandville who will make the decision about who is to get the Washburn farm."

Susan's pretty face was full of anticipation. "Is it true, then, my lady? Is Mr. Stephen really coming home?"

"Lord Weston named him to be Giles's guardian," I said. "Under the circumstances, I cannot see any reason for him to remain in Jamaica."

"It will make us all so happy," Susan said, "to have Mr. Stephen home again."

The sun had burned off the rest of the clouds while I was inside Susan's cottage, and after offering Elf a drink and tightening her girth, I mounted. Instead of returning home by the Weston Road, however, I turned my mare onto the well-trodden dirt path that led from the village to the Downs. Her ears pricked as she realized where we were going, and her trot became bouncier.

I let Elf break into a canter as we drew closer to the rolling hills that marked the skyline to the north, and very soon we were cantering over the close, fine turf of the Sussex Downs. I felt the surge of Elf's hindquarters under me as we began to climb. I was riding sidesaddle today, as I always did except when I was hunting, and I was careful to keep my weight balanced forward so as not to weigh her down as she drove uphill.

We reached the level top of the Downs and turned toward the double row of juniper bushes that made a sort of natural lane, about fifty yards wide, along the top of the hill.

Elf's ears flicked forward until they were almost touching. She knew what was coming, and the instant I moved my hands forward, she accelerated into a full gallop. The wind whipped past my ears, and I clicked to Elf to go faster.

She stretched out, a Thoroughbred in flat-out run, one of the fastest things in the world, and I bent low over her neck, and the ground streamed past beneath us, and the blood pumped strongly through my veins, and I wanted never to stop.

We did about a mile at full speed, and then we began to slow down. At the end of a mile and a half we were cantering easily. By the time we reached the point where I could pick up the path that would take me home, Elf was trotting.

The sky had turned a deep cobalt, with a few high white clouds sailing with infinite grace across an endless expanse of blue. I pulled Elf up and together we looked out across the small and sunny valley that was our home.

Weston Hall and Park occupied almost all of the eastern part of the valley. I could see the great stone house quite clearly, as well as the stables, the horse pastures, and the lake. I could even make out the fishing pavilion on the lakeshore and the icehouse as well.

The village of Weston lay to the west of the park. From my vantage point on the Downs it looked like a mere cluster of trees and houses amid the spreading farmland. The church lay on the outskirts of the village, and its spire jutted up toward the blue heavens with graceful authority.

To the north of the village, nestled right up against the Downs, lay the second most important house in the neighborhood: Stanhope Manor, the home of Sir Matthew. I could see the beginning of the park, but the house itself was hidden from my view.

The rest of the valley comprised rich farmland, most of which was owned by the earl of Weston and leased out to tenants. I could not see beyond the ridge that formed the southern wall of the valley, but I knew that on the far side of that steep, wooded hillside the land sloped away for several miles before it reached the Channel and the small port town of West Haven. It was this ridge of land that sheltered the valley from the Channel winds and made it one of the most clement places in all of England.

After a few minutes, I sent Elf forward and we made our way downhill over the turf until we reached the dirt path that would take us back to Weston Park.

CHAPTER
three

When I reached home, Hodges, our butler, met me at the door to inform me that Gerald's cousin, Jack Grandville, had come to visit. Hodges had put him in the library.

"He came with a portmanteau, my lady, but I have not yet sent his bag upstairs." Hodges had a great beak of a nose, which had fascinated me ever since I was a child. It was a perfect indicator of his moods, and at the present moment it was quivering with indignation.

Jack had been visiting Weston for as long as I could remember. He was the only son of Gerald's father's only brother, and as such, he stood next in line after Giles and Stephen to inherit the earldom. As the son of a younger son, Jack was chronically short of money, and he had long made a habit of coming to stay at Weston when he needed to live cheaply for a while. I didn't understand Hodges's sudden disapproval.

"Why haven't you sent his bag upstairs, Hodges?" I inquired as I stripped off my gloves.

"He is an unmarried gentleman, and he should not be staying in the house with you while you are alone, Miss Annabelle," Hodges said. His slip into the old childhood name was the measure of his distress.

"Nonsense," I said. "Mr. Jack is family."

The beak veritably quaked with outrage. "It isn't proper, Mi... my lady. If he stays here, there will be *talk*."

As I regarded Hodges's nose, it occurred to me that I did not particularly want Jack underfoot from morning until night. I slapped my gloves thoughtfully against my riding skirt, then said, "I suppose he could stay with Mr. Adam."

The beak stopped quivering. Hodges smiled and said, "I will have Mr. Jack's portmanteau sent to the Dower House immediately, my lady."

"You had better check with Mrs. Grandville first," I warned.

"Of course, my lady."

I tossed my gloves onto a delicate Louis XIV table and said, "Have some lemonade sent to the library, Hodges, will you? I am rather thirsty from my ride."

He was as pleasant as he could be now that he had gotten his way. "Of course, my lady." He gave me a benign smile. "It is good to see you with some color in your cheeks."

I couldn't resist. I looked around the immense marble entrance hall in which we were standing, with its Roman-style columns and classical statues poised in pale green niches, and asked innocently, "Where *is* Mr. Jack's portmanteau, Hodges?"

He said immediately, "It is under the stairs, my lady."

We looked at each other. I knew, and he knew I knew, that he had sent it over to Uncle Adam's even before I came in.

"It is nice of you to keep up the pretense that I am in charge here, Hodges," I said amiably.

He had the grace to look abashed. I grinned and went across the gleaming black-and-white marble floor, past the great formal staircase, and into the corridor. Instead of crossing the corridor into the formal salon, I turned left and went along the passageway that led to the family part of the house. The door opposite the bedroom staircase was open, and I walked into the library, an enormous, chestnut-paneled room with book shelves that reached all the way up to the high, gilt-ornamented ceiling. Above the green and white marble fireplace hung a portrait of the first Earl of Weston, a man who looked remarkably like Gerald dressed in the gaudy finery of the Restoration.

There was a man standing by the front window, and even though my feet made no sound on the thick, Turkish carpet, he turned to face me. The sunlight glinted off his fair hair, and for a moment, even though I knew who he was, my heart leaped into my throat.

"Annabelle," Jack's voice said. He came toward me, then frowned in quick concern. "What's wrong?"

"It's just... when the sunlight caught your hair... I thought for a moment that you were Gerald."

"Oh, my dear. I am sorry. Sit down, you look alarmingly pale."

I managed a smile. "I'm all right." But I let him take my arm and lead me toward the group of four Chippendale armchairs that were arranged in a square next to the great globe. I sat and looked up into the face that bore the stamp of Gerald's blond-haired, blue-eyed, good looks without Gerald's geniality. There was a hardness about Jack's mouth, a faintly hawk-like look about his nose that had not been present in my husband.

"Let me pour you a glass of Madeira," he said.

My knees still felt a little shaky. "All right," I agreed, and watched as he went to the Sheraton cabinet that always held a few bottles of wine and glasses. He poured, then handed me the glass in silence. I took one sip, and then I took another. I looked up into his concerned face and repeated, "I'm all right."

He touched the bridge of my nose with a light finger, said, "You've been riding without a hat again, your freckles are out," and went to pour some Madeira for himself.

I fortified myself with another sip of wine and watched him as he took the chair opposite to mine. "You probably think I'm here because I'm on a repairing lease to save some money," he said, and took a healthy swallow.

"The thought had crossed my mind," I replied frankly.

He grinned. "Not this time, Annabelle. In fact, I did fairly well at Watier's last week. I rather think I won enough money to last me for a while."

"My congratulations," I said.

He settled his broad shoulders against the rose silk chair back. "I came because I was worried about you."

I twirled the stem of my glass with my fingers. "There is no need to worry about me, Jack. I am going on very well."

"London isn't the same without you, Annabelle." He looked at me over the top of his wineglass. "Even that muttonhead Byron wrote a poem about you—called it 'Farewell Brightness,' or some such nonsense."

"Have you taken to reading *poetry*, Jack?" I asked in amazement.

The grin dawned again. "Not likely," he said.

The door opened and a footman came in bearing a tray with a pitcher of lemonade and two glasses.

"*Lemonade?*" Jack said in horror.

I said firmly, "Thank you, William. You may set it down on the table there."

William placed the tray of lemonade on a piecrust table close to my chair. He straightened and said in a wooden voice, "Mr. Hodges said I was to tell you that Mr. Jack's portmanteau has been sent to the Dower House."

Hodges, that wily old devil, was making sure that Jack knew he was not welcome. My gently spoken, "Thank you, William," clashed with Jack's much louder, "What the devil do you mean by sending my portmanteau over to Adam's! I'm not staying with Adam, damn it."

30

I nodded to William to go, which he did. Hastily. Then I turned to confront Jack. "Hodges says that you cannot stay in the house with me, as I am not chaperoned."

His blue eyes blazed. "Damn it all, Annabelle, I'm your cousin! Of course I can stay with you."

"You are not my cousin, Jack, you are Gerald's cousin. And Gerald is..."

I could not say the word.

The quick anger left Jack's face, and he leaned forward to take my fingers into his own hard grasp. "Annabelle, love, I'm sorry. You know I wouldn't do anything to distress you."

I thought as I left my hand in his for a moment before withdrawing it gently, Hodges is right. I ought not to be alone with Jack.

He gave me a charming, crooked grin. "I will even stay with Adam, if that will make you happy."

I took a deep, unsteady breath. "It isn't a penance to stay with Adam, Jack." I took another breath, and this time my voice came out steadier. "He has been very good to me."

Jack pushed himself out of his chair and paced restlessly to the window. He said, "I cannot understand why Gerald named Stephen and not Adam to be Giles's guardian. The very thought of Stephen *guiding* anyone is enough to make one shudder."

"He has done very well in Jamaica these last five years." I poured myself a glass of lemonade. "Gerald said that ours was one of the few sugar plantations that has not had to declare bankruptcy."

"My grandfather made a fortune out of that sugar plantation, but its time is finished," Jack

31

said. "Napoleon killed the sugar market when he barred British goods from Europe. You might just as well declare it bankrupt and be rid of it."

I drank some lemonade and did not reply.

"I really don't think I can stand more than two days of Aunt Fanny," Jack said gloomily.

"Why not?" I said in surprise. Adam's wife did talk a bit, but she was an extremely good-hearted woman who had kept an open house for all the Grandville children when we were young. We had all liked Aunt Fanny far more than we liked my mother.

"Because," Jack said, "she will tell me—in great detail—all about Nell's come-out. She has told me all about it the last three times we have met."

"Nell had quite a success in London, Jack. She had *four* offers of marriage!"

"I know all about them," Jack said. "I even know the color of each suitor's eyes."

I had to bite my lip to keep from laughing.

Jack went to the cupboard where the wine was kept and poured another glass. "One can't help but wonder why Nell hasn't accepted one of these desirable suitors," he commented as he turned to face me again.

I shrugged. "Perhaps she didn't care for any of them."

"She hasn't said anything to you?"

I shook my head.

"Well, she is certain to get other offers," Jack said. "The word around town is that Adam has come up with a handsome dowry for her."

The dogs, who had been whining pitifully from behind the door that led into the morning room, now began to bark. I went to the door and opened it to let them in.

"The ubiquitous hounds," Jack said with resignation as they circled around his feet, reacquainting themselves with his smell.

"They're spaniels, Jack, not hounds."

"I say, Annabelle, must they slobber all over my boots?"

I snapped my fingers and the dogs came to my side.

Jack said, "Who was it that Fanny inveigled into helping her bring Nell out? Some old relic of a cousin, wasn't it?"

"Yes." I went back to my chair, and the dogs settled themselves on the floor at my feet. "Her name is Dorothy Grandville and she lives in Bath." I bent down to scratch Portia's long silky ears. "I offered to help with Nell's come-out, but Aunt Fanny didn't seem to want me."

I tried not to sound hurt, but the fact was I had been hurt. After all, Nell was almost like my little sister. I had always assumed that I would assist in her come-out.

Jack was regarding me with amusement in his pale blue eyes. "Annabelle, darling, no mama in her right mind would want to exhibit her daughter with you alongside for comparison. The point of coming out is that people are supposed to pay attention to you—not to your chaperone."

Merlin pushed his muzzle against my hand, and I switched from Portia's ears to his. I didn't reply.

Jack said, "Do you think you might coax this Dorothy Grandville to come and stay with you at Weston Hall?"

I looked up in astonishment. "Why should I want to do that?"

"To chaperone you, of course," Jack said. "You can't keep asking me to put up at Adam's, Annabelle. Aunt Fanny will drive me straight to Bedlam."

"I wasn't expecting you to be visiting quite so frequently, Jack," I said tartly. "The hunting season is over."

"Stephen will expect to stay here when he comes home," Jack pointed out.

I gave Merlin's head one last pat and folded my hands in my lap. "I don't even know if Stephen is coming home."

"Gerald is dead," Jack said. "Of course Stephen will come home."

I kept my eyes on my folded hands. "I suppose he will have to. After all, he is Giles's guardian."

"He would have come home anyway, Annabelle," Jack said, "and you know it."

I felt myself getting into dangerous waters and tried to extricate myself by saying briskly, "Weston is Stephen's home. Of course he will stay here."

"Your mother will kick up stiff if you and Stephen are alone together," Jack said.

I remembered Mama's words the day of the reading of the will and had to acknowledge that Jack was probably right.

I said bitterly, "I am twenty-three years of age. I have a four-year-old child, and my husband has not been dead a month. Why is everyone treating me as if I were a girl in her first Season?"

Jack said bluntly, "You aren't a fool,

Annabelle. You must know how many men would love to take Gerald's place."

I could feel the pulses beginning to throb in my temples. I stood up. "If you will excuse me, Jack, I've promised to join Giles in the school-room for luncheon."

Jack accepted his dismissal gracefully. "Very well, I will make my dutiful way to the Dower House." He gave me a pained look. "Do I have to dine there as well?"

I found a smile. "No, come to the hall for dinner. In fact, if you wait a moment, I'll write a quick note to Aunt Fanny and ask her and Adam and Nell to join us."

Jack made a face, but he waited while I wrote the invitation. We went out of the library together, and in the passageway in front of the staircase we ran into Giles and Miss Stedham.

"We were out in the garden getting a little air before luncheon," Miss Stedham explained.

"Miss Stedham, allow me to introduce my cousin, Mr. Jack Grandville," I said.

The two of them shook hands, Jack's eyes glinting with appreciation of Eugenia Stedham's deep auburn hair and magnolia fresh skin. A little color stained her cheeks at the frank look of admiration in his blue eyes.

"Good-bye Jack," I said with amusement.

As he turned to leave he murmured to me, "Invite Miss Stedham to dinner, too, Annabelle."

I thought it was a good idea, so I did.

My maid, Marianne, laid out an evening dress made of plain black bombazine, one of several that my mother had had made for me after

Gerald's death. I had scarcely worn any of them, as I was in the habit of dining in the school-room with Giles when I was alone at the hall.

"Such a dull material," Marianne said as she ran her finger up and down the sheenless bodice of the gown.

"In another month or so I can wear black silk," I said.

Marianne nodded glumly, and I knew she was thinking of all the colorful dresses I would be wearing if I were in London. My young maid adored pretty clothes, and when I was home I tended to live in a riding skirt.

"I expect you are missing the Season this year, Marianne," I said sympathetically.

"It is that London is so exciting, my lady," she said. "So many different clothes to wear to so many different places! Balls and routs and Almacks—" Her voice stopped abruptly, and she sank her teeth into her lower lip. "I am sorry, my lady. I should not be speaking of pleasures when you... when my lord..." She gathered herself and finished with dignity, "I should not have spoken so. You are not interested in parties now, my lady."

In fact, I had never been interested in parties. It was Gerald who enjoyed London, not me. I would have been much happier spending April through June in the country, where the beauty belonged to nature and not to artifice.

I finished dressing and went along to the drawing room a little early, as Uncle Adam was famous for being exactly on time.

When Weston Hall had been built in the middle of the last century, it had been designed with a family section in the west part of the house, grouped around one staircase, and a formal section in the east part, grouped around another staircase. The family section contained the library, the morning room, the master bedroom with attached dressing rooms for the earl and the countess, and the room that was now my office. The public section of the house consisted of the hall, salon, drawing room, long gallery, and dining room.

The drawing room, where I received my guests, was a large, elegant room, painted a soft gray color, with a high rotunda ceiling set with gold medallions. Four long windows opened onto a terrace that faced south toward a vista of trimmed shrubbery interspersed with marble statues and flower beds.

I chose a gilt, tapestry-covered chair and sat down to wait for my guests to arrive. At precisely six-thirty, Aunt Fanny arrived in the drawing room, followed by Uncle Adam, Jack, and Nell.

"Annabelle, my dear girl," Aunt Fanny said in her soft, breathless voice, "how *good* of you to invite us to dinner. Of course, you must be lonely in this great house all by yourself. Please do not ever hesitate for a *moment* to come to visit me. Or certainly you may ask me to visit you. You know how fond I am of you...."

Aunt Fanny was capable of continuing in this good-hearted fashion for at least another ten minutes, but her monologue was mercifully interrupted by her husband. "You must give the rest of us a chance to greet Annabelle, Fanny," he said. Then, when Aunt Fanny stepped aside, Adam took my hand and kissed my cheek. "How are you, my dear?" he asked. "Good of you to ask us."

I am tall, so I did not have far to raise my eyes to meet Uncle Adam's calm, experienced gray gaze. He was in his late fifties, his blond hair was mixed with gray, and his square, genial face bore the look of a man who is well pleased with his world and his ability to deal with it.

Gerald and Stephen had always called Adam "Uncle," even though he was their father's cousin and not his brother. He had managed the Weston estate for the last twenty years, first for Gerald's father and then for Gerald. He and his family resided in the Dower House, which was located at the eastern edge of Weston's park.

He had always been kindness itself to me, and the smile I gave him was genuine. "It is always good to see you, Uncle Adam," I said, and turned to his nineteen-year-old daughter, Nell.

She was a small girl in whom the Grandville blond hair was set off by an unusual pair of slightly tilted brown eyes. Nell had always put me in mind of an elf. I smiled at her now, and we exchanged a cousinly kiss.

Jack looked around the room and said, "Don't tell me we are to be spared the dogs?"

I gave him an irritated look.

"Some fine ladies are preceded by liveried pages," Adam said humorously, "Annabelle is usually preceded by dogs."

This drew a laugh from everyone. I spotted Miss Stedham hovering uncertainly in the doorway and beckoned her in, and the rest of the family greeted her in a friendly fashion. The governess was wearing a gray evening dress trimmed in black ribbons and her auburn hair had been pulled into a smooth chignon at her nape, a simple style I myself favored when I was dining at home.

Now that the entire company was assembled, Hodges appeared in the doorway and announced to me that dinner was ready. We lined up for the formal procession to the dining room, with Adam escorting me, Jack escorting Aunt Fanny, and Nell and Miss Stedham bringing up the rear. In this order we crossed the passageway to the dining room, where we took our seats around the mahogany table from which all the leaves had been removed.

It was the first time I had sat at this table since the funeral, and I found myself glancing across the expanse of polished wood, expecting to see Gerald sitting opposite to me.

Gerald had excelled at social occasions like dinner parties. He had been a man of easy temperament and lavish charm—"the sun child," Jack used to call him, not without bitterness. It must have been difficult for less fortunate men not to have envied Gerald.

Adam's voice recalled me to the present. "I was talking to Matthew Stanhope today, and he tells me that the hunt subscription price is going to have to go up to a thousand pounds."

"That's a big increase, isn't it?" Jack asked.

Adam explained about Susan Fenton's shrubbery and the solution I had come up with.

"You can't eliminate visitors from riding out with the Sussex Hunt, Annabelle," Jack said sharply. "Where is that going to leave me?"

Jack was a keen huntsman, and he often came down to Weston in order to ride out with us. He could do this cheaply, as he could always count on me to provide him with a horse.

"I'm afraid you'll have to join if you want to ride with us next year, Jack," I said.

His blue eyes blazed with sudden temper, and he slammed his fist down on the table, making the dishes jump. "I can't afford a thousand pounds! You know that, Annabelle!"

Aunt Fanny chattered in distress as a footman hastily came forward to wipe up the wine that had spilled from her glass when Jack's fist struck the table.

"If you don't watch that temper of yours, Jack, you're going to find yourself in real trouble one of these days," Uncle Adam said grimly. "Annabelle is right. The Fenton child could have been badly hurt. Killed, even."

"What does one farmer's brat more or less matter?" Jack said rashly.

Nell's breath drew in with a small, shocked sound.

"You don't mean that, Mr. Grandville," Miss Stedham said quietly.

Jack shot her a look, and his mouth, which had thinned dangerously, relaxed a trifle. "I suppose I don't," he grumbled.

"Of course you don't," I said. I drummed my fingers on the napkin in my lap, thinking. I did not want Jack deprived of his hunting. He helped me keep my horses fit.

"I know," I said brightly. "The Weston estate will pay for your subscription, Jack." I knew Gerald would never have paid for Jack's subscription, but surely this huge estate could bear the cost of a meager thousand pounds. I looked at Adam. "That will be all right, won't it, Uncle Adam?"

"I am no longer the proper person to consult about such matters, Annabelle," Adam said gravely. "According to Gerald's will, the only person who now has the right to make decisions about estate disbursements is Stephen."

My brow smoothed out. "You have been running Weston for over twenty years, Uncle Adam. I rather doubt that Stephen will wish to step in and replace you."

"I should hope not," Aunt Fanny said in an unusually forceful voice.

"Well," Jack drawled, "I don't know if I agree with you, Fanny. I know I have a much better chance of getting a thousand pounds out of Stephen than I do out of Adam."

We all laughed.

"That is certainly so, Jack," Aunt Fanny said with a sigh. "A softer-hearted boy than Stephen never lived. I could never understand how he came to be embroiled in smuggling!"

"I have often wondered if the evidence against him was contrived," Nell said.

"Stephen admitted responsibility," I replied in a flat, hard voice. "I know because I heard him."

In fact, I had been listening at the connecting door between the morning room and the library while the earl and a government officer questioned Stephen.

I am responsible, Papa. There is no one else.

Those were his words and he had stuck to them, even when he was told the government would not press charges if he left the country and went to Jamaica.

He had chosen to go to Jamaica.

And I had chosen Gerald.

"...do you think, Annabelle?"

I blinked and pulled my attention back to the table.

"I beg your pardon, Aunt Fanny," I said. "I did not hear you."

She repeated herself, and dinner went on.

CHAPTER
four

At the end of May a ship docked at Southampton with letters from Stephen. One was addressed to Uncle Adam, and one was addressed to me.

I retreated with mine to the privacy of my dressing room, annoyed to discover that my hands were shaking so badly that I had difficulty opening the envelope. Finally I managed to extract a single sheet of paper that was only half-covered with writing. In his familiar, sprawling scrawl, Stephen wrote that he was sorry to hear about Gerald, that he understood and shared my grief, and that he would be home as soon as he could complete some unfinished business pertaining to the plantation. I was to give his regards to Giles.

His regards.

I crumpled up the letter and tossed it into the fireplace.

Adam came to see me later in the day with *his* letter, which, I was interested to note, ran to five closely written pages.

"Stephen writes that he is divesting the estate of the sugar plantation," Adam said in an expressionless voice as he took his usual chair in the library.

"Divesting the estate?" I blinked. "Do you mean he is declaring bankruptcy after all?"

"No," Adam said deliberately. "Stephen says that he is giving the plantation to the slaves."

I rubbed my nose and regarded Adam's impassive face. "Giving?" I said after a while.

"That is what he writes." Adam rattled the pages he was holding clenched in his fist. "Apparently, Stephen has not been planting sugar for the last several years. Instead he divided the plantation into plots, which he then turned over to the slaves, and they have been cultivating crops for their own sustenance as well as to sell. He has even," Adam said grimly, "imported some English livestock for them."

"Are slaves allowed to own property?" I asked curiously.

"Stephen is giving them their freedom first, of course," Adam replied.

I couldn't help my grin. "How like Stephen," I said.

"This is not amusing, Annabelle," Adam said. And indeed, he did not look amused. His nostrils were pinched and his face was flushed. "That plantation is worth a great deal of money."

"It was worth a great deal of money," I corrected. "None of the Jamaican sugar plantations have been making money for decades, Uncle Adam. First they were hurt by the American war, and then, when Napoleon closed all of Europe to English trade there were not enough markets to buy all the sugar that Jamaica produces. The plantation may have been a gold mine for Weston at one time, but it's been nothing but a dead loss for many years."

Adam looked annoyed. "I certainly know all

43

of that, Annabelle. The plantation may well be profitable again, however, now that it looks as if Napoleon is finally beaten." Adam tapped the pages of his letter against the mahogany wood of his chair. "I am telling you now, Annabelle. Stephen's action is directly contrary to Giles's best interest. He should not be allowed to do this."

"The question is, *can* he do it?"

"Are you asking if he is legally empowered to give the plantation away?"

I nodded.

"Yes," Adam said bitterly, "he is."

I shrugged. "Then there is nothing I can do to stop him, Uncle Adam."

The intelligent gray eyes held mine, and then he expelled his breath and sat back in his chair, the tension draining visibly from his shoulders. "I suppose there isn't," he said. "By the time a letter from you could reach Jamaica, Stephen would probably be on his way home."

"We don't need the plantation," I said. An unpleasant thought struck me. "Or *do* we? Are we in dun territory, Uncle Adam?"

Merlin, hearing the sharp note in my voice, lifted his head from his paws and gazed at me alertly. I bent to give his silky black head a re-assuring pat.

"No, no, my dear, there is nothing like that. I did not mean to alarm you. Giles's future is very well secured."

Merlin's head dropped back to his paws.

"There are no nasty debts or mortgages that I don't know about?" I said.

"Nothing like that, Annabelle," Adam re-peated firmly. "The earl's income is about twenty thousand pounds a year—and that is the sum that is left after all the costs of the estate and the pensions to old servants have been paid."

This was a very healthy income indeed. "You have done well by us, Uncle Adam," I said warmly.

He smiled faintly in acknowledgment and said, "Thank you, my dear."

Portia got up, stretched, and went to lie down in the sun in front of the window.

"Have you heard from Jasper?" I asked.

Jasper was Uncle Adam's son, a captain of cavalry who had been in Spain with Wellington for the past two years.

"We had a letter just yesterday." Adam smiled. "It seems that Stephen is not the only Grandville who will be coming home."

"Jasper is coming home?"

Adam nodded.

"That's wonderful news, Uncle Adam! Aunt Fanny must be in alt."

He grinned. "She is. We all are."

Merlin had decided that his sister had a better spot than he. He got up, padded across the Turkish carpet to the patch of sun where Portia was dozing blissfully, and stretched out beside her. They looked like twin inkspots on the red carpet.

"This wretched, wretched war," I said. "But it does seem as if it is finally coming to an end."

"Now that the Allies have taken Paris, I should think it inevitable," Adam said.

"It will be so good to see Jasper again," I said.

Uncle Adam shot me an enigmatic look and did not reply.

I said next, "I wonder if Jasper will want a subscription to the Sussex Hunt?"

At that, Adam threw back his head and laughed. "Annabelle, you are so predictable!"

"I am only thinking of Jasper," I defended myself. "He won't be able to hunt with us if he doesn't have a subscription."

"I will buy a subscription for Jasper," Adam said. "I wouldn't want the lad to miss his fun. He's had a rough enough time in Spain these last few years." He got to his feet. "Who is collecting the subscription money—you or Stanhope?"

I was delighted. "I am, Uncle Adam. But you don't need to pay me until August." I rose to see him to the door, and both dogs opened their eyes and yawned.

Adam gave me a humorous look. "I'm sure I don't have to tell you to remind me, Annabelle."

"You are a terrible tease," I replied.

He laughed and patted my arm. "You must forgive an old man who has known you since you were a solemn-faced little girl."

I smiled at him affectionately. "I'm glad about Jasper," I said.

"So am I." He patted my arm once more and went out the door. I called to the dogs and we went up the stairs to the nursery to have luncheon with Giles.

The day Stephen came home, the hazy August sun was shining on golden fields of wheat, ripe for harvesting. The air was sweet with the smell of cut grass, and the horses in the paddocks were standing head to tail, lazily swishing away the flies. In the distance the turf of the Downs looked like green velvet against the blue of the sky.

Giles had recently become interested in fishing, and the two of us had spent the afternoon out at the lake. I was wearing an old, grass-stained gown, my hair was done in a single braid down my back, and my bare feet were thrust into a disgraceful pair of ancient leather slippers. It was the sort of costume that would invariably provoke Gerald to complain that I looked like a farmgirl.

As soon as we came in I sent Giles upstairs to the nursery while I lingered for a moment in the Great Hall to consult with Mrs. Nordlem, our housekeeper, about cooking the fish Giles had caught. I was still in the hall when a hired carriage came rolling up the drive and stopped in front of the stately front steps of Weston Hall.

Hodges heard the carriage, went to one of the tall narrow windows that flanked the front door, and glanced out. He clicked his tongue in disapproval of the shabby equipage. Then his back stiffened.

"Good God," he said, "it's Mister Stephen!"

I stood as if rooted to the marble floor.

"Mr. Stephen?" Mrs. Nordlem's small, trim figure was quivering with delight. "My lady, did you hear? Mr. Stephen has arrived!"

"Yes," I said, "I heard."

Hodges had already thrown open the front door as wide as it would go and gone outdoors into the hot afternoon sun. "Mr. Stephen!" I heard him cry. There came the tapping of his feet as he ran down the stone stairs. "Welcome home!"

Then, for the first time in five years, I heard Stephen's voice. "Thank you, Hodges," he said. "It is good to see you again."

My legs felt as if they would not bear me up. My mouth was dry and my heart was hammering.

Stop this, Annabelle! I commanded myself. I breathed slowly and deeply, trying to get myself under control.

Stephen walked in the open front door, saw me, and stopped as suddenly as if he'd been shot. We stared at each other across a seemingly endless expanse of black-and-white marble.

He looked the same, yet somehow he was different. The mahogany brown hair, the level brows, the narrow, slightly arched nose, which bore a distinct bump where it had once been broken, the thin, beautifully chiseled mouth, the familiar deep blue eyes: all of these were the same. Yet they looked sharper than I remembered, as if all of the softness of boyhood had been burned away by the hot Jamaican sun.

He said my name, and his voice sounded unsteady.

Portia, who had once been Stephen's dog, recognized his voice and hurled herself across the marble floor, barking ecstatically.

"Portia! How are you, girl?" He bent to pet her, but she was too excited to stay still. She raced back to me, barked three times to tell me the wonderful news of Stephen's arrival, and then tore back to him, skidding along the marble floor in her excitement. Merlin decided to get in on the fun, and he also went to greet Stephen. Both dogs' tails were wagging so hard, their whole bodies shook with the force of it.

The dogs gave me a chance to gain my composure. I crossed the marble floor after them, and conscious of the watching eyes of Hodges and Mrs. Nordlem, I held out my hand. "Portia missed you," I said. "Welcome home, Stephen."

Even to my own ears, my cool voice did not sound particularly welcoming.

I felt his familiar thin, hard fingers close around my hand, and then he dropped it as if the brief contact had scalded him.

"I am so sorry about Gerald," he said. His eyes flicked upward, in the direction of Gerald's old bedroom. "I still can't believe that I will never see him again."

I nodded, incapable of summoning up words of comfort on the death of his brother.

Two footmen came in the front door, carrying Stephen's bags. Mrs. Nordlem asked, "In what room shall I have them put Mr. Stephen's bags, my lady?"

Stephen looked surprised. "Can't I have my old room?"

I said, "Giles and his governess have the nursery now, Stephen."

The shuttered look that I had seen him wear so often in the years of our growing up settled across his face. "Oh, of course."

He had never before put up that shuttered look for me.

"Take the bags to the blue bedroom," I said, and the footmen went obediently toward the corridor that led into the family part of the house. Mrs. Nordlem and Hodges followed.

Stephen and I were alone in the hall.

He was staring at my face. "You haven't changed at all, Annabelle," he said in wonderment.

The power of his flesh-and-blood presence was beginning to take its toll on my nerves. I said in a hard voice, "You're wrong, Stephen. I've changed a great deal."

A slight narrowing of the eyes was the only indication he gave that he had heard the open hostility in my voice.

The door that led from the library directly into the west side of the hall suddenly opened and Adam came striding in. "Stephen! Hodges told me you were here! My dear boy, how wonderful to see you!"

"Uncle Adam." Stephen smiled for the first time since he had walked in, and I felt my heart twist in my breast. He was holding out his hand, but Adam ignored it and enveloped him instead in a huge bear hug. Then he put his hands on Stephen's shoulders and held him for inspection.

"Why, you've grown. You're taller than I am!" Adam said in surprise.

"It must have been all that sunshine," Stephen said.

"Or the rum," Adam retorted, and they both laughed.

Aunt Fanny's breathless voice came from behind me. "Is it true what Hodges has told me? Is Stephen really home?" I heard the sharp intake of her breath "Why, Stephen, you're as brown as an Indian!"

He was holding out both his arms. "Aunt Fanny. How wonderful to see you again."

She ran to receive his hug. "Do you know that Jasper is home also?" she said as she emerged from his embrace.

"No, is he really? That is excellent news."

Aunt Fanny fluttered around him, chattering excitedly about "having both my boys home again," and he regarded her with affectionate amusement. In all the years of our growing up, Adam and Fanny had always been very fond of Stephen.

"Come along to the morning room and have some tea," Fanny said now, and Stephen's eyes moved to me in obvious surprise that Fanny should be acting as hostess in my house.

"Adam and Fanny are staying at the hall while the Dower House is being refurbished," I said.

This was the arrangement I had come up with to satisfy my mother about the propriety of Stephen living in the same house as I. Aunt Fanny had been delighted when I suggested redecorating the Dower House, and although her constant chatter could be wearing at times, she was infinitely preferable to some unknown cousin from Bath.

Adam and Fanny and Nell had moved in the previous week. Jasper had arrived yesterday.

Stephen and I would be well chaperoned.

Stephen said, "Tea would be wonderful, Aunt Fanny."

"How was your voyage?" Adam asked as they began to move toward the door that would take them through the library and thence into the morning room.

I did not move, and Aunt Fanny turned to ask, "Annabelle? Are you not coming, my dear?"

I shook my head and gestured to my clothes. "I would like to change first, Aunt Fanny."

"Did you and young Giles catch anything?" Adam asked genially.

"Yes, Giles caught four fish. He was delighted."

Fanny and Adam smiled. Stephen said nothing.

"Jasper and Nell have gone for a ride, but they will be back soon," Aunt Fanny said. "How pleased they both will be to see you, Stephen! I must tell you about Nell's come-out. She had four offers, you know...."

Their voices died away as they disappeared through the library door. I realized that I had stopped breathing and inhaled sharply.

The initial meeting was over.

I had gotten over the first jump.

Now it was simply a matter of staying the course.

I picked one of my five interchangeable black silk dresses to wear to dinner and let Marianne put me into it. I sat in front of my dressing table mirror as she dressed my hair.

"Perhaps I will get it cut after all," I said as she wove it into a sleek arrangement of layers on the top of my head. "Long hair has been out of style for an age now."

"You have such beautiful hair, my lady," Marianne said. She pinned the last strand into place. "It would be a shame to cut it off."

I had not cut it because Gerald had not wanted me to. He had loved to take down my hair in bed....

I shut my eyes, not wanting to remember.

"It is the exact color of honey," Marianne said.

I stared at myself in the mirror, assessing my face, trying to see if the changes inside were at all reflected by the outward flesh.

I had been seventeen years old when Stephen

had gone to Jamaica, and this afternoon, in an old sprig muslin dress, with my hair in a plait, I had probably not looked much older than seventeen. But I was twenty-three now, a widow with a four-year-old son. I had suffered. Surely the changes had to show.

"Does my face look thinner to you, Marianne?" I asked. "Do you think I am looking older?"

We both looked in the mirror. The face that looked back at us had my father's gray green eyes and was lightly tanned with a sprinkling of golden freckles marching across the bridge of its straight nose. The tan and the freckles were scandalously unfashionable, but they certainly did make me look young and healthy.

"No, my lady," Marianne said. "You are not looking older."

Damn, I thought crossly.

My maid turned to remove a pair of earrings from my jewelry case. She slipped them into my ears, then picked up a single strand of pearls and clasped it around my throat.

I stood up.

"Thank goodness I don't have to wear the bombazine any longer," I said. "It would be stifling on a warm summer night such as this."

My dressing room windows were open, and a light breeze was coming into the room, but the night was indeed warm. It wasn't just the weather that accounted for the small beads of perspiration that had formed on my upper lip, however. Tonight I would have to face Stephen across the dining room table.

I was suddenly very glad that Adam and Fanny would be there.

53

I went from my dressing room through the door into the bedroom next door and thence out into the corridor. I looked for a moment at the wide oak staircase, then I set my foot resolutely on the bottom step.

This had to be done, and the sooner I did it the sooner I could cease worrying about it. I made my mind a blank, marched up the stairs to the first bedroom along the second-floor passageway, and knocked briskly on the door.

There was no sound of footsteps within, but the door opened, suddenly and silently, and Stephen was there.

He *was* taller, I thought. When he had left for Jamaica my eyes had been on a level with his cheekbones. Now they were on a level with his mouth.

My heart began to hammer in my chest.

He looked at me and didn't say anything.

I spoke. "Before we eat, I would like you to meet Giles."

He still didn't say anything.

I stiffened my knees to keep them from trembling. "Will you come up to the nursery with me?"

He stepped out into the corridor and closed the door behind him. "Yes," he said.

We proceeded in silence back to the staircase and climbed the steps to the next floor, were we found Giles alone in the playroom working on a new puzzle.

"Mama!" Giles cried, and ran to hug me.

I stroked his shining blond hair. "Giles, here is your uncle Stephen come to say hello to you."

Giles turned eagerly to face Stephen, and for the first time Stephen looked upon the child who had cost him an earldom.

"How do you do, Uncle Stephen," Giles said shyly. "I am very glad you have come home."

Stephen's face was once more wearing its shuttered look, but he held out his hand and said, "I am very glad to meet you, Giles." Then, as Giles confided his small hand into his uncle's larger clasp, Stephen said, "You have a great look of your mother."

Giles did not appear pleased. During the last six months he had become very conscious of the fact that he was a boy, and he did not like being compared to a girl, even if the girl was his adored Mama.

Stephen immediately registered Giles's displeasure—he had always been extraordinarily quick at reading people. "I meant that your coloring is like your mother's," he amended easily. "Your features are all Grandville."

Giles smiled, placated. "Are you going to live with us, Uncle Stephen? Mama says that you are my guardian."

"I shall be living with you for the present, Giles," Stephen said. "Your papa wanted me to take care of the estate for you until you are grown up enough to do it for yourself."

"Do you like to fish, Uncle Stephen?" Giles asked eagerly.

"Yes, I do." For the first time, Stephen smiled at my son. "I did a great deal of fishing in Jamaica."

"We have fishing right here in our park," Giles informed him, "in our very own lake. And there is fishing in West Haven, too. On the *ocean*."

"Uncle Stephen grew up at Weston Hall, darling," I said. "He knows all about the fishing."

"Perhaps you would like to come fishing with Mama and me, Uncle Stephen," Giles said, and the hopeful expression on his face caught at my heart. "I caught *four* big fishes today. I ate them for dinner, Mama," he added in an aside to me.

A little of Stephen's initial stiffness had subsided in the face of Giles's childish chatter. He said now, "Surely you didn't eat all four of them, Giles."

"Yes," Giles said. "I did."

"They were not quite as big as you may be imagining, Stephen," I murmured.

His eyes swung around to me in a quick flash of blue, and my heart gave an unwelcome jolt.

Giles reverted with unswerving determination to his original question. "Will you come fishing with us, Uncle Stephen?"

Stephen's gaze returned to Giles. Part of me was anxious for him to say yes, so that my son would not feel rebuffed, and part of me wanted him to say no, so that I would be spared the excruciating agony of his company.

"I would love to go fishing with you, Giles," Stephen said. His gaze brushed my face again. "I have many very happy memories of Weston's lake."

Anger, sudden, hot, and welcome, swept through me. "I think it would be even more fun for you two boys to go without me," I said firmly. "It will give you a chance to get to know each other."

Giles, who was thirsting for male companionship, said eagerly, "Will you, Uncle Stephen?"

I could see the reluctance in Stephen's face. But he could see the hope in Giles's, and

Stephen had never had it in him to be cruel.

Except, of course, to me.

"Of course I will go," he said to Giles. "It will be fun."

CHAPTER
five

Dinner was not quite as dreadful as I had feared. Jasper and Uncle Adam sat on either side of me, and Nell and Aunt Fanny sat on either side of Stephen. This left Miss Stedham alone in the middle, facing an empty chair, but since this was a family party, the conversation was general and so wasn't awkward.

My mother had redone all the formal rooms at Weston Hall, and the dining room was resplendent in pale green and gold. The large two-pedestal mahogany table was surrounded by gilt-and-green silk chairs, and overhead a huge crystal chandelier hung majestically from the domed ceiling. A carved mahogany sideboard, impressively loaded with silver servers, stood against the north wall. The pièces de résistance, however, were the matching portraits of my mother and Stephen's father that hung next to each other on the east wall, facing the sideboard.

Sir Thomas Lawrence had done the portraits a few years after they were married. The earl, blond and handsome, looked just as Gerald would have looked had he lived to forty. It was not only the good looks that caught one's attention when one looked at the earl's portrait, however. Lawrence had captured the easy look

57

of aristocratic confidence that had character-
ized the man, the sort of confidence that can
belong only to someone who is supremely certain of himself and of his own high position in
the world.

Lawrence's portrait of my mother was already
famous. He considered it one of his master-
pieces, and it probably was. He had painted
her in a soft green-colored morning dress, holding a King Charles spaniel in her arms. (She
had borrowed the spaniel from Lady Morton.
My mother does not care for dogs.) It was a
perfect matching portrait to the earl's. She
seemed, in all her immense feminine beauty
and elegance, to be the very essence of a great
aristocracy.

Mama was very proud of the portrait, and it
had been praised and admired by legions.

I sometimes wondered if I were the only one
who saw the other thing that Lawrence had
managed to capture in the portrait, the thing
that revealed his genius and marked him as a
truly great painter and not just a social recorder.
If you looked closely enough at the pictured
woman, you could see the selfishness in her
beauty, the coldness in her smile, the shallow-
ness in her lovely green eyes.

The footmen came in with the first course,
a delicate beef broth that our cook did very
well. William and James filled each individual
bowl at the sideboard and brought them to the
table.

Aunt Fanny said, "You are so brown, Stephen!
I shouldn't have thought your skin capable of
turning so very brown."

"The sun in Jamaica is very hot," Stephen

replied. His soup dish was set in front of him, and he picked up his spoon.

"I know a few fellows who were out in India," Jasper remarked. "They all came home just as brown as Stephen."

Aunt Fanny said, "When Stephen was a little boy his skin would burn when he was out in the sun for too long."

"I stopped burning after a few months, Aunt Fanny," Stephen said.

"I think Stephen looks very nice with his tan, Mama," Nell said loyally. She had always been one of Stephen's partisans.

Stephen gave Nell a friendly smile, then said to Miss Stedham, "A great friend of mine in Jamaica had the name of Stedham. Could he be any relation of yours, Miss Stedham?"

Miss Stedham replied in her quiet, well-bred voice, "He is my brother."

I stared at her in amazement. "You never mentioned to me that you had a brother in Jamaica, Miss Stedham," I said.

"He is employed as an agent for one of the English-owned plantations on the island, my lady," she said matter-of-factly. "When my father died, Tom had to find employment, and Lord Northrup offered him the post."

Miss Stedham came from a family that was impeccably blue-blooded and desperately impoverished. Her father had lost his entire fortune at gaming and then had killed himself, leaving his children to make their way in the world as best they could. Miss Stedham had become a governess. Her brother, it seemed, had become a plantation agent.

"Tom Stedham is one of the very few decent white men I encountered during all the years I spent in Jamaica," Stephen said forcefully. "I was damn glad to have him for a friend."

"Stephen!" Aunt Fanny protested.

He gave her a bewildered look.

"Don't say 'damn' at the dinner table," I interpreted.

"Oh." He gave his aunt an apologetic smile. "Sorry, Aunt Fanny. I fear I have grown unaccustomed to the company of ladies."

Nell's exotic dark eyes were glued to his face. "Surely there were *some* ladies in Jamaica, Stephen."

He shrugged. "As I couldn't abide their husbands, Nell, I'm afraid I didn't see much of them."

I was annoyed by the twinge of pleasure that went through me at those words.

"Surely things weren't as bad as that, Stephen," Adam protested mildly.

"They were every bit as bad as that, Uncle Adam," Stephen said bitterly. "I have never met a more despicable group of men in my life than the agents, attorneys, and overseers hired by absentee owners to run the sugar plantations in Jamaica." He put down his spoon. "The first thing I did after I arrived was to fire our own overseer. The man was a perfect brute."

Aunt Fanny smiled at him. "Dear Stephen, you haven't changed at all."

"Did he ill-treat the slaves, Stephen?" Nell asked.

Stephen's mouth set in the way we all knew. "Yes."

"That is unpardonable, of course," Adam said.

Miss Stedham said quietly, "The really un-

60

pardonable thing is the enslaving of another human being in the first place."

Stephen regarded her with warm approval. "You are very like your brother," he said.

"The slave trade has been abolished in British territories since 1807, Miss Stedham," Jasper reminded her.

"That act may have halted the importation of new slaves, Jasper, but the breeding of present slaves still goes on." The bitter note was back in Stephen's voice.

Aunt Fanny glanced at me, and when she saw I was not going to intervene, she once more took it upon herself. "This is hardly a topic fit for the dinner table, my dear Stephen. There is a young lady present."

"Oh, Mama!" Nell protested.

Stephen said, "Sorry, Aunt Fanny. Sorry, Nell."

"I don't mind at all, Stephen," Nell said.

He winked at her.

The footmen approached the table to remove the soup. A roast beef was brought in and set before Stephen.

His whole face froze and he looked at the meat as if he didn't know what it was.

There was an awkward silence, and then Uncle Adam asked kindly, "Would you like me to carve it for you, Stephen?"

He shook his head once and didn't reply.

I understood what emotion Stephen was struggling with. The last time he had eaten at this table, his father had carved the roast. In Stephen's absence, the earl's position as carver had been filled by Gerald.

His father and his brother. He would never see them again.

Stephen lifted his eyes from the roast and looked at me. He was white under his tan.

I said softly, "I imagine Stephen can manage to carve a roast, Uncle Adam."

"Yes," Stephen said. He picked up the knife, grasped the fork, and correctly sliced the first piece.

The footmen took our plates and brought them to Stephen, who put the meat on them. When our plates had been returned, our wineglasses refilled, and the side dishes put out, I said, "Tell us, Jasper, what do you think of this scheme of making Napoleon the ruler of Elba? Do you think it will satisfy him?"

Jasper put down his fork and turned to me. "I don't know, Annabelle." His strong, square face was grave, his gray eyes thoughtful.

Ever since his boyhood all Jasper had wanted was to join the army. Uncle Adam had bought him a commission when he was nineteen, and he had not lived at Weston above a few weeks ever since. It was good to have him safely home again.

He said now, "A man like that, one who has almost ruled the world... well, one wonders if he will be content with just one small island."

The conversation turned to the end of the war and then to the local harvest.

Thank God, I thought, for Uncle Adam and his family. Thank God there was someone to stand between Stephen and me.

We gathered in the drawing room after dinner, and Adam and Jasper and Fanny and I sat down to a game of whist. Nell and Stephen went to look at the rose garden. Miss Stedham went upstairs to Giles.

I had a headache and played badly, which annoyed Adam, who was my partner.

"Sorry, Uncle Adam," I said as I neglected to lead back into the ace that he was holding. "I'm rather tired. I think I'll go to bed."

As I finished speaking Stephen and Nell came in through the French doors. Nell looked very animated; her dark eyes were sparkling. Stephen was smiling.

"The moon is out," Nell said. "The sky is very beautiful."

My headache began to pound.

"Poor Annabelle has the headache," Aunt Fanny announced to the room.

I looked at her in surprise; I had said nothing about a headache.

"One can always tell when you have the headache, dear," Aunt Fanny said sympathetically. "You get dark shadows under your eyes."

"How attractive that must be," I said lightly. I stood up. "Will you dispense the tea, Aunt Fanny?"

"Certainly, my dear Annabelle. Don't worry about us—you need your bed."

I smiled at her and said a general good night to everyone else. I went out into the passageway, along past the saloon and the Great Hall, and into the family part of the house. The master suite was in the southwest corner, and I let myself into my dressing room, closed the door behind me, and leaned my shoulders back against it, as if I were keeping someone out.

The back of my head felt as if it were being squeezed by a vise.

I cannot live like this, I thought. Even with the others present in the house, it was impossible.

Stephen was going to have to go.

I can't just throw him out, though, I thought miserably. He is Giles's guardian. He has a right to live in the house.

Stephen, I thought. Oh God, Stephen. How did we ever come to such a wilderness?

I rang the bell and Marianne came to help me undress. When I dismissed her, however, I did not get into bed but went instead to the open window. The night was warm and the sweet scent of the cut roses that Mrs. Nordlem had arranged in the crystal bowl on my nightstand filled the room.

I didn't want to get into the big bed that I had shared with Gerald. Instead I turned one of the chintz-covered chairs around to face the window, curled up in it, and allowed the soft, moist, fragrant summer air to carry me back over the years.

And once again I am eight years old, and Mama has taken me to Weston Hall and told me that this is where I am going to live.

My father had been dead a year when Mama married the Earl of Weston. Papa was a soldier. His family was a good one, but he was the younger son of a younger son and so had no money. Mama had married him when she was eighteen years old, and she was twenty when she had me. When he died she determined that next time she would marry better. She took a lodging in Bath, showed her beautiful face in the pump room and at the assemblies, and at the end of the Season she had managed to snare the widowed Earl of Weston.

A week before the wedding, the earl sent a

coach to Bath to bring Mama and me to Weston. I will never forget the fear I felt as we drove up the immense circular drive and for the first time I saw the huge gray stone house rear up before me. Later I would discover that Weston was actually laid out in a friendlier, cozier fashion than many of the country homes of the aristocracy, but that first view of symmetrical stone walls, glittering windows, and multitudes of chimneys struck me mute with terror.

The butler met us in the great entry hall, which by itself was larger than most of the lodgings I had lived in. He then escorted us through a huge gilded room that he called the saloon and thence into the drawing room, where the earl and his sons awaited us.

The rooms all had immensely high ceilings that were decorated with either paintings, plasterwork, or both. The house seemed to me to be as grand as a palace, and the thought of living here made me feel quite ill.

The earl took my hand, kissed my forehead, and told me that I looked just like my mama. I dropped my eyes to the tips of my too small boots and mumbled some reply.

I remember that Mama exerted herself to be charming to the earl's two sons. Gerald gazed at her as if enchanted, which of course endeared him to her immediately. She rhapsodized over his good looks, his intelligence, his charm; she asked him about his school.

Stephen stood silently and listened. His face was grave, but I thought I could detect the faintest trace of scorn in his eyes as he watched my mother. Then he looked at me.

Dark blue eyes in a thin, little boy's face.

65

Looking at me. Seeing me.

"How old are you?" he asked me.

"Eight," I said.

"I'm nine."

I nodded.

The earl made an attempt to draw Mama's attention to his other son. "Stephen is not yet at school, Regina," he said. "But the rector tells me he is a very promising scholar."

"How nice," my mother said. "And why are you not at school, Stephen?"

Stephen didn't answer, just gave her that grave, faintly scornful look.

"Stephen was ill last year and we thought it best to keep him home for another year or so," the earl replied.

My mother regarded Stephen's thin body. "I am sorry to hear that you were ill, Stephen," she said.

Stephen said, "Thank you."

"What was wrong?"

"I had a fever for a long time," Stephen said. "But I am all better now."

My mother raised her perfect brows and looked at the earl.

"We never did find out what it was, but he seems to have recuperated very well," Stephen's father confirmed. Then, in a low voice, "I think part of it was missing his mother."

Stephen shot his father a distinctly annoyed look.

I thought that perhaps that was why Stephen seemed so unimpressed by Mama. He did not like her for the same reason that I did not like the earl.

Gerald said, "It will seem strange to call so young and beautiful a lady 'Mama.'"

Stephen looked as if he would die before he called her any such thing.

I was liking him more and more.

My mother said to Gerald, "You may call me Regina if that would make you more comfortable, Gerald."

I knew I would never call the earl anything but 'sir.'

A footman in blue-and-gold livery came into the room, bearing a tray.

"Ah," the earl said genially, "here is our refreshment." He looked at Stephen and me. "Sit down, children, and your mother will pour you some lemonade."

There was a circle of extremely uncomfortable gilt chairs arranged in front of the French windows, and the butler was setting a table in front of one of them so the footman could put down his tray. The earl sat on one side of my mother, and Gerald sat on the other. Stephen and I automatically took the two chairs that were on the opposite side of the circle.

My mother poured lemonade from a silver pitcher for the three children, and then she poured tea for herself and the earl. The day was hot, and I felt horribly sick to my stomach from the ride, but she looked as cool and fresh as if she had just stepped out of her dressing room.

The earl couldn't take his eyes off of her.

My feet did not reach the floor, and I sat straight, my spine not touching the back of the chair, my lemonade clutched in my sticky, sweaty hands. I looked around the room, at the ornate chimneypiece, the carved moldings, the expensive, uncomfortable furniture. The French door opened onto what seemed to be acres and acres of lush green lawns and flower gardens.

How can I live here? I thought in despair.

In a low voice Stephen said to me, "Do you go to school, Annabelle?"

I brought my eyes back to him. There was a beading of sweat on his forehead, and he had finished half his glass of lemonade. I shook my head. "Mama says that she will get a governess for me," I said. I had had a governess briefly, before my father died, but Mama had not been able to afford one since.

Strange house.

Strange governess.

I stretched my eyes wide, forcing back the threatened tears. I would rather die than cry in front of the earl.

Stephen said, "You don't need to be afraid of coming to live at Weston, you know." His crisp voice was matter-of-fact. "I will be here to show you how to go on."

He had stripes of sunburn on his nose and along his high cheekbones.

My mother said something, and both the earl and Gerald laughed.

I said to Stephen, "Do you have a pony?"

He looked amazed that I should ask such a question, as if in his world ponies were as common as lemonade. He nodded. "His name is Peaches."

"Peaches?" I asked in amazement.

"He likes peaches."

"Isn't that... unusual?" I asked.

"Very," Stephen said.

He took another big drink of lemonade.

"Do you have a pony, Annabelle?"

I shook my head.

"Well, we shall have to get one for you, then," he said.

I stopped breathing.

He looked at me a little anxiously. "Are you afraid of horses?"

I shook my head vigorously, and my breathing started up again.

"I have never learned to ride," I confessed in a constricted little voice. "We always moved too much for me to be able to have a pony."

I would never tell the earl's son that my own papa hadn't been able to afford a pony for me.

"Do you... do you think I might learn?" I asked.

He gave me that amazed look again. "Of course," he said. "I'll get Grimes to teach you. He is our head groom, you know, and a good 'un."

He must have seen the response in my face, because suddenly he grinned.

The wonder of Stephen's smile.

I smiled back.

"I have a dog, too," he said. "He sleeps in my room in the nursery."

"They *allow* you to have your dog in your bedroom?" I asked in awe. Mama would not even let a dog in the house.

"My mother said I could," he replied.

I glanced at my own mother. "Your mother sounds nice," I said.

His lips tightened and he nodded.

"What is your dog's name?" I asked.

"Rags," Stephen said.

"Do you think that perhaps I could have a dog?" I asked daringly.

"You have to get the right governess," he said.

We had looked at each other in perfect comprehension, already allies against the grown-up world.

It was pain to remember. I leaned back in my chair and shut my eyes and inhaled the scent of the summer night deep into my lungs. An unbridgeable chasm lay between the children I was remembering and the adults we had become. Nothing could give us back our innocence. Nothing could make us Annabelle-and-Stephen once again.

It wasn't until I brushed my hand against my cheek that I realized I was crying.

CHAPTER
six

I took Giles for a ride early the following morning. Before Gerald died, Giles had been happy to ride in front of me on my horse, but these last months he had insisted on being allowed to ride his pony. For the last few weeks he had not even allowed me to hold a lead line.

"I'm a big boy, Mama." They were his favorite words. In a few weeks he would be five years old.

We took the ride through the park that went in the direction of the Brighton Road, as Giles wanted to check to see if the unusual bird he had spotted a few days ago was still in the same tree.

It wasn't.

"I wonder where he is, Mama?" he asked as we walked our horses side by side along the grassy ride. The trees, thick with summer foliage, made a canopy over our heads. Cuckoos called from within the wood, and squirrels raced madly up and down the trees.

"Perhaps he is out searching for seeds, Giles. Or for worms."

"He was pretty," Giles said wistfully. "His feathers were all blue. But he wasn't a bluebird, was he, Mama?"

"I don't think so. I don't know what kind of a bird he was, Giles. But I agree that he was very pretty."

We rode for a few minutes in silence.

Then, "Uncle Stephen is nice, isn't he, Mama?" Giles said.

"Did you think so?"

"His eyes are the same color as that blue bird's feathers," Giles said.

I cleared my throat. "Yes, I suppose they are."

We were coming out of the park now onto the local road that connected up with the main road to Brighton. Farms lined the northern side of the dirt road; to the south rose the wooded hillside that stood between the valley and the Channel.

These were the farms that belonged to the Earl of Weston and were leased by tenant farmers. August was the time for harvesting, and the fields were filled with people working hard under the early sun. Even the tradesmen from the village pitched in for the harvest.

Giles and I stopped our horses and looked out at the men, women, and children who were

71

cutting their laborious way through the field of billowing wheat. They worked with sickle, reaping hook, fagging hook, and scythe. All of this wheat must be cut by hand and then stacked in sheaves before nightfall. Wheat could not stand unsheaved overnight.

During the war years the wheat crop had represented a substantial amount of money to farmers, but now that the war was over, prices were falling. All of this work would reap less of a reward than it had in the past, and our tenant farmers would likely find themselves considerably less prosperous than they had been.

Topper, my bay gelding, kicked his near hind foot forward, trying to reach a fly that had landed on his belly.

"Let's go a little farther, Mama," Giles said, and he trotted his pony forward.

The Washburn farm was the next farm on the road, and I didn't want to pass it.

"No, Giles, it's time to go back," I called to my son. Instead of stopping, however, his pony accelerated from a trot into a canter and then, almost instantly, from a canter into a gallop.

My heart jumped into my throat, and I sent Topper after the pony.

The sound of hoofbeats behind him only spurred the pony to run faster. He was galloping flat out now, with Giles standing in his stirrups, holding on to the pony's mane.

I passed the pony in two strides, planted Topper's rear in the pony's face, and began to slow down. From a gallop we went to a canter from a canter to a trot and then down to a walk. Finally I turned in the saddle to look at Giles.

His eyes were glowing, his expression radiant. "I've never gone that fast before, Mama. That was fun!"

He was, after all, my son.

"You shouldn't go that fast until you can hold on to your reins and steer," I said sternly.

"When will I be able to do that?" he demanded.

"In another year or so, I expect."

He looked outraged. "Another *year?*"

"Well, if you practice very hard on keeping your seat, perhaps it will be sooner. Now, let's turn these horses around."

But Giles's eyes were caught by the overgrown fields on the north side of the road. "How come there is nothing growing on this farm, Mama?" he asked.

"Mr. Washburn, the farmer, is very ill," I said. "He never got the seed in."

"Nobody helped him?" Giles asked, clearly surprised. The valley was a small community, and people were in the habit of helping each other out.

"I'm afraid that no one likes Mr. Washburn very much. He is not a very nice man."

We were still facing west on the road, and now a cart drawn by a cob I didn't recognize came into sight. As the road dead-ended at Weston Park, the cart's destination could only be the Mapshaw farm or this derelict one. I resigned myself to the meeting.

The cob pulled up in front of us and Jem Washburn's face looked into mine. "Miss Annabelle," he said, and took off his cap. His hair, black as a raven's wing, was clean and shining in the morning sun. His bony face was a man's now, not a boy's, but his deep-set pale blue eyes were the same.

"How are you, Jem?" I said.

"I'm good, thank you." His eyes moved to Giles, who was regarding him with undisguised curiosity.

"This is my son," I said. "Giles, this is Mr. Washburn. He used to be a great friend of your uncle Stephen's when we were children."

"I am sorry that your papa is sick," Giles said politely.

Jem shot me a startled look.

"Giles was wondering why there was nothing growing in your fields," I said. "I told him that your father was sick."

"He died this morning," Jem said in a flat voice. "I was just into the village to see the rector."

"He couldn't have picked a worse time," I said frankly. "Everyone is busy with the harvest."

Jem shrugged. "It won't matter," he said. "We'll bury him tomorrow, and if nobody comes it can't be helped. He never made friends while he was alive; no reason for folk to put themselves out now that he's dead."

Giles's eyes were huge as he listened to Jem's cold assessment of his father.

I said, "Stephen came home yesterday. I'll tell him that you're here." I heard the chilly note in my voice, but I couldn't help it.

Jem's face was somber. "If he doesn't want to see me, tell him I'll understand."

"Of course he will want to see you," I said. I shortened my reins and prepared to turn away. "If there is anything we can do for you, you have only to let Adam know."

His eyes were as cold as my own. "Thanks, but I doubt I'll need anything from you"—a significant pause—"my lady."

"Come along, Giles," I said, and trotted Topper back down the road in the direction of Weston Park. Giles and his pony trotted alongside, and, daunted by what he must have seen on my face, he didn't ask me another question the entire way back to the stable.

The afternoon was very warm, and I decided to take the dogs down to the lake so they could swim. Jasper offered to come with me, and we set off together along the graveled path that led through the acres of landscaped parkland that Capability Brown had created for Gerald's grandfather on the north side of the house. A herd of over a hundred deer grazed on lush grass beneath clumps of splendid beeches, chestnuts, and oaks. The lake itself was set like a jewel in the midst of this woodland masterpiece. Beyond the lake the land rose gently but inexorably toward the heights of the Downs.

Jasper and I walked to the edge of the water, and Jasper picked up a stick to throw for the dogs. Merlin and Portia panted with anticipation, their eyes glued to the stick. Jasper threw it and both dogs splashed into the water and began to swim. I noted with satisfaction that Jasper could throw much farther than I; the dogs would get a good workout.

The sun was hot, and I was glad of my wide-brimmed straw hat and thin cotton dress.

Jasper was dressed in breeches, boots, and rust-colored coat: correct attire for a country gentleman, but warm for this August afternoon. I said, "If you wish to take off your coat, Jasper, I won't mind."

He looked at me and said, "Only if you promise not to tell my mother."

That made me laugh. "Is this the hero whose courage didn't flinch in the midst of battle?"

He was sliding his coat from his shoulders. "It is that Mama always manages to look so *disappointed* when one doesn't live up to her expectations."

"I shall have to remember that strategy when I am dealing with Giles," I said.

Portia had retrieved the stick this time, and both dogs came splashing out of the water so she could return it to Jasper and have it thrown again. I held out my hand for his coat, noticing that he did not owe the breadth of his shoulders to any artificial padding as so many of the London dandies did. He gave me the jacket, then once more threw the stick into the water. I folded the coat neatly and put it down at a decent distance from the dogs.

Merlin was the first to reach the stick this time. I watched the twin black heads of my spaniels as they swam toward us, and I said to Jasper, "What will you do now that the war is finished?"

"I don't know," he replied soberly.

I looked up at him from beneath the brim of my hat. "For as long as I can remember, Jasper, all you ever wanted was a commission. Have you had enough of it, then?"

There was a dark, brooding look to his Grandville face, an expression that had not been there before the war. He said, "Do you know,

Annabelle, I rather think I have. I had enough of it after Burgos, actually. So much death...." He shook his head as if trying to clear it of an ugly vision.

I looked out over the lake. "Yes," I said. "Too much."

He said in a roughened voice, "I was so sorry about Gerald, Annabelle."

"It was a terrible shock," I said.

"I wished I could have been with you."

"I appreciated your letter, Jasper. It helped—truly. And your mother and father have been wonderful to me."

With extreme delicacy, Merlin deposited the stick at Jasper's feet. Once more he threw it into the lake.

"What will you do if you stop being a soldier?" I asked curiously.

He hesitated. Then he said, "Papa owns a small property in Northhamptonshire, and he wants to make it over to me."

"I didn't know that Uncle Adam had a property in Northamptonshire," I said in surprise.

"He came into possession of it only recently. I believe it belonged to a distant cousin of my mother's. The house is in good repair and there are a few farms attached to it." A light breeze began to blow off the lake, and it stirred the tawny hair at Jasper's temples. Stephen was the only Grandville who was not a blond.

"Northamptonshire." I said the place name with reverence. "Northamptonshire is wonderful hunting country, Jasper."

"I can't afford to hunt in the shires, Annabelle," Jasper said shortly.

I bit my lip, annoyed with myself for being

so insensitive. Hunting in the shires was pro-hibitively expensive. I should have had enough sense to keep my mouth closed.

Jasper was going on, "I'm on indefinite leave presently, so I have time to make up my mind as to what I will do. In the meanwhile, I am going to relax and enjoy my time at home."

The dogs were back, but Jasper ignored them, turning instead to face me. There were fine wrinkles in the corners of his gray eyes, as if he had spent many hours squinting into the strong Spanish sun, and his skin was lightly tanned. The open collar of his shirt showed the strong, muscled column of his neck.

Here is another one who went away a boy and has returned a man, I thought.

"Weston will always be home to me," he said a little huskily.

I gave him an unshadowed smile. "We were such happy children," I said. "Sometimes I wish we could turn back time and all be children again, with nothing more to worry us than how many muffins we could squeeze out of your mother's cook."

"The ever good-natured Mrs. Sprague," he said, returning my smile. "She never minded us underfoot in her kitchen."

"You *always* got the biggest muffin," I reminded him. "Stephen and I used to think it was unfair."

"It was my house," Jasper said.

The dogs, realizing their game was over, proceeded to give themselves a thorough shake. Jasper and I backed away from the shower of drops. "Let's walk to the fishing pavilion," I said.

We began to stroll along the shoreline, with the dogs racing ahead of us. "Remember the summer of the Club?" Jasper asked suddenly.

The "Club" he was referring to was started by Gerald two summers after I came to Weston. Gerald had heard his father talking about "his club" in London (the earl belonged to White's) and had decided to emulate his papa and start his own exclusive club in Weston. He enrolled himself, Jack, Stephen, and Jasper as members and got my mother to allow him to use one of the empty bedrooms as his clubhouse.

I had been furious that he wouldn't allow Nell or me to join.

"Females do not belong to clubs," Gerald had declared with all the lofty arrogance of the spoiled young adolescent male.

"Fine," I had replied with hauteur. "Nell and I will have our own club, and *you* can't join."

I had recruited Susan Fenton (she hadn't been Fenton then, of course) and Alice Thornton (the daughter of the earl's wealthiest tenant), and we had adopted the fishing pavilion as our headquarters.

All summer long the two clubs had vied with each other, each trying to demonstrate that it was having more fun than the rival club. Escapade had followed escapade. The boys jumped from the top of a barn roof into a hayrick. The girls made a raft out of some lumber we roped together and rode it out into the middle of the lake. The boys spent the night in the village graveyard. The girls "borrowed" one of Susan's father's wagons, and I daringly drove it into the village, right under the boys' noses. I had been ten years old.

"It was a miracle that none of us got hurt," I said now to Jasper. "When I think that someday Giles might do some of those things, my blood runs cold."

He laughed. "It was so much fun, though. I can still remember the four of us, huddled in that bedroom, plotting our little hearts out. And no matter what we came up with, you always managed to top it."

I grinned. "It was fun."

"The bonfire was our best effort, I thought," Jasper said.

"I liked our ghost impersonation best," I returned.

Jasper ran a hand through his hair. "I used to think of that summer when I was in Spain," he said. "In the early morning, waiting for a battle to begin, I would go over it in my mind. It was my talisman, my good-luck memory."

I felt sadness descend on me like a cloak. "We have all come so far since that summer," I said. "You have been to war. Stephen was sent to Jamaica. And Gerald is... dead."

Jasper slowly shook his head. "I still can't quite believe that he is gone, Annabelle. Not Gerald— the sun child, the golden boy. Everything the rest of us wanted came pouring into his lap." He was walking with bent head, his eyes fixed on the ground under his feet. "Somehow one always thought that Gerald would live forever."

I tried for a lighter note. "At least you and Stephen are safely home."

He gave me a look that I couldn't read. "Yes," he said. "Frankly, I was surprised that Gerald named Stephen to be Giles's guardian. He and Stephen were hardly close."

I shrugged. We had rounded a small clump of trees, and the fishing pavilion came into sight. Portia and Merlin began to race each other to see who could get there first.

I said, "There is other good news. Jack has recently won quite a large sum of money, and, as I am sure you must have heard, Nell has had four offers of marriage."

At that he grinned. "I've heard something about them," he said.

We both laughed.

"There's someone at the pavilion," Jasper said.

The dogs were barking and yipping. Then a small figure was running across the grass toward us.

"Mama!" Giles called. "I catched another fish!"

He barreled into me, and I staggered a little under the onslaught of his weight.

"Caught, not catched, Giles," I said.

Jasper caught my arm and steadied me. "Whoa there, youngster. You almost knocked your mother down."

"Sorry, Mama," Giles said. He beamed up at me, his light gray green eyes shining, as they did when he was happy. "Uncle Stephen and Genie didn't catch anything, but I did!"

I looked over at the pavilion, which was nothing more than a summer house with a single interior room surrounded by a roofed porch. A man and a woman were standing on the steps of the porch, watching us. The dogs raced from the pavilion back to me, and the man and woman descended the steps and waited for us in front of the pavilion.

"Good afternoon," Jasper said to Stephen and

Miss Stedham as we came up to them. "I'm sorry to hear that you didn't catch any fish."

Miss Stedham laughed. She looked very lovely in a straw sunshade and a lavender muslin dress. "Giles seems to have a special talent for fishing," she said.

Giles laughed gleefully.

Portia had returned to Stephen and was sitting at his feet, looking up at him. Like Jasper, he had taken off his coat and rolled up his sleeves in the heat. He was taller than Jasper and thinner, and his face and throat and forearms looked very dark against the white of his shirt.

"I told Uncle Stephen about that man we met this morning, Mama," Giles said.

I put my hand on my son's shoulder. "Yes, Jem Washburn is back, Stephen," I said coolly. "His father died this morning."

"I already *told* him that, Mama," Giles said with annoyance.

Both Stephen and Jasper looked at Giles, obviously startled by his tone of voice. My fingers tightened on his shoulder. If I wanted to spoil my son, it was my business and no one else's.

"Jem said that if you didn't wish to see him, he would understand." My own voice had gone from cool to cold.

Giles looked up at me uneasily, and I forced my fingers to relax on his shoulder. I gave him a reassuring smile.

"Why would he think you wouldn't want to see him?" Jasper asked Stephen. "The two of you were always such great friends."

Stephen shook his head in professed bewilderment. "I can't imagine why he would say such a thing."

I could imagine very well, but I said nothing.

"I don't know if you heard, but shortly after you left for Jamaica, Jem ran away from home," Jasper told Stephen. "We heard nothing of him until a few months ago, when he suddenly came back. He must have heard that his father was dying."

Stephen's expression was totally detached. He nodded.

"He paid my father the overdue farm rent," Jasper said.

That caught everyone's attention.

"*Jem* paid the rent?" I asked.

"So my father said—two quarters' worth. He asked Jem what he had been doing these last few years, but Jem's reply was evasive."

"Susan Fenton told me that he wanted to take over the farm," I said abruptly.

Jasper nodded. "That is what he told my father."

Giles shuffled his feet, impatient with a conversation in which he was not included.

Stephen said, "Well, if Jem wants the farm, then of course he must have it."

"Of course he must," I said.

This time everyone looked at me.

"Don't you *like* Jem Washburn, Mama?" Giles asked anxiously.

In fact, I disliked Jem Washburn intensely.

"I never think about him," I said. "Now, where is that fish you caught, Giles? I want to see it."

He was instantly distracted. "It's in the bucket, Mama!" He grabbed my hand and began to drag me forward. "Come and see!"

We all were happy to have something else to

talk about, and even Giles was satisfied that he had received enough credit for catching his fish.

The fishing party gathered up its equipment and we all walked back to the house together, Stephen carrying the poles and Giles carrying his fish. My son surprised me by choosing to walk between Stephen and Miss Stedham and not with Jasper and me.

Jasper and I and the dogs went first, and we both were silent as we listened to the conversation being conducted behind us.

It was actually more of an inquisition than a conversation, with Giles asking Stephen relentless question after relentless question, most of them starting with the words "Uncle Stephen, did you ever..."

Stephen answered all the questions with a patience that was truly heroic.

The gravel path crunched under my shoes, and Jasper's arm brushed lightly against mine. Lawn and trees stretched away on either side of us. A small group of deer were standing in the shade of a clump of magnificent chestnuts, and behind them, in the distance, one could just make out the stone building that was the old bathhouse.

Behind us Miss Stedham said gently, "Giles, it is not good manners to monopolize the conversation."

"Oh," said Giles. Then, charmingly, "If you want to ask Uncle Stephen some questions, Genie, you can."

The sound of Stephen's low chuckle caused the muscles in my abdomen to tighten. The sun was hot on my head and shoulders, and I could feel beads of moisture forming on my upper lip.

Stephen said, "Go ahead, Miss Stedham. Ask me."

I could hear the smile in her voice as she answered, "To be truthful, I should very much like to hear about my brother, Mr. Grandville. I have not seen him in six years, you know."

Stephen said, "What would you like to know?"

The deer left the shade of the chestnuts and began to flow over the grass, grazing with delicate particularity.

"I would like to know if he is going to find himself unemployed shortly," Miss Stedham said bluntly. "His letters have been painting an increasingly gloomy picture of the Jamaican economy."

"Unfortunately, it is true that, economically, things are not good in Jamaica, Miss Stedham," Stephen said.

"That is what I keep hearing. But what does 'not good' really mean?" Miss Stedham asked. I heard the tension in her voice and for the first time realized that she was genuinely worried about her brother losing his position.

Stephen said, "I'll give you an example. My own family's plantation, which made a twelve percent profit during the late 1700s, was barely meeting operating costs when I went out there five years ago. And Westover was always one of the most profitable plantations on the island."

Jasper whistled. He turned his head and asked, "What was the situation when you left, Stephen? The same? Or worse?"

"I got out of the sugar business," Stephen said. "Remember?"

Jasper grunted. "That's right."

"It's worse for everyone else, though," Stephen said.

I stuck my tongue out and licked away the perspiration on my upper lip. It tasted salty. I glanced sideways and caught Jasper staring at me. He looked away immediately.

Stephen was going on, "Since the turn of the century, over a hundred estates have been given up in Jamaica for unmet debts, and suits are now pending against one hundred and fifteen others." He paused and his voice gentled. "I am afraid that one of those estates is Lord Northrup's, Miss Stedham."

I knew that gentle voice. I pressed my lips together hard and stared intently at the gravel under my feet.

Miss Stedham said in a low voice, "That is what I feared."

Jasper turned his head again and said, "But won't the end of the war help the sugar planters, Stephen? Now that Napoleon is defeated, the whole continent is once more an open market."

"It will undoubtedly help the planters in Cuba and Brazil, who have access to an unending supply of slaves," Stephen said in a bitter voice. "I do not think it will help Jamaica."

"Because Jamaica is British and so is barred from importing new slaves?" Jasper asked.

"Yes," said Stephen.

Giles gave up on regaining Stephen's attention and skipped forward to take my hand. Some water sloshed over the top of his bucket, and he bent his head to check that his fish was safe.

I said over my shoulder, "Do not worry about your brother, Miss Stedham. If he finds himself without employment, Stephen will help him. Stephen always helps his friends."

I said this in an extraordinarily sweet voice, so I didn't understand why everyone was suddenly staring at me. I felt myself flush and was glad that my face was shadowed by the wide brim of my hat.

Stephen said pleasantly, "In fact, Tom and I have indeed discussed a plan for his next position, Miss Stedham. I do not think you need to fear for his future."

"That is wonderful news." The relief in Miss Stedham's voice was embarrassingly obvious. "Is... do you think Tom might be coming home, Mr. Grandville?"

"He will stay in Jamaica until the plantation is officially foreclosed," Stephen said. "But I expect you will see him by Christmas, Miss Stedham."

I turned my head to catch a glimpse of Miss Stedham's glowing face. Stephen was smiling at her. Once more I turned my back to them. I looked up at Jasper and made some inane comment about the weather.

He answered, bless him, and we chatted away about nothing at all for the rest of the way back to the house.

CHAPTER
seven

I was awakened in the night by a thunderstorm.

Good, I thought sleepily as I rolled over on my back. Perhaps it won't be so hot tomorrow.

My windows had been opened as far as they could go, and the cool air of the storm was streaming into the room. I yawned, then struggled out of bed to see if the rain was wetting the draperies. When I saw that it wasn't, I left the windows as they were and got back into bed.

The room had cooled sufficiently for me to pull the quilt up over my shoulders, and I cuddled down under it, inhaling the fresh chilly air deeply into my lungs.

Lightning flashed, followed a few seconds later by the rumble of thunder.

These days I rather liked thunderstorms, although there had been a time when I had been afraid of them.

The room was filled with the sharp, distinct smell that a thunderstorm always brings. I snuggled my head into my pillow, closed my eyes, and let the smell carry me back over the years.

And once again I am nine years old, and the thunder is crashing outside my bedroom window, and I am afraid.

The fear of thunderstorms started with the death of my father. I do not remember ever worrying about storms until then. It was a fear that grew worse when we moved to Weston, where the storms were fiercer because of its proximity to the Channel.

The sick, frightened feeling would begin with the first sound of distant rumbling. Afternoon storms, when I was with other people, were just bearable. It was the nighttime storms, when I was all alone, that were the worst.

The July day had been sultry, and I awoke in the middle of the night to the sound of thunder. Then lightning flashed, so brightly that for one brief moment it illuminated the whole of my nursery bedroom. I saw quite clearly the big walnut dresser, the pictures of horses I had hung on the walls, the shelf that held my favorite books. The crash of thunder that followed the lightning was deafening.

I pulled the covers up over my head and huddled under them, quivering all over inside my cotton nightdress.

The next lightning flash was so brilliant that it even brightened the dark under the covers, and I whimpered.

"Annabelle."

He had to repeat my name twice before I heard him.

"Don't be afraid, Annabelle," he said. "It will be over soon."

I peered cautiously from beneath my covers. I saw him clearly in the next lightning flash, standing next to my bed, his hair ruffled from sleep, his blue eyes concerned.

"I d-don't like thunders-storms, Stephen," I said.

"I know. But you're quite safe in the house, Annabelle. Nothing can hurt you in here."

I nodded.

He could see from my face that I didn't believe him.

A crack of thunder made me jump. I stared at him imploringly.

"Would you like me to stay with you until it's over?" Stephen asked.

"Yes!"

"Well, move over," Stephen said.

I wiggled to the far side of the feather mattress, and Stephen climbed in beside me. He had been sleeping in only his drawers, because of the heat, and his upper body gleamed as white as a candle in the next flash of lightning. He appropriated one of my pillows, turned his back to me, and curled up, and in two minutes he was asleep.

I put my hand on his warm bare back.

The thunder crashed. The lightning blazed. And safety and comfort radiated all through me from that thin, bony, boy's back. Before the storm was finished, I too had fallen asleep.

The next time there was a thunderstorm at night, I didn't bother to wait for Stephen to come to me. I took my pillow and went along to the bedroom next to mine.

He was stretched out on his stomach in the middle of the bed, deeply asleep. I had to shake him before his eyes opened.

"It's thundering, Stephen," I said. "Can I stay with you until it's over?"

He blinked. "Um," he said.

The thunder rumbled. It was coming closer.

Stephen rolled over to the far side of the bed, and I crawled in.

In five minutes we both were asleep.

Until I was sixteen years old, Stephen and I were all alone in the nursery, except for Miss Archer, my governess. My bedroom was directly next to Stephen's at the end of the passage. Gerald's old room lay between mine and the playroom, and the room next to Stephen's on the passage was the bathroom. The governess's bedroom was farther down the corridor, between the playroom and the schoolroom.

In later years I would wonder about my mother's lack of perception in allowing Stephen and me to share the nursery wing for all those years. Of course, Mama had her own plans. She had determined from the first that I should marry Gerald.

It had simply never crossed her mind that I would be fool enough to want the younger son.

Now, fearless of thunderstorms at the age of twenty-three, I lay awake in the dark, remembering, until the storm had passed through the valley. In my heart there was such a confusion of emotions. Once I had loved Stephen beyond all measure, and he had failed me. I blamed him bitterly for that. I would probably never forgive him. But when I thought of what we once had been, my heart bled and bled and bled.

I wanted those times to return. And they never could.

For as long as I could remember, breakfast was put out in the dining room from seven-thirty to ten, and people could wander in whenever they chose. So when I walked in the following morning at eight I was surprised to find the entire family eating together around the uncovered mahogany table. I filled my coffee cup, took a muffin from the sideboard, and appropriated the empty chair next to Nell.

Stephen looked up from his grilled kidneys and announced that he was leaving later in the morning to pay a visit to his uncle Francis in Kent for a few days.

Nell was dismayed.

I was relieved.

Aunt Fanny approved. "It is right that you

should go," she said. "Mr. Putnam is your god-father and he has always been very fond of you, Stephen dear. He will be anxious to see you again."

"Thornhill is a nice little property," Uncle Adam said. "You will inherit it one day, Stephen. It is only right that you show an interest in the place."

I might mention here that Stephen's expectations were better than those of most younger sons. His mother had left him fifty thousand pounds, and his mother's brother, Francis Putnam, was a childless widower who had made Stephen his heir.

Stephen said quietly to Adam, "Uncle Francis wrote to me faithfully every month during the five years I was in Jamaica. I owe him a great deal."

"I did not mean to suggest that you did not care for your uncle," Adam said stiffly.

"I know that, sir," said Stephen with a fleeting smile. He lifted his coffee cup.

"How long will you be gone?" I asked.

He looked at me over the rim of the delicate china cup. He was sitting between Adam and Fanny and directly across from Nell, but when our eyes met it was as if no one else were present in the room.

I felt the treacherous tightening of my stomach muscles. No one in the world had eyes like Stephen's, so dark and yet so blue.

He lowered the cup. "I don't know for certain," he said. "We will be going up to London to meet a few people. I'll let you know."

"London?" Aunt Fanny said in surprise. "There is no one in London in August, Stephen.

92

Everyone has left for Brighton or the country."

"There is an abolitionist meeting that I particularly want to attend," Stephen said.

Adam put down his fork, having finished his lamb cutlet. "Abolitionist as in antislavery?" he asked.

"Yes, sir," Stephen said. "Now that the war is over there is talk of the revival of the French slave trade. This is the time to press for the international abolition of slavery, and all the old abolitionist committees are reviving. They are particularly interested in gathering information about the consequences of the British abolition of the slave trade on the slave population of the islands. This is why they are anxious to talk to me."

"There was a letter in *The Times* just the other day urging the abolitionists' cause," Jasper said. "Something about 'Let the voice of the British nation once declare itself and the African slave trade must universally cease.'"

"It won't be as easy as that," Adam said.

"No, it won't be," Stephen agreed. "Thomas Clarkson will be going to the congress at Vienna, however, and there is hope that he will be able to exert enough moral pressure to force an international agreement to outlaw the slave trade."

"You sound quite knowledgeable about all this, Stephen," Jasper said.

Stephen leaned back in his chair and said quietly, "I have been in touch with Clarkson since my first year in Jamaica."

There was a little silence as we all digested the implications of that remark.

Then Jasper said, "Look out, world, Stephen has a Cause."

He was only half joking.

Stephen said, "You would feel the same way I do, Jasper, if you had seen what I have seen."

Everyone's attention was focused on Stephen, and for a few brief unnoticed minutes, I allowed myself to gaze at him, too. Contrary to the present masculine fashion, which called for short curls to be worn on the forehead, his brown hair was brushed softly off his brow and behind his ears. My hand remembered the feel of its thick smoothness very clearly, and I closed my fist in my lap so tightly that my nails cut into my palm.

"I saw some pretty dreadful sights in Spain," Jasper said in a suddenly harsh voice. "But I'm not as selfless as you are, Stephen. All I want out of life now is a little peace for myself."

We were all silent for a moment, a little startled, I think, by the raw pain that had sounded in Jasper's voice.

I broke the tableau by pushing back my chair and getting to my feet.

"Annabelle dear, you haven't eaten your muffin," Aunt Fanny protested.

"I'm not hungry," I said.

"Are you going to the stables?" Jasper asked in his normal voice.

"Yes."

"I'll go along with you, if you don't mind."

I nodded, and Jasper also got to his feet.

"Show him whatever horses you have for sale, Annabelle," Adam said. "He'll need at least two for the hunting season."

"Jasper doesn't have to *buy* horses from me, Uncle Adam," I said. "I will be happy to mount him for the season."

"You are always so generous, my dear," Adam said. "But I can afford to buy horses for my son."

Jasper gave his father an odd, searching look.

Adam went on mischievously, "Of course, if you don't want to sell to him, we can always look elsewhere."

"If you look elsewhere, you'll get inferior horses," I said instantly.

Adam threw back his head and laughed.

I had to smile at him. "You certainly know how to get round me, Uncle Adam."

"Everyone knows that Weston hunters are the best hunters anywhere," Adam said comfortably. "I would take it as a compliment if you would sell two of them to Jasper."

I was pleased at the compliment, which was not wholly flattery. These days I always had more buyers than horses to sell to them. I could afford to be particular about where I placed my horses, and I was.

"You can have them only if you continue to stable them with me," I said. The Dower House did not have its own stable.

"You drive a hard bargain, my dear," Adam said.

A footman came into the room with a fresh pot of coffee and another plate of muffins.

"I didn't know that Annabelle had gone into the horse business," Stephen said to no one in particular.

Aunt Fanny said, "It is not a business! Annabelle simply finds nice horses, teaches them to hunt, and then sells them to a few friends. I would not call that a business, Stephen."

The footman exited silently, taking with him an empty silver serving tray.

Stephen's eyes were on my face. "Do you make money?" he asked.

"Yes."

He turned to Aunt Fanny. "It certainly sounds like a business to me."

Aunt Fanny looked distressed. Society did not consider it at all proper for ladies to be "in business."

The truth was, in recent years I had made quite a lot of money out of my hunters. It was a good, safe feeling to have money that was all one's own.

Of course, I had also come into a substantial amount of money when Gerald died. That was not a good feeling at all.

"Come along, Jasper," I said now, turning on my heel to leave the dining room, "and I'll show you some hunters."

The formal gardens to the south of the house were partitioned by several long walks edged with yew and hornbeam. One of these walks led to the stables; the other led into the wooded, hilly terrain of the Ridge.

A plantation of beeches screened the Weston stables from the view of the house, and Jasper and I walked together between carefully laid out and colorful beds of asters, petunias, phlox, and snapdragons and entered under the shade of the beeches. In the summer, when the trees were in full foliage, it was always a delightful surprise to walk out from beneath their canopy and see the gray stone stable buildings and the acres of fenced paddocks suddenly spread out before one. Merlin and Portia raced ahead of us, crossing the bridge over the stream and heading for the water trough, where they always took a drink.

I had slept later than usual because of the thunderstorm, and Grimes, the head groom, was waiting for me, metaphorically tapping his foot.

"There you are, Miss Annabelle," he said reprovingly when I passed through the open gate that led into the graveled stableyard.

I would never be anything but "Miss Annabelle" to Grimes. He had taught me to ride, and he took enormous pride (and most of the credit) for my equestrian accomplishments.

He noticed that Jasper was with me and added pleasantly, "Good morning, Captain."

Grimes had taught Jasper to ride also. The old groom had been delighted when Jasper went into the cavalry and never referred to him as anything but "Captain."

Jasper returned Grimes's greeting, and the two men exchanged a few pleasant words about the weather.

A groom passed close to us, carrying two buckets of well water to the stable. He smiled at me as he passed and ducked his head.

"Good morning, Frank," I said.

"Mornin', Your Ladyship."

The storm had cleared the air, and the sky was a uniformly brilliant blue. The sun felt pleasantly warm, not hot and stuffy as it had the day before.

"Captain Grandville is in the market for some hunters, Grimes," I said, "and I promised Mr. Adam that I would sell him two."

"Two!" Grimes said. His narrow, weathered face regarded me in some distress. "I don't think

97

we have two hunters that are not yet spoken for, Miss Annabelle."

"All of the horses may be spoken for, but none of them are yet sold," I reminded Grimes. I always waited until cubbing season before I let my horses go. "I think Captain Grandville deserves precedence over my other customers, don't you, Grimes?"

The old groom grinned.

Jasper said in surprise, "You really *do* have a business."

Grimes drew up his small, whipcord-thin body with pride. "Every master of foxhounds in the country wants a Weston horse," he declared.

"That is amazing," Jasper said. He looked at me. "You were such a faithful correspondent while I was in Spain, Annabelle, but you never once mentioned that you had gone into the horse-breeding business."

Another groom came by, pushing a wheelbarrow filled with manure. We said our good mornings.

I said to Jasper, "I do very little breeding, actually. I mainly buy Thoroughbreds who have not been very successful in racing and retrain them to hunt."

"Thoroughbreds?" Jasper said. His eyes moved beyond the stable building to the fenced paddocks, registering the clean-limbed elegance of many of the horses turned out there.

I said, "Today's huntsman wants a horse that can go fast and jump high, and Thoroughbreds do both of those things very well."

"Thoroughbreds are also high-strung and nervous," Jasper said, bringing his eyes back to my face. "We used a lot of Thoroughbred

98

crosses in the cavalry, but very few purebreds."

"Get working on the harnesses, now, Tommy," Grimes ordered a stableboy who was raking the already smooth gravel.

The boy trotted off in the direction of the carriage house, and Grimes brought his attention back to our conversation.

"Miss Annabelle knows how to pick 'em, Captain," he said. "Then she rides them for a season and teaches them their manners. They turn out a treat."

I had been considering all my horses on the walk from the house, and now I said to Grimes, "Let's go and take a look at Snap. I think he has the size to carry Captain Grandville."

Grimes looked thoughtfully at Jasper, then nodded slowly. "He's in the second paddock."

The three of us turned our steps in the direction of the graveled path that led out of the stableyard. Colorful herbaceous borders lined the wide gateway entrance to the stableyard. We passed under the gate and turned west on the path to the paddocks.

Two of my mares were turned out in the first enclosure, and one came galloping up to the fence as soon as she saw me.

"Good morning, beautiful," I called to Elf.

The dogs went over to sniff her.

Elf's ears were pricked so far forward that they almost touched. The morning sun made her chestnut coat gleam like burnished copper. She nickered at me.

The second mare, afraid she might be missing something, came tearing up next to Elf. I had purchased her in the spring, thinking to hunt her this season. She was a dark dappled gray with a short back and a strong hind end. I thought she would have a good jump in her.

The two mares followed us as far as they could along the fence line, then stood watching as we stopped at the next paddock, where two geldings were turned out together.

"Snap is the liver chestnut," I said to Jasper. The other horse was Topper.

We leaned on the fence, and the two geldings trotted over to us.

"You always did have a magical way with horses," Jasper said as I rubbed Topper's neck. "I remember the way your pony used to follow you around as if he were a dog."

"Bounce," I said nostalgically. "He was the most wonderful pony. It broke my heart when he died."

Elf, disgusted that she was losing out on any potential treats, squealed, kicked up her heels, and bucked her way across the first paddock. The gray mare, whom I had appropriately named Shadow, copied her exactly.

Snap lunged away from us and galloped to stand at the fence that separated his paddock from the mares. He called to them, but they ignored him.

Topper nuzzled my hand for a treat, which I produced from my skirt pocket.

Jasper's gray eyes were filled with amusement as he watched Topper poke his nose between the rails to try to get at my pocket to find another piece of carrot.

He said, "Tell me, Annabelle, what does your mother have to say about this business of yours?"

Grimes snorted rudely.

I laughed. "Grimes has expressed it very well.

She doesn't like it, but there's not a single thing she can do about it."

"Shall I just trot him around for you, Miss Annabelle?" Grimes asked.

"Do you want to see him move?" I asked Jasper.

"Please."

"Go ahead, Grimes," I said.

Jasper and I watched as the head groom climbed into the paddock and made his way to where Snap was standing, still watching the mares. He attached a lead line to the gelding's leather halter and began to walk him into the center of the paddock.

"I'll get in so I can keep Topper out of the way," I said to Jasper. I had to hold up my riding skirt to climb between the rails, but I was wearing high boots, so modesty was preserved. Once in, I took a firm hold of Topper's halter.

Jasper had followed me in, and he stood beside me as Grimes trotted Snap around in a big circle in the center of the paddock. We both watched the Thoroughbred intently. Topper once more nuzzled my pocket.

"How big is he?" Jasper said.

"Sixteen hands."

"He's very nice, Annabelle."

Topper snorted and tried to put his head down to graze, but I held tight to his halter.

"I hunted him last season," I said. "He's got a wonderful stride, as you can see, and a big jump. His major flaw is that he's insecure. You have to be very clear with him, Jasper. He needs to know exactly what you want him to do all the time. He's not a horse you can leave to figure things out for himself."

Jasper nodded.

"I've hesitated about selling him because of that," I said. "He could go very sour if he got the wrong rider."

I motioned to Grimes that he could stop jogging. He slowed and began to walk Snap in our direction.

Topper put his chin on my shoulder and blew in my ear.

"What would you get for a horse like that?" Jasper asked curiously.

I hesitated.

Grimes was close enough to have heard the last question, and when he saw me hesitate, he said firmly, "Eight hundred guineas."

Jasper's head snapped around to me. "*What?*"

I nodded with a little embarrassment. "Of course, I won't charge you that price, Jasper."

He was flabbergasted. "Do people really pay that much for *one* hunter?"

"For a Weston hunter they do," said Grimes with satisfaction.

Jasper's eyes went up and down the acres and acres of paddocks, each of them containing two horses. "Are all of these horses worth that much?"

"Of course not," I said. "The carriage horses aren't worth that, or the hacks. Just the hunters."

"And how many hunters do you have?"

"I usually keep sixteen," I said, "but two of them are mine, and not for sale at any price."

I could see Jasper totting up sums in his head.

"How on earth did you ever get such a lucrative business established?" he asked me.

Grimes unbuckled the lead line from Snap's

halter, and I released Topper. The two geldings wandered off to graze. We began to walk back toward the fence.

"The biggest obstacle I had to overcome was my sex," I said honestly. "Very few women hunt—well, you know that, Jasper. I believe that Lady Salisbury and Mrs. Farley and I are the only ladies who hunt regularly with established packs."

The main reason why so few women hunted was the insecurity of one's seat in a sidesaddle. I rode astride when I hunted, with a medium-full skirt over a pair of breeches.

"Good God," Jasper said, "don't tell me Lady Salisbury is still hunting? She must be at least a hundred years old!"

I grinned. "Not yet. She is quite blind, however. Gerald and I hunted with her pack last year and a groom holds her horse on a leading rein."

"She's blind and she hunts?"

"When they came to a fence, the groom shouts, 'Jump, damn it, my lady, *Jump*,' And she does."

"Amazing," said Jasper, laughing and shaking his head.

I leaned my shoulders against the fence and went back to answering his question. "When I first realized that I had a few nice hunters I could sell, no one wanted to buy them from a woman."

Snap was back at the fence that was next to the mares. They were still ignoring him.

I looked up at Jasper, who was standing at right angles to me, facing the mares. "It was very frustrating, I can tell you that."

He was watching Snap. "How did you overcome the prejudice?" he asked.

"Perseverance," I replied.

Grimes was not about to let me get away with
such a minimal reply. "She hunted with the
Quorn," he said to Jasper. "Took four Thoroughbreds and went up and by damn hunted
with Assheton Smith himself. He didn't want
her at first. Ended up giving her his hunting
button, inviting her back, and offering to buy
two of her horses!"

Jasper grinned at me. "Good for you,
Annabelle."

I smiled back. "In the hunting world, if the
master of the Quorn approves of you, you are
golden. I haven't had any trouble selling a horse
since."

"Would you like to try him, Captain?" Grimes
asked. "I can have him saddled for you."

Jasper hesitated.

"Yes, do that, Grimes," I said. "And have
Topper saddled as well. The captain and I will
ride out together."

Grimes nodded and climbed out of the paddock to walk back to the stable. He would have
two grooms bring saddles out to the paddock.

Once Grimes was out of earshot, Jasper said
to me, "My father can't possibly pay eight hundred guineas for a horse, Annabelle!"

"I said I wouldn't charge eight hundred to
Uncle Adam."

Jasper's eyebrows were drawn together. His
mouth looked hard. For a moment there was
nothing in his face of the boy I had grown up
with. He said, "I will not permit you to take a
loss on your horse."

"I bought Snap a year ago for a hundred guineas," I said frankly. "I won't take a loss on him."

The gray eyes rounded in astonishment, and he was once more the Jasper I knew.

"In one year you can make a profit like that?"

"He looked perfectly awful when I picked him up. All his ribs were sticking out, poor thing. He was nothing like the horse you see before you now."

We both looked at Snap, whose burnished dark coat shone with red in the bright sunlight. He walked along the fence line, following the mares, and we could see the muscles flex under his skin.

"What did Gerald think of his wife being in business?" Jasper asked. "He was always such a stickler for how things looked, and there's no denying that what you have here is a business, my dear."

I shifted my shoulders into a more comfortable position. I said easily, "Oh, Gerald and I never interfered with each other."

Jasper's gray eyes regarded me gravely.

"It has become *fashionable* to have a Weston horse, Jasper," I explained. "Gerald might not have been keen on my horses when I first started selling them, but he soon came around." I shrugged. "You know how affable Gerald was. Nothing ever put him out of countenance for long."

"There was no reason for Gerald not to be affable," Jasper said austerely.

"He was a man who preferred to be happy," I returned. "There is a great deal to be said for such a temperament."

105

In the next paddock the mares began to graze. Snap still stood at the fence line, watching.

"Poor fellow," Jasper said strangely, "I know just how he must feel."

CHAPTER
eight

When Jasper and I got back to the house, the curricle was standing at the bottom of the front steps with a groom holding the horses' reins. Inside we found Stephen in the front hall making his good-byes to Uncle Adam and Aunt Fanny. His portmanteau was lying next to the front door.

"Haven't you left yet?" I asked.

Stephen just looked at me.

The atmosphere in the hall was not friendly, and Adam said with forced lightness, "Jem Washburn stopped by to see Stephen and me this morning, Annabelle, and we spoke for some time about his taking over his father's lease."

I could feel my back go rigid. I did not want Jem Washburn in my house.

Stephen was watching my reaction, but when he spoke it was not to me, but to Adam. "I will make a start on the estate books as soon as I return, Uncle Adam. I assure you, I do mean to assume my responsibilities."

Adam looked at him in obvious surprise.

"I actually do know how to read account books." Stephen's smile deliberately did not include me. "That is one useful thing I learned in Jamaica."

Adam said, "My accounting system may be a little different from what you are accustomed to, Stephen."

"We'll go over them together, then, and you can explain what I don't understand."

Jasper said from the doorway, "Did you know that the curricle is standing in front of the house, Stephen?"

"Yes," Stephen said, "I was just leaving when you came in."

I folded my arms across my chest. "I did not know you planned to take the curricle," I said.

Stephen had been walking toward the door, and now he stopped.

He turned.

He looked me straight in the eyes and said, "I was led to believe that you did not use the curricle, Annabelle."

His voice was courteous. Too courteous.

He continued in the same odious tone, "Would you prefer that I take the phaeton? Or perhaps the coach?"

In fact, the curricle had belonged to Gerald, and I never drove it.

"Oh, I suppose it had better be the curricle," I said ungraciously.

Aunt Fanny wrung her hands, and Adam looked from my face to Stephen's, clearly not understanding the tension between us. I glanced at Jasper, but his expression was impenetrable.

A footman picked up Stephen's portmanteau to take it out to the curricle.

Jasper said, "I'll walk out with you, Stephen."

Stephen nodded and once more said good-bye to Aunt Fanny and Uncle Adam. For a brief, charged moment our eyes met again.

"Annabelle," he said emotionlessly, and turned to follow Jasper out the door.

I told myself that I was very glad to see him go.

It was a Weston tradition, begun by Gerald's father, for the earl and countess to hold an annual August festival for the servants, the laborers, the tenantry, the local townspeople, and the yeomanry. Like so many other English aristocrats, the earl had been horrified by the excesses of the French revolution, and this annual festival for the lower orders had been his way of showing them how different the Earl of Weston was from those decadent French nobles who had had their powdered heads so rudely parted from their necks.

As Giles had been born on August 23, for the last four years Gerald and I had combined the festival with a celebration of the heir's birthday.

I had not intended to have the festival this year.

No one expected me to have the festival this year.

Stephen had not been gone above an hour before I decided that I would have the festival after all.

I immediately sought out Aunt Fanny to share my decision with her. Hodges directed me to the drawing room, where I found Nell practicing on the pianoforte. Aunt Fanny was seated on the sofa behind her daughter, writing letters on the mahogany drop-leaved sofa table.

The cherubs in the painted roundels upon the ceiling looked down with approval on this peaceful scene.

Aunt Fanny was horrified when I told her what I proposed to do.

"Gerald is not dead six months, Annabelle!" she said, sitting back on the yellow tapestry sofa and wringing her hands in the way she always did when she was distressed. "People will be scandalized if you entertain so soon."

Nell stopped playing the piano and turned to listen.

The dogs went to lie down under the rosewood table with the inlaid chessboard, their favorite spot in the drawing room.

"It will be just for our own tenants and servants this year, Aunt Fanny," I explained. "They enjoy it so much, and they look forward to it all year long. It does not seem fair to deprive them."

The hand-wringing continued. "They don't expect a birthday festival this year, Annabelle, so they will not feel deprived."

I chose a mahogany shield-back chair close to Aunt Fanny's sofa and sat down, folding my own hands in my lap.

"Giles has been very disappointed that we are not going to celebrate his birthday this year."

I looked at Nell in surprise. I thought that in fact Giles had been extraordinarily quiet about his birthday this year.

Nell saw my expression. "I expect he did not want to worry you, Annabelle," she said. "He understood perfectly why you could not have the celebration, but he wouldn't be a normal child if he hadn't been disappointed."

"I suppose that is so," I said. I did not like the idea that Giles would confide in Nell and not in me.

Aunt Fanny was still looking worried. "You are not planning a party of your own?"

Gerald and his father had always invited a houseful of friends to stay for the festival.

"No," I assured her. "It will be just for our own people."

Nell said, "The tenant children have also been disappointed that there was to be no birthday festival this year. Annabelle is right, Mama. They look forward all year to the pony rides and the games."

"What about the rector?" Aunt Fanny asked me.

"Of course the rector must come."

Aunt Fanny pinched her lips. "And the squire?"

My voice was firm. "Sir Matthew must come as well."

"I suppose you will feel obligated to invite the rest of your fox-hunting friends also?"

I said soothingly, "Just Sir Matthew, I promise."

Aunt Fanny's mouth relaxed and her hands quieted. "Well, I suppose it will be all right if it is just for our own people."

"There is absolutely no reason for you to be concerned, Mama," Nell said. "You must realize that no one in the vicinity of Weston would ever dream of criticizing Annabelle."

I thought I detected a trace of bitterness in Nell's voice, and for the second time in a minute I looked at her in surprise.

Aunt Fanny apparently heard only the words

110

and not the tone. "Dear Annabelle." She smiled at me. "Nell is right. You are universally loved in Weston, my dear."

I said slowly, "I am glad that you approve of my having the festival, Aunt Fanny."

"Dear child." Aunt Fanny reached forward and patted my hands. "You are the mistress here; you do not need my permission to hold your festival. It is just your kindness that makes you ask for my opinion."

"I have always valued your opinion, Aunt Fanny."

She laughed merrily. "What a whisker, my dear. The only people whom you ever listen to are Grimes and Sir Matthew. And, when you were children, Stephen."

I began to protest, but she waved her hand to silence me. "You must do as you wish with the birthday festival, my dear, and Nell and I will help you in any way we can."

My eyes moved to Nell. She said, "I'll organize the children's games if you like."

"Thank you, Nell," I said with gratitude. Nell had done the games for the last two years, and they had never been better organized or more fun. She was wonderful with children.

As I looked into her familiar slanting brown eyes, I thought I must have imagined that trace of bitterness.

Giles was ecstatic when I told him that we were going to have his birthday festival after all. It was only when I saw the joy in his face that I realized how disappointed he must have been that I was not going to have it.

"It is only going to be for the servants and

the tenants, Giles," I said, thinking that perhaps I should have gone ahead and held the whole thing.

"That is all right, Mama."

We were in the playroom and he picked up his hobby horse, straddled it, and began to prance around the room, chanting, "We're going to have my birthday party! We're going to have my birthday party!"

I said to Miss Stedham, "I had no idea he felt this way."

"I don't think he wanted to distress you, Lady Weston," she said. "He understood that you would not be in the mood for a party."

It was exactly what Nell had said.

I looked at the little boy who was galloping so gaily around the room and thought, I shouldn't be so surprised by this reaction.

It wasn't that Giles had not grieved for Gerald, but Gerald had been a very small part of Giles's life. Gerald had spent at least half of the year in London, and when he wasn't in London he was visiting friends or having friends to visit Weston. I had always thought that one of the reasons Giles loved his birthday festival so much was that, for however brief a time, it made him the focal point of Gerald's attention.

Gerald had been the same kind of father as he was husband: affable, benevolent, undemanding, uninvolved.

I said to the moving figure on the hobby horse, "I thought we might ride around the valley this afternoon and tell the tenants that we will be having the festival after all."

The hobby horse came to a halt.

"Me and you, Mama?"

"You and I," I corrected him.

"Can Genie come, too?" Giles asked. "She never gets to leave the house, Mama."

I looked at Miss Stedham in time to see color stain her cheeks. She said quickly, "That is not true, Giles. I walk in the gardens every day, and you and I go for walks also. Why, I even went fishing with you and your uncle!" Her eyes moved to my face, and I saw apprehension reflected in their warm brown depths. "Your mama will think I have been complaining," she said.

I felt a pang of guilt as I looked back at the lovely young woman before me. Miss Stedham had come to us only two months before Gerald died, and I had been so involved with my own feelings ever since that I had had little thought for her.

She was clearly worried that I would think she had been trying to manipulate Giles.

"Do you ride, Miss Stedham?" I asked.

"Really, Lady Weston, there is no need—"

"Giles is right. You need to get out more. If you don't ride, we will take the phaeton. There is room for three of us on the seat; we're all thin enough."

"Actually," Miss Stedham said in a low voice, "I do ride."

"Splendid." Next, I realized that she probably did not own a habit. "If you don't mind wearing one of my skirts, we'll ride."

The color was still flying in her cheeks. She had the kind of skin that one saw occasionally on redheads: so translucent that one could almost see through it.

"You don't want me to wear your clothes, Lady Weston," she protested.

"You know what my riding skirts look like, Miss Stedham," I said humorously, gesturing to the ancient garment I was wearing at the moment. "If you don't mind being seen in one, I don't mind you wearing it."

That earned a smile.

"What about boots?" I asked next.

"I have some half-boots."

"Fine. I'll have one of the chambermaids bring a skirt up to you." I smiled at my son. "You can come along with me now, Giles. We'll meet Miss Stedham in the Great Hall in twenty minutes."

He pranced to my side, still fancying himself a horse. He continued to prance as we went down the stairs. I waited until we had reached the second floor before I said to him, "I'm proud of you, Giles, for thinking about Miss Stedham's welfare."

He turned his face up to me. "Are you, Mama?"

"Yes. You were right. We must try to get her out of the nursery more."

"I like Genie, Mama," he said. "She's fun."

I had deliberately engaged a young governess for him for just that very reason: I did not want him taught by an inflexible and joyless tutor. I thought again of that apprehensive look in Miss Stedham's eyes.

Poor girl, I thought. I shall have to pay more attention to her in the future.

The prospect of finding new employment should she lose her position with me was not bright for a young woman like Miss Stedham. A lovely exterior was an asset when one was looking for a husband; it was a decided nuisance when one was looking for a position as a governess. There were not many employers who would deliberately place a face and form such as Miss Stedham possessed into the orbit of their husbands.

In fact, Miss Stedham had been released from her last position without a character. She had told me, with choking voice and flaming face, that the master of the house had got drunk one night and tried to get into her bedroom. Once this reprehensible behavior had come to the attention of the mistress of the house, the blameless Miss Stedham had been escorted to the door.

I had hired her because I thought she would be good for Giles, and I had known I could trust Gerald to keep his hands off her. Not that Gerald wouldn't notice her; he was a man who always noticed a pretty woman. But he would not take advantage of a well-bred young woman who had no protection.

Besides, I was always present at Weston to keep an eye on him.

"It is very important to think of others," I said now to my son as we stood together in front of a small piecrust table upon which was placed a priceless Chinese vase from some dynasty whose name I could never remember.

"You are a fortunate little boy, Giles," I continued. "You have been born into a great position and one day you will have great wealth. That is why it is so important for you to be mindful of others, because you will have it in your power either to help or to harm them."

We continued to descend the stairs until we reached the main floor. Giles had ceased to prance like a horse, and the look on his face was as sober as his gait. He didn't speak until we had turned to the right to go to my suite of rooms.

Then, "I want to be just like you, Mama," he said. "Everyone loves you because you are so kind." We stood before the door to my dressing room, and he gazed up at me trustingly and smiled. "And so pretty."

I looked down into eyes that were a mirror reflection of my own. "Thank you, darling," I said, accepting with forced graciousness a compliment that I knew I didn't deserve.

It took us all afternoon to ride around the valley delivering our invitations. By four o'clock I was hot, crabby, and too full of lemonade. I heartily wished I had given the invitations to a servant to deliver.

Our tenants' wives and children had been uniformly delighted to see Giles and me, which was why I had undertaken the chore in the first place, of course.

The only farm we missed was the Washburn farm. I got around having to go there by asking Susan Fenton if she would have her husband tell Jem about the festival. Susan had agreed and invited us in for lemonade.

Miss Stedham proved to be an excellent horsewoman, which made me feel guilty for never before having given her an opportunity to ride. I tried to make up for my thoughtlessness by telling her that she could take a horse out anytime she pleased, but she demurred.

"I am perfectly serious, Miss Stedham," I assured her as we stood together in the

116

stableyard and watched our horses being led into the stable. "I have five just-off-the-track Thoroughbreds eating their heads off in my stable, and they all desperately need steady work. You would do me a favor by riding them."

She smiled politely and thanked me, and I could see that she would never ride one of my horses unless I specifically invited her to accompany me.

Damn, I thought crossly. Why did she have to be so afraid of encroaching? I did not want the responsibility of making certain that Miss Stedham got opportunities to ride. I already had too many people whose welfare I felt responsible for.

I tried again. "Shadow, in particular, could use miles and miles of steady trotting. You could take her up to the Downs."

Her eyes glimmered. She would have loved it. The glimmer died, and once more the polite smile appeared. She wouldn't do it.

Giles said, "Perhaps Genie could come with us, Mama, when we go up to the Downs."

I liked the time I had alone with my son. I did not want to include his governess.

"What a good idea, Giles," I said.

He beamed. He was a truly generous and thoughtful child, and I was proud of him.

Miss Stedham said, "This has been a lovely afternoon. Thank you, Lady Weston, you are very kind."

I managed some sort of innocuous reply and sent the two of them off to the house, as it was almost time for Giles's dinner. I stayed at the stable to talk to Grimes for a while, and then I too turned my steps toward home.

117

I was frowning as I walked along the gravel path under the shade of the beeches. Too many people had called me kind today, and my conscience was bothering me.

Giles was kind.

Stephen was kind.

I wasn't kind. True kindness came from the heart. My care for people came from a sense of duty.

It was easy for a countess to seem kind. It was easy to give a party, to send a footman to the dentist, to give a Saturday off to a young chambermaid who was homesick. It was easy to be generous with your horses when you had a stableful of them. It was easy to be pleasant to people. It was easy to live on the untroubled surface of a financially comfortable life.

I emerged from the beeches and the south wing of the house rose before me, framed by gardens and bathed in the golden light of the late afternoon sun. The gray stone with which the house was built glowed with warmth and radiance, the large many-paned windows glittered, and I remembered suddenly how terrifying Weston had seemed to me the first time I beheld it.

I halted and stood there in the late afternoon sunshine, gazing at the house that had sheltered me since I was eight years of age. The trickle of water in the marble fountain that marked the center of the rose garden intruded into my consciousness, and I turned my head to look at it.

The sunlight caught something bright in the grass to the left of the walk, and I went to investigate. It was a sixpence. On impulse I picked it up, carried it along the flower-lined walk-way to the fountain, closed my eyes, made a wish, and threw it in.

The scent of the roses was strong in my nostrils, and I went to sit on one of the four stone benches that surrounded the fountain. The rose garden fountain consisted of a marble basin with three figures of youthful Greek sea gods in its center, each one spouting water into the basin out of a horn held to his lips.

The sun was warm on my back and the scent of roses heavy in my nostrils.

I stared at the marble figures in the fountain and thought of Jasper's words at dinner the other night: *Stephen has found a Cause.*

When we were growing up Stephen had always had a cause, but this time would be different, I thought. This time Stephen was a man and not a powerless little boy. Thanks to his mother's money and his prospects from his uncle Francis, he now had what he had wanted all his life: a position from which he could command attention and effect change.

If Stephen had decided to commit himself to the abolition of slavery in British territories, I had little doubt that the days of slavery were numbered. His father had not known what he was unleashing when he sent Stephen to Jamaica.

My vision blurred and slowly a picture of a much younger Stephen formed before my mind's eye. I shut my eyes and bent my head.

And once again I am eleven years old, and Stephen is being sent home from school in disgrace.

Stephen had not gone up to Eton until he was

twelve. This was unusual, but he had not wanted to go away to school at all, and the earl had allowed him to remain at home because he was a companion to me. The earl and my mother lived a life of relentless sociability, and neither of them wanted to be saddled with the encumbrance of a child (me). I think it was chiefly the earl who felt guilty about the prospect of leaving me alone for months at a time, and this was why he had agreed to Stephen remaining at Weston and continuing his lessons with the rector.

Finally, however, the time had come when the earl felt he could procrastinate no longer, and Stephen had had to enter Eton.

The first inkling the earl had that something was wrong was the arrival of a letter from the headmaster asking him to come up for an interview in regard to his son Stephen. The earl had left a house full of guests in order to drive to Eton, and he had returned to Weston looking distinctly grim around the mouth.

I suppose he told my mother what had transpired between him and the headmaster, but he would tell no one else. This didn't matter to me, however, as I already knew all about Eton from Stephen's letters.

The expensive, exclusive school he described sounded like the worst sort of barbarian hell. Approximately seven hundred upper-class boys lived at Eton, and as they were largely unsupervised, the strong preyed upon the weak with a callousness that Stephen described as utterly uncivilized. The tough thrived; the weak lived in fear and misery.

Stephen couldn't stand it. The sound of a

frightened and humiliated child pitifully crying himself to sleep drove him wild. So, being Stephen, he decided to do something to rectify the situation.

He began by making an official complaint to the headmaster. The headmaster was not pleased to be reprimanded by one of his own students, and this was the reason he had sent for the earl.

His father upbraided Stephen for his impudence, and the headmaster had him flogged.

As the term advanced, Stephen continued to stand up for the weak, and consequently he was beaten up regularly by all of the school bullies.

Physical pain never stopped Stephen, however. The next thing he did was write to the prime minister and the home secretary. On his father's crested stationery.

He threatened the prime minister that he would write to the newspapers.

He was twelve years old.

Eton couldn't get rid of him fast enough. The earl collected him two weeks before Christmas and brought him home to Weston to stay.

I will never forget what his face looked like as he walked in the door of the nursery schoolroom. He had two black eyes, and his formerly straight nose was badly swollen, and so was his mouth. He was holding one shoulder higher than the other, as if it hurt.

My heart leaped with fierce joy at the sight of him.

"I hope you didn't get your teeth broken, too," I said.

He looked up from patting Rags, and though

his face was pale under all his bruises, his eyes were blazing. "I don't care what Papa says," he said defiantly. "I'm not sorry about any of it. I'm only sorry I couldn't make them listen."

I was sitting on the old blue sofa that had been in the nursery for at least fifty years. I said with conviction, "One day they will listen to you, Stephen."

He stared across the room at me, his cut mouth set into a straight line, and he did not look young at all. "They will, Annabelle," he said. "One day they will have to."

I didn't doubt him. I never doubted him.

"I missed you," I said. "I had no one to talk to."

He let out his breath in a great gusty sigh and came across the room to sit beside me on the sofa. "I know," he said. "I missed you, too."

He reached over and picked up my hand. I noticed that his knuckles were swollen, too. Stephen had always been one to fight back.

I closed my fingers gently around his, and we leaned back on the sofa together, shoulders touching, hands entwined, and he told me about everything that had happened at Eton.

I had been perfectly happy. Stephen was mine once more.

The voice of one of the gardeners brought me back to the present. "Beg pardon, my lady," he said. "I don't wish to disturb you, but Mrs. Nordlem asked me to cut some roses for the dining room table."

I stood up. "Go right ahead, Simon. It is time I returned anyway."

I left him there, bent over the roses, and walked slowly home, telling myself how relieved

I was that I would not have to face Stephen over the dinner table.

CHAPTER
nine

I had under a week to get Giles's birthday festival organized, and I went to work with all the determination of a general organizing a major campaign. Nell and Aunt Fanny and I spent every morning in my office, making lists of the food and the various other supplies that needed to be ordered. In the afternoon we would separate, each of us attending to the different responsibilities we had assumed.

The weather held good and I prayed it would remain that way. We had never yet had rain on the day of the festival. It was bound to happen eventually, of course, but, Not this year, Lord, I begged.

Of course I said that every year.

The food for the lower orders had always been served in a tent on the lawn, while the family's private guests dined indoors. This year, however, I ordered all the food to be laid out in the house.

"So many people will be sure to track mud onto the floor, Annabelle," Aunt Fanny protested when I first proposed using the long gallery, which had French doors leading directly onto the east lawn, where the main part of the festival was always staged.

"We'll take the rugs up," I said. "Remember, Aunt Fanny, there will be fewer people at the festival this year than usual, and you know how our tenants will enjoy being entertained in the house."

"It will be easier for the servants if the food is in the house, Mama," Nell said in support of my idea.

I gave her an appreciative smile. "None of us ever goes into the long gallery, Aunt Fanny," I said persuasively. "We might as well put it to *some* use."

Aunt Fanny finally gave in to "her girls," as she usually did, and the three of us went along to the gallery in order to decide how we could best set up for serving.

"See how easy it will be," I said as we stood in the center of the long, narrow room that ran the entire width of the east side of the house. "The doors lead directly out to the terrace and the lawns. The rugs"—I pointed to the three Turkish rugs that were placed at measured intervals down the length of the room—"can be taken up, and then, if the floor gets dirty, it can easily be cleaned."

"We can place a line of tables right down the middle of the room," Nell said. "That will enable people to serve themselves from either side."

"It will be much less crowded than a tent," I said.

"Yes, you girls are right, it will be easier to serve the food in here," Aunt Fanny agreed. "We can have people enter by that door"—she pointed to the French door at the south end of the long, windowed wall—"and leave by this one. That will facilitate an even flow of traffic."

"We must be sure to leave room for people to look at the pictures," Nell said.

The long interior wall of the gallery was lined

with the portraits of Grandvilles, past and present.

"Do you really think anyone will be interested in looking at family pictures, Nell?" I asked doubtfully.

"Weston people are interested in anything that has to do with the Grandvilles," Nell said. "I am certain we will have many people who will want to look at the family portraits."

"They will particularly want to look at your portrait, my dear Annabelle," Aunt Fanny said generously. "Although I still don't understand why you did not leave it hanging in the drawing room."

My eyes flicked toward the spot on the wall on which hung the portrait Aunt Fanny was referring to. Lawrence had done it shortly after my marriage, and Gerald had given it a place of honor in the drawing room. I had had it removed to the gallery several months ago, and it now hung beside the portrait of Gerald that had been done when he left Oxford.

"I never enjoyed looking at myself while I was playing cards or drinking tea," I told Aunt Fanny. "It belongs in the gallery with the rest of the Grandville portraits."

"Everyone else certainly likes looking at you, Annabelle," Nell said. And once again I heard that oddly bitter note in her voice.

This time Aunt Fanny must have heard it, too, for she gave her daughter a measuring look.

Nell moved away from us to straighten a picture and said over her shoulder, "Have you notified Stephen about the festival, Annabelle? He is Giles's guardian after all; it will look odd if he is not here."

"I did send a note to Uncle Francis's house, but he and Stephen had already left for London," I replied.

Aunt Fanny said to her daughter, "There is nothing wrong with that picture, dear, and it is rude to turn your back upon the people with whom you are conversing."

Nell turned. "I beg your pardon, Mama." She looked at me. "Didn't you send to them in London?"

"I don't know where they are staying," I replied.

"Surely Mr. Putnam's servants must know where he is," Nell said.

"I believe they are putting up at a friend's house."

The dogs spied a squirrel on the lawn and began barking to go out. Nell frowned as she went to open one of the French doors for them. After the two spaniels had streaked outside, she closed the door and said with barely concealed impatience, "Well, didn't you get the direction of the friend?"

"I have no intention of sending my servants up to London in search of Stephen," I said. "He knows when Giles was born. If he chooses to spend his nephew's birthday in London, that is his affair."

Silence descended on the room. This was such an unusual state of affairs when Aunt Fanny was present that I looked at her in surprise.

She was gazing at the rug and refused to meet my eyes.

I turned to Nell, who was intently watching my spaniels as they raced around on the lawn.

"What is the matter?" I said sharply.

"Oh dear," said Aunt Fanny.

"Surely someone informed Stephen when his nephew was born," I said. "It was certainly a matter of interest to him that he was no longer Gerald's principal heir."

The silence stretched unbearably. Finally Aunt Fanny could endure it no longer. "Stephen knew that Giles had been born, Annabelle." She met my eyes fleetingly and once again looked away. "He may be uncertain as to the date."

I stared at my aunt's averted face. I was beginning to feel grim.

"Why would he be uncertain as to the date?" I said.

"Oh dear," Aunt Fanny said again. She started to wring her hands. "It was Gerald's idea, Annabelle. He only did it because Giles was born five weeks too soon and he didn't want Stephen to leap to the wrong conclusion."

I could feel the blood drain from my face. I said through stiff lips, "May I ask what was the imaginary birthdate Gerald gave to Stephen?"

"Oh dear. You are angry, Annabelle."

I supposed I would be angry shortly, but it wasn't temper that was making my body tremble and my heart thump right now. I swallowed. "It seems to me I have cause to be angry," I said.

"Gerald was only thinking of your reputation and Stephen's peace of mind." Nell's tilted dark eyes glittered as she turned to face me in the afternoon light. "Gerald knew that Stephen would be upset if he thought his brother had seduced you," she said bluntly. "It was to spare Stephen's feelings that we went along with Gerald's suggestion."

"*I did not go to bed with Gerald before our marriage,*" I said between my teeth.

"Oh dear, oh dear, oh dear," wailed Aunt Fanny. "Nell, you should not be talking this way! It is not proper for a young girl!" Then, to me, "None of us ever thought such a dreadful thing of you, Annabelle!"

Nell ignored her mother's protests and shot more words at me. "Gerald had been after you for months to marry him. Stephen knew that very well. And he also knew Gerald's reputation with women. As Mama just told you, Annabelle, Gerald didn't want his brother to leap to the wrong conclusion. That is the only reason he misled Stephen about the date of Giles's birth."

I made myself breathe slowly and deeply. There was only one fact that mattered to me at the moment, and I needed to be certain of it.

I said clearly, "When does Stephen think Giles was born?"

Aunt Fanny wrung her hands again. "Gerald told him early October, dear."

Stephen thought that Giles had been born in early October.

It had never occurred to me that he might not know the correct date.

Nell's intelligent eyes were watching me closely, and I struggled to keep my expression from betraying me.

"Well, it is of no importance now," I managed to say with a semblance of calm. "We are still several days away from the festival. Doubtless Stephen will return in time."

"I am sure that he will, my dear Annabelle,"

Aunt Fanny said. Her voice was trembling with relief that I was letting the matter drop. "I am sure that he will."

It was not Stephen, however, but Jack who appeared unexpectedly in my office the day before Giles's birthday. He came over to the desk where I was making a menu for the cook, kissed my cheek, and upbraided me for not letting him know about the festival.

"I only decided to go ahead with it last week," I said. "I did send to London to inform you, but there was no one at your lodgings and I didn't know where else to look for you."

"I was at Rudely," Jack said.

He was lounging with one hip against my desk, and I looked up at him with my eyebrows lifted in surprise. Rudely was the small estate in Hampshire that Gerald's grandfather had bought many years ago for Jack's father, who was his younger son. It had been a nice little property once, Gerald had told me, but after Jack's mother had died his father had let it go badly. This was the reason Jack had been brought up at Weston with his cousins and not at his own home.

"Sit down, Jack," I said. "I didn't know you ever went to Rudely."

He shrugged and went to sprawl lazily in the comfortable old velvet chair that faced my desk. "I haven't been there since my father finally succeeded in drinking himself to death last year. I thought it was time to take a look at the wreck and see what needs to be done to salvage it."

I was shocked. "I never knew your father drank himself to death!"

He gave me a humorless smile. "It's one of those little secrets the Grandvilles like to keep hidden from the rest of the world."

"I'm not the rest of the world," I protested indignantly. "I'm a Grandville!"

He shrugged again. "I suppose no one wanted to sully your beautiful ears with so sordid a tale."

I gave an annoyed exclamation; he looked back at me out of somber eyes and said nothing. Belatedly, I understood that I was being tactless. "Is the house really in such bad condition?" I asked hurriedly.

"Yes," came the uncompromising reply.

His hard mouth looked even harder than usual. I turned away from him, picked up my pen, and began idly to sketch on the edge of my menu. "Gerald once told me that Rudely was a nice little property when your grandfather bought it," I remarked. "Perhaps you can make it a nice little property again."

"It could be restored, but it will take money," Jack said in a voice that was as hard as his face. "And even if I repaired the house sufficiently to make it livable, I wouldn't have the money to keep it going."

I added a few flourishes to the design I had drawn. "Doesn't it have any farms attached to it?" I asked. I knew that the income to keep Weston running was derived largely from the farms we leased out to tenants.

"It did," Jack replied grimly. "I sold them last year to pay off the mortgage my father had taken on the house."

"Oh," I said.

"Precisely." I heard his big body shift in his chair. "The house and the gardens and the home

130

farm are clear, but without rents I have no way to keep them going."

I returned my pen to its holder and returned my gaze to his face. Jack had never before discussed his finances with me, and I felt compelled to try to come up with a helpful suggestion.

"Perhaps you could sell Rudely and buy something smaller," I said.

His expression told me instantly that I had not been helpful. "Rudely *is* small, Annabelle," he said. "It's about as small as a house can get and still be regarded as the residence of a gentleman."

I bit my lip and thought about assuring Jack that he would always have a home at Weston, but I knew such a reassurance wouldn't help. In the world in which we lived, a gentleman owned his own property. It was his badge of respectability. Jack needed to be "Mr. John Grandville of Rudely," not Jack Grandville, poor relation of Weston.

Surely, I thought, the rest of the family understood that.

"Don't look so worried, Annabelle," he said. "I didn't mean to saddle you with my problems."

"Did Gerald know that you had to sell the farms to pay off the mortgage?" I demanded.

The blond head, so like Gerald's, nodded an affirmative.

Gerald knew and had done nothing.

"What about Uncle Adam?" I asked next. "Does he know?"

"I discussed the situation with Adam. He was the one who advised me to pay off the mortgage to save the house."

131

"For goodness' sake, Jack," I said in distress, "didn't either of them offer you any help?"

He looked at me as if debating what to tell me. "They offered me advice," he said at last.

"What kind of advice?" I asked in bewilderment.

"They told me to marry a girl with money."

It was the second time in this conversation that he had shocked me. "*What?*"

He actually laughed. "I wish you could see your own face, Annabelle. Such scandalized disapproval!"

"Will you do it?" I asked baldly.

"I don't know." A muscle flickered along the line of his jaw, as if he had just clenched it. "The only girl I've ever loved married someone else. If I have to marry without love, I suppose it might as well be to a girl who has money."

I dropped my eyes to my decorated menu and said with a little difficulty, "I suppose I am a romantic, but I believe one should marry for love."

He replied with slow deliberation, "Annabelle darling, you of all people should understand that sometimes it is necessary to marry for expediency."

I went perfectly still, staring as if mesmerized at my unfinished menu.

The silence seemed to go on for a very long time. Then Jack said, "They told me in the stable that Stephen was home."

"Yes." I cleared my throat. "He's not here at the moment, however. He went on a visit to Francis Putnam."

"How does he look?" Jack asked.

"He is very brown," I said, and looked up.

"Mmmm?"

The blue eyes on my face were much too knowing. I said, "I've finished buying this year's batch of horses."

Mercifully, he followed my change of subject. "Have you had them out yet?"

"I've hacked them through the woods a bit," I said. "Physically, they are very talented. They know absolutely nothing, however."

"They never do when you first get them," he reminded me.

I leaned back a little in my chair. "The cubbing season is almost on us," I said. "I bought a big bay from the Egremont stud that I think you will particularly like."

"Is that an invitation?" he asked.

"It's more like a plea," I retorted. "You know how much I appreciate your help during cubbing season."

Cubbing season was the time during late summer and early autumn when the young hounds were first taken out to learn their business from their elders. There was no hunt field present during cubbing, only the hounds, the master, and a few assistants. I had found cubbing to be a good time to introduce my new horses to both hounds and woods, and Jack was one of the few people other than myself whom I trusted to do this the right way. Thoroughbreds who have done nothing all their lives except run as fast as possible can be very excitable, and Jack was very good with excitable horses.

"I take it I am a member of the Sussex Hunt, then?" Jack asked sardonically.

"You most certainly are."

"Stephen agreed to pay my fee?"

"I paid your fee," I said.

He straightened up in his chair. "Damn it, Annabelle, I didn't want you to do that!"

"I really need your help, Jack," I said matter-of-factly. "I consider your subscription a business expense."

I looked calmly back at him, and after a moment he relaxed. He lifted his thick blond eyebrows. "Oh well, as long as I'm a business expense," he drawled.

I picked up my pen. "Tell Mrs. Hodges to put you in your usual bedroom," I said. "I can't sit here talking to you any longer; I have got to get this menu done for Cook."

"Yes, ma'am," he said mockingly, and rose to his feet. "I understand that Adam and Fanny are staying here also?"

"Mmm," I said. "Jasper and Nell, too."

The corners of his eyes crinkled. "How delightful."

"Dinner is at the usual time," I said, and once more regarded my menu.

"Is Giles in the nursery?" he asked.

I looked up, surprised by the question. "Why?"

"I brought him a birthday present," Jack said. "It's the reason I came. I didn't know you were having the festival and I thought the poor little beggar might be feeling a bit blue-deviled."

I felt a warm glow in the region of my heart. It always made me happy when people thought of Giles. "How kind of you, Jack," I said.

His lids were half-lowered, so I couldn't see the expression in his eyes. "Is he in the nursery?" he repeated.

"Probably not at the moment," I said. "He

134

and Miss Stedham went to the lake to fish. I haven't seen the dogs yet, so they mustn't have returned."

"I was wondering where the ubiquitous dogs had got to," he commented.

"Why don't you walk down to the lake and meet them?" I suggested.

He surprised me by replying, "Perhaps I will."

I watched his broad back until the door had closed behind him, then I sighed and returned to my menu.

It was the night before Giles's birthday, and still Stephen had not come home. The family group in the drawing room broke up at eleven and I went along to my bedroom. I did not get undressed, however, but told Marianne that I was going to take the dogs for a walk. I often did this before I went to bed, so no one thought it unusual when I let myself out the small door that lay between my office and the saloon.

The moon was full and I could see perfectly as I walked along the path that skirted the south gardens, the dogs trotting faithfully at my heels. I could hear the splash of water in the rose garden fountain as I set my feet on the path that would take me to the Ridge.

The summer night was very still. The scent of August roses hung heavy on the air, and I could hear the crunch of gravel under my feet as I started out along the garden path. Somewhere in the garden a nightingale began to sing. The dogs streaked past me and disappeared into the darkness.

They were nowhere in sight when I finally reached the woods. The gravel path turned at a right angle here and began to run directly east, forming a boundary between landscaped park and natural woodland. A narrow dirt track continued on into the woods, and I knew that if I followed it for several miles, I would end up in a small secluded cove on the Channel.

It had been a cold January night more than five years ago when Stephen had been surprised on this track by a party of revenue officers. He had been leading a train of three horses, all of them loaded with brandy smuggled from France. Someone had informed the authorities that a shipment was coming into the cove that night, and they had been waiting for him. The rest of the smugglers, hard-bitten professionals all, had gotten away. Stephen, at eighteen, had been left to face the music alone.

Free trading was an old and established pastime in Sussex, but the government had expanded its presence on the Channel coast in order to be ready should Napoleon decide to attempt an invasion. We were a country at war, and the government was coming down hard on free traders, who had been known to smuggle gold into France so that Napoleon could pay his mercenaries. If Stephen had not been an earl's son, he might well have hung.

I was wearing an evening dress and shoes and did not want to go into the woods. I crossed my arms against the cool breeze that had sprung up and waited for the dogs on the edge of the gravel path. The moon was hanging full and bright in the starry summer sky, and the softly rustling leaves in the woods before me seemed to give voice to the restlessness that I felt within myself. I pressed my hand beneath my left breast and felt the beating of my heart.

I drew in one deep, slow breath of the moist night air, and then another. I thought I could smell the salt from the Channel. I remembered how the salt used to taste on my skin, how it used to sting all the scratches that I seemed always to be covered with when I was young. I closed my eyes, my senses filled with the smell and taste of the sea.

And once again I am fifteen years old, and Stephen and I have gone to the cove so that the spaniels can swim.

Merlin and Portia had been eight weeks old when Sir Matthew gave them to the earl as a present for me. I had been helping Sir Matthew with the hounds since I was ten, and I began to ride out with the hunt when I was twelve. Sir Matthew had seen the two ink black spaniel puppies at a friend's house and had known I would adore them.

Since Stephen's old dog had died the year before, I gave him Portia and kept Merlin for my own. Now the puppies were a fully grown fourteen months old, and during the hot summer weather we often took them to the cove so they could swim in the cold seawater. They liked it better than the tepid lake.

It was a hot August day, and I had taken off my shoes and kilted up my dress's sprig muslin skirt and was standing next to Stephen in knee-deep water, watching him throw a stick for the excited dogs.

The sun was glinting off the shimmering

water, and out deep in the Channel a yacht was slowly gliding by.

"I hate it when you go away," I said.

He had just returned the previous day from a month-long visit to his uncle Francis Putnam in Kent.

"I know," he replied absently. He was squinting into the sun, his eyes on the black heads of the swimming dogs. The breeze off the water blew his dark hair back from his brow, and his face looked preoccupied.

I bent forward to plunge my hands in the cold water, and the front hem of my kilted-up dress got wet. "What did he say about Oxford?" I asked.

Stephen didn't look at me. "He thinks I should go. He says that if I am ever to be an effective reformer, I need to train my mind."

Two seagulls floated on the water about twenty feet from shore, watching the dogs.

"Your mind is trained," I said sharply. "The rector says you're the smartest person he knows."

His lips curved into a wry smile. "The rector is partial," he said.

I turned, splashed out of the water, in the process getting my dress even wetter, and began to walk westward along the shore, my head bent, my eyes on my bare feet.

"Annabelle!" I heard Stephen call. "Wait!"

I didn't want him to see that I was crying, and when I heard him coming after me, I broke into a run. At fifteen I had long legs and a body that had been trained to stay in the saddle for eight hours at a time. It took him quite a while to catch me.

"Annabelle... ," he said breathlessly after he had dragged me to a halt.

I wouldn't look at him but stared instead at his hand on my bare arm. With his other hand he touched the salty wetness on my cheeks, a wetness that was not from the sea. "Oh God," he said in a voice I had never heard him use before. "What are we going to do?"

At that I raised my tear-streaked face to his, and he bent and put his mouth on mine.

We stayed like that for a long moment, frozen into immobility by the sheer daring of what we were doing. Then he lifted his head and his blue eyes looked searchingly into mine.

"Stephen," I breathed. I raised my hands until they were resting on his shoulders. His lips moved, forming my name, but no sound came out. Then he bent over me once more.

I closed my eyes. I leaned against him and felt his hard young body pressed against mine. Our arms were locked around each other, our mouths pressed together with fierce necessity.

I don't know what would have happened between us next if the spaniels had not come racing up and tangled themselves in our feet, abruptly recalling us from our first dizzying journey into adult passion.

We laughed unsteadily and backed away from each other. Merlin pressed himself against my legs, his wet fur tickling my bare calves.

Stephen ran his fingers through the damp salty hair on his brow, and the laughter left his face abruptly.

"Why do we have to be so young?" he said despairingly.

A gull circled in the air above us, and the

dogs jumped and barked at it. I looked at Stephen and had no reply.

Tonight, the dogs came racing out of the woods to break up my reverie, just as they had broken up that first kiss so many years before.

I thought again of the startling fact I had learned that afternoon. "He never knew," I said to the dogs. "*He never knew.*"

Merlin, who was always particularly sensitive to my moods, gave a little questioning whine and looked up at me.

"Come along," I said to the two spaniels, "it's time for bed." And we walked through the fragrant summer night all the way back to the house.

CHAPTER
ten

I woke early on the morning of Giles's birthday to find that clouds had rolled in from the Channel overnight.

"They will clear by afternoon, my lady," Hodges assured me when I met him by the stairs. Hodges fancied himself a weather expert, and I prayed that today his forecast would prove to be a correct one. I had made contingency plans for bad weather, of course, but most of the fun would be spoiled if we had to move everyone indoors.

I went up the stairs to the nursery floor and on into Stephen's old room, which now belonged to Giles. I found him awake but still in bed. He leaped up as soon as he saw me and began to jump up and down on the mattress, chanting: "Today is my birthday! Today is my birthday!"

I laughed. "Five years old. My goodness, Giles, you're turning into an old man right before my eyes."

He shouted, "No, I'm not, Mama! No, I'm not!" And, leaping off the bed, he threw himself against me, his arms hugging my waist.

I smoothed his tangled blond hair. "Why don't you get dressed, darling, and then you can come down to breakfast with me."

His head tipped back. "What about my gift, Mama?"

"Gift?" I lifted my brows. "What gift?"

"*Mama!*"

"If you get dressed and come down to breakfast, then perhaps you will find a gift." I went over to the chair where the nursery maid had laid out his clothes the night before and said, "I'll help you."

I had arranged for the rest of the family and Miss Stedham to be in the dining room when Giles and I came in, and everyone chorused "Happy Birthday!" at once. Giles beamed. Both Nell and Aunt Fanny came to kiss him and the men shook his hand, which pleased him mightily. I had had a place for Giles set next to mine, and his chair was heaped with birthday gifts.

Giles was thrilled with his loot: new fishing equipment from me; a new bridle from Uncle Adam and Aunt Fanny; a wooden whistle from Nell; a cricket bat from Jasper; some unusual stones for his collection from Miss Stedham; and a carved statue of a Thoroughbred from Jack.

His high spirits were infectious, and we all

141

lingered around the table, laughing and talking. It was ten-thirty when Hodges entered the dining room, bringing news that effectively destroyed everyone's holiday mood.

"My lady," he intoned, "the Duke and Duchess of Saye have arrived."

Silence, heavy as a wet horse rug, fell in the dining room as my mother walked in with her husband at her heels. They made a stunning-looking couple. The duke was ten years older than Mama, but he had kept his figure, and though his hair had gone gray, his eyebrows were still startlingly black. He was the most incredibly arrogant man I had ever met. He and Mama were a perfect match.

"You cannot have this festival, Annabelle," my mother announced. "Gerald is not yet dead six months."

Giles gave me an anxious look.

"As it is due to begin in less than two hours, I am most certainly having this festival, Mama," I replied.

"Whatever were you thinking of?" she demanded. "We were visiting the Ashtons when we heard about it. Everyone is scandalized!"

Adam said in his genial way, "Goodness, Regina, how on earth did news of a local event in Weston carry so far so fast? Annabelle only decided to have the festival a week ago."

"I believe there is an intermarriage between a Weston farmer and one of the Ashton tenants," my mother said disdainfully.

Her words jogged my memory. "That's true," I said to Adam. "Bob Fenton's sister Alice is married to an Ashton farmer."

"Really, Annabelle," my mother said, "the

142

marriages of tenant farmers are of no interest to me. What does interest me is your reputation. You should not be holding this festival!"

I gave her a steely smile. "Well, I am."

Silence fell once more.

"Good going, Annabelle," I heard Jack mutter.

Giles's small hand slipped into mine and I squeezed it.

The duke spoke. "Disgraceful," he said.

"Have you come to stay?" I asked the ducal couple. "Would you care for some breakfast? Or are you too anxious to shake the dust of this scandalous household from your feet?"

"You are not amusing, Annabelle," my mother informed me. "We most certainly are staying. Our presence will help to ameliorate the scandal to some degree."

"I am sure it will, Regina," Adam said gravely.

"I told Hodges to put our things in the red suite," my mother continued. "We have been traveling since seven and will take tea in our rooms."

The red suite was Weston's most luxurious bedroom suite, which had once actually been graced by visiting royalty. Mama had annexed it after my marriage to Gerald had forced her to vacate the earl's chambers.

"The festival begins at noon," I informed them.

The duke looked disgusted.

Giles's hand tightened around mine.

Silence continued to reign in the dining room until the door finally swung closed behind the unexpected visitors.

Nell spoke first. "Really, I think the duke is quite the most unpleasant man I have ever met," she said.

Giles said, "I once heard Papa call him an 'old fart.'"

We all burst into wild whoops of laughter.

Giles clapped his hands with glee, delighted to have provoked such a satisfactory response.

"Oh dear," said Aunt Fanny as she wiped the tears from her face. "We must not encourage Giles to say such things."

"I didn't say it, Aunt Fanny," Giles said virtuously. "Papa did."

Nell said, "The sun just came out! Thank God."

I got up and went to look out the window. "The sky to the south is all blue," I reported.

Giles had come to stand beside me. "Grandmama brought the sun with her," he said.

He had to be the sweetest child in the world. I put my arm around him and hugged him to my side.

"Whatever are we going to do with them?" I asked Aunt Fanny despairingly. "There aren't any other guests of a rank elevated enough to keep them occupied."

"They can talk to Sir Matthew," Jack said wickedly.

I threw him an exasperated look. My mother and Sir Matthew hated each other, and Jack knew it.

Jasper said to me, "I don't see why either you or my mother have to worry about entertaining the ducals, Annabelle. After all, your mother is scarcely a stranger to Weston."

"'The ducals,'" Jack said. "I like that, Jasper."

They grinned at each other.

"Jasper is right," Adam said firmly. "You ladies are going to be busy enough. Regina can take care of herself and her husband."

"She won't offend anyone, Annabelle," Nell said. "The tenants all know her too well to take her seriously."

I sighed. "That's true enough."

Nell set aside her napkin and stood up. "I'd better check to see that the children's games are being set up properly."

I said, "And I had better make certain things are going smoothly in the kitchen." Since the festival was for the servants as well as the tenants, I had hired extra help so that our own people could have the day free.

"I will be happy to assist you in any way I can, Lady Weston," Miss Stedham said in her pleasant, well-bred voice.

"I'm sure that Nell could use some help with the children's games," I said, lifting an enquiring eyebrow at my cousin.

"I certainly could. Come along, Miss Stedham," Nell said.

"Me too! Me too!" Giles went rushing across the floor to Nell's side. The three of them left the room together.

Adam said, "I'd better make sure the tents are being properly secured."

Aunt Fanny said, "I'll supervise in the gallery."

Jasper said, "I'll make sure the extra boats have been put on the lake."

"My God," said Jack as the room began to empty, "if only the Horse Guards had put Annabelle in charge of the army instead of Wellington, Napoleon would have been defeated years ago."

145

Jasper retorted as he went out the door, "Be sure to give Jack *his* orders, Annabelle."

"You can go down to the stable and make sure the carriage is ready, Jack," I said. Every year we took out the great black coach, with its gold coat of arms on the door, and gave carriage rides around the estate. It was always a popular event.

He gave me a mock salute and went.

I stood for a moment in the deserted dining room, my eyes on the gifts heaped next to Giles's chair.

His fifth birthday, I thought, and his father isn't here.

A wave of loneliness washed over me, and I buried my face in my hands. Oh God, I thought despairingly, is it never going to end?

Hodges spoke from the doorway. "Are you finished in here, my lady?"

I dropped my hands and lifted my chin. "Yes, Hodges, you can have the dishes cleared."

I went downstairs to check on how things were progressing in the kitchen.

By three in the afternoon the festival was in full swing. Hodges had indeed proved to be an accurate forecaster, and the afternoon sun shone brightly on the two big blue-striped tents we had pitched on the north lawn for use in case of a shower. Beyond the tents the deer watched from a safe distance as a game of cricket was hotly contested, and in the gardens on the west side of the house a number of husbands and wives were matching their skill at archery.

To my surprise, the Grandville portraits in the gallery had proved to be as popular as Nell had predicted. To the family's great amusement, Mama's nose had been out of joint because no one was able to see *her* portrait, and she had made poor Aunt Fanny escort groups of people into the dining room so that they could admire the twin portraits of my mother and the earl.

The five rowboats we had on the lake were busy all afternoon, as was the coach. Grimes even had to change the horses midway through the afternoon. The pony rides also did a brisk business, with Giles's two ponies and a steady old hunter of mine giving delighted children rides up and down the front driveway.

I left the supervision of these various activities to my able lieutenants and set about performing what was my own particular duty on festival day—making sure that I talked to all the guests.

At five o'clock, when the musicians were in place on the terrace outside the gallery and people were gathering on the lawn to listen, I made my way into the house, planning to seek refuge for a while in the quiet of the morning room.

In the Great Hall I ran into Nell, obviously intent on doing the same thing. We looked at each other and laughed.

"You have been wonderful, Nell," I said with fervent gratitude. "Every child I've seen is carrying a prize and wearing a huge smile. You must be utterly exhausted."

"I am a bit weary," she admitted. "I was going to take a brief respite in the morning room."

"Have you eaten—" I was beginning when someone began to hammer the knocker on the front door. As there were no servants in sight, I went to open the door myself.

My son was standing on the front step. "Mama!" he cried. "Guess who I met coming up the drive?"

My fingers closed convulsively around the doorknob. I didn't need to be told, but I asked anyway.

"Uncle Stephen!" came the triumphant reply.

My heart gave one hard thump and then began to beat rapidly.

Nell's voice, warm with pleasure, said from behind me, "Stephen is here? How wonderful."

My knuckles on the doorknob were white with pressure. I looked down into Giles's bright, observant eyes and said with a pitiful attempt at brightness, "What a nice surprise."

Nell came to the doorway and stood beside me, scanning the empty front drive. "I don't see him, Giles."

"He took the curricle to the stable." Giles gave an excited little bounce, extended his arm, and pointed. "Look, here he comes now!"

The three of us obediently looked in the direction of Giles's guiding finger and saw a solitary figure approaching the house from the stable path.

"Uncle Stephen!" Giles shouted in a voice loud enough to carry across three hunting fields. "Here we are!"

Stephen, who had been heading for the side door, changed direction and came around the front of the house.

"I ran into the pony rides on the front drive," he said as he stepped into the hall. He was hatless and there was a stripe of sunburn on the bridge of his nose. "I had completely forgotten about the August festival."

"Annabelle sent to Mr. Putnam's to tell you,

Stephen, but you had already gone to London," Nell assured him earnestly.

I closed the front door and made a conscious effort to let go of the knob.

As I turned to face the others, Giles said, "It's not just an August festival anymore, Uncle Stephen. It's my birthday festival."

A faint line appeared between Stephen's brows as he focused his attention on my son. "Your birthday, Giles?"

"Didn't you know?" Giles was amazed.

"Giles turned five years old today, Stephen," I said quietly.

The line between Stephen's brows deepened and he looked at me. "I thought Giles was born in October," he said sharply.

"So I have just discovered," I said.

"Why did you think I was born in October, Uncle Stephen?" Giles asked.

"Your cousin Nell will explain," I said.

Nell gave me an incredulous look.

I was implacable. "Go on," I said, and rested my hands on Giles's shoulders.

"Yes," Stephen said in a clipped voice that sounded suddenly very tense. "Tell me, Nell."

She fidgeted with one of the pale ringlets she wore clustered in front of her ears. "It was Gerald's idea, Stephen," she finally said with palpable reluctance. "He let you think it was October instead of August because..." She wound the ringlet around her finger in a nervous gesture and looked worriedly at Giles.

"Go on," I said again.

She bit her lip. "It was just that Gerald didn't want you to jump to the wrong conclusion, Stephen."

Silence. Beneath my fingers I felt Giles shift his weight, but he didn't speak.

"And what conclusion might that have been?" Stephen asked in a dangerous-sounding voice.

Nell cast another quick look in the direction of Giles. "You know what Gerald's reputation was, Stephen. He just didn't want you to think that he hadn't... respected... Annabelle."

There was a slight tense frown between Stephen's eyebrows. All the endearing softness of boyhood was gone from his face. I thought with surprise that he had the look of a man used to being in charge.

Nell said, "Gerald did not wish to upset you when you were so far from home." She took a step closer to him and touched his arm in a brief, apologetic gesture. "That's all there was to it, Stephen, I promise you."

I gave Giles's shoulders a warning squeeze to stop him from talking and watched Stephen's face. I could see the exact second when he realized the truth. His head jerked up, as if someone had struck him on the chin, and his eyes sought mine. For a brief moment of charged, vibrating silence, I let myself look into the shocked blue eyes of my child's father.

I said to him, "I didn't know until a few days ago. I always assumed you had been informed of the correct date."

He was visibly pale under his tan, and a pulse had begun to beat in his temple beneath the unfashionably smooth, brushed-back hair.

Giles broke the silence, "It's all right if you don't have a gift for me, Uncle Stephen," he said. "You didn't know."

Stephen looked at his son. "I'm sorry, Giles," he said. His face was stark.

"Are you feeling well, Stephen?" Nell asked solicitously. "You look pale. If you were driving all afternoon without a hat, you probably had too much sun."

"There is lemonade in the gallery," Giles said helpfully. "Georgie and me drank it all afternoon and it's good."

I didn't even attempt to correct his grammar.

"Stephen?" Nell said.

"I'm fine, Nell," Stephen said impatiently, his eyes still riveted on Giles.

Of course, my son interpreted this attention as an invitation to talk. "I got a new fishing pole for my birthday, Uncle Stephen," he began. "And I got..."

I let him rattle on, hoping that his chatter would distract Nell's attention from the look on Stephen's face.

Hodges, who always refused to take festival day off, came pacing gravely into the hall. "Your presence is requested on the terrace, my lady," he said.

"Thank you, Hodges. I will be right there."

"Goodness," said Nell, "is it time for the presentation already?"

Every year the tenants presented me with an enormous bouquet of flowers to thank me for the festival.

"It must be," I said. "Nell, why don't you make sure Stephen gets something to eat?"

"I'm not hungry," Stephen said.

Nell put her hand on his elbow and pushed him gently in the direction of the library. "You

151

still look too pale. Come and sit down and I'll get you some food and drink."

I left Stephen to Nell's tender ministrations and made my escape to the terrace and the gallantry of Edmund Burres, the most senior of all our tenant farmers.

By eight o'clock the music was finished, the August light was beginning to fade, and the party was fast thinning out. I could not endure the thought of facing Mama in the drawing room, so I collected the dogs from my office, where they had spent most of the day, and walked toward the lake to make certain that no one was still out on the water.

The lake was deserted. Someone had dragged the boats up onto the shore, where they rested, upside-down, in front of the icehouse. We usually kept only one boat in the water during the summer and stored the others in the fishing pavilion, to be used as needed.

I sat on the steps of the fishing pavilion and watched the dogs. They kept racing back to me, as if to assure themselves that I was really there, and then they would tear up and down the shore, stretching legs that had been unusually confined all day. The setting sun was low in the sky, touching the tops of the trees with a reddish glow. I wrapped my arms around my knees and listened to the gentle sound of lakewater lapping against the shore.

In my mind's eye I saw again Stephen's shocked face.

He really had not known.

I hugged my knees tighter and wondered what he was going to do.

Portia came up for a quick check-in. "I'm still here," I told her softly, and, reassured, she ran back to join her brother. Both dogs were wet by now. Mama would have an apoplexy when she saw them.

I heard voices coming from the direction of the house, and the dogs went racing past me on their way to greet the newcomers. I stood up and smoothed my skirt with fingers that trembled slightly. One of the voices had belonged to Stephen.

He was accompanied by Jasper and Nell.

"Is everyone hiding from Mama?" I asked brightly as they came up to me.

Nell shook her head. "It isn't so much your mother, Annabelle. We're accustomed to her. It's the duke."

Jasper turned to Stephen. "You should have heard Giles at breakfast, Stephen. He told us that Gerald once called the duke an 'old fart'!"

Stephen produced the expected smile. I realized I was staring at his mouth and made myself look instead at Jasper. I had not seen him all day, as he had been stationed here at the lake to make certain everyone behaved themselves in the boats.

"You performed heroically, Jasper," I said. "We managed to get through the entire day without anyone falling into the water."

Jasper chuckled. "I gave everyone instructions in my best commanding officer voice before I let them get into a boat. Even the friskiest youngsters were afraid to stand up, with me posted on the shore glowering at them."

"Were you out here all day, Jasper?" Stephen asked.

"Jack relieved me for a while."

"It is one of my greatest fears on festival day that someone will drown in the lake," I confessed.

Merlin shook himself, showering us all with drops of lakewater. Nell squeaked and jumped out of the way.

The four of us stood talking for a while longer, but I scarcely heard a word that was said. All my senses were centered on Stephen. I didn't look at him, but I felt him there. I had never needed to look at Stephen to know where he was.

"I have been wondering where the four of you were hiding yourselves!"

It was Adam, approaching us from the direction of the house.

"Oh dear," I said, "have we left Aunt Fanny saddled with Mama and the duke?"

Adam chuckled. "The rector had that chore for most of the day, but he left about an hour ago. I told him he had earned himself a halo."

We all laughed.

"Miss Stedham asked me to tell you that Giles is not feeling well and is asking for you, Annabelle," Adam said.

I felt the sudden tension in Stephen.

I sighed. "Too much food and too much excitement and then he can't go to sleep. I'll read to him for a while; that usually does it."

Nell said, "He was running around with Georgie Miller the whole day, and every time I saw them they had something in their mouths."

I moved to Adam's side, and together we turned and began to return along the gravel path. Jasper moved to my other side, and Nell and Stephen fell in behind us.

The sun had gone down, and the sky was that soft shade of gray it turns before the true blackness of night sets in. I walked between Uncle Adam and Jasper and listened to the sound of Nell's voice chatting away to Stephen and wondered how he was going to manage to get me alone.

CHAPTER
eleven

It was close to ten o'clock when I came back downstairs, looked into the drawing room, and discovered my mother, the duke, Aunt Fanny, and Uncle Adam having an early tea. I stepped into the room, planning to say good night, but Aunt Fanny gave me such a piteous look that I changed my mind and reluctantly accepted a cup of tea from Mama.

"How is Giles?" Aunt Fanny asked.

"Asleep," I replied. "He was overexcited, that is all."

"You should not allow him to fraternize with the tenants' children, Annabelle." The duke managed to look down his nose and at the same time balance a Wedgwood china plate containing a slice of cake on his knee. Remarkable.

I sipped my tea and answered mildly, "He is a child and he needs to play with other children."

The ducal eyebrows drew together in an awe-inducing frown. "Before he is a child, he is the

155

Earl of Weston. He should be taught never to forget that."

My mother seconded her husband. "Saye is giving you good advice, Annabelle. You have always been overinclined to socialize with your inferiors. It is to be hoped that you don't encourage Gerald's son to do the same. *Gerald* never demeaned himself by pretending he was the equal of a farmer."

I said pleasantly, "Gerald had a brother and cousins to play with. Giles is not so fortunate."

My mother and I stared at each over the teapot.

Aunt Fanny said in a breathless voice, "The day went beautifully, Annabelle."

Adam nobly seconded his wife's effort. "Yes," he said, "you gave happiness to a great many people. It was the right decision to hold the festival."

Dear Aunt Fanny and Uncle Adam. I smiled at them and said, "It did go smoothly, didn't it?"

"I don't know what possessed you to allow all those people into the house," Mama complained. "I was in terror that something would be broken. Or stolen!"

"I'll have a little more of that cake, Regina," Adam said.

As my mother deftly slipped a slice of lemon cake onto a plate, I said, "The only things in the gallery besides the food were the portraits, Mama."

In fact, I had ordered the gallery cleared not because I feared theft, but because I knew how difficult it was for parents to keep inquisitive little fingers from touching. I would not have grieved if a vase was broken, but the parents of the child who broke it would have been horrified.

Aunt Fanny made another valiant contribution to the conversation. "My, those portraits were popular. There was a queue of people all afternoon waiting to look at them."

Mama said, "And those people also came into the dining room, Fanny, where the Weston silver was displayed on the sideboard!"

I raised my brows in a charade of elaborate surprise. "It was not in my plan to allow people into the dining room," I said. "Who let them in there?"

My mother did not look at all chagrined but replied with regal dignity, "It was only natural for people to wish to see the portraits of Weston and myself. I authorized Fanny to allow them in the dining room."

Adam winked at me from behind his lemon cake, and I had to bite my lip to keep from smiling.

The duke said, "The duchess and I felt obligated to remain in the dining room ourselves, to keep a watch on the silver."

The thought of the ducal pair spending their entire afternoon guarding the silver struck me as so humorous that I had to raise my hand and feign a cough to keep from laughing out loud.

"Mr. Davies joined us," Mama said. "He is a learned man, I suppose, but his conversation is scarcely lively."

I made a mental note to contribute a healthy donation to the rector's favorite charity. I hadn't realized that the poor man had been cooped up with Mama all afternoon.

157

Aunt Fanny tried heroically to suppress a yawn.

"Come along, my dear," Adam said. "You are exhausted and need your bed."

"I am rather weary," Fanny confessed as she allowed Adam to assist her to her feet.

"I too am ready to retire," Mama announced. "Do you come with me, Saye, or shall I order you some wine?"

The duke was looking tired. "I shall come upstairs with you, Regina," he said. "It has been a long day." His tone made it clear that we could substitute the word "dreadful" for "long."

We all walked out into the corridor together. "Sleep well," I said to the four of them as I left them at the bottom of the stairs. My mother compressed her lips and favored me with a terse nod.

I knew what was behind that nod. As much as Mama had wanted me to marry Gerald, it had almost killed her to relinquish the master suite. It still irked her every time she had to go up the stairs and leave me behind.

As I passed the library I heard male laughter coming from behind the closed door. I opened the door, peeked in, and saw Stephen, Jasper, and Jack clustered around the desk upon which reposed several bottles of what looked to be port. Jasper, sprawled comfortably in the big chair behind the desk, was the only one of them facing the door, and he stood up when he saw me.

"By Jove, if it isn't Lady Bountiful herself." He picked up his half-full glass. "A toast to Annabelle"—he pointed the glass in my direction—"the most beautiful lady in all of England."

His voice was faintly slurred, and I realized that this was not his first glass of wine.

Jack and Stephen were half standing, half sitting, on either side of the desk. Jack's blond head turned toward me, and he lifted his glass as well, seconding amiably, "To Annabelle."

Stephen also lifted his glass, but he looked in the direction of the wing chair. "And a toast to Nell," he said, "the kindest lady in all of England."

For the first time I realized that someone was sitting in the wing chair in front of the desk.

I heard Nell say softly, "Thank you, Stephen."

"To Nell," her brother said, swinging his glass in her direction with a motion so lavishly sweeping that it almost caused the wine to slop over the rim.

"To Nell," said Jack.

The three of them drained their wineglasses, and I tried vainly to suppress a surge of jealousy. I didn't like it that Stephen had called Nell "kind."

I walked slowly across the Turkish carpet to stand beside Jack on the opposite side of the desk from Stephen.

"Aren't these wretches sharing their wine with you, Nell?" I asked. She was curled up in the wing chair, with her legs tucked under her.

"I didn't want any," she said. Her boneless posture, combined with the exotic tilt of her eyes, made her look like a sleepy kitten.

I shot a glance at Stephen and found him looking at me. His expression was not pleasant.

I thought perhaps I could do with some wine and asked Jasper to pour me a glass.

"I need one," I said. "I have spent the last half hour drinking tea with Mama and the duke." I let my gaze flick quickly from one cousin's face to the next. "You ought to be ashamed of yourselves, deserting poor Aunt Fanny and Uncle Adam like that."

Jasper placed the new glass of wine he had just poured on the desk in front of his chair, stood up, and gestured for me to take his seat, which I did. He stood beside me and filled up his own glass.

"Jack?" he said. "Stephen?"

Jack extended his glass for a refill.

"No, thank you, Jasper," Stephen said.

He was sitting on the edge of the desk, close enough for me to reach out and touch him. I shot him a defiant look and drank down half of my port. The wine burned hot and strong in my throat and stomach.

"Whoa, Annabelle!" Jasper said, reaching out to curl his fingers around my wrist. "Na—*not*—good to drink it so fast."

I looked up into his gray eyes, which were noticeably darkened by drink. He was close enough for me to smell the port on his breath. "Jasper," I said affectionately, "I believe you're foxed."

I felt his fingers tighten around my wrist, and his head bent closer to mine.

Nell's voice said practically, "Better let Annabelle go before you tip over and fall in her lap, Jasper."

Jasper let go of my wrist and straightened up. "I am not foxed," he said slowly and clearly.

"Just a trifle castaway, old fellow," Jack said soothingly.

160

Jasper steadied himself on his feet. "Well," he admitted thickly. "P'haps a trif-trifle."

I looked around the room at the companions of my childhood and felt a sudden rush of love. I said, "It has been a long time since we were all together like this. It brings back so many happy memories."

Everyone looked at me in surprise.

Nell said, "We aren't children anymore, Annabelle. You can't expect us to be as we were when we were younger."

Her impatient voice annoyed me. I know that better than anyone, I thought. I didn't understand why Nell seemed always to be in opposition to me these days.

Jack pushed away from the desk, stood up, drained his glass, and announced, "I'm for bed."

"If I remain one minute longer in this chair, I will be here for the night," Nell said as she uncurled herself. She stood up, then yawned, her hand coming up belatedly to cover her pink mouth. With her smallness and her ruffled curls she looked more like a kitten than ever.

Stephen was at her side. As I watched, he gently took her arm. "Come along, Nell, and I'll see you to your room."

She smiled up at him sleepily. "Thank you, Stephen."

He smiled back.

I said to Jack, "I think Jasper may require some assistance."

He turned to Jasper and carefully removed the half-full glass from between his fingers. "Come along, old fellow. Time you turned in."

"I don't want to," Jasper said.

"It's late," Jack said. "Annabelle is tired."

Jasper sighed and said mournfully, "I feel so good now, Jack, and I'll feel so wretched in the morning."

Jack chuckled. "Too true, my boy, too true."

"You were all wonderful today," I said from my seat behind the desk. "I cannot thank you enough for your assistance."

"Anything for you, Annabelle darling," Jack said lightly. He aimed Jasper in the direction of the door.

"Yes." Jasper resisted Jack's encouraging push for a moment, looked at me, and gave three distinct nods. "Anything for Annabelle."

"Thank you both," I said.

Nell gave me a stiff smile.

"Good night," Stephen said. He didn't look at me at all.

After they had all exited, I sat behind the desk and wondered whether I should remain in the library or seek the shelter of my own rooms. I had no doubt that Stephen would be back. The question was, did I want to face him tonight?

I steepled my fingers and regarded them with detached interest as I pondered this question. The fingers seemed a little out of focus, and I blinked to clear my vision. Then I blinked again. Finally I realized that I had indeed drunk the port too quickly.

I was going to have to face Stephen sooner or later, I thought. Perhaps I ought to get it over with tonight, while I was protected by this pleasant, wine-induced detachment. I propped my elbows on the desk, opened my fingers, and lowered my forehead into my hands. I shut my eyes.

Twenty minutes later I heard the library door click closed. Slowly I raised my head. Stephen was standing in front of the closed door, and across the room his gaze locked with mine. All the hazy fumes left by the wine burned instantly away with that blazing look. I had expected anger. I had not expected this.

"How could you have done this to me?"

The words were spoken with such intense, concentrated fury that they struck me like a blow. I sucked air into my lungs and tried to form a reply.

He began to walk toward me. "Giles is mine, isn't he?"

I sat as still as a hunted animal trying to evade a predator. I didn't answer him. I couldn't.

He leaned his hands on the top of the desk, bending over them, bringing his face closer to mine. *"Isn't he, Annabelle?"*

I had imagined this scene between us so many times. How often had I pored over all the bitter, wounding words that I would say to him when finally we confronted each other about Giles.

Not a single one of those words came to my mind as I confronted the reality of Stephen's burning blue gaze.

"Y-yes," I managed to say in a low, shaking voice, "Giles is your son."

He shut his eyes to hide them from me and straightened up, drawing away from me to the far side of the desk.

"Jesus." He said the word as if it were a prayer for help. He thrust his hand through his hair in such a familiar gesture that it sent a shiver of pain through my heart. *"Jesus,* Annabelle!" There was a white line around his mouth, always a bad sign with Stephen. *"Why?"*

163

His voice was anguished.

My stomach was in a knot. I had not thought our meeting would feel like this.

"I told you earlier that I did not know Gerald had misled you," I said breathlessly. "I always assumed you knew the correct date of Giles's birth, so when you didn't write to me I assumed you didn't care."

"That is not what I meant," Stephen said grimly. "What I want to know is"—his voice measured each word precisely—"why... did... you... marry... Gerald?"

I gripped my hands together in my lap. "I was with child, Stephen! I had to marry some-one, and Gerald was available." I added, my own bitterness finally coming to the fore, "You were in Jamaica, if you recall."

His eyes skewered me to my soul. "Did you know about the baby before I left?"

"No," I said, "I did not."

He turned abruptly away and went to the window. He stood there with his back to me, staring out into the dark. He had removed his coat and his neckcloth upstairs, and I could see the tension in his shoulders right through the fine white linen of his shirt. It was surprising how wide those shoulders had grown in the last five years.

He said without turning around, "And how did you account for Giles to Gerald?"

I replied in a steady voice, "Gerald thought that Giles was his."

At that he swung around to face me. His hair had slipped forward over his temples, and his bare throat looked very brown against the opened collar of his shirt. Desire struck me, like an unexpected blow to the stomach, and hastily I lowered my eyes so that he shouldn't see it.

"Gerald wasn't stupid," I heard him say forcefully. "He had to know you weren't a virgin when you married him."

"I told him it must be because I rode horses astride," I said, my eyes focused on the jade paperweight that reposed on the corner of the desk blotter. "I told him I had never lain with a man."

"Dear God," he said.

We both knew very well that riding horses astride had not impaired my virginity.

He continued, "Did you tell him the baby was early?"

"Yes."

"And he believed you?"

I said slowly, "I have always thought that he believed me."

Stephen began to walk back toward the desk. I picked up the smooth round paperweight and sat back in my chair, holding the jade in my lap. My grip on it was so tight that my fingers felt cramped.

He sat in the wing chair that Nell had been sitting in earlier, and we regarded each other over the barrier of the desk. He repeated, emphasizing my use of the past tense, "*You have always thought.*" He ran his fingers through his hair, pushing it back. "And what do you think now?"

"I was shaken when I learned that he hadn't told you the truth about Giles's birthdate," I admitted.

The white line had faded from around his

mouth. It was set now in pain, not in anger. "I went berserk when I learned you had married Gerald," he said with difficulty. "I couldn't understand it. I had no idea you were with child."

"Surely it would have been a reasonable surmise," I said.

"We had been safe for over a year," he returned. "I just didn't think..."

"It was a shock to me, too," I said grimly.

For some unfathomable reason, my monthly flow was more like a trimonthly flow. My mother had told me she was the same, which was why I was her only child. I had worried sometimes that I would never have children, but there was no denying that my unusual biology had facilitated the sexual relationship between Stephen and me.

He said abruptly, "Gerald couldn't have known. Good God, Annabelle, Giles was his heir! Gerald would never have accepted the child if he had had suspicions regarding his paternity."

"If Gerald did indeed have suspicions, he also would have known at whose door to lay them," I returned coolly. "He would have known that Giles was a Grandville."

Stephen shut his eyes.

"After all, Stephen, what could he have done?" I continued remorselessly. "As it was, everyone simply thought that Gerald and I had slept together before our wedding day. Given Gerald's reputation, that was not an unreasonable assumption for people to make. Gerald had far too much pride to hold himself up before his world as a duped husband. It was much easier for him to believe me when I said that the baby was early. He believed what he wanted to believe." I shrugged again. "Gerald was so handsome and charming and amusing that most people didn't realize how ruthlessly selfish he was at heart."

"But you did."

"Yes, I did. And I admit I took advantage of it. But Gerald got what he wanted, too, Stephen. He got my face."

Silence. I stared at the green stone in my lap, smoothing my thumbs over its surface again and again.

When finally Stephen spoke it was in a quiet voice from which all anger had been expunged. "Annabelle, I am so sorry."

I looked up. I said fiercely, "I will never forgive you for leaving me like that. Never."

I stood up. I put the paperweight back on the desk. "I hate you," I said, and walked out of the room.

CHAPTER
twelve

I went into my dressing room, dismissed the waiting Marianne, flung myself onto the chaise longue, and began to weep. These were tears that had waited a long time to be shed, and there was a cathartic quality about the uninhibited violence that I allowed them this night.

I wept for the seventeen-year-old half-child half-woman whose mother had once grabbed her by the chin, stared pitilessly into her face, and demanded, "Annabelle, are you increasing?"

"N-no, M-mama," I had stuttered in shocked denial. "How can you ask me such a thing?"

"It's your skin," my mother had replied grimly. "It has a sheen to it, almost a pearly look. I had that look once—when I was expecting you."

I wept for the girl who, out of anger and out of fear, had married a man she did not love and had lied to him.

"I had a fall yesterday, Gerald. I didn't tell you about it because I didn't want to worry you, but I think the baby is coming early."

I wept for the young mother who had held her child in her arms and longed with agonizing intensity for his father to be with her to share in her joy.

I wept for all the happiness Stephen had destroyed when he had uttered those fateful words, "I am responsible, Papa. There is no one else."

I was exhausted when the tears finally slowed and stopped. My head hurt and I didn't think my legs had the strength to carry me to my bedroom, so I curled up on the chaise longue instead, closed my eyes, and let my thoughts drift into memory.

And once again I am sixteen years old, and Stephen and I have gone to the lake to be alone.

Weston was always beautiful in April. The woods were full of bluebells, wild hyacinths, and violets, and the beds of orange-and-white tulips in front of the house stood at colorful attention to greet a new arrival. The south garden was transformed into carpets of brilliant color separated from each other by neat gravel paths. The oak and elm trees were lightly furred with incipient foliage, and the cherry trees near the kitchen garden were frothy with blossoms.

It was early morning when Stephen and I crept out of the house together to go to the lake. Thrushes and blackbirds were singing as we made our way to the fishing pavilion, where the porch was decorated with trellises of pink and white wallflowers.

The dogs trotted off to explore the shoreline. I leaned my arms on the porch rail and gazed out at the lake, shining so peacefully in the early morning sun. "It's wonderful to be home again," I said.

My mother had taken me up to London with her in the middle of March so that she could buy me some new clothes at a London dressmaker's. The previous Christmas she had decreed that the time had come for me to put up my hair and put aside my schoolgirl frocks, and she was intent on adding to my new wardrobe.

I had been furious about missing the end of the hunting season. Ever since I had turned sixteen, it had seemed to me that my nice, undisturbed life at Weston had been continually disrupted. And when I actually was at home, more and more often it seemed as if Stephen were not.

In fact, Stephen and I had not seen each other since January. After Christmas he had gone on a visit to his uncle Francis, then I had been in London when he had returned to Weston in March. This was the first chance we had had to be private together since my arrival early yesterday evening.

"Didn't you enjoy London?" Stephen asked now. He was leaning on the rail beside me, and when I glanced at him his nostrils and the line of his mouth looked tense.

"Some of it," I said slowly. "Mama bought me tons of clothes. She is talking about letting me go to some assemblies and dances this year, so that I will be ready for my come-out next spring."

Stephen scowled and didn't reply.

I said, "He isn't going to help us, is he?"

Stephen still wouldn't look at me. "No. He isn't."

I said in a quiet voice, "I see."

We had put so much faith in Francis Putnam, who had always been exceedingly fond of Stephen. Surely, we had told each other, surely he would help us to convince the earl and my mother that we should marry. Surely he would allow us to live with him after we were indeed man and wife. He had already made Stephen his heir. He had always seemed to like me. Surely Francis Putnam would take our part.

That we would need help to convince our parents that we should marry was obvious to us both. My mother's plans for me definitely did not include marriage to a younger son. The fact was, both she and the earl fully expected me to marry Gerald. My mother, of course, had decided years ago that I should marry her husband's elder son; the earl had reached his decision more recently, when he had seen how Gerald had reacted to the new, grown-up Annabelle over the Christmas holiday.

It was Gerald's reaction, and our parents'

obvious expectations, that had driven Stephen to talk to his uncle Francis.

The tension in Stephen's shoulders was visible through the fabric of his old russet jacket. His thin, ringless hands were clenched hard on the porch railing. "He said we were too young to know our own hearts, that we had to give ourselves opportunities to meet other people. He said I should go to Oxford and you should make your come-out. Then, if we still felt the same way after I was finished with school, then he would help us."

"Did you tell him about Gerald?"

"He said no one would make you marry Gerald if you didn't want to."

"He doesn't understand," I said despairingly.

Stephen pushed his hair off of his brow. "I tried to explain to him how we felt about each other, Annabelle, but he wouldn't listen! He said it wasn't wise of the earl to have thrown us together so much, that it was a good thing I was going away to Oxford."

"Why don't we just run away to Scotland, Stephen?" I asked.

In England, minors could not marry without the consent of their parents or guardians, but this was not the case in Scotland. Scotland had no requirements of age or of the posting of banns. Scotland required only a mutual declaration exchanged before witnesses for a marriage to be legal. Runaway couples from England traditionally headed for the border town of Gretna Green, which was only ten miles north of Carlisle.

"If we try to make a run for Scotland, and

we are caught, they will separate us completely," Stephen said grimly. At last he turned to face me. "Do we want to take that chance?"

My mouth quivered and I shook my head.

"Don't, love...." Stephen stepped forward and gathered me into his arms.

I pressed against him and then we were kissing, our mouths open to each other, our arms holding on to each other as if our very lives depended upon it.

We had learned a lot about kissing in the last six months, but this was different from anything we had known before. There was a frantic quality to this kiss that reflected not only our three-month separation, but also the blow our hopes had taken from Francis Putnam's refusal to help.

I felt the heat of his body through the thin cotton of my dress. It was an old dress and the bodice was too tight. His hand moved tentatively to cup my breast. Shocks of sheer delight shot through me. With a little murmur of pleasure, I pressed myself against his fingers.

"Annabelle—" He pulled his mouth from mine, and I found myself staring into narrowed glittering eyes that were almost black with desire. "We have to stop this now," he said in a harsh, laboring voice. "If we don't, I won't be able to stop at all."

"I don't want to stop," I said.

He drew a deep, shuddering breath. "You don't know what you're saying."

I punched him on the shoulders with both my fists. "Don't you dare say that to me, Stephen Grandville! You sound like all the rest of them." I punched him again, hard. "I know what I want. I have always known what I wanted. I want you!"

And I punched him one more time.

He captured my fists in his hands.

"Annabelle. Oh dear God, Annabelle. I love you so much." And he bent his mouth to mine once more.

There was an old chaise longue inside the pavilion, and that is where we went. It was not a smooth lovemaking. We neither of us had any experience; all we had was a great and urgent need. All those years of riding astride did not make Stephen's penetration any easier for me, and I bled.

But neither the pain nor the blood mattered. What mattered was that we had done it; we had pledged ourselves in the most irrevocable way either of us could imagine. I belonged to Stephen and Stephen belonged to me.

"Nothing can ever part us now," he had said to me as we lay pressed against each other on the narrow chaise longue that smelled faintly of mildew and fish.

And I had believed him.

I lay now on another chaise longue next door to the bedroom where I had slept with Stephen's brother. Gerald had been a master at making love—unlike Stephen, he had had plenty of practice—but his love had been counterfeit coin. My body had responded to Gerald, but afterward I would lie awake for hours, suffocated by a fog of depression, longing with all my being for the gold that I had lost.

I had told Stephen tonight that I hated him, and I had spoken the truth. I did hate him. But I loved him, too. I always would.

My head was pounding, and I rang the bell

for Marianne and asked her to bring me a cold cloth to put on my forehead.

I slept late the following morning. When I finally awoke the headache was gone, but my scalp felt tender and I decided against joining the family in the dining room. Instead I had tea and a muffin in my dressing room.

I had been surrounded by such a constant press of people the day before that this morning I felt the need to be alone. So I collected the dogs, slipped out the back door of the house, and went for a meandering walk around the estate, ending up at the lake.

I was surprised to find that Stephen and Giles were before me. As I approached the fishing pavilion from along the shoreline, I saw the two of them, standing knee-deep in the water in front of the pavilion, throwing stones.

Giles's clear, childish treble carried easily through the soft summer air. "I think I know how to do it, Uncle Stephen! Watch me!"

"Go ahead," Stephen said.

Giles threw the stone with a flick of his wrist, and as we all watched intently, the stone skipped once, twice, then three times before it sank beneath the water.

"Did you see that?" Giles said excitedly. "I made it skip!"

"That was perfect," Stephen said. "Three skips is excellent."

Stephen was obviously trying to make friends with his son. I ignored the sudden cramp around my heart and walked forward. The dogs announced my presence.

"Mama!" Giles came splashing out of the water to jump up and down in front of me. "Did you see that? Did you see me skip the stone?"

"I did, darling. Three times! I'm impressed."

"Uncle Stephen showed me how."

I said, "I don't know why it should be so, but there is something about stones and water that triggers an irresistible compulsion in the male animal to throw."

Stephen grinned, turned to face the lake, and flung the stone that was in his hand far out into the water.

Giles made a noise that was indicative of great admiration.

I said austerely, "Fortunately, females are not burdened by so primitive an urge."

My loyal son felt that I was belittling myself and tried to reassure me. "You throw good, Mama," he said. "For a girl."

"Thank you, darling." I looked at Stephen, who was still standing in the water. "Did you come to the lake just to teach Giles to skip stones?"

"No." He began to wade toward me. "Actually, we came to try out Giles's new fishing pole. We just got distracted by the stones."

"Uncle Stephen is going to take me out in the boat, Mama," Giles said. "I told him I would catch him a fish for his dinner."

"At the rate you have been catching fish, Giles, there won't be any left in the lake," I said.

Giles laughed gleefully. "Then I will have to fish in the ocean!"

Stephen had come to stand beside Giles. Before commencing the stone-throwing lesson, he had removed his blue single-breasted morning coat, his neckcloth, his stockings, and his boots, and he had rolled his shirtsleeves up to

175

his elbows. He appeared completely indifferent to the fact that his neck, his forearms, his feet, and his calves were still bare.

Well, I thought irritably, why shouldn't he be? God knows, Annabelle, you have seen him wearing less than this.

But I was uncomfortable. My own green jaconet gown, worn with only one petticoat, was extremely lightweight, and I was wearing only green walking shoes and no stockings. I folded my arms across my breasts, forming a protective shield against my own acute awareness of him, and said, "You haven't fished yet?"

"Not yet," Stephen said.

"Come with us, Mama," Giles urged. "There is room in the boat for you, too."

"You know I don't like boats, Giles."

"The lake is as smooth as glass, Annabelle," Stephen interrupted. "You can't possibly feel ill on a surface as calm as the lake is today."

Giles looked up into his father's face and smiled approvingly.

Sudden emotion caught at my throat, clogging it, and tears stung my eyes. I shaded my eyes with my hand and stared out at the lake as if trying to make up my mind.

"All right," I said at last. "But I don't want to go out too far."

"It's a small lake, Annabelle," Stephen said. "It isn't possible to go out too far."

Stephen and Giles picked up their poles and we all began to walk in the direction of the single rowboat that was floating in the water at the end of the small wooden dock.

"The oars are in the fishing pavilion," I said. "I'll go and fetch them."

By the time I returned with the oars, Stephen and Giles had put their fishing poles in the boat and Giles was sitting on the small front bench seat, looking expectant.

Stephen said, "Shall I help you, Annabelle?" and put his hands on my waist as if he would lift me down into the boat.

The material of my summer dress was thin, and there was no way I could disguise the shock that jolted through me at the touch of his hands. I jerked away from him and said in a voice that sounded unnecessarily shrill, "I am perfectly capable of getting into the boat by myself, Stephen."

He didn't answer, just stood there watching me. I gathered up the green skirt of my summer morning dress and stepped into the boat. It rocked under my feet, and I reached out blindly, trying to find something to balance myself with. Stephen's hand caught mine and held me steady.

"Just sit down, Annabelle," he said. "You'll be fine."

Still holding tightly to his hand, I cautiously lowered myself to the wooden plank that formed the main seat of the boat. Stephen stepped in after me, balanced himself easily as he fitted the oars into the oarlocks, then sat next to me and pushed away from the dock.

"I really do not like boats," I muttered as we moved smoothly away from the shore.

"*I* like boats," Giles informed us. He was sitting with his back to the front, facing us. "May I row, too, Uncle Stephen?"

Stephen's "In a little while" clashed with my "*No*, Giles."

Giles stuck out his lower lip. "Why not, Mama?"

"Because no one is going to stand up and change places in this boat as long as I am in it," I said.

"But—" Giles began.

"I mean it, Giles," I said.

We had been out on the water for perhaps fifteen minutes, and I was just beginning to relax, when the boat started to leak. The first indication I had that we were in trouble was the sudden chill wetness of my feet. I looked down and saw that they were reposing in at least two inches of water.

"Stephen," I said tensely, "the boat is leaking."

"I noticed," he said. He was rowing strongly. "I'm taking us in."

"I told you not to come so far out," I said as I gauged the distance to shore. It was too far away.

He continued to row and didn't reply.

"The water is coming in *fast*, Mama," Giles said.

It was now up to my ankles.

"Stephen?" I said.

"See if you can find the hole, Annabelle, and stuff it with something."

I immediately slid to my knees on the floor of the boat and began to feel around.

"I think it's here, Uncle Stephen," Giles said. He was looking at the floor on the other side of his seat. "One of the boards is sticking up."

"Can you push it down, Giles?" Stephen said. His voice was very calm. "Put your foot over it."

Giles scrambled to do as Stephen had asked.

"I am, Uncle Stephen," he said in a small, frightened voice. "But the water is coming in anyway."

The water in the boat was now up to our knees, and no matter how hard Stephen rowed, the boat was scarcely moving.

It was my worst nightmare come true.

"Stephen," I said, trying to keep the panic inside me from sounding in my voice, "Giles can't swim."

Stephen pushed the useless oars out of his way and said, "This is what we are going to do. First I will swim to shore with Giles. Annabelle, you are going to have to keep yourself afloat until I can come back for you."

I searched his face. I knew that Stephen could swim, but what he was suggesting seemed impossible. "Can you get Giles in as well as yourself?" I asked.

"Yes. I did a great deal of swimming in Jamaica. I will take Giles in and come back for you." He blue eyes commanded me. "You can swim a little, Annabelle. Remember?"

When we were children I had sometimes paddled in the water, imitating the dogs. I had no idea if I could keep afloat for more than a few minutes. I said, "Of course I remember."

The boat was slowly sinking.

Stephen said, "Giles, you must lie very still, with your head on my shoulder, and I will swim you to shore. You must not struggle or you might sink us both. Do you understand?"

Giles said in a frightened voice, "We can't leave Mama, Uncle Stephen."

"I will come back for her, Giles, I promise. Now, are you ready?"

Giles looked at me.

"I will be all right, Giles," I said firmly. "Please, do as Uncle Stephen says."

"A-all right," Giles whispered.

I looked back at Stephen. "Float on your stomach, Annabelle," he said. "Let your face rest in the water and lift it only when you need to breathe. Kick your feet a little."

"Yes," I said.

We looked at each other.

"Just don't panic," he said. "You'll be all right as long as you don't panic."

I nodded. "Take care of Giles for me."

We were all standing now as the boat was slowly sinking beneath the water.

"Tie the skirt of that dress around your waist so you can kick," Stephen said, and, cupping his hand under Giles's chin, he pushed away from the boat and began to swim.

I had just enough time to do as he said before the boat completely disappeared from beneath my feet and I was left to stay afloat on my own.

The lakewater felt very cold as it closed over my shoulders. I kicked my feet and paddled my hands as fast as I could and managed to hold my head up out of the water long enough to see Stephen moving smoothly toward the shore, with Giles's small head braced against his shoulder.

Giles would be safe.

Thank you, God, I prayed. Then I turned my attention to myself.

I knew I could not keep up this kicking and paddling for very long; it was too tiring. I remembered what Stephen had said about resting my face in the water, but every instinct I possessed was telling me that if I put my face in the water, I would drown.

I swallowed some water and kicked and paddled frantically trying to stay afloat.

Don't panic, Annabelle, I told myself firmly. Whatever you do, don't panic.

Float on your stomach, Stephen had said. Only lift your face when you need to breathe.

I filled my lungs with air, shut my eyes and my mouth tightly, put my face into the water and lay still.

My legs began to sink.

Don't panic, Annabelle. Kick. Keep your face in the water and kick.

I did this and my legs floated upward. I paddled with my hands for a minute, lifted my face, and took another breath. I put my face back in the water.

I can do this. It's easier to stay on top of the water if I'm not trying to hold up my head. I can keep this up until Stephen comes back.

I never doubted that he would come back. I was out on the lake for what seemed to be hours, and I was very, very frightened. But I didn't panic. I kept on floating and breathing because I knew that eventually Stephen would come back.

His hand on my shoulder announced his arrival. I lifted my head and swallowed some water. "Your turn," he said, gripped me, and turned me until I was lying on my back with my head pillowed on his shoulder. Then we began to move toward the shore.

He was tired. I could feel the effort in his muscles, and I kept as still as I could. Even when the water washed over my face, as it did occasionally, I didn't struggle. Slowly, laboriously, the shore drew closer.

Finally Stephen gasped, "We can stand up here," and released me.

The solid feel of the lake bottom beneath my feet was one of the most beautiful things I had ever known.

"*Mama! Mama!*" Giles was screaming at me from the shore. He ran into the water as if he would come out to meet me.

"Stay where you are, Giles," I called back to him in a hoarse, breathless voice. "I'm coming in." And I began to stagger toward the shore.

Giles remained where he was, in chest-deep water, until I reached him. Then he wrapped his arms around my waist, clung to me tightly, and began to sob.

I rocked back and forth with him. "It's all right, darling," I kept saying. "It's all over now. We're safe. Thanks to Uncle Stephen, we're safe."

Finally, when the storm was spent and Giles was able to command himself again, the both of us tottered out of the lake and collapsed beside Stephen on the shore.

He was lying on his back, his knees bent, one arm outstretched and the other flung across his eyes to shade them from the sun. His chest rose and fell in rapid succession as he drew shallow gulps of air into his exhausted lungs.

I put my hand over his heart and felt its heavy hammering right through his soaked shirt. "Thank God you can swim," I said, leaving my hand where it was.

"One other... (pant)... useful thing I... (pant)... learned in Jamaica."

"Dear God, Stephen," I said. "Dear God."

He lifted his arm from his face. His blue eyes looked up at me from between spiked wet lashes. He said, "Thank God you don't panic."

I could feel his skin through his soaking wet shirt, could feel the rise and fall of his chest as he took the precious air into his overworked lungs. His hand closed over mine and he said, "Annabelle, we have to talk."

"Yes." My voice was shaking.

A small voice said, "Mama, I'm cold."

The sun was hot. "It's a reaction," Stephen said. "My coat is in the fishing pavilion. Wrap him up in that and let's get him home."

CHAPTER
thirteen

The three of us attempted to slip unnoticed into the house, but before we could reach the side door we ran into Jasper, Jack, Nell, and Miss Stedham, all of whom were setting out for the stables. We might have managed to avoid them, but as soon as Giles saw Miss Stedham he called out, "Genie! Wait till you hear what happened! I almost drowned!"

The four of them looked our way, so we had to continue along the path. Their shocked expressions told us exactly how horrific we must have appeared. Stephen, who had been carrying Giles, set him on his feet, removed the coat in which he was wrapped, and handed it to me with the brief comment, "Put it on."

I slid my arms into the sleeves and wrapped its length around my damp frock, achieving at least a modicum of modesty, I hoped. My hair was hanging down my back, and I pulled it out from under the coat in order to get the wet mass away from my skin.

Jasper was staring at me. "Good God, Annabelle!" he exclaimed. "What happened?"

Miss Stedham knelt in front of Giles, so that their faces were on a level, and asked with genuine concern, "Are you all right, Giles?"

Giles nodded. "Uncle Stephen saved me, Genie. He saved Mama, too."

Nell's shocked intake of breath was clearly audible.

Jasper repeated his question: "For God's sake, what happened?"

"The boat sank while we were in it," Stephen replied.

There was a moment of stunned silence. The water in the rose garden fountain dripped steadily in the background.

"It sank?" Nell echoed. "Do you mean all the way?"

"Yes," Stephen said.

"To the bottom?"

"Yes."

"Oh, my God."

A few strands of my hair had dried and were falling over my forehead and cheeks, tickling me. I pushed up the sleeves of Stephen's coat so that they wouldn't cover my hands and tried to brush my hair off my face. Jasper watched this maneuver, his face a study in absorbed fascination.

Jack said, "How far out were you?"

"Much too far, Jack," I replied firmly.

"Uncle Stephen swimmed me in first and then he swimmed back for Mama," Giles said.

Miss Stedham felt the wetness of Giles's clothes, stood up, and said, "I'll take him up to the nursery, get him into dry clothes, and give him some hot soup, my lady."

"Thank you, Miss Stedham," I said.

The governess took Giles's hand into her own. "What an adventure you have had, Giles! I am dying to hear all about it. Come along upstairs and you can tell me everything that happened."

Giles looked at me and said, "Will you come, too, Mama?"

"I'll come as soon as I change my own clothes," I promised.

He went off with Miss Stedham, leaving the rest of us facing each other on the stable pathway.

Jack's eyes raked me up and down, and I was very glad I had the protection of Stephen's coat. "What in the name of God were you doing in a boat, Annabelle?" he demanded. "I thought you hated boats."

"Giles was going to try out his new fishing pole and I went along to watch," I replied. "Needless to say, no one will ever get me into a boat again."

"But what happened?" Nell repeated. "How on earth did the boat come to sink?"

"Apparently one of the boards in the bottom of the boat was loose and no one noticed it," Stephen said. "It came up when we were out in the middle of the lake. The boat was swamped and it sank. I swam in with Giles and then went back for Annabelle."

"Thank God the boat didn't sink until you

185

could get back for Annabelle," Jasper said in an unusually harsh voice.

Stephen glanced at me, and I shook my head slightly. I said, "Much as I am enjoying this conversation, I am going to excuse myself so that I may change my clothes."

"Actually," Jack said with a gleam in his eyes, "you look rather tasty the way you are."

"Your humor is badly misplaced, Jack," Stephen said coldly.

Jack's blond eyebrows lifted and he gave Stephen an appraising look.

"I will see you all at dinner," I said, and squished off in the direction of the house.

Adam was horrified when he learned of our accident, and he immediately made inquiries as to why no one had noticed that the boat wasn't safe.

"It was used all day long at the festival and it never took on water," he reported to me later in the day when he ran me to earth in the stable office, where I was going over the feed charts for my hunters. "It was just chance that that particular boat was the one left in the water while the others were put back into the fishing pavilion. No one realized that one of the bottom planks was loose."

"The whole plank came up suddenly, Uncle Adam," I said. "It was almost as if someone had loosened it, the way it gave all at once."

He frowned. "Surely, Annabelle, you don't think that it was done deliberately?"

"I wonder if some of the boys who were out on the lake yesterday might have thought it would be a lark to try to sink one of the boats,"

I said. I put down the pen I was holding and gave Adam my full attention. "It wouldn't have been so dangerous if it had happened yesterday, when there were other boats in the water and plenty of people on the shore. It was just bad luck that the plank held until today, when there was no one available to attempt a rescue."

"Perhaps you are right," Adam said slowly. "I can assure you that I had all the boats inspected before the festival, and there were no problems reported with any of them." He shifted his weight on the narrow chair that was the office's only other seating besides the desk chair I was using. "I have always thought that the men I assigned to check the boats were reliable."

"I am sure they are. Please don't dismiss anyone over this," I said. I glanced out the window, trying to assess the height of the sun. "Do you have the time, Uncle Adam?"

He took out his watch. "Getting on for five o'clock, my dear."

I sighed. "Almost time to dress for dinner."

He quirked a humorous eyebrow. "Been hiding out from Regina?"

I had to grin. "How did you guess?"

"Natural genius," he replied, smiling back at me.

We walked together to the office door. "Just let it be known around the estate that we almost had a drowning due to a damaged boat, Uncle Adam. If any of the tenant children were in fact responsible, they will be frightened enough not to attempt anything so foolish again."

The office was in the middle of the stable, and as we walked toward the yard, the horses in the boxes nickered at us expectantly.

"Almost the equine dinner hour, I see," Adam commented.

The horse in the last box kicked his door imperatively as we walked by. "Stop that, Marshall!" I commanded sternly.

We stepped out of the stable and into the late afternoon sunshine. Adam said apologetically, "I'm afraid it will be impossible for me to find out just who was in that particular boat yesterday, Annabelle."

"Of course it will be impossible. Don't even think of attempting such an inquiry."

We began to walk along the path that would take us back to the house. Adam said, "Well, we must just thank God that you are safe, my dear. Stephen told me the whole story of what happened. You were very brave."

"I was petrified," I said frankly. "No more boats for me, Uncle Adam. I will stick to my horses."

"Speaking of your horses," Adam returned, "Jasper tells me he likes that liver chestnut you showed him."

"Snap?"

"That's the one. How much do you want for him, Annabelle?"

We had crossed the small bridge and were entering under the shade of the beech trees. "You don't have to buy him from me, Uncle Adam," I said earnestly. "Please believe me when I say that I will be very happy to keep him over the season for Jasper to ride."

Adam's well-shaped gray blond head shook

in a firm negative. "I wouldn't think of asking you to do such a thing, Annabelle. I will take you up on your offer to stable him, but my son must ride his own horses."

It was clearly a matter of pride with Adam that Jasper not ride a borrowed horse.

I thought that I understood my uncle's feelings on this matter. He was a good-humored, easygoing man, but he liked his position as a local power. In our little part of the world, he was king. It was Adam whom the tenants saw when they needed a repair, or a new well, or an extension on their lease. It was Adam to whom the villagers took off their hats, whom the rector consulted about local problems, whom Sir Matthew invited to an evening of cards and brandy. Both Gerald and his father had passed at least three-quarters of the year away from Sussex. All the local power belonged to Adam.

It was evident to me that he thought it would damage his reputation if it became known that his son could not afford his own horses.

I said, "I was going to ask four hundred guineas for Snap."

Adam's gray eyes regarded me shrewdly. "You get more for your horses than that, my dear."

We had reached the gardens. "I do for some of them," I said, "but Snap is not the kind of horse who is easy to place. He has gone very well for Jasper, and I am happy to be able to find the right rider for him. I think four hundred guineas is a fair price, Uncle Adam."

"Then four hundred guineas it will be," Adam replied. "I will give you a draft on my bank."

I smiled and nodded.

"Jasper may not have a title, Annabelle," Adam said gravely, "but he will have quite a respectable place in the world when he leaves the army. Fanny came into a nice little inheritance a while back, and Jasper will have a house in Northamptonshire"—he laid heavy emphasis on the word "Northamptonshire"—"as well as an income to keep it up."

"That is wonderful," I said, trying not to look as mystified as I felt. Why on earth was Adam telling me all of this?

I noticed that one of the gardeners was diligently trimming some of the ornamental shrubbery, and I called, "Rather late today, aren't you, John?"

He turned at the sound of my voice. "Afternoon, my lady, Mr. Grandville," he greeted us. "It's cooler now than it were earlier, my lady," he answered my question.

"Well, don't miss your dinner."

"Never, my lady," he said with a grin.

We were almost at the back door when Adam said, "Did you have another horse in mind for Jasper?"

"I really do not have any other horses left from last year's batch," I said regretfully. "But Jasper is welcome to ride one of my new purchases, Uncle Adam. They need schooling, but usually you can get some fun out of them. Jack rides my new horses all the time."

"Jack can count himself fortunate to have anything to ride at all," Adam said.

I was a little taken aback by the hard note in Adam's usually pleasant voice and did not know how to reply.

"What is Jack going to do about hunting this

season?" Adam asked. "Have you spoken to Stephen about paying for his subscription?"

"No." We had reached the back door of the house, and I waited for Adam to open it for me. "I decided to pay for Jack's subscription myself," I said.

Adam's hand fell away from the door. I glanced up at him and was dismayed by the angry look I saw in his eyes.

"You should not have done that, Annabelle," he said. "It isn't proper."

I stared at him in bewilderment. "I beg your pardon?"

"Jack should not have accepted such a sum of money from you," Adam said.

I felt my spine stiffen. "My goodness, Uncle Adam, you are beginning to sound like Mama." I was careful to keep my tone humorous, but I was annoyed at his presuming to lecture me.

He didn't take the hint. "Have you paid for the subscription yet?"

I said firmly, "I have paid for it. I consider it a business expense, Uncle Adam. I need Jack's help with my new hunters. He has a very nice way with green horses."

Adam's mouth set in a straight line and he did not look as genial as he usually did. "Annabelle, I hope you don't take offense at what I am going to say, but I must say it because I am fond of you and I don't want to see you hurt."

I stared at him in utter bafflement.

"You have always been a beautiful woman, my dear, and now you are a wealthy one as well. Don't let your soft heart overrule your extremely intelligent brain."

191

A little light was beginning to dawn in my extremely intelligent brain. "Are you by any chance implying that Jack is a fortune hunter, Uncle Adam?"

Adam's graying brows were drawn together in a worried frown. "He needs money desperately, Annabelle. He has virtually no private income, and he had to sell the farms that were attached to Rudely in order to save the house. Jack cannot survive unless he marries a wealthy woman."

"Jack told me all those things himself," I said, and this time I did not try to conceal my annoyance.

The fine, straight brows, which Jasper had inherited, lifted. He said softly, "I had not thought Jack to be so clever."

"He also told me that it was you who advised him to marry for money!" I shot back.

"It was very sensible advice," Adam replied calmly. "But I most certainly did not mean that Jack should target you, Annabelle."

I did not at all like the disturbing picture that Adam was painting of Jack. I said rather haughtily, "This is not a discussion I care to continue, Uncle Adam."

And I put my own hand on the door, pushed it open, and walked briskly into the back hall.

Dinner was dreadful. Mama was irritating and the duke was offensive. Both of them blamed Stephen for taking Giles and me out in an unsafe boat.

"You're right, it was my error. I should have checked the boat," Stephen agreed. Long experience of my mother had taught him that agreeing with her was the only way to survive.

"I hope you dismissed the men who were in charge of removing the boats from the lake after the festival," the duke said to Adam. "It was sheer negligence that such an unsafe boat was allowed to remain in the water."

"All of the boats were used for the entire day yesterday, Duke," Adam replied. "Stephen said there was no water in the bottom of the boat when he and Annabelle got into it. There was no reason for anyone to suppose the boat was unsafe."

The duke's slanted black eyebrows drew together in a way that made him look positively satanic. He said, "Nevertheless, someone must be held accountable, Grandville."

How charming, I thought. My mother's husband would dismiss people just because "someone must be held accountable"!

Adam said, "Annabelle thinks that perhaps some of the children loosened the planks yesterday for a lark."

I winced and thought, Now we're in for it.

"A lark!" my mother said in outrage. "The Earl and the Countess of Weston were almost killed—for a lark!"

I could not help but notice that Giles and I did not figure as "my daughter and my grandson." No, we were "the earl and the countess."

Stephen said gravely, "The earl's uncle and guardian was in the boat as well, Regina."

Across the length of the table, our eyes met.

Don't let her upset you. The familiar blue eyes flashed the familiar old message. I felt the tightness in my neck begin to relax.

"If that is so," said the duke, "then the children must be found and punished."

"There were children in and out of that boat all day yesterday, Duke," Jasper said with ill-concealed annoyance. "I know because I was the one who was on duty at the lake. If Annabelle is correct, and the boat was sabotaged yesterday, it would be completely impossible to narrow down the list of potential culprits."

"I cannot believe that any of the children here yesterday would be guilty of such a dreadful thing," Nell said in distress.

"You know children, Nell," I said. "They have no idea of the consequences of the things that they do. I just thought that perhaps some of the boys might have thought it would be jolly to see someone take a dunking. I'm sure they thought it would happen yesterday, when there were plenty of other boats in the water and people on the shore to make a rescue."

"Disgraceful," the duke said. "Those children must be found and made an example of."

Jack's blue eyes were glittering wickedly. "If I had thought of such a prank when I was a boy, I would have done it," he said.

"I would have helped you," Jasper said.

They looked at each other and grinned.

I said to Nell, "Don't you remember our raft? If that had gone down, we all would have drowned."

Nell turned to me, and for a moment the little sister I had loved was looking at me out of her eyes. "I had forgotten all about that raft, Annabelle," she said. She laughed. "Remember how sick you were when we finally managed to get it to shore?"

"I shall never forget," I said fervently.

My mother said, "What raft are you talking about, Annabelle?"

Aunt Fanny had been quiet for most of the dinner (my mother was the only person who could silence Aunt Fanny), but she spoke up now and echoed Mama's demand, "Yes, Nell, *what* raft?"

"That must have been the summer of the clubs," Stephen said.

Nell nodded. "It was."

"Those wretched clubs," Aunt Fanny groaned. "You were into trouble all summer long because of those clubs."

All the members of my generation shot surreptitious looks at each other.

"You don't want to know about the raft, Mother," Nell said.

"*I* most certainly do not want to know about this raft," the duke said. "It sounds a dead bore."

We all knew who the dead bore was, and it wasn't the raft.

Nell was not quite successful in stifling a giggle, and I had to stare at my plate to keep my countenance.

My heart felt lighter than it had in months.

My mother said, "I believe it is time for the ladies to excuse themselves, Annabelle."

"Yes, Mama." I stood up.

Stephen surprised us all by asking, "Would you gentlemen care to join the ladies?"

This was a serious breach of etiquette; the gentlemen always sat for at least half an hour over their port. Stephen, of course, was trying to get out of a cozy session with the duke.

Jasper said heartily, "A grand idea, Stephen.

195

In the Peninsula I got out of the habit of drinking port after dinner, and now I find it doesn't agree with me."

Jack said, "And I promised young Giles I would play him a game of cards before he went to sleep."

I gave him a delighted smile. "How kind of you, Jack."

Adam scowled, and his earlier words about fortune hunters popped into my brain.

Jack had never before shown any interest in Giles, I thought. Could he possibly be trying to impress me?"

I shook my head, as if to clear it of such a nasty suspicion.

The duke was looking outraged. "*I* should be glad of some port," he said.

"So should I," Adam said mildly.

Stephen said, "Then of course we will join you."

"You youngsters can go ahead if you like," Adam said. "Saye and I will do very well on our own."

He made it sound as if Stephen and Jasper and Jack were ten years old.

The three youngsters exchanged looks.

I struggled to keep from smiling.

"We shall be happy to bear you company, Papa," Jasper said heroically.

"You don't have to drink port if you don't want to, Jasper," Jack said kindly.

Jasper scowled. I knew that if I remained one more minute in the dining room, I should disgrace myself by laughing.

"Ladies," I said, and swept the women before me to the door.

CHAPTER
fourteen

"Take the dogs and meet me at the fishing pavilion," Stephen murmured in my ear as I made my good nights after evening tea had been served.

I left the drawing room without looking at him, and when I reached my dressing room I dismissed Marianne. I was wearing a white evening dress of sprigged muslin trimmed with broad lace over a satin slip, and I simply flung an old riding jacket over my shoulders for warmth and quietly went out the back door with the dogs.

The moon had an odd, greenish look to it that I had never noticed before. Perhaps we will have a storm tomorrow, I thought.

The dogs were surprised when I did not set out on our usual walk to the Ridge but detoured instead around the house to the path that would take us to the lake. Once they realized where we were going, they raced happily ahead of me, darting off the path here and there to check the stands of trees that Capability Brown had scattered so gracefully all over the north lawn. I followed more slowly, searching for something to think about to take my mind off the coming meeting with Stephen.

I thought of this evening's dinner and of how the presence of my mother and the duke had acted as a catalyst to bring together all the cousins, much in the way we had banded together when we were children.

I had made many acquaintances during the years that I was married to Gerald, but my stepcousins always remained my best friends. We shared that most unbreakable of all bonds, the bond of a common childhood.

An image of Jack flashed suddenly into my mind, Jack and the way he had looked tonight, sitting around the nursery table with Giles and Miss Stedham, laughing and playing cards. Giles's little face had been bright with happiness.

I had known Jack forever, and I was convinced that he did not have it in him to exploit a child's feelings for his own advantage. I was furious with Adam for planting such an ugly suspicion in my brain.

Portia and Merlin barked joyfully and began to run toward the pavilion. I looked, and the moonlight showed me the glow of a white shirt on the pavilion porch. I followed the dogs and mounted the wooden stairs. Stephen was leaning on the railing, watching me.

"How did you manage to get here ahead of me?" I asked.

"I slipped out the French doors right after you left us," he replied.

"Oh."

He straightened as I approached, and the two of us stood face-to-face on the wooden porch in the strange green moonlight and looked at each other.

"It is driving me mad, being near you like this and not being able to touch you," he said.

The concentrated passion in his voice struck

an answering spark deep within me, but I steeled myself against desire. I said in as cold a voice as I could command, "Whatever was between you and me was finished five years ago, Stephen. You killed it when you left me to go to Jamaica."

The moonlight was bright enough to illuminate the tenseness of his fine-cut nostrils, the tautness of his mouth, the glitter of his eyes as he looked at me. "I don't believe that," he said. "I won't believe it."

"I don't care what you believe." I could hear the anger vibrating in my voice. "You left me," I repeated. "You just got on that boat and sailed off to Jamaica without sparing one single thought for me!"

"That's not true," he defended himself. His long dark eyelashes were making shadows on his cheeks in the moonlight. "Of course I thought about you! I had every intention of writing to you after I reached Jamaica."

I folded my arms across my chest, trying to ward off the treacherous feelings that his nearness was provoking in me. "Well, you didn't write," I said bitterly.

"Christ, Annabelle, you married my brother! What did you expect me to write? Congratulations?"

The light breeze blew a loose tendril of hair across my face, and I lifted my hand to brush it away. Stephen groaned audibly, and before I quite realized what he was about, I found myself in his arms and his mouth was coming down on mine.

I had suspected that Stephen might try something like this, and I had fully intended to repulse him. In fact, I had expected to derive a good deal of pleasure out of rejecting him the way he had rejected me five years before.

At least, that is what I had told myself when I had agreed to meet him here at the lake tonight.

Stephen's mouth covered mine. I made a pitiful attempt to push him away, an attempt that he quite rightly ignored. He kept kissing me and kissing me, and when the force of his kisses bent my neck backward, he put one hand behind my head to support it and his other hand came up and covered my breast.

I had forgotten what it was like to feel like this. I forgot all about my anger with him, all about my plan for revenge. I kissed him back. I pulled his shirt out from his waistband, slipped my hands under the soft white linen, and ran them up and down his rib cage, feeling his skin under my fingers. He was burning hot to the touch. I inhaled the smell of him. I licked his skin.

"Annabelle." His voice came out like a croak. "The chaise longue. Inside..."

I was trying to undo my bodice so his hand could get inside, could touch my bare skin.

"Yes," I said.

My knees were so weak that when I took a step, I staggered. Stephen scooped me up in his arms and carried me into the octagonal room that constituted the main part of the pavilion structure.

Fishing poles were stacked against the walls, and extra line, and two empty buckets, and four unlit lanterns. There was a low chest in one of the points of the octagon, and the extra rowboats from the lake were stored in three of the other points. Even though the windows were open, the room smelled of damp and mildew and fish. The cushions on the longue smelled of damp and mildew and fish, too, but Stephen and I were not in any state either to notice or to care.

We fell together onto the longue, pushing and shoving at our clothes, trying to get them out of our way, and all the while Stephen was kissing me. My heart was beating so hard that it made my breasts tremble. He pulled the combs out of my hair, and it came loose from its chignon and tumbled all around us. Then Stephen was pushing up my skirt.

I arched my back and lifted my hips. I wanted him every bit as badly as he wanted me. Then he drove, deep into the moist heat at the heart of me, again and again, lifting me with the power of his thrusts, and the pleasure of that pounding was absolutely excruciating.

I said out loud the name that, for five long barren years, I had only been able to whisper in my heart.

"Stephen," I said. "Stephen, Stephen, Stephen..." Then, triumphantly, as my whole body was shaken by shock after shock of explosive pleasure, "*Stephen!*"

The only noise in the room was the ragged sound of our breathing. We lay as close together as it was possible for two people to get, flesh buried within flesh, my legs encircling his waist, our arms wrapped around each other. It seemed we could not get close enough.

He said in my ear, "When I had to leave you today on the lake, it was the worst moment of my life. It was even worse than when I heard you had married Gerald."

201

My eyes were tightly shut, my face was pressed against his neck. I muttered something meant to sidetrack him from that particular line of thought.

Typically, Stephen would not be distracted. He said, "I would wake in the night sometimes, and pictures would come into my mind—pictures of you and Gerald together—and I would want to kill him." I felt the shudder that went all through him. "No one should feel about a brother the way I felt about him then."

I supposed it had to be said, so I shut my eyes even tighter and said into his neck, "Every time I lay with him, I pretended that it was you."

He groaned and his embrace actually managed to tighten. "Oh God, Annabelle," he said. "Oh God."

I felt him growing big within me. I lifted my head so that my mouth was next to his ear. "Kiss me," I whispered.

We needed each other so badly. The night passed in a fury of passion, and after a while the dogs gave up waiting for us to leave and just lay down on the floor and went to sleep.

It was Merlin's voice in my ear that finally woke me from an exhausted sleep shortly before dawn.

Whimper, whimper, I heard. Then a little whistle. Then a squeak, followed by a long whine. Then another whimper.

I opened my eyes and Merlin barked joyfully. He obviously could see me, although I could not see him. The moon was down and the sun hadn't yet risen, and the spaniel's black face blended into the darkness that blanketed the pavilion.

I fought my way back to complete consciousness. The chaise longue was narrow, but Stephen and I had managed to fit together so that we both could sleep. At one time we had had a great deal of practice sleeping together on this particular piece of furniture.

His right arm and leg were draped over me, and I couldn't move.

I had no idea what time it was.

"Stephen," I said urgently. "*Stephen!* Wake up. I have to get back to the house before I'm missed."

He didn't answer and didn't move. No one slept as soundly as Stephen.

I was lying on my stomach and I began to squirm, trying to roll over so I could push him off me. Merlin barked again, and this time Portia joined him. The combination of the dogs' voices and my squirming finally got through to Stephen. He grunted.

"Stephen, *get up!*"

"Annabelle." Once Stephen's eyes opened, he was always completely awake. "We fell asleep," he said.

"The moon is down. It must be late. I can't see a thing, Stephen, and I have to get home!"

"Don't panic," he said. I felt his weight come off me, and I scrambled to a sitting position. At some point during the night we had removed all of our clothes, and I felt around for mine on the floor beside the longue.

Stephen said, "I'll see if I can light one of the lanterns."

A floorboard squeaked under him as he crossed the pavilion floor. To my eyes the darkness was impenetrable, but Stephen had always had excellent night vision. I heard him lifting the lid of the chest.

"The tinderbox is here," he said.

"Thank God."

I heard him moving again over to where the lanterns were stored. A minute later we had light.

I blinked and looked at Stephen as he straightened up from lighting the lantern. His man's body, illuminated by the yellow glow of burning oil, had the same flat stomach and narrow hips as the boy's body I remembered, but the chest and shoulders were a good deal broader and more muscular. His torso was tanned a deep, Indian brown, but between waist and knees he was English white.

I was scandalized. "Did you walk around half-naked the whole time you were in Jamaica?"

He glanced down at himself and laughed. "I told you I did a great deal of swimming." He left the lantern where it was and started back toward me. "The beaches in Jamaica are beautiful, Annabelle. The sand is so fine and white and the water is the color of turquoise."

"It sounds like paradise," I said.

He sat next to me on the chaise longue, and the mattress made a little crunching sound as it took his weight. His mouth set. "The physical setting may resemble paradise, but I can assure you that the living conditions are far from heavenly for the unfortunate Negro people who live there."

I leaned over and kissed his sternly set mouth. Then I pulled my dress over my head without bothering to put on my petticoat or drawers. I stood up to smooth down the dress, then bent to pick up my discarded jacket. "Thank God I had the presence of mind to take the key to the back door," I said, feeling in the jacket's pocket to make certain it was still there.

Stephen had stood up to button his shirt, and now he looked down at me and grinned. He didn't say anything.

The grin annoyed me. "I didn't take it because I planned to spend the night with you," I said haughtily.

"No?"

"No."

"If you say so."

He didn't sound as if he believed me. I wasn't sure I believed myself. Why had I taken the damn key? Hodges usually locked all the doors at midnight, before he went to bed, and I was always in from my evening walk by midnight. Tonight, however, for some reason I had lifted the key from its hook by the door and slipped it in the pocket of my riding jacket as I went out.

We finished dressing in silence, and then Stephen said, "Do you want me to take the lantern?"

If we took the lantern, we would be required to explain away its presence in the morning. I said, "Do you think you can see well enough to get us home without it?"

"Yes."

"Leave it, then," I said.

Birds were beginning to call to each other as we left the pavilion and walked together through the darkened park. Stephen put his arm around my shoulders, and I pressed the length of my body against him and matched my steps to his. I could hear the dogs' panting as they trailed at our heels.

He said, as if we were continuing a conversation that had been interrupted earlier, "Do you have to wait a year before you can marry again?"

"Yes," I said.

"That is six more months."

"Yes."

He released his breath with a long whistling sound. "Six months is a damn long time, Annabelle."

I didn't say anything.

As we were walking, the first streaks of gray had appeared in the sky. The world was beginning to take shape around me, and by now I could see well enough to find my own way. I stayed where I was.

"Giles is a brave little fellow," Stephen said. "He didn't want to leave you today, Annabelle. You should be proud of him."

"I am." I took a deep breath and then I said one other thing that needed to be said between us. "You should be the next earl, Stephen, not your son."

"I don't want to be an earl," Stephen said.

I went on as if he had not spoken, "I have been wondering if perhaps we might do something legally to reestablish your right."

He stopped walking. He tipped up my face with his finger so that I had to look at him. "What are you talking about?"

"Well..." I watched him closely to gauge his reaction. "Perhaps we could have Giles recognized as your son."

His brows snapped together. His eyes blazed

blue fire. He said incredulously, "Are you mad, Annabelle? To do that you would have to brand him a bastard. I would never do that to Giles."

I could feel two tears spill out of my eyes and begin to roll down my cheeks.

"Stop it," he said crossly, and began to walk me forward again. "I don't want to be an earl," he repeated. "I want to sit in the Commons and agitate for reform."

I turned my head a little so that my lips touched his collarbone.

Two deer appeared out of the mist and crossed the path in front of us. I spoke sharply to the spaniels, who nobly refrained from giving chase.

"There is one thing in all of this I don't understand at all, Annabelle," Stephen said. "Why do you think Gerald named me to be Giles's guardian?"

I said honestly, "I have no idea."

We walked for a few more paces. It was light enough now to see the roofline and chimneys of the house.

Stephen said, "I always thought that Gerald regarded me as nothing short of an idiot."

It was true that Gerald had never had any patience with Stephen's causes. He had been particularly livid when Stephen had caused his famous uproar at Eton. Gerald had been at Oxford at the time, but he had heard about his brother's folly from far too many people to forgive Stephen easily.

"I was extremely surprised when Mr. MacAllister read out your name," I confessed. "Like everyone else, I expected the guardian to be Adam."

A pinkish glow had now appeared in the sky

above the eastern horizon. "Oh dear," I said, "the servants will be getting up. Someone is bound to see us coming in, Stephen."

"Adam would have been the logical choice," Stephen said. He had always had a one-track mind.

I humored him. "All I can surmise is that Gerald suspected you were Giles's father and wanted you to have some say in his upbringing."

"No." Stephen rejected that idea. "It doesn't add up, Annabelle. Gerald wouldn't first try to throw me off the scent by misleading me about the date of Giles's birth, and then do a complete about-face and name me as Giles's guardian."

"Well... when you put it like that, I suppose it doesn't make sense."

I had not bothered to fix my hair before we left the pavilion, thinking I would be able to make it back to the house before anyone was up. "Wait a minute, Stephen," I said now, and stopped and fished in my jacket pocket for the combs Stephen had removed from my chignon last night. I stuck the combs between my teeth and began to braid my hair, pulling it forward over my shoulder.

Stephen watched me. "I wonder," he said slowly, "if Gerald suspected there was something wrong with Weston's books."

It took a moment before I understood what he was implying. Then my hands stilled and I said, as sharply as I could around a mouthful of pearl-encrusted combs, "You cannot mean that Gerald mistrusted Adam!"

"I don't know, Annabelle." Stephen ran his

fingers through his own tossled hair, pushing it back from his forehead. "But why didn't Gerald name Adam?"

I pulled the thick braid I had just created up to the top of my head and secured it with the pearl combs. I said, "First of all, Stephen, you must realize that Gerald certainly did not expect to die at such an early age. When he made that will he probably thought that, should he die before Giles was twenty-one, Adam would be too old to act as an effective guardian for the boy Giles would still be. Gerald probably wanted someone who would be more sympathetic."

"Perhaps that is it," Stephen said.

I began to walk forward again. "I am sure it is."

"Nevertheless," Stephen said, "I am going to go over Adam's books with great care."

I stopped once again and swung around to face him. I planted my hands on my hips and said, "I cannot believe that you can be so suspicious!"

I recognized the stubborn look on his face. "This is my son's inheritance we are talking about, Annabelle, and I don't want to find that Adam has been gambling it away."

"Adam does not gamble!"

"I hope you're right. I hope I don't find anything. But I am damn well going to look."

We were now within sight of the house. I said, "I will go first and leave the back door open for you. Wait at least fifteen minutes before you follow me, Stephen."

He nodded. We looked at each other. I swayed a little, and his arms came around me and we kissed.

How could we possibly feel like this again so soon?

"I have to go," I said huskily.

I saw him swallow. He nodded. "Go."

I called softly to the dogs and left Stephen standing beside the stone urn filled with pink petunias that marked the beginning of the gravel path to the lake.

CHAPTER
fifteen

I had slept for only a few hours, and I should have been exhausted, but instead I felt more alive than I had in years. I breakfasted with Giles, thus managing to avoid the rest of the family, and repaired to my office to await Sir Matthew, who was coming to discuss hunt business with me. Almost the first thing he said when he came in the door was, "You look radiant this morning, Annabelle."

This was not good news. If I was altered enough for Sir Matthew to notice, I most certainly would not escape the sharp eyes of my mother.

"It must be the weather," I said. "I thought I smelled autumn in the air."

This was very clever of me, as any mention of autumn infallibly made Sir Matthew think of hunting. "Did you?" he said hopefully.

I grinned at him. "How are the pups coming along?"

"Very well indeed," he said. "I really think we have the makings of one of the best packs in the country, Annabelle."

After a bit more chitchat about the hounds, we proceeded to the business that was the reason I had asked him to come to the hall. I said, "Most of the farmers we were counting on could not come up with the subscription money, Sir Matthew."

He had been regarding with approval the painting that hung over my desk—a hunt scene that he had given me as a wedding gift—but at my words his eyes snapped back to my face. "Who couldn't come up with the subscription money?" he demanded.

"Roger Whitelaw, for one."

"*Whitelaw* is not taking a subscription?"

"It's not that he doesn't want to, Sir Matthew," I explained, "but he told me that money is tight. Now that the war is over, wheat is not fetching the price it once did."

"This is terrible," said Sir Matthew, and I understood perfectly that he was not referring to the drop in the price of wheat.

"We cannot afford to exclude our farmers from the hunt," I said. "Their goodwill is too important to us."

"I realize that, Annabelle," Sir Matthew said testily. "Damn it all, it was trying to placate the farmers—or, more exactly, the farmers' *wives*—that got us into raising the price of the subscription in the first place!"

I sighed. "We can't seem to win, can we? I wonder if other hunts have these problems."

"I don't know about the shire hunts, but the local hunts certainly do," Sir Matthew replied. "Just look at the terrible time Hartly had last year over Aldesley Wood."

Lord Henry Hartly was the master of the West

Sussex Hounds, and Aldesley Wood, which belonged to the Marquis of Highdon, was an important part of his hunt territory.

"I have heard nothing about Aldesley Wood," I replied. Sir Matthew looked at me incredulously. "You never heard that poisoned meat was put out in the wood and two of Hartly's hounds died?"

I was aghast. "How dreadful! Why did I never hear about this?"

Sir Matthew drummed his long, elegant fingers on the velvet chair arm. "Well, now that I think of it, Annabelle, I only learned of it myself at the very end of the season, and at that time you had other things on your mind."

There was a moment of silence as we both remembered Gerald.

Then, "Tell me what happened," I demanded. "All the world knows that Lord Henry regularly draws Aldesley Wood. Who would do such a dreadful thing as to put down poison in such a place?"

"Hartly suspects the marquis's agent," Sir Matthew replied ominously.

"*What?*"

Sir Matthew nodded. "Fellow by the name of Appleby. He complained to Hartly that no one was killing the foxes and they were becoming a nuisance to the local farmers. But Hartly said that he wasn't drawing any foxes because the keepers weren't stopping the earths."

Foxes are nocturnal creatures that normally return to their dens, or earths, in the morning. If the earths are not stopped up to keep the foxes from going into them, then there would be no foxes abroad for hunters to hunt. Most large landowners, like the Marquis of Highdon, cooperated with the local hunt by having their keepers stop the earths on their property during hunting season. If the marquis's keepers were not stopping the earths in Aldesley Wood, then obviously Lord Henry would not have found any foxes. They would all have been sleeping peacefully belowground while the hounds cast around in vain, trying to draw them.

"What makes Lord Henry think the marquis's agent is responsible?" I asked.

"Well, when Hartly first received an impertinent letter from Appleby, complaining that the foxes were not being killed, he was naturally enraged, and he wrote directly to the marquis to object that his keepers were not doing their duty by the hunt. Hartly continued to draw Aldesley Wood while he was waiting to hear back from the marquis, and that was when his hounds were poisoned. You can imagine his fury."

I shuddered to imagine his fury. Any master who sees his hounds die of poison wants vengeance, and Lord Henry was not known for his temperate personality.

"What happened then?" I demanded.

"Hartly went up to London to see the marquis in person. Highdon is an old man now, and he never was much of a sportsman, but he knows his duty to his country. He refused to dismiss the perfidious Appleby, but he instructed his keepers to stop the earths in Aldesley Wood." Sir Matthew's thin, ascetic face looked as lucent as that of a monk who has just had a vision of heaven. He said, "If I were Appleby, I would take care to keep out of Hartly's way."

I nodded fervent agreement.

"Getting back to this business of the farmers," Sir Matthew said briskly. "I take it that *none* of your tenants have subscribed?"

"That is right."

Sir Matthew snorted.

"Precisely," I agreed.

"Well, we must have 'em," Sir Matthew said grumpily. "I suppose we could offer a reduced subscription rate to those farmers over whose property we hunt."

This was precisely the solution I had come to myself. "That is an excellent idea, Sir Matthew!" I said warmly.

He narrowed his eyes at me. "Is this going to leave us short of funds, Annabelle?"

"It might," I confessed. "Since last I spoke to you I have only collected subscription money from my cousins Jack and Jasper."

Sir Matthew looked surprised. "Shouldn't think either of them would have that kind of money. It's well known that Jack ain't got a feather to fly with, and Jasper can't have anything above his army pay."

"Adam tells me that Fanny has come into a little inheritance," I explained. "He bought Snap for Jasper to ride."

Sir Matthew pursed his lips. "Well, well, well."

A little silence fell and my eyes went, as they so often did, to the Stubbs painting on the opposite wall.

"What about Stephen?" Sir Matthew said. "He must have come into his mother's money by now. Do you think you might convince him to take a subscription?"

I lowered my eyes from the painting and looked at Sir Matthew.

"I suppose not," he said.

Stephen hated to hunt. He felt bad for the fox. I had learned never to get into a discussion about hunting with Stephen. He always left me feeling guilty that I loved it so much.

"I suppose I could ask the duke," I said slowly. "He hunts."

Sir Matthew shuddered. "Don't do that, Annabelle," he begged. "I'd rather go short of funds than ride out with Saye."

Since this was my own feeling, I did not try to change his mind.

"Well," he said, "we must just do the best we can with what we have."

"I'm afraid so," I agreed.

Instead of getting ready to leave, Sir Matthew settled himself deeper into his chair and sipped the wine I had given him when first he'd come. "How are the new horses coming along?" he asked chattily.

"Slowly," I answered with a wry smile. "I always forget how green Thoroughbreds are when they first come off the track."

"By the end of the season you will have them going like lambs," Sir Matthew said heartily.

"First I have to get them out," I said. "They badly need to clock some miles in the woods. And my regular hunters need conditioning before the season opens."

"I have to get my young hounds out, too." Sir Matthew leaned forward eagerly, balancing his wineglass on his knee. "There's no reason why we can't start cubbing season a little early. You don't mind getting out of bed at four, do you, Annabelle?"

"Of course not," I said gamely.

One of the main drawbacks of cubbing season is that the weather is still warm and you have to get the hounds out very early, while the air is cool and the scent is still on the ground. In late August this meant that I would have to be at the stable by five in order to meet Sir Matthew by six.

Needless to say, not very many people turned out for cubbing.

"Actually, it would be a good thing to start cubbing now," I said. "Jack is staying with us, and I can get him to take one of the new horses for me."

Sir Matthew gave me a long, level look. "You never mentioned how Jack came up with the subscription money."

"He had a lucky turn at the gambling table," I said.

For some reason, I found that I did not want to tell Sir Matthew that I had paid for Jack's subscription.

"Hmmm," said Sir Matthew. His expression was skeptical.

"Perhaps I can convince Stephen to come out cubbing with us, too," I said. "You always make certain that we don't draw a fox, so his sensibilities won't be outraged."

"Damn fool ideas that boy has," Sir Matthew fumed. "Foxes are vermin, damn it!"

This was not a discussion I wanted to pursue. I said, "I have some reservations about one of the horses that I bought. He's much more

216

highly strung than what I usually look for, and I'd like Stephen to ride him. Stephen is always so good at getting a horse to relax."

"I've never been able to understand it," Sir Matthew grumbled. "The boy does nothing but lounge about in the saddle, and horses will do anything for him."

It was true that Stephen was not a serious horseman, in the way Sir Matthew understood serious. But Stephen had a great natural ability to sense what a horse was feeling. You could almost see a tense, fearful horse heave a sigh of relief when Stephen picked up the reins.

The door behind Sir Matthew was pushed open and Jasper looked in. "Oh, I say, Annabelle, I'm sorry. I didn't know that Sir Matthew was with you." He began to close the door again.

"Do come in, Jasper," I said. "We have finished our business, and I'm sure Sir Matthew would like to have you join him for a glass of hock."

"Come along in, boy," Sir Matthew said genially. "I hear you are going to hunt with us this year. That is splendid news."

"Yes, Annabelle has signed me up," Jasper said. He went to the cabinet where I kept the wine and poured himself a glass.

"Have you sold out of the army, then?" Sir Matthew asked.

Jasper sat down on the ladder-back chair that was the room's only other seating. "Not yet, sir. I probably will, though. My father wants me to take over this new property he has inherited."

Sir Matthew raised his eyebrows. It constantly amazed me how like a medieval scholar he looked, when, to my certain knowledge, he never read anything except stud and pedigree books.

"This is the first I have heard of a new property," he said.

Jasper shrugged. "Some old relative of my mother's popped off."

"Aha."

Jasper's eyes rested on my face. "You're looking particularly radiant this morning, Annabelle."

Damn, I thought.

"We've decided to push up cubbing season, Jasper, my boy," Sir Matthew said. "The thought of hunting always gives Annabelle a glow."

Thank you, Sir Matthew, I thought, giving him a grateful smile.

"Where is Stephen?" Sir Matthew asked me next. "I haven't seen him since he got home from Jamaica."

"He is going over the estate books with my father," Jasper said.

"Good heavens," said Sir Matthew. "Why would he want to do that?"

"I have no idea." Jasper's voice was flat, and his gray eyes looked unusually cold.

"You know Stephen's sense of responsibility," I said humorously to Sir Matthew. "Gerald named him to be Giles's guardian and trustee, so naturally he feels it is his duty to familiarize himself with the way the estate is run."

"Well, I suppose that is sensible," Sir Matthew said, and I blessed him for the second time in less than a minute.

"I believe that Stephen may safely leave the running of the estate to my father," Jasper said.

"Of course he can," I replied. "But what if something happened to your father, Jasper? I certainly don't mean to ill-wish Uncle Adam, but he is not immortal. If he got thrown from his horse tomorrow and broke his neck, there would be no one who knows anything at all about Weston's books. I know I certainly do not. I only keep the housekeeping records."

I felt quite pleased with the reasonableness of this explanation and added, "I think it is quite sensible of Stephen to ask Adam to teach him something about the way the estate is run."

Some of the coldness left Jasper's eyes. I gave him my most beguiling smile and said, "Would you like to come out cubbing with us?"

His strong, square face warmed into an answering smile. Jasper had turned into a very good-looking man, I thought. He would break hearts at the local assemblies this fall.

"I should love to come cubbing with you, Annabelle," he said.

I looked at Sir Matthew. "When shall we start?"

"Tomorrow morning," he said heartily.

"Good heavens, that *is* soon."

"You said you wanted to get your horses out," he said.

I sighed. "So I did."

"Just make certain you get to bed early," Sir Matthew advised.

"I'm not sure I like the sound of that," Jasper said. "What time do we have to get up, Annabelle?"

"Four," I said baldly.

Jasper pretended to choke on his wine. It was a trick he had perfected when he was a boy, and it had always made me smile. It made me smile now.

"You can't fool me, my boy," Sir Matthew said. "An army man is quite used to early morning risings."

"I don't consider four a.m. 'the morning,' Sir Matthew," Jasper retorted. "I consider it the middle of the night!"

"Nonsense," came the brisk reply. Sir Matthew finished his wine and stood up. "I had better get going so I can pass the good news to Clinton."

Mr. Clinton lived on the other side of Weston village at Whiteoak, a very pretty property that had been in his family since Domesday Book. He had acted as assistant master to Sir Matthew for years.

"We'll meet you at the usual place?" I asked.

The usual place was the Market Cross near Weston village.

Sir Matthew's grin made him look like a little boy. "Usual place," he said buoyantly.

Jasper chuckled as the door closed behind the squire. "I do believe Sir Matthew is the most uncomplicated man I have ever met," he said.

"He's not stupid, Jasper." I was quick in defense of my friend.

"I did not mean to imply that I thought he was."

"I am excessively fond of Sir Matthew," I said sternly.

His level blond brows drew together. "I hope you are not entertaining the thought of becoming Lady Stanhope, Annabelle," he said.

I stared at him in utter stupefaction. "*What?*"

A little color crept into his cheeks, and he shifted uncomfortably on the ladder-back chair. "I beg your pardon. But you said you were excessively fond of him, and I thought for a moment..." His color deepened as he met my eyes. "Dash it all, Annabelle. I just wanted to make certain that Stanhope was not taking advantage of your... fondness."

I said coldly, "Sir Matthew's feelings for me are paternal, not lascivious."

Jasper looked infuriatingly unconvinced.

I snapped, "Try to remember that you are Nell's brother, Jasper—not mine."

He surged to his feet and stood looking at me, his hand gripping the back of his chair so tightly that his knuckles showed white. "You don't have to remind me that I am not your brother, Annabelle. Believe me, I know that very well indeed!"

There was a real edge to his voice, and I felt a rush of contrition—he had meant to protect me, not to insult me.

I said, "I did not mean to hurt your feelings, Jasper. I know you meant well."

His gray eyes were unreadable. "I always mean well as far as you are concerned."

I smiled. "I know. It is a great comfort to me to have all my cousins here with me at Weston."

His return smiled looked forced.

At that moment Nell looked around the office door. "I'm sorry to interrupt, Annabelle. I just wanted to tell Jasper that Mama is looking for him."

Jasper turned to face his sister. She smiled sweetly and informed him, "Mrs. Clinton has called, and Mama wants to show off her soldier son."

Jasper groaned.

"Such are a hero's wages," I said with a laugh. Mrs. Clinton was the wife of the hunt's assistant master and the biggest gossip in all of Sussex.

"I suppose you couldn't tell Mama that I am out?" Jasper suggested.

Nell gave him her best "virtuous little sister" look. "Are you asking me to *lie* to Mama, Jasper?"

"God forbid," he muttered. "Where are they?"

"In the salon."

"Excuse me, Annabelle," Jasper said. He walked out the door with the mien of someone going off to the gallows.

Nell and I looked at each other and giggled. Nell came farther into the room.

"I am going into the village this afternoon to pick up some new books I ordered," she said. "Would you like to come with me, Annabelle?"

"I'd love to," I said warmly. "What books did you order?"

She came all the way into the room and sat down. I was delighted. It would make me very happy to have Nell's friendship back again.

CHAPTER
sixteen

Nell and I had a very pleasant afternoon together shopping in the village, and on the way home I asked if she had plans to attend the autumn assemblies in Brighton. I felt very bad that Gerald's death had forced Aunt Fanny to cancel Nell's second London Season last spring.

"Are you worried that I am going to turn into an old maid, Annabelle?" Nell retorted.

"Of course not!"

But the fact was, Nell had turned twenty the previous month. She was not exactly "on the shelf," but she would be in another year or so.

"You certainly did not lack for suitors during your first Season," I said, "and there is every reason to suppose that other suitors more to your taste will be forthcoming in the future. But you need to go out into society in order to meet them, Nell!"

Nell stuck her round little chin in the air. "What makes you think that I want to get married at all?"

This was a patently absurd remark. Every woman living in England in the second decade of the nineteenth century wanted to get married. There were simply no other viable options open to one.

"You adore children, and the only way you can have your own is to get married," I returned promptly.

Nell sighed. "I suppose that is true."

"What was wrong with all the suitors from your first Season?"

"I didn't love them," Nell said. "And frankly, Annabelle, I cannot imagine anything as miserable as being forced to live in deep intimacy with a man one doesn't love."

My fingers must have tightened on the reins because Monarch's ears suddenly twitched, as if he were waiting for a command. I clicked to him, and his ears went forward again and he trotted on.

"I would not advise it," I said quietly to Nell.

She said, "If I can't marry the man I love, then I would prefer to marry no one."

It was her careless choice of article that betrayed her. "*The* man I love," she had said, as if that man already existed.

Good God! I thought. Could Nell be secretly in love with someone right here in Weston?

I stared at the road between Monarch's alert chestnut-colored ears and considered the possibilities.

Might Nell be in love with the son of one of our tenant farmers? I knew that Adam would never countenance her marrying beneath herself like that, which would certainly account for her silence on the subject.

To the south, storm clouds from the Channel had been pushed far up the Ridge and now they were spilling over the top of it and advancing into the valley.

Nell said, "It looks as if we will have rain later. The farmers will be glad of that."

"Now that the festival is over, it can rain any time it likes," I returned absently.

Acres of rich farmland stretched away on either side of the road. I ran the names of all the eligible men in the valley through my mind and couldn't come up with anyone whom I thought could conceivably have captured Nell's heart.

The air smelled of the approaching rain. I raised my hands a little and called, "Trot on," to Monarch, who obliged me with a brisker pace.

"We're going to make it home just in time," Nell commented.

If it wasn't one of the farmers, then who else could it be? I thought.

The answer came to me in a flash of blinding insight.

Jack! My God, Nell is in love with Jack!

That had to be the answer, I thought, and in that answer lay only heartbreak for my little cousin.

Jack was a well-known rake. He could charm the birds off the trees if he wanted to, and he had charmed more aristocratic matrons into his bed than I for one cared to count.

"Jack doesn't believe in paying for sex when he can get it so easily for free...."

I remembered Gerald saying that to me one night after we had been to a ball and met Jack, who was escorting his latest mistress, the young wife of an elderly earl. I remembered that Gerald had laughed.

Jack was far too sophisticated, and far too heartless, for a girl like Nell.

Another memory flashed suddenly into my mind: *The word around town is that Adam has come up with a handsome dowry.* Those had been Jack's exact words to me when we had been discussing Nell's marriage prospects.

And Adam had told Jack to marry money! What an incredible irony it would be if Jack chose Adam's own daughter to achieve that ambition.

We turned off the road into Weston Park. The sun was now completely hidden under the cloud cover.

"The temperature must have dropped ten degrees," Nell said. She was shivering.

"Why don't you take out that shawl you bought for your mother and put it on?" I suggested.

"Good idea." Nell began to rout through the parcels that were piled under the seat.

The trees on either side of the ride were rustling with the increased wind, and the first roll of thunder sounded in the distance. Nell found the parcel she wanted and unwrapped the pretty ivory-colored shawl she had bought this afternoon for Aunt Fanny.

"Aren't you cold, Annabelle?" she asked as she settled the soft wool around her shoulders.

"I am outdoors so much that I don't chill easily," I returned.

"You have always liked to be outdoors," Nell said affectionately. "I remember Mama once saying to me, 'I sometimes think that Annabelle is really a horse in disguise.' "

I grinned. "Damn. You have discovered my secret."

"Annabelle dear," Nell said in a passable imitation of Aunt Fanny's voice, "watch your language, please. There is a young lady present."

We both laughed.

I did not want to say anything that might spoil this precious harmony between me and Nell, so I kept my own counsel about Jack. But I made a private vow to be vigilant. I had no intention of letting Jack marry Nell for her money.

We pulled up to the front steps of the house just as the first drops began to fall. One footman collected our parcels from under the seat while another climbed into the driver's seat to take the gig down to the stables.

Nell and I scurried up the stairs through the increasingly heavy raindrops. Hodges himself was holding the door open for us. The first person I saw as I stepped into the hall was Jack.

I untied my straw bonnet and said lightly, "We outran the rain."

Hodges came to take the bonnet from my

hand, and Jack said somberly, "Come into the salon with me, both of you."

My heart gave one big warning thump and then began to race. "What has happened?" I asked breathlessly. "Is it Giles?"

"Giles is fine, Annabelle," Jack said. "Come into the salon and I will tell you about it."

He strode across the passageway and into the salon, with Nell and me hard on his heels. Once we were inside the privacy of the room, Jack closed the door, turned to us, and said, "Stephen has been shot."

I could feel all the blood congeal in my veins.

"He is all right, Annabelle," Jack said quickly. "The doctor is with him now. He even managed to walk part of the way home."

"Shot?" I said in disbelief.

"I am afraid so."

Beside me Nell made a little mewing sound, but neither Jack nor I looked at her.

My hands had closed into fists. "Where was he shot?"

"The bullet grazed his temple."

"*Oh, my God!*" I stared at Jack, appalled.

"Grazed it," Jack repeated. "It did not enter into his skull. Stephen was very, very lucky."

"Where was he when this happened?" I demanded.

"On the Ridge. He had gone for a walk with Giles."

My heart literally stopped beating. "You are certain that Giles is all right?"

"Giles is perfectly fine," Jack said. "As a matter of fact, it was Giles who ran to fetch help."

I thought: Stephen is going to be all right. Giles is safe.

My first rush of terror subsided, to be replaced by a surge of absolute rage.

"*What bloody fool was shooting in those woods?*"

I almost shouted the words I was so furious.

Jack said, "Whoever it was disappeared quickly once he realized that his shot had gone astray and hit someone."

Beside me, a thin, breathy voice said, "I believe I need to sit down."

Belatedly Jack and I turned our attention to Nell. She was pale as a sheet and looked as if she were about to faint dead away.

I reached out to grab her, but Jack was before me. He scooped her up in his arms as easily as if she had been a child, carried her over to one of the salon's sofas, and gently laid her down. I went to the door and sent a footman flying to fetch some smelling salts.

"I f-feel so foolish," Nell said weakly from her supine position on the sofa.

"Nonsense." Jack was sitting on his heels at her side, and now he stroked her head reassuringly, in much the same way that I stroked my spaniels. "It was quite a shock."

"Is Giles in the nursery?" I asked Jack.

He turned his head to look at me. "Yes. Eug... er, Miss Stedham, has him safe and sound, Annabelle."

"Where is Aunt Fanny?" I asked next. "She should be here with Nell."

Jack bestowed one last pat upon Nell's head and rose effortlessly to his feet. "Aunt Fanny is upstairs with Stephen and the doctor."

"And Mama?" I asked.

"The ducals, thank God, have gone into Brighton for the day."

I shut my eyes for a moment, the relief was so intense. Then I said, "I'll go upstairs and send Aunt Fanny down to the salon, Jack. Will you stay with Nell?"

"Of course," he said.

As I whirled out of the room I heard Nell asking feebly, "Jack, are you certain that Stephen is all right?"

The door to Stephen's room was open, and I stood for one unobserved moment upon the threshold, looking in. Stephen was sitting in a straight-backed chair, with the blue silk seat covered by a towel, presumably to protect the delicate material from blood. Dr. Montrose was winding a strip of white linen like a headband around Stephen's temples, and Aunt Fanny was standing next to the door, holding a tray. They both were completely concentrated upon the doctor's handiwork, and it was Stephen who saw me first.

"Come in, Annabelle," he said calmly. "We're almost finished here."

At the sound of his voice the muscles in the back of my neck, which had tightened the moment I first saw Jack, began to relax.

I walked over to stand beside Dr. Montrose and regarded the bandage, which looked very white against the darkness of Stephen's skin and hair.

I shuddered to think what two more inches would have meant.

"I have just been telling Stephen how lucky he is that this bullet did not go any deeper," Dr. Montrose said, echoing my own thoughts. He was an old man who quite literally had known Stephen since he was born, having been the doctor who delivered him.

"I don't feel very lucky," Stephen said wryly. "I have the world's worst headache." He was indeed looking very haggard under his bandage.

I said fiercely, "I want to know what idiot was shooting in those woods."

Dr. Montrose replied, "That is something we all would like to know, Annabelle."

"Adam and Jasper are out in the woods now, looking for some sign of the culprit," Aunt Fanny said.

Her voice reminded me of my errand. "Nell needs you in the salon, Aunt Fanny. She became quite faint when Jack told us about the shooting."

"Goodness me," Aunt Fanny said with a worried frown. "What can have happened? Nell is not the fainting kind."

"I don't know, but she went as white as snow. If Jack hadn't caught her in time, she would have fallen."

"I shall go down to her immediately," Aunt Fanny said.

Dr. Montrose asked, "Do you want me to have a look at her before I leave, Fanny?"

"Please, Martin, if you would."

Aunt Fanny departed.

Dr. Montrose said to me, "See that this young fellow gets enough sleep in the next few days, Annabelle. He looks to me as if he were up all night."

The acuteness of this observation caused Stephen's eyes and mine to meet in guilty alarm.

"Yes, Dr. Montrose," I said.

The shrewd hazel eyes looked me over. "I

am glad to see that you are looking better, my dear. You've regained some of that sparkle you used to have when you were a girl."

"Thank you, Dr. Montrose," I said.

While Dr. Montrose had not delivered me, he had delivered Giles, and he knew me very well. I lowered my eyes, fearful of what he might discover in them.

"Well then," he said briskly. "I had better go and attend to Nell."

"Good-bye, Dr. Montrose," Stephen and I chorused. "Thank you, Dr. Montrose."

The elderly doctor went out, leaving the bedroom door open. After a moment I went to peek out into the passageway. When I saw no one, I closed the door quietly and turned once more to look at Stephen.

"Something is wrong here," he said. "You sparkle and I look tired."

His words were so very far from what I had on my mind that it took me a moment to understand what he meant. When his comment finally registered, I put my hands on my hips and retorted, "It seems to me that you should be complimented and I should be insulted."

He grinned.

A lightning flash lit up the lawn outside the window, and a moment later the thunder boomed.

"Frightened, Annabelle?" Stephen said softly. "Want to get into bed with me?"

What frightened me was the intensity of the desire that shot like a bolt of lightning through all my entrails. I said a little shakily, "No, I do not. I want you to tell me all about what happened out there on the Ridge today."

He sighed. "You were more fun when you were younger."

"You and Giles had gone for a walk... ," I prompted.

More lightning and another boom of thunder punctuated my words. I sat down on the arm of the comfortable chair that stood in front of the fireplace and regarded Stephen expectantly.

"Oh, very well," he said. "We were on the path to the cove because I had promised to show Giles the place where Jasper and I had built that tree house when we were children." He moved his head cautiously, as if trying to find a more comfortable way to hold it. "We were having such a good time together, Annabelle, telling each other silly jokes and laughing our heads off. We had reached the track that led to the tree house, and I was just turning my head to point out the marker we had always used, when we heard the sound of a gun going off. I felt a burning sensation on my forehead, but I didn't realize I'd been hit until the blood began to stream into my eyes."

"Dear God," I said softly.

"I grabbed Giles and hit the ground as fast as I could. Then I shouted, 'Don't shoot. There are people here.' "

"Did anyone answer?"

"No. I thought I heard the sound of someone moving through the trees, but then it became silent. Whoever it was must have been frightened off when he realized he had shot at a person and not a deer."

"Deer don't talk and laugh and tell jokes," I said grimly.

Stephen sighed and picked at his bandage.

"Leave it alone," I said. "What happened then?"

He let his hand drop to the mahogany chair arm. "When I felt it was safe, I got up. When no shots erupted I let Giles get up, too. We began to walk back toward Weston, but I'm afraid I became rather light-headed. I didn't want Giles to go off on his own, but he wouldn't listen. He ran on ahead of me and came back very shortly with Jack in tow."

Another flash of lightning. Another boom of thunder.

"How did Giles find Jack so quickly?" I asked.

Stephen's hand moved restlessly. He said, "Giles ran into him as soon as he reached the garden."

We stared at each other.

"Where in the garden?" I asked.

Stephen was beginning to look rather gray. "On the west side, where the track to the Ridge comes in," he said.

The stable path, where one might expect to find Jack, was to the east of the garden.

"Jack wouldn't shoot at you, Stephen," I said. But I could hear the uncertainty in my own voice.

His blue eyes were steady on mine. "Annabelle, I really do not think he would."

"It was probably just a poacher. He saw movement and thought that you and Giles were deer or grouse or something."

"That is the most likely explanation."

I got up and went to stare out the window. The rain was pouring down outside; the flowers in the garden were bent with the force of it.

I turned back to Stephen and asked the question that frightened me the most. "What would have happened if you had not turned your head to look for the marker?"

His silence gave me my answer.

I said desperately. "If... someone... truly meant you harm, then he would have followed up on his advantage. You had no weapon. You were a sitting duck."

"That is my thought precisely," Stephen said.

We stared at each other again, each of us reluctant to give reality to our suspicions by admitting them out loud.

The next flash of lightning was not so bright, and the thunder sounded farther away. "The storm is passing," I said.

Stephen grunted.

I remembered something. "Good God, Adam and Jasper must have been caught in this storm!"

"One way or another, the Ridge has not been a very safe place today, has it?" Stephen said in a tired voice.

I walked briskly over to his bed, turned down the covers, and plumped the pillows. "Doctor's orders are for you to go to bed," I said.

His eyes glinted.

I added firmly, "Alone."

He made a wry face. "Oh, all right."

I looked at the tray Aunt Fanny had put down on the bedside table. "Did Dr. Montrose leave anything to help with the headache pain?"

"Not that I am aware of."

I sighed. "I adore Dr. Montrose, but he always expects one to be such a Spartan."

"I'll survive," Stephen said nobly.

"Hmm." I regarded him critically. "I have some laudanum you can have if you want."

He gave me a suspicious look. "Why do you have laudanum?"

"I have been known to get a headache myself."

He frowned. "You never used to get headaches."

"Well, I do now."

His frown deepened. "And you take laudanum for them?"

"Well... not anymore. I got some from a London doctor a few years ago, and when I innocently asked Dr. Montrose to give me some more, he ranted and raved for ten uninterrupted minutes about the evils of laudanum. He frightened me so much that I haven't taken any since."

"Well, I don't want any either," Stephen said.

"It is perfectly safe to use it once," I said.

His whole expression said *No*.

I sighed and walked to the door. "I will send Matthews to you directly." Matthews was the valet Stephen had engaged when he was in London.

He said softly, "Can't I at least have a kiss?"

I wavered.

"Annabelle... ," he said coaxingly.

I went over to his chair and took his face between my hands. I bent and very gently laid my lips against the linen that covered the wound in his temple. Then I moved down to his mouth.

He looked so terrible that the hunger of his kiss startled me. His hand came up to cup my breast. Desire stabbed through me once more, and it took all the willpower I possessed to straighten up and step away from him.

"You are incorrigible," I said, trying to look stern.

"Five years is a long time, Annabelle," he said.

I backed farther away. "You and I have some talking to do, Stephen. Don't think you can just walk back into my life and pick up where you left off, because you can't."

His eyes were narrow slits of midnight blue under the startling white of the bandage. "Then let's start over again," he said.

My heart was racing and my pulses were pounding. "I must go to Giles," I said.

"I won't take very long," he said.

I wanted to give in to him so badly that it frightened me. I shook my head. "You need to get some rest, and I need to see my son."

He let out his breath in an exasperated sigh. "Oh, all right. Send Matthews to me and I will go to bed. But I probably won't sleep."

"Blackmail is an ugly thing," I said.

His whole face lit with his sudden, radiant smile. "It is, and I apologize. Tell Giles I said he is a very brave little boy."

"He takes after his father," I said softly. And closed the door firmly behind me as I left.

CHAPTER
seventeen

I found Giles in the nursery, having tea and cakes with Miss Stedham. My first impulse was to put my arms around him and hold him as tightly as I could, but that would be certain to alarm him. So instead I kissed the top of his head and said lightly, "I hear you have had another adventure, Giles."

"Somebody shot Uncle Stephen," he said, looking up at me with solemn eyes. "Have you seen him, Mama? Is he all right?"

"I have just come from him, and he is fine, darling. He said I was to tell you that you are a very brave boy."

"He got shot in the head," Giles said.

"I know, but the bullet did not go into his head, Giles. The doctor said that he is going to be perfectly fine."

Giles looked away from me and began to stir his tea, which he always half-filled with sugar. "It was scary, Mama," he confessed. "Uncle Stephen pushed me down on the ground, and then he lay on top of me. He wouldn't let me get up for a long time."

"He was right to be so cautious," I said. "Whoever was poaching in the woods was stupidly and criminally careless."

Giles said in a small voice, "You don't think the person meant to shoot at Uncle Stephen?"

"Of course not!" I said too heartily.

"My goodness, Giles," Miss Stedham said, "why would anyone want to shoot at your uncle Stephen?"

Giles stirred his tea with intense concentration and refused to look at us. "Do you think that perhaps the person meant to shoot at me?"

An appalled look passed between Miss Stedham and me.

I struggled to keep my voice calm and sensible. "Of course I don't think that, Giles. Why would anyone want to shoot at you?"

He stared into his well-stirred tea and shrugged.

Silence fell like a pall on the room.

I said briskly, "Uncle Stephen told me he thought it was probably some local who was looking to poach a deer."

Giles nodded and took a slow, deliberate sip of his heavily sugared tea.

"Would you care for a cup of tea, Lady Weston?" Miss Stedham asked.

"Thank you." I pulled out one of the old wooden chairs and sat down.

For the rest of the meal, Miss Stedham and I kept up a determinedly bright and cheerful conversation while Giles maintained an unusual silence.

I left the nursery in an uneasy frame of mind. Giles's behavior had made it painfully clear that he did not think Stephen had been shot by a poacher.

My mother and her husband had returned in time for dinner. We had sat down without Stephen or Nell, and naturally their absence had to be explained to the ducal pair.

The duke's comment was typical. "Poachers should be hung. Transportation is not a strong enough penalty to deter the commission of such a crime. String a few poachers up at the Market Cross, I say. Then you'll see a lessening of poaching incidents."

I saw Jasper's and Jack's eyes meet across the table. Neither of them needed to say a word to express to each other their mutual opinion of my dear stepfather.

Adam said quietly, "Surely a few grouse are not worth a man's life, Duke."

"It's the principle of the thing," the duke said. "Let them steal your grouse, and the next thing you know, they'll want your house, too. Look at what happened to the Frenchies."

"You didn't see any signs of who it might have been?" I asked Jasper.

He shook his head. "I regret to say we did not, Annabelle. The heavy rain washed away any signs the intruder might have left."

My mother said bitterly, "One would think that Stephen might have matured at least slightly during those five years he spent in Jamaica. But no, he is just as troublesome now as he was when he was a boy."

We all stared at her in stunned surprise.

"Surely, Regina, you can't think that it was Stephen's fault he was shot at," Adam said feebly.

"All I know is that he is upstairs now with a bullet in his head," my mother returned. "And yesterday the boat he was in sank. These things never happen to anyone else. They only happen to Stephen." She turned to me. "I do not think you should permit Giles to be alone in Stephen's company, Annabelle. It appears to be dangerous."

"What are you implying, Mama?"

"I'm not implying anything, I'm saying it straight out," my mother returned. "Stephen doesn't have the common sense of a booby bird, Annabelle! That is why these things happen to him all the time! The boat sank because he didn't look at it properly. He got shot at because he was tramping around the woods looking for a tree house! Good God." Mama's disgust was written all over her lovely face. "When most men go into the woods they have a gun with them and they are looking to be the ones who do the shooting."

No one could make me as angry as my mother. I said, "If you find the family members who live in my house so unpalatable, Mama, then perhaps you ought to leave."

There was absolute silence in the dining room. I held my mother's eyes, and the message in mine was uncompromising. I would not tolerate any disparagement of Stephen.

The duke was amazed to find that someone else could be as rude as he was. "Apologize to your mother this instant, young lady," he demanded.

My mother said, "I never cease to wonder how I could have given birth to such a stupid child."

"Annabelle is not stupid." My eyes swung with surprise to Aunt Fanny's face. She rarely crossed swords with my mother.

"Annabelle is a fool," Mama said bitterly, and I knew then for certain that she had noticed the change in me.

Adam said mildly, "Regina, you know that no one has ever been allowed to say anything against Stephen to Annabelle. They are as close as any brother and sister could possibly be. Now, why don't we stop this silly squabbling and enjoy our dinner?"

Jack and Jasper once more looked at each other across the table, but this time I was not able to interpret the silent message they exchanged.

"You mean well, Adam, but you are as big a fool as my daughter." My mother stood up. "Come along, Saye. We are leaving."

The duke was horrified. "I have not finished my meal, Regina!"

I picked up my wineglass and drank off what was left in it. "You don't have to leave right now, Mama," I said.

"I wouldn't dream of remaining for another moment in *your house* if I am not wanted," my mother said haughtily.

I had known perfectly well when I said it that the phrase "my house" would hit Mama hard.

All the men at the table had struggled to their feet when my mother rose. They stood now in front of their chairs, looking on uncomfortably as my mother and I had it out with each other.

I said, "You are more than welcome to remain, Mama. I only ask that you refrain from making disparaging remarks about my other guests. Surely that is a reasonable request."

She was really irritated now. She had never considered herself a guest at Weston. "Saye," she said to her husband in ominous tones.

The duke was still clutching his napkin. "But where are we to go at this hour?" he asked plaintively.

"To an hotel in Brighton," my mother said grandly.

"But Regina... cannot I at least finish my dinner?"

My mother was merciless. "You can eat when we reach Brighton."

Aunt Fanny produced a few words begging Mama to change her mind, which Mama ignored. Fanny threw me a beseeching look. I

241

sat like stone and uttered not a word as Mama, followed by her ruffled husband, stalked out of the room.

Silence.

Then all of the men, who were still standing in deference to my mother, turned to look at me. Jack picked up his glass. "A toast to the victor," he said, his face alight with malicious laughter.

I said irritably, "Oh, sit down, all of you, and finish your dinners."

"Annabelle dear," said kind Aunt Fanny, "surely you don't wish your mother to go off in such a fashion!"

I gestured to my empty wineglass, and one of the footmen emerged from the trancelike state they had all fallen into during the quarrel and came hastily to fill it.

"The choice is hers," I said, and picked up my wine.

"I cannot believe that you mean such a thing! You have always been such a warmhearted girl."

"When it suits her, Annabelle can be every bit as calculating and coldhearted as Regina," Jack said with the same malicious delight in his voice that I had seen in his face.

I threw him an annoyed look over the top of my glass.

"Stop it, Jack," Jasper said.

"What a shame that Nell wasn't here to witness Regina's defeat," Jack said irrepressibly. "She will be furious when she finds out what she missed."

I put down my wineglass a little too firmly, and the wine almost sloshed over the top and onto the table. I said, "I will ask you to leave, too, if you don't stop it, Jack."

"You can't ask me to leave," he replied cheerfully. "You need me to help school your new horses."

Adam leaped at the possibility of a new topic. "What is this I hear about Sir Matthews starting cubbing season early this year, Annabelle?"

I replied at some length, pointedly ignoring Jack's attempts to be witty. He could be very annoying when he got into this mood.

By the time dinner was finished, and Aunt Fanny and I had left the dining room so that the men could drink their port, Mama and the duke were gone.

I supposed that I ought to feel guilty about driving my own mother away from my house. I didn't feel guilty, however.

I felt safe.

After we left the men in the dining room, Aunt Fanny and I went upstairs to check on the invalids.

Nell was sitting up in bed, reading a book. She closed it as we came in and returned it to her bedside table.

"How are you feeling, my love?" Aunt Fanny asked solicitously as she laid a practiced hand on Nell's brow.

"I am fine, Mother," Nell replied. She looked at me and said apologetically, "I don't know what came over me, Annabelle. I don't believe I have ever fainted before in my entire life."

I went to stand next to Aunt Fanny. The bedside lamp shone on Nell's short blond curls, which were brushed neatly off her face. Sitting there in bed, in her prim white nightdress, she looked so like the little girl I remembered that I had to smile.

"Well, the news was certainly shocking enough," I said. "But both Giles and Stephen are going to be fine, Nell."

"I know. I looked in on Stephen a little while ago and it does seem that he will be all right."

"You should not be visiting a gentleman in his bedchamber, Nell," Aunt Fanny said immediately.

"Oh, Mama! Stephen was hardly in a fit enough state to ravish me," Nell said with exasperation.

I remembered his hungry kiss and thought that Nell had underestimated him.

Aunt Fanny was thoroughly shocked. "Of course Stephen would not ravish you! I never thought such a thing!"

I said, "Nell only means that there was nothing improper with her looking in on Stephen."

"In her nightdress!"

"She looks very sweet in her nightdress," I said. "Like a little girl."

Aunt Fanny's brow smoothed out.

Nell scowled.

I said, "I am going to look in on Stephen myself. Do you want to come with me, Aunt Fanny?"

"He should be sleeping," she said.

"If he is, we won't wake him. I only want to make certain that he is all right."

"Why is Annabelle allowed to go into Stephen's room and I'm not?" Nell demanded.

Aunt Fanny looked both surprised and dismayed at her daughter's belligerence. "This is Annabelle's house, Nell," she replied quietly. "And Annabelle is a married lady, not a young girl."

Nell's lower lip was stuck out, making her look more than ever like the child she had been. "She isn't married any longer," she said.

A chambermaid, carrying a can of fresh water for Nell's bedside table, opened the door. She stopped on the threshold when she saw us.

"I think it will be best if we ignore that unforgivable remark," Aunt Fanny said to me. "Perhaps by the morning Nell will have recovered her manners."

Nell's cheeks turned pink, and I gave her a sympathetic look. Aunt Fanny's infrequent reproaches always stung far worse than my mother's invective ever did. It was because one cared what Aunt Fanny thought, of course, that made the difference.

"Good night, Nell," I said.

"Good night, Annabelle," she replied politely. But she wouldn't look at me.

"You may come in now, Mary," I said to the maid with the water, and together Aunt Fanny and I walked down the passage to Stephen's room. I knocked softly on the door, and when there was no response I pushed it open and we peeked in. The room was dark, except for the narrow strip of moonlight that was coming in through the open window.

"Stephen?" I said gently.

No reply.

I went over to stand beside the bed, holding my candle so that I could see him. He was lying on his back, deeply asleep. His hair was

245

tangled, his thin face looked haggard, and he needed a shave. I thought he was the most beautiful thing I had ever seen in my life.

"Poor boy," Aunt Fanny murmured at my side.

I curbed my impulse to touch him.

"We'll let him sleep," I whispered. "It's the best thing for him, the doctor said."

The two of us quietly left the room.

"Would you care to take tea with me in my sitting room?" Aunt Fanny surprised me by asking.

I accepted, trying not to look too curious. At the beginning of their stay at the hall, I had given my aunt and uncle two large bedrooms with a connecting door. Aunt Fanny had decided to use one bedroom for sleeping and to turn the other one into a sitting room. I had been happy to have the room furnished for her use; I perfectly understood her need for a retreat of her own.

The two of us retraced our footsteps down the passage, and Aunt Fanny opened the door that came directly after Nell's. We sat in the comfortable upholstered chairs I had had installed, and she ordered tea.

I chatted lightly about this and that, and after the tea had been poured and the chambermaid had gone, Aunt Fanny brought up what was on her mind.

"I feel that I must apologize for Nell," she said. "I don't know what has gotten into her lately, Annabelle. I never had to correct her for rudeness when she was a child!"

"You don't have to apologize to me, Aunt Fanny," I said firmly. "Nell is like my little sister, and sisters, you know, are allowed to be frank with each other."

"Frankness and rudeness are not quite the same thing, my dear Annabelle," Aunt Fanny said.

I sipped my tea. "I have been known to be rude on occasion myself," I murmured. "There is no reason for you to distress yourself on my account, Aunt Fanny."

She said, "I suppose I am also asking your advice, Annabelle. Nell has become so rebellious of late, and I don't understand why."

"I don't think I would call Nell rebellious," I said slowly.

Aunt Fanny put down her teacup, folded her hands in her lap, and stared at them all the while she was telling me her real concern.

"Perhaps rebellious is too strong a word," she agreed. "But she has certainly changed from the eager-to-please child she once was. When we gave her that expensive London Season, she would not cooperate at all." Aunt Fanny glanced up at me fleetingly, then went back to staring at her hands. "You know about the offers she received. They came from four very eligible men, Annabelle!"

"I know," I said. In fact, I did know the men who had offered for my cousin, and they were indeed extremely eligible.

"She told me she didn't love them," I went on. "She isn't wrong to wish to marry for love, Aunt Fanny. You loved Uncle Adam, didn't you?"

On this topic she could meet my eyes. "I thought he was a very nice young man," she said primly. "He was kind and handsome and he had good manners. I was pleased that he wanted to marry me. I was disposed to love him, and it wasn't long before I did."

"I see," I said a little feebly.

"If the young man is amiable, and the girl is disposed to love him, love almost always comes. The problem," Aunt Fanny said, "is that Nell was *not* disposed to love any of the young men who offered for her. In fact, she was dead set against them from the start."

"I see," I said again.

Aunt Fanny gazed with some distress at the picture of a younger Nell that she had hung on the sitting room wall. "I very much fear that she is in love with someone else."

"Goodness," I said.

"Do you have any idea who such a man might be?" Aunt Fanny asked.

I tried to look as if I were racking my brains. I most certainly did not want to alarm my aunt by mentioning Jack.

I said, "Could it be someone else she met in London? Someone who did not offer for her?"

"I really do not think so. She did not want us to give her that Season, you know. She told her father not to waste his money." Aunt Fanny's eyes glittered. "Really, Annabelle, can you think of one single reason why a young girl like Nell would not jump at the chance of a London Season?"

I bit my lip. "I am afraid I cannot help you," I said. "It's true that we were close when we were children, but Nell has not confided in me for rather a long time, Aunt Fanny."

"Do you think that Nell might be harboring a *tendre* for Stephen?" Aunt Fanny asked.

248

My mouth dropped open. "*Stephen?*"

She nodded. "She wrote to him every month while he was in Jamaica."

I hadn't known that.

"Nell was only fifteen when Stephen went away," I managed to say. "Surely that was too young to form a lasting attachment."

"I didn't say 'lasting attachment,' " Aunt Fanny said irritably. "I said '*tendre*.' "

I opened my mouth to tell Aunt Fanny she was wrong, but the words wouldn't come out.

"She fainted this afternoon when she heard that Stephen had been shot," I said instead.

"Oh dear, oh dear, oh dear." Aunt Fanny almost wailed the words. "What am I to do?"

She sounded so distressed at the thought of Stephen as a prospective son-in-law that I leaped to his defense. "Don't you consider Stephen an eligible *parti*, Aunt Fanny? He is far from being poor, you know." When she didn't reply, I added accusingly, "I thought you liked Stephen."

"Of course I like Stephen. I like him very much. It is impossible not to like Stephen. But as a husband for Nell—no, no, and no."

I would have murdered Nell before I allowed her to marry Stephen, but I was incensed at Aunt Fanny's rejection of him. "There is nothing wrong with Stephen!" I said fiercely.

Aunt Fanny finally realized that she had offended me. "I have nothing against Stephen, Annabelle," she assured me. "There is no need for you to fly tooth and nail to his defense. It is just that, with all his splendid qualities, I do not think that he is the husband for Nell."

That comment about "splendid qualities"

249

mollified me a little. "Why not?" I asked more quietly.

"Because the most important person in Stephen's life will always be you." Aunt Fanny said.

I stared at her and had no reply.

"Nell has played second fiddle to you all her life, my dear. That is why I wanted her to have a London Season—so she could get away from Weston and out from under your shadow. That is why I would not let you assist me with her come-out. And that is why I do not want her to break her heart over Stephen."

I pressed my hand to my own heart, as if it hurt. As indeed it did. "It sounds as if you thought I were bad for Nell," I said.

"You never meant to be," Aunt Fanny returned. "I know that, my dear. And I know that you have a real fondness for her. As she does for you."

I turned my head and looked at the picture on the wall. A twelve-year-old Nell looked solemnly back at me. She was wearing breeches and sitting on a shaggy roan pony. I remembered very clearly the summer that portrait had been done.

"You can't help what you are, Annabelle," Aunt Fanny said. "But you present an impossible standard for a younger girl to measure herself against."

"Looks aren't everything," I protested strongly.

Aunt Fanny raised her graying brows. "I was not talking about looks," she said.

I stared at her in utter bewilderment. "Then

I have no idea what you are talking about," I said.

She smiled at me with a fondness I could have sworn was genuine. "You are an extremely formidable young woman, my dear. All the more so because you don't realize it."

Her comments were making me feel very uncomfortable, and I tried to steer the conversation back to our original topic. "There will be assemblies in Brighton all through the winter," I said. "You ought to take Nell to those. Perhaps she will meet a man more to her taste than the London beaux she rejected."

Aunt Fanny sighed. "Yes, I am planning to do just that. In fact, I have been thinking of renting a house in Brighton for the winter, Annabelle. I think it would be a good idea to get Nell away from Weston, particularly now that Stephen is home."

I had to agree. Whether my cousin was in love with Stephen or with Jack, the outcome for her was going to be heartbreak. It was definitely best that she go to Brighton with her mother.

CHAPTER
eighteen

After I left Aunt Fanny I went straight downstairs to my own rooms. Marianne did not even attempt to disguise her horror when I told her to awaken me at four-thirty the following morning.

"I am meeting Sir Matthew and the hounds

251

at six," I said, "and it is a thirty-minute hack to the Market Cross. Four-thirty."

"Yes, my lady."

"Don't look like such a martyr," I advised. "You can go back to bed after I've left."

She brightened a little at that news. "Shall I lay out your riding habit now, my lady?"

"Yes. Neither one of us will feel like searching for misplaced articles of clothing at four-thirty in the morning."

After she had left, I curled up in bed and snuggled my cheek into my favorite pillow. But even though I was very tired, sleep didn't come. Over and over again, last night's scene with Stephen replayed itself in my mind.

Six months is a damn long time.

Stephen had made his intentions very clear with that remark. We were both of age now, and the only thing that stood in the way of our marriage was six more months of official mourning.

"Let's start over again," he had replied when I accused him of thinking he could pick up where he had left off five years before.

I rolled over in bed, flung my arm across my forehead, and stared upward into the cool darkness. The soft night breeze rustled the pages of an open book I had left on the table by the window.

Stephen and I couldn't just start over, I thought sadly. His betrayal would always lie between us, like a shadow on the deep clear well of our love.

I would marry Stephen. I loved him. I had always loved him. I always would love him.

But nothing could bring back those sunlit

years when I had rested secure in the knowledge that I belonged to Stephen and Stephen
belonged to me.

*The most important person in Stephen's life will
always be you.*

Once I, like Aunt Fanny, had thought that
to be true. I didn't think that way any longer.
And that was what I would never forgive.

Four-thirty came much too soon. I struggled
out of bed in the dark and let a cranky, sleepy
Marianne help me dress. It was exactly five when
I walked into the dining room, where Hodges,
bless him, had set out coffee and muffins. Jack
and Jasper were already there, drinking coffee
in bleary-eyed silence.

"Good morning," I said cheerfully.

Two grunts were all the responses I got.

I had enough sense not to tease them about
their lack of courtesy, filled a cup for myself,
and drank the coffee as if it were the nectar of
the gods.

At five-fifteen, as the sky was beginning to
brighten, the three of us walked down to the
stables. The horses were ready. We mounted,
and by five-thirty we were on our way to join
Sir Matthew and the hounds.

We had an enjoyable morning. Cubbing is
rewarding, but not exciting. Sir Matthew had
each of his young hounds coupled with a more
experienced partner, and the point of the exercise was for the young hounds to learn their
business from their elders. The horses did some
trotting, but mainly we walked.

This slow, uneventful teaching exercise was
the perfect way to introduce green horses to

the hounds and to the woods. Snap had hunted all last season, so Jasper had a more relaxed morning than either Jack or I. We were both riding inexperienced Thoroughbreds, and we had to be extremely careful that the nervous horses never got an opportunity to aim a steel-shod hoof at one of the hounds.

I never liked Jack as much as I did when I rode with him. He was so intolerant of most people that it was a constant surprise to see how patient he could be with a horse. He was particularly excited about the colt he was riding this morning and told me at least twenty times during the three hours we were out that "this Aladdin is going to be something, Annabelle."

Jasper was a fine horseman also, but he rode like the cavalry officer he was. There was never any doubt who was in charge when Jasper was in the saddle. This attitude suited Snap perfectly, and as I watched them I felt all the gratification of a matchmaker who had arranged a successful marriage.

The young hounds did very well, the horses all behaved themselves, and by nine o'clock Sir Matthew announced that he thought we had had a very successful morning. We parted company a few miles from Stanhope, Sir Matthew and Mr. Clinton to return the hounds to their kennels, the rest of us to return to Weston Hall for a real breakfast.

Stephen was sitting at the dining room table, eating a plate of grilled kidneys, when Jasper and I walked in.

"Should you be up?" Jasper asked in the gruff voice that men used to each other to conceal concern.

"I feel fine." Stephen's eyes moved from Jasper's face to mine.

I felt the thrill of that blue-eyed glance go all through me and walked over to the sideboard so that no one could see my expression. I put some food on my plate, came back to the table, and unthinkingly sat next to Stephen.

"Hungry?" he asked softly, and I heard the amusement in his voice.

I gestured to my full plate. "I was up at four-thirty, unlike some people I could mention."

"I was exhausted," he said reproachfully, and I knew that he was not referring to his head wound.

I took a bite of bacon and refused to answer.

Adam peeked out from behind his newspaper and said, "Do any of you want to look at the *Post*?"

Jasper took a section and propped it next to his cup so he could read it as he ate.

Hodges entered the room with a silver tray bearing an envelope, which he brought to Stephen.

"This letter came for you in the afternoon post yesterday, Mr. Stephen," he said. "I am afraid it was forgotten in the... er... excitement."

Stephen took the letter and looked at the seal. "Thank you, Hodges," he said. He glanced at me. "Do you mind if I read this, Annabelle?"

"Of course not."

Silence descended while Stephen read his letter and Adam and Jasper read their newspapers.

I worked my way steadily through the food on my plate and wondered idly what had become of Jack.

Stephen refolded his letter. "Tom Clarkson is going to be in Brighton tomorrow afternoon," he said. "There is to be an antislavery rally, and he wants me to drive over and join him."

Adam put down his paper. "You cannot possibly think of going to Brighton, Stephen. You took a bullet in your head yesterday!"

His voice was resonant with paternal authority.

"I feel fine this morning, Uncle Adam," Stephen replied absently. He tapped his letter against the tabletop and looked as if his thoughts were many miles away.

"I thought Clarkson was supposed to be going to the Vienna congress," I said.

"He is," Stephen answered, returning his attention to the breakfast table. "And he will be taking antislavery petitions with him that carry upward of one and a half million signatures."

Jasper lifted his eyes from his newspaper. "That may sound impressive, Stephen, but I rather doubt that the other European nations at the congress are going to be persuaded by petitions which bear only British signatures."

I finished my last bite of bacon and picked up my coffee cup.

Stephen said, "All the rallies and petitions this summer have put tremendous public pressure on our own ministers to make the abolition of the slave trade a priority in the coming peace negotiations, Jasper. Clarkson says that he doesn't believe the country had ever before expressed a feeling so general as it has done about the slave trade."

Jasper looked unconvinced.

Adam repeated firmly, "You cannot drive into Brighton tomorrow."

I didn't bother to waste my energy warning Stephen against something he was obviously bent on doing. I said instead, "Clarkson doesn't want you to go with him to Vienna, does he?"

"No. He thinks I will be of more use to the cause here in England," Stephen replied. "He says I'm too young to make any kind of meaningful impression on the delegates in Vienna."

The note of bitterness in his voice was so achingly familiar. *Why do I have to be so young?* He had been saying that since he was ten years old.

"You're not too young to make your mark in Parliament," I said. "Look at Pitt. He was prime minister when he was only twenty-four."

"Are you going to run for Parliament, Stephen?" Jasper asked curiously.

Stephen's reply was brief. "Yes."

Adam put his section of the paper next to Jasper's plate. "I did not realize that Parliament was your ambition, my boy," he said, frowning thoughtfully. "Pettigrew has held the seat for Weston these last fifteen years; but if you want it, then of course we shall have to find a seat for him somewhere else."

"I don't want the seat from Weston, Uncle Adam," Stephen said. "You must know that I could never run as a Tory, and Weston has been solidly Tory for as long as I can remember."

"Weston would vote for a Grandville no matter what party he belonged to," Adam said matter-of-factly.

This was indisputably true.

Stephen said, "I am going to run for my uncle Francis's seat in Kent. He, as you know, has always been staunchly Whig."

257

"He has been *quietly* Whig," Jasper said with amusement. "I have a feeling that his replacement will be rather more vocal."

Stephen grinned.

My heart cramped with love.

Jasper said, "I'll lay odds you already have your first speech written."

"I have the topic," Stephen returned serenely. He picked up his coffee cup, realized it was empty, and put it down again.

I picked up the silver pot that was on the table and poured him more coffee. Then I poured a second cup for myself.

"Is it a secret?" I inquired.

He shook his head. "Not at all. I would like to speak in favor of a slave registration bill." He took a sip of his newly poured coffee.

I was puzzled. "What good would registering slaves accomplish?"

Stephen turned his head to look at me. "A census would enable us to measure the consequences of the abolition of the slave trade on the slave populations of the islands. Specifically, it would show us if planters were smuggling new slaves into the Caribbean in defiance of the law. Do you see, Annabelle? Slave registration will yield the data we need in order to win freedom for all Negro slaves in British possessions."

Adam said calmly, "The planters will never accept a registration bill."

The stubborn look we all knew settled across Stephen's face. "Then they must be compelled to accept it," he said.

Silence fell.

I stood up and gestured that the men should keep their seats.

"Where are you going?" Stephen asked me.

"To the nursery to see Giles."

He nodded as if he approved.

I looked next at Jasper to give him a parting smile and was shocked by the bleak expression that looked back at me from his gray eyes. "Is anything wrong, Jasper?" I asked.

He blinked, and the look was gone. "Of course not," he said. "I enjoyed our outing this morning very much, Annabelle. Thank you for inviting me."

Stephen said, "Do you have some time you can give to me this morning, Uncle Adam?"

"Surely you don't want to look at ledgers this morning, Stephen!" Adam replied. "Doesn't your head hurt?"

"Not much," Stephen replied.

"Well, I am sorry, my boy, but I promised Charlie Hutchinson that I would take a look at his roof this morning. He says it leaked badly in yesterday's storm."

Their voices faded as I went out into the passage and made my way toward the stairs.

I was surprised to find that breakfast was still on the table in the nursery. I was even more surprised to find Jack there, cozily sharing the meal with Giles and Miss Stedham.

He pushed back his old wooden chair and stood up as I came in.

I stared at him and demanded ungraciously, "What are you doing here?"

He lifted his thick blond eyebrows. "I just looked in to see how Giles was doing after yesterday's incident, and he invited me to join him and Miss Stedham for breakfast."

I surveyed the table, taking in the standard

nursery breakfast that had been served at Weston ever since I was a child; a big pot of hot chocolate and muffins with butter and jam. I thought of the feast that had been laid out in the dining room and regarded Jack incredulously.

"Are you actually drinking *chocolate*?"

"It is very tasty," he replied with a dangerously smooth smile.

Giles said, "Jack said he would take me and Genie to West Haven this afternoon, Mama. We are going to buy a kite at Fullham's and fly it down at the cove!"

West Haven was the small port town on the Channel that lay on the other side of the Ridge directly to the south of Weston.

Miss Stedham said, "Of course, I was going to consult with you first, Lady Weston."

I looked at my son's governess. Her magnolia skin was flushed and her eyes were bright. My eyes moved on to Jack's too handsome face and narrowed.

What's your game, Jack? I thought.

He returned my look, his light blue eyes full of the malicious humor I so distrusted.

Giles said, "May I go, Mama?"

I said, my eyes still on Jack, "You may go to West Haven, but I would rather you kept away from the cove."

Giles's voice took on a distinct whine. "But I want to fly my kite!"

At my comment about the cove, all of the humor had disappeared from Jack's eyes. He frowned, started to ask me a question, glanced at Giles, and changed his mind. He said instead, "You can fly your kite on the beach in

260

West Haven, Giles. There is really no need for us to go to the cove."

"I like the cove better than the beach in West Haven," Giles said stubbornly.

Miss Stedham said in her calm, reasonable way, "Perhaps it would be better if we stayed at home."

Giles squeaked in alarm as he saw his outing disappearing before his eyes. "No, Genie! Mama didn't say we had to stay home. Did you, Mama?"

"I said you may go to West Haven, Giles. Not to the cove."

"Jack just said we wouldn't go to the cove. Didn't you, Jack?"

"That is what I said," Jack replied gravely.

"See, Genie." Giles's voice was urgent. "We will only go to West Haven."

Miss Stedham said, "In that case, Giles, we will go."

Across the table my eyes met the eyes of Giles's governess, and the both of us repressed a smile.

After I left the nursery I went back downstairs and asked Hodges to bring a pot of tea to my office. Then I settled down at my desk to spend the rest of the morning working on my housekeeping books.

It took only a few minutes to read through Cook's suggested menus for the following week and to scrawl my approval. I made only one change, substituting a fish soup for mulligatawny, which I knew Stephen did not like.

Then I started on the accounts.

Adam was the one who paid the household bills, but I was the one who kept the records. It was a time-consuming business, but one I discharged faithfully every week. Accounts for everything pertaining to the immediate household passed over my desk: servants' wages book; tax accounts; dairy accounts, etc. I kept monthly, quarterly, and yearly account books, which I divided into categories—foodstuffs, wages, apothecaries' supplies, charitable donations, and so on.

I picked up my pen, picked up the first paid bill, and entered the amount.

Five minutes later I was staring blankly at the July bill for beeswax candles, with my thoughts on something entirely removed from the household accounts.

Jack was up to something. Of that I was certain. He was not showing all this flattering attention to Giles because he yearned for the company of my small son. I loved Giles dearly, but I recognized that the conversation of a five-year-old was likely to be of little interest to a sophisticated man like Jack.

Upon reflection, I was able to entertain several possible explanations for Jack's sudden interest in Giles.

One explanation was that Adam was right: Jack was trying to fix his interest with me. He was certainly clever enough to realize that the one sure way to endear himself to me was by befriending Giles.

On the other hand, I really couldn't imagine why Jack would confide in me that he needed to marry money, if the money he intended to marry belonged to me.

I leaned back in my chair, gazed at Stubbs' elegant Thoroughbreds on the wall, and thought some more.

If pleasing me was not the object of Jack's sudden interest in Giles, then what was?

The answer to that question flashed with sudden, blinding clarity into my mind. Jack's real interest was Miss Stedham!

And, as Miss Stedham was even poorer than Jack himself, his intentions toward her could not be honorable.

I thought of the governess's bright eyes and flushed cheeks when I had walked in on the breakfast scene in the nursery this morning.

Poor girl, I thought sympathetically. I certainly did not blame her for falling under Jack's spell. He could be very charming when he wanted, and of course he had his full measure of the Grandville looks. And Miss Stedham's life was so dreadfully limited.

I sighed and rubbed my temples. Just what I needed, I thought gloomily. Something else to worry about.

I forcibly returned my attention to the bills on my desk, picked up my pen, and entered into my housekeeping ledger the amount of money it had cost to keep the household in candles for the month of July.

Miss Stedham's face had looked as bright as a candle this morning, I thought.

Once more I put down my pen, leaned back in my chair, and regarded my beloved Stubbs. I simply could not allow that poor girl to be seduced by Jack.

And how was I to prevent this disaster? I wondered. I couldn't get Miss Stedham out of

Jack's way by dismissing her. She needed her position in order to eat.

What she *really* needed, I thought grimly, was a husband. Unfortunately, governesses had very few opportunities to meet eligible men. Miss Stedham had met Jack, of course, but Jack's intentions were not likely to include marriage to a girl who was even poorer than he.

Jasper was an eligible man, I thought. And if he was really thinking of settling down in Northamptonshire, surely he would need to find a wife. Miss Stedham would be a perfect match for him, I thought with growing enthusiasm. She liked country life as much as he did.

The only drawback to this brilliant idea was that I had not detected the slightest interest in the lovely governess on Jasper's part.

I glanced at the small gold clock that perched on the corner of my desk and realized with dismay that the morning was almost gone. Resolutely I returned my eyes to the next bill.

It was for sugar. I looked at the sum and thought that if all English households consumed as much sugar as mine, the Jamaican sugar plantations would be making millions.

I really must speak to Giles about the amount of sugar he heaps into his tea, I thought as I wrote down the sum and went on to the next bill.

Perhaps I can arrange to throw Jasper and Miss Stedham together occasionally.

The thought flashed into my mind as I was frowning at the amount of money it had cost to replace the morning room draperies.

I had a feeling that Uncle Adam would not be pleased to see his son marry a poor girl like

Miss Stedham, but I didn't agree. In my opinion, any man who won a girl as lovely and warm-hearted as Giles's governess should count himself lucky.

Before I could implement this plan, however, I would have to get rid of Jack. I tried very hard not to think that there might be other reasons that necessitated the quick removal of Jack from Weston.

Once more I put down my pen and stared at the horses on the wall. Surely I could not seriously think that Jack would ever mean harm to Stephen and Giles?

CHAPTER
nineteen

I took a much needed nap after luncheon, and when I awoke I decided to drive into Weston village to pick up a pair of leather gloves that I had seen in Mr. Wyatt's shop the day before. The dogs jumped onto the front seat of the phaeton with me, delighted to be included in the outing.

I ran into Susan Fenton in Wyatt's, and I left the dogs sleeping in the phaeton as we both repaired to Mrs. Compton's tea shop for a cozy gossip.

She was shocked to hear that Stephen had been shot.

"Nobody poaches in them woods, my lady," she said positively.

"Do you know, Susan," I said casually, "I think we can dispense with the 'my lady' from now on."

We looked at each other. We both knew that she had adopted the formal title only because Gerald did not like to hear his tenants calling his wife by her first name.

"All right," she said with a faint smile. "Nobody poaches in them woods, Miss Annabelle."

I smiled back before returning to the topic that was preying on my mind. "I have been wondering if there is still smuggling going on in the cove." I added meaningfully, "Jem Washburn is back, you know."

"Jem would *never* shoot Mr. Stephen," Susan said instantly. I noticed that she did not object to my connecting Jem's name with smuggling.

"I'm not saying that Jem was the one who shot Stephen," I said. "It could have been someone else connected with a smuggling gang. Someone who was in the process of concealing a shipment in the woods and was afraid that Stephen would stumble upon his hiding place."

Susan stirred her tea, a thoughtful line between her brows, "I don't know...."

Another voice said, "Do you have everything you want, my lady?"

I looked up to see Mrs. Compton, the shop's owner, regarding me with a pleased-as-punch look. She loved it when I came to tea and always made a point of placing me in the front window, directly in the view of everyone passing on the street.

"Everything is lovely, Mrs. Compton," I assured her.

She treated me to the gap-toothed smile that always gave her elderly face an endearingly urchinlike look. "I just made them muffins ten minutes ago, my lady."

"They are utterly delicious, Mrs. Compton.

You know I have always adored your hazelnut muffins."

The old lady's smile broadened. "You have that, my lady. From the time when you was a little girl you have always asked for my hazelnut muffins."

Mrs. Compton moved on to take an order from another customer, and I turned back to my conversation. "I know smugglers are still operating in the area, Susan. Gerald got all his brandy from the free traders, as did his father."

This had always been a sore point with me. The earl and Gerald had been so outraged when they had discovered that Stephen was involved with smugglers, yet neither one of them had hesitated to buy goods from the very people they supposedly condemned!

"Bob still gets some things from the 'gentlemen,' too," Susan said. "But I don't think they have ever used the Ridge woods to hide their shipments, Miss Annabelle. The Ridge woods belong to the hall; everyone knows that."

"Stephen was caught on the Ridge path," I reminded her.

She finished chewing her own hazelnut muffin. "Well, might be it's true that the gentlemen have used the Ridge path to move the goods from the cove to wherever they was being hidden," she admitted. "But I'm certain sure they never hid nothing in the Ridge woods."

"Then what about this, Susan? Someone was transporting smuggled goods through the woods, and when he heard Stephen coming he got off the path and hid. Then, when it looked as if Stephen were going to leave the path as well, the smuggler shot him."

Susan's response to this idea was depressingly lukewarm. "Maybe, but what smugglers would be doing abroad in plain daylight is a mystery to me, Miss Annabelle."

I stared glumly at my tea, annoyed with Susan for not supporting my idea and afraid that she was right and I was wrong. When I looked up again I saw Sir Matthew's sister coming into the shop. Our eyes met and we both smiled and nodded a greeting.

I began to shred my muffin with my fingers. Susan drank her tea and waited. She had always known when to be silent. It was this last thought that decided me to tell her the whole story. I knew I could trust Susan to keep a secret.

I said in a low voice, "This is not something we want to get around, but the only reason Stephen wasn't killed was that at the very moment the shot was fired, he turned his head to look at something."

Susan had been reaching for the teapot to refill her cup, but at my words she went perfectly still.

"It is difficult to believe that such a close shot could be an accident." My voice trembled. "It looks as if someone were shooting to kill."

Susan withdrew her hand and put it in her lap. She stared across the table at me with widened eyes. "Oh, Annabelle," she said.

I bit my lip. "It is—rather worrying."

Susan slowly began to shake her head. "I'm not saying there ain't smuggling going on at the cove," she said, "but I won't believe that any of the gentlemen would deliberately fire a shot at Mr. Stephen."

"Perhaps they didn't know it was Stephen."

I wasn't ready to give up my smuggling theory yet. "They may have caught only a glimpse of a figure through the trees, and fired because they were frightened."

"If the shooter couldn't see who was there, then the chance was it was you on that path, Miss Annabelle," Susan said bluntly. "And no one would dare to fire a shot at you."

I felt as if someone had kicked me in the stomach. It had never once occurred to me that I might have been the target of that deadly shot.

"I never thought of that," I breathed. "And Stephen had Giles with him, too."

Susan was appalled. "*Giles* was there? Is he all right?"

My muffin had been reduced to a heap of crumbs on my plate. Mrs. Compton would be very upset.

"He was frightened," I said. "He believes the shot was deliberate, Susan."

"No one would fire at you, Miss Annabelle," she repeated.

"Someone might fire at me if he thought I was going to find him in possession of illegal goods," I said stubbornly. "Particularly if the shooter was someone who knew I disliked him." Someone like Jem Washburn, I thought to myself.

I was not going to give up my smuggling theory without a fight. Frightening as such a possibility was, the other possibility was even more terrifying.

"I don't believe it," Susan said. "I don't believe anybody was taking illegal goods through the Ridge woods, and even if they was, I don't believe anyone would try to kill you, or Mr.

Stephen, either, just to protect their own selves."

To be honest, I had a hard time believing it, too.

"There is another possibility," I said, aware that I had my back against the wall. "Perhaps it wasn't a chance meeting at all. Perhaps someone was actually lying in wait for Stephen— one of the smugglers whom he sheltered five years ago." One of the reasons the magistrate had insisted that Stephen must be punished so strictly was that he had refused to give the authorities the names of his associates. "Perhaps this smuggler was afraid that now that Stephen was back he would reveal the names of his confederates. Perhaps he decided it would be safest to make certain that Stephen remained silent permanently."

"Miss Annabelle," Susan said patiently, "no one who knows Mr. Stephen would be that stupid."

I looked at her bleakly. "You don't think it was smugglers?"

She shook her head.

"Or poachers?"

Another head shake.

"Do... do you think that someone else was lying in wait for Stephen?"

Susan's eyes were huge in her white face. "It looks that way, don't it?"

"But if the shooter really wanted to kill Stephen, then why didn't he follow up on his advantage?" I objected. "Stephen was unarmed. He and Giles were sitting ducks."

"The shooter couldn't know whether or not he was armed, could he?" Susan pointed out. "Most gentlemen take a gun when they go out into the woods."

I stared at her unhappily.

"There is also the chance that the shooter was someone Stephen and Giles knew, and he didn't want to take a chance on being recognized," Susan said.

At the sound of my worst fear spoken out loud, an icy hand gripped my heart.

"It could have been a complete stranger," I said desperately. "There are a lot of soldiers and sailors coming home now that the war is over. Someone may have been camping out in the woods and panicked when he heard voices."

Susan gave me a look filled with pity and said chillingly, "Tell Mr. Stephen it's best for him to be careful."

Emily Stanhope, Sir Matthew's spinster sister, was leaving the shop, and she stopped at our table to say a few words. She greeted Susan and asked me pleasantly, "How did the cubbing go this morning, Annabelle?"

"Very well, thank you, Miss Stanhope," I said. "I believe Sir Matthew was pleased."

"Oh, Matthew is always pleased if he can get up in the middle of the night and go galloping through the woods after his beloved hounds," his sister said with an ironic look. Miss Stanhope did not hunt.

I forbore to point out that one rarely galloped while one was cubbing. I said instead, "Sir Matthew is a wonderful master of foxhounds."

"He was born for it," Emily Stanhope agreed, the irony sounding in her voice as well.

After a little more chitchat, Miss Stanhope moved off and Susan and I were alone once more.

I said, "I hope you didn't suffer any damage in yesterday's storm."

Susan obligingly followed my lead. "The pig-pen was swamped, but otherwise we're all right. Not everyone was as lucky as we, though."

"Yes. Mr. Grandville told me that the Hutchinsons' roof sprang a leak. I hope there was no permanent damage done."

"Emma said she had pots everywhere. Charlie has been after Mr. Grandville these last four years to reroof that cottage. Maybe now it will get done."

"I am sure it will," I said. I signaled to Mrs. Compton that I was ready to leave.

"I have some news that might interest you, Miss Annabelle," Susan said.

She was wearing her "You're not going to believe this" look, so it couldn't be ordinary news, like another baby on the way. I leaned toward her, full of breathless attention. "What?"

"Marietta Adams is going to marry Jem Washburn."

"No!"

"Yes. They started walking out a few weeks after Jem came home."

"I can't believe that George Adams would agree to such a match." George Adams was the village's only blacksmith, and he had a very prosperous little business. His daughter was one of the valley's "catches."

"Evidently Jem come home pretty plump in the pocket," Susan informed me. "He paid up all that was owing on the farm, and he's goin' to work it himself. Mr. Grandville give him the lease on it."

I said bitterly, "I for one would be interested to know just how Jem Washburn earned enough money to make him 'plump in the pocket.' "

"Well, howsoever he may have earned it, he's honest now," Susan said. "The Washburn farm's been neglected, of course, but it's good land. Jem says he's going to grow hops. The way the price of wheat has been falling, Bob says maybe he'll try hops, too."

"When is this wedding to take place?" I asked.

"Soon as Jem gets back."

My eyes widened. "Jem's gone?"

"Just for a week. He's gone up to Kent to look at some farm there that's growing hops."

Was Jem in Kent? I wondered. Or was he perhaps involved in some lucrative smuggling scheme closer to home?

I had never had any doubts about who had embroiled Stephen in that smuggling venture five years ago. It was because of Jem Washburn that Stephen had been forced to spend five years in Jamaica.

I had good cause to dislike and distrust Jem Washburn. Nor was I as certain as Susan was that Jem was Stephen's friend.

Mrs. Compton was hastening toward our table, and I braced myself for the reproaches that were sure to come over the sadly mashed muffin on my plate.

When I got home, I looked into the nursery and found Giles and Miss Stedham at tea— without Jack. Giles's face was rosy with sunburn, and he told me in great detail about his kite-flying experience in West Haven. He had clearly had a wonderful time.

Before I left I invited Miss Stedham to have dinner with the family. I would arrange things so that Uncle Adam took in Aunt Fanny and

273

me, Jack took in Nell, and Jasper took in Miss Stedham.

Next I looked into the housekeeper's room to tell Mrs. Nordlem to set an extra place for the governess and was caught for almost half an hour as she regaled me with news of all the damage the storm had done to the local farms.

My housekeeper was a bosom bow of Mrs. Clinton's housekeeper, and between the two of them every inhabitant of the valley was kept apprised of what was happening in the hall, the farms, and the village.

Miss Stedham wore the same gown to dinner that she had worn every time I had invited her before, and I made a mental note to make certain that the poor girl got some new clothes. She looked lovely, however, and I was delighted to see Jasper conversing with her with every evidence of pleasure.

Jack did not look pleased at all. In fact, he scowled at Jasper in a very intimidating manner. Jasper was clearly startled when he looked up and caught Jack's belligerent look.

I said from my place at the top of the table, "The storm evidently did quite a bit of destruction yesterday."

Adam said in a surprised way, "We lost some flower beds, of course, but there was no serious damage done, Annabelle."

"I meant to the farms, Uncle Adam. Mrs. Nordlem spent at least half an hour reporting to me all the sad tales of how the tenants suffered."

Stephen spoke from his place opposite to mine. "What tenants were hurt, Annabelle?"

"Well, the Hutchinsons, of course. Their roof

leaked. But even worse was what happened to the Benningtons. The stream behind their house rose and flooded the whole first floor of the house. Mrs. Clinton's housekeeper told Mrs. Nordlem that there was mud all over everything."

Sometime during the course of the day, Stephen had removed the bandage that the doctor had wound around his head. All he was wearing now was a patch of white plaster over the wound on his temple. He said quietly, "I thought that stream had been dredged, Uncle Adam."

Adam said, "It was, my boy, but evidently not enough. I'll see that it gets done again."

"All of the Benningtons' furniture will have been ruined by water and mud," Stephen said. "Tell Florrie Bennington that we will replace everything she lost."

His voice was very soft and gentle. There was no reason for Uncle Adam to turn so red, but he did. "All right, Stephen," he said gruffly.

I ran my eyes quickly around the other faces at the table to see if anyone sensed the sudden tension between Uncle Adam and Stephen the way I did.

Jack was looking at Miss Stedham, who was studiously not looking back. Nell was looking at Stephen. Aunt Fanny was eating her roast lamb with obvious enjoyment. My eyes reached Jasper's face and stopped.

Jasper was looking at his father with a very grim expression about his mouth.

I hate this, I thought with sudden fury. I hate looking at my family, at people I love, with all this monstrous suspicion in my heart!

But I couldn't help it. There was one fact about yesterday's shooting that I couldn't seem to get out of my mind, no matter how hard I tried. It bothered me so much that I hadn't been able to mention it to Susan.

The only people who could have known that Stephen was going to be in the Ridge woods yesterday afternoon were the people who lived in this house.

I insisted that Miss Stedham accompany us to the drawing room after dinner, where I had the happy inspiration of asking if she played the piano.

"Yes, I do, Lady Weston," she replied.

I regarded her with approval. There was no fuss about Miss Stedham, no simpering false modesty. It occurred to me suddenly that she was someone I would like to have as a friend.

"We would all enjoy hearing some music," I said. "If you would not mind?"

"Of course I don't mind." She went to the piano and sat down.

Jack began to walk toward the piano to join her, but I stepped in front of him to cut him off.

"Jasper," I said sweetly, "perhaps you would turn the pages of Miss Stedham's music for her?"

"Of course," Jasper said courteously, and he went to stand next to Miss Stedham's piano bench.

Jack gave me such a murderous look that I was startled.

"Excuse me, Annabelle," he said in a hard, angry voice.

I stepped out of his way, and he strode to the piano.

"Do you have music that I might fetch for you, Miss Stedham?" he asked the governess, using a very different tone of voice from the one he had used to me.

"I am afraid I do not, Mr. Grandville," she said with a smile. "I shall have to rely on my memory." She turned her head a little to look at me. "What kind of music would you like to hear, Lady Weston?"

"I have always been fond of the Mozart A major sonata," I said, naming a piece that even I had learned in the days when my mother forced me to take piano lessons.

"Do you know that, Miss Stedham?" Jasper asked kindly.

"Yes, Captain Grandville, I know it," Miss Stedham returned quietly. She flexed her fingers a few times before she placed them on the keys. She began to play.

She was a marvelous pianist. I am not at all musical, but I could easily recognize the superiority of her talent. I looked over at Stephen, who was sitting on the sofa next to Nell. His eyes were half-closed and he was listening with absorbed attention. Stephen loved music.

Suddenly, as if he had felt my glance like a physical touch, he lifted his lashes and looked at me. The faintest of smiles touched his mouth. Then he went back to listening to the music.

My heart contracted with love, and my stomach cramped with fear.

Could it really be true that someone had deliberately tried to kill Stephen? Someone in this room?

My heart said no, but my brain said yes.

Miss Stedham finished the Mozart and was loudly urged by everyone in the room to play something else. She obliged gracefully.

When I next glanced at the clock on the mantelpiece I realized that we had kept the poor girl playing for over an hour. I mentioned this and apologized to the governess for being so demanding. "I can only offer the excuse that your playing gave us such delight that we did not know how much time was going by," I concluded.

"It was my pleasure, Lady Weston," the governess replied. "I am never so happy as when I am playing the piano."

There was a glow about her face that testified to the truth of her statement.

"A talent such as yours cries out for an instrument to play upon," Jasper said. He looked at me. "Is there by any chance an extra piano around the house that you could have installed in the nursery, Annabelle?"

I was very happy with this sign of attention to Miss Stedham's needs, and I gave Jasper my warmest smile. "I am afraid there is not, but there is no reason why Miss Stedham cannot use the piano here in the drawing room."

The governess had gone very pale, and I realized abruptly how much the use of a piano must mean to her. "I could not impose upon you like that, Lady Weston," she said stiffly.

"No one goes near the drawing room until after dinner," Jack said in a tight voice. "You would not be imposing."

"Jack is right," I said. "Nell is the only one who ever plays the piano, and I am certain she will not mind if you play it as well."

"Of course I don't mind," Nell said promptly. "In fact, I would enjoy hearing Miss Stedham practice. I'm sure I can learn something from her."

A piano was evidently more important to Miss Stedham than a horse. She accepted my offer. "Thank you, Lady Weston. I would very much appreciate having use of the piano when Giles does not need me."

"It wouldn't hurt Giles at all to sit quietly for a while and listen to some music each day," Stephen said mildly.

Aunt Fanny said, "I believe it is time to send for the tea tray, Annabelle dear."

As I rang for a footman, Miss Stedham rose from the piano and tried to excuse herself, but I refused to allow her to escape. She finally settled gracefully into an upholstered chair. Jasper sat on the sofa on the other side of Nell, and Jack chose a chair where he would have an unimpeded view of Miss Stedham.

The tea tray came in and I poured.

And wondered how long Stephen would wait before he came to me tonight.

CHAPTER
twenty

Someone was already in my bed, and I knew it couldn't be Stephen because I had just left him going into the library with Jasper and Jack. Besides, the mound revealed by the bedside lamp was much too small to be a man.

"Giles?" I said softly as I came all the way into the room.

The mound moved, and a blond head peeked out from under the quilt.

"What are you doing here?" I asked.

"I had a bad dream, Mama, and I couldn't find Genie. So I came down here to wait for you." His voice had none of its characteristic self-confidence. He sounded afraid.

I sat down on the bed and put my hand on his back. "What kind of a dream, Giles?"

"I dreamed that a man was chasing me," he said. The lamplight turned his hair into a ruffled golden halo, and his eyes looked very gray, always a sign that he was troubled. "He had a gun," my son said in a very small voice, "and I knew he wanted to kill me."

My heart ached for him. "Oh, darling," I said. "It's because of what happened in the woods yesterday. You're dreaming about that."

"I know," he said in an even smaller voice than before.

I began to rub his back between his shoulder blades. "It was an accident, Giles. Someone mistook Uncle Stephen for a deer."

"I don't think so, Mama," he said in that same strained little voice. "We were talking and laughing. Deers don't talk and laugh."

My hand stilled on his back. "No," I said, "they don't."

"We were loud, Mama. Loud enough to be heard."

I took one deep breath and then another. "Darling," I said to my small son, "do you think someone was trying to kill Uncle Stephen?"

His voice was so low that I had to bend my head closer to his in order to hear. "Yes," said

Giles, "I do." Pause. "And maybe me, too."

I reached my arms around him and held him close. He pushed his face into the hollow between my breasts and burrowed against me.

"You are just a little boy, Giles," I said as calmly and as reasonably as I could. "Who could possibly want to hurt you?"

"I don't know," he said in a muffled voice. "But I almost drowned, Mama. And then someone shooted at me."

I bent my head and rested my lips on the top of his golden head. I shut my eyes.

"I'm afraid," Giles said.

I was horribly afraid that he might have cause to be.

"Can I stay here with you tonight, Mama?" he asked.

I said what I believed to be true. "You are perfectly safe in your own house, darling. Miss Stedham is in her room now, so you won't be alone in the nursery, and I will leave the dogs with you if you like."

"I want to stay here with you," he said, and burrowed closer.

I didn't have the heart to send him away. "You can stay here until you fall asleep," I said. "Then I will have Uncle Stephen carry you upstairs."

"Can't I stay here all night?"

"No," I said. "You can't."

"But what if I have that dream again, Mama?"

"Then Genie will make you some hot milk to help you go back to sleep again."

That seemed to satisfy him. I went next door to my dressing room and let Marianne put me into my nightdress and robe. Then I sent her to the nursery to inform Miss Stedham that Giles was with me and that I would return him after he had fallen asleep.

When I got into bed next to Giles, he reached out and closed his fist around a fold of my robe. I bent to kiss him. "Good night, darling," I murmured.

Then I settled back against my pillows to wait for Stephen.

The library was almost next door to my bedroom, but the walls of the hall were too thick for me to hear doors opening and closing in the passageway. At one point I thought I heard the rumble of men's voices, but I couldn't be certain.

Half an hour after I thought I had heard the voices, my bedroom door opened silently and Stephen came in. He stopped dead when he saw that Giles was in bed with me.

"It's all right," I said softly, "he's asleep."

Stephen crossed to the bed, moving out of the shadows and into the circle of light cast by the bedside lamp. I saw that he was wearing a white shirt without a neckcloth and the dark trousers he had worn at dinner. He looked for a moment at his son's sleeping face, then raised his eyes to me.

"What happened?" he asked.

"He had a nightmare." I recounted what Giles had told me. "He's afraid that someone is trying to kill him, Stephen," I concluded. "And he definitely thinks that someone is trying to kill you."

"If yesterday's shooter wanted to kill Giles, then he would have come after us," Stephen said. "I think the very fact that he did not is a good indication that he does not wish to hurt Giles."

The rush of relief I felt at his words left me momentarily dizzy. "Do you really think so?"

He nodded and sat on the edge of the bed, his eyes still on Giles's peaceful face.

"On the other hand, he might have been afraid that you had a gun with you," I said. "His retreat might have had nothing to do with Giles at all."

"Anyone who knows me knows I never go out with a gun," Stephen said.

I thought about that for a minute.

"Does that mean you think someone you know is trying to kill you?" I demanded at last.

"I'm not sure yet," he said.

I was feeling physically ill. "Stephen," I said, "I keep thinking that if something happened to you and Giles, then Jack would be the next earl. He would inherit Weston. And Jack needs money."

He repeated, "I do not think that Giles is in danger."

"He *has* been in danger. Twice," I snapped.

"I think that was because he was with me."

I said a word that I occasionally heard around the stables when the men didn't know I was within earshot.

Stephen gave me a startled look, and then he began to laugh.

"It's not funny," I said furiously.

The laughter drained from his face. "I'm sorry, Annabelle. Believe me, I know it isn't funny. I have instituted inquiries and I should know something shortly. I'd rather wait until I had some facts before I said anything."

"You can tell me," I said.

"Of course I can, but I'd rather wait. I may be wrong, and then I will have upset you for nothing."

I debated within myself whether or not I wanted Stephen to give me a name and decided that it would be too difficult to try to act normally toward someone whom I suspected of being a murderer.

Stephen said, "I suppose you told Giles he could stay with you for the night?" His face and voice were so glum, it was almost comical.

"Actually, I told him that he could stay here until he fell asleep. I said that you would carry him upstairs to his own bed."

Stephen's lugubrious expression disappeared like magic. "I will be happy to do that," he said.

"I thought perhaps you might be," I said with amusement.

"Poor little fellow," Stephen said, able to feel pity for Giles now that he knew his rival was being evicted.

"He is quite certain that whoever shot at you meant to kill you," I said grimly. "That is what has made him think that someone may be after him, too."

"I'll keep away from him until we have this… problem… resolved, Annabelle."

Stephen gently pulled the quilt off Giles and lifted his son into his arms. Giles stirred and half opened sleepy eyes. "Where's Mama?" he said.

"I'm right here, darling," I said softly, coming around the bed to stand next to Stephen. "We're going to bring you up to your own bed

284

now. Just go back to sleep. You'll be perfectly safe with Genie and the dogs."

Giles's eyes closed and his head nestled against Stephen's shoulder. I opened my dressing room door and called to the sleeping spaniels to come. Then we all exited into the passageway and climbed the two flights of stairs to the nursery.

Giles was asleep when Stephen lowered him carefully into his bed. I pulled the quilt over him and tucked it in. Then Stephen and I stood side by side next to the bed and looked at our sleeping son. I felt Stephen's hand close around mine.

Warmth and happiness filled my heart, except for that one small cold place that couldn't—or wouldn't—forget the pain of his silent departure and the five long years I had endured without him.

"This room brings back so many memories," Stephen murmured in my ear.

"Yes," I breathed.

We were in Stephen's old bedroom, and the bed where Giles was sleeping was quite probably the place where he had been conceived.

I wished, with sudden and painful intensity, that we could turn back time, that we could become once more those two young innocents who had embraced each other with such eager passion inside the sheltering walls of the Weston nursery.

I won't think about the past, I told myself. Just for tonight I would forget Stephen's failures and think only that he was alive, and beside me, and that I loved him. I swayed a little and felt his arm go around my shoulders.

"Let's go downstairs, Annabelle," he said.

"Yes," I replied.

The house was perfectly silent as we went back down the stairs and let ourselves into my bedroom. The lamp was still burning on the bedside table, and moonlight was coming in through the open window. We neither of us needed help to get out of our clothes. I was going to get into the bed when Stephen stopped me, turned me around, and simply stood there, drinking me in with his eyes.

I had hated it when Gerald had looked at me like that. It had always made me feel as if he were admiring a possession.

Stephen, I knew, was looking at me.

"I thought about you all the time," he said in a shaken voice. "And the most amazing thing is—you're even more beautiful than I remembered."

"So are you," I said. And I meant it. Just looking at his body caused the heat to rise inside me. He bent his head to kiss me, and our naked bodies came together. I felt him pressed against me, hard as a spear, and a ripple of sensation fluttered through my loins. "Annabelle," he said, and his tongue came deeply into my mouth.

Another ripple of sensation spread through me, then another. He picked me up and laid me on the bed. He began to kiss my breasts.

The ripple turned into waves of intense feeling.

"I love you," he said. He kept on saying it while he continued to kiss me all over, and my heart began to race so swiftly that I thought it would jump right out of my body.

I said his name in a hoarse voice that didn't

sound like mine at all. I ran my fingers up and down his bare arms, stopping as I touched the familiar ridged scar above his right elbow that had been left by an arrow badly aimed by Jasper when Stephen was eleven.

His mouth came back to mine, and his kiss was so hard that it drove my head back into the pillow. I answered his urgency by opening myself so he could enter.

He surged into me, and little sobs of relief and anticipation caught in my throat. I could feel my internal tissues softening around the iron hardness that was Stephen, and I held tightly to his upper arms as I lifted my legs to take him even deeper inside.

He groaned.

His skin was hot and slippery with sweat. Inside, the core of me quivered and began to yield.

"Dear God," Stephen said. It sounded as if he were talking through clenched teeth. "Annabelle."

I believe I might have sobbed.

"Now?" he said, still in that clenched-sounding voice.

My fingers tightened their grip on his arms. "Yes," I said, and he began to drive into me with such intensity that he pushed me all the way up the bed until my head was pressed against the headboard and we could go no farther. I felt the final explosion beginning to roll through me, shooting out in all directions from the part of Stephen that was responsible for making all of this fierce pleasure. I cried out.

Stephen responded, his voice sounding hoarsely in my ear. He drove into me once more, and I felt his own passion explode within mine. We clung together in our extremity, helpless as leaves driven before the typhoon of our mutual desire. Very, very slowly, Stephen collapsed on top of me. I felt the heat of his body, the laboring of his breath, the heavy hammer strokes of his heart, and was violently, triumphantly happy.

I reached my arms around him and held him close, and we lay together, unmoving, for a long time. My mind was empty of everything except the knowledge that we were together.

Finally Stephen's heartbeat began to slow, and I heard him say, "I'm too heavy for you."

"You're not as light as you used to be," I agreed.

He rolled off me, then once more gathered me close, so that my cheek was pillowed on his shoulder. I sighed and noticed that a few strands of my hair were spread across his chest, looking very pale against his deeply tanned skin.

"Do you think you are going to stay brown forever?" I asked curiously. My lips brushed against the bare skin of his collarbone, and it tasted salty from sweat.

I could feel the laugh rumbling in his chest. "I expect the color will fade eventually," he said.

I was glad to hear this. I didn't like anything that reminded me of the years he had spent in Jamaica.

Stephen said, "Annabelle, do we really have to wait for six more months?"

I don't know what caused me to hesitate. After all, I had already made up my mind that I would marry him. "I... I don't know," I said with uncharacteristic indecision.

"You don't care the snap of your fingers for what people think," he said persuasively. "You know you don't."

I sat up. My loose hair streamed over my shoulders and breasts, giving me the illusion of modesty. "Stephen," I said abruptly, "why didn't you communicate with me before you left for Jamaica?"

He raised his brows, as if surprised by my question. He replied in a soft, reasonable voice, "Papa locked me in my room, and the following day he packed me off to Southampton to board a ship. You know that, Annabelle."

I knew it, and I also knew that he could have seen me if he had tried. At the very least, he could have gotten a message to me. I had not attempted to see him because I had not realized that he was to have only the one more night at home. But Stephen had known. He had known, and still he had not tried to communicate with me.

I looked down into the deep, familiar blue of his eyes. Desire looked back at me, and tenderness, and love.

How could you have done this to me?

I wanted to scream the words at him, but I knew he would give me no answer.

He reached up one hand and tangled it in my hair. "God in heaven," he said with suppressed violence. "I look at you, Annabelle, and I feel like a man who has been dying of thirst in the middle of the Sahara. All I want to do is drink, and drink and drink..."

He reached up with his other hand and began to caress my breast. The touch of his fingers was gentle, but I could feel the urgency he was trying to restrain.

"Good heavens, Stephen," I said faintly. "Don't you need some time to recuperate?"

"After five years of drought, I could do this all night," he assured me. "Easily."

I had sworn a solemn oath to myself that I would never ask him whether or not he had been with a woman while he was in Jamaica. If he had, I told myself, I didn't want to know about it.

Consequently I was horrified to hear my voice asking, "Are you telling me that you remained celibate for the entire five years that you were gone?"

His finger lightly teased my nipple. "Yes," he said in a preoccupied kind of voice. "I did."

I believed him. Under similar circumstances I would not have believed any other man in the world, but I believed Stephen. He didn't lie. Which, of course, was why I had been afraid to ask him that question in the first place.

"Why?" I demanded. "It couldn't have been loyalty to me—not after you had learned I was married to Gerald."

He ran his finger back and forth along the place where my breasts swelled out above my ribs, and the caress made me shiver.

"All of the white women were married, and the Negro women weren't free to make their own choices," he said. "I would never force myself on a woman who couldn't say no."

I couldn't imagine any woman wanting to say no to Stephen, but I felt curiously satisfied by his reply.

I smiled down at him, and my hair streamed all around us, enclosing us inside a lavender-scented tent. I bent my head and fluttered a row of tiny kisses along the line of his jaw. He turned his face and captured my mouth with his own. He ran his hand down my side to my hip, then across my right thigh to rest between my legs.

Desire shuddered through me.

He murmured into my mouth, "Let's do it again," and before I quite knew what was happening, he had rolled me over, pressed me flat back upon the bed, and was entering me once more.

My body closed around him, and the delicious pleasure began to build again.

"God," he said, "it feels so good."

I arched my back and my neck, lifting the lower part of my body toward him.

"I love you, Stephen," I said. Sensation sizzled through me, and I gasped out loud. His face was hard and concentrated.

"It's you and me," he said. "Just you and me, Annabelle."

"Always," I told him. "Always."

He didn't leave until an hour before dawn. "I don't know what I'm going to say to the chambermaid," I complained as he buttoned his shirt by the light of the lamp that we had never extinguished. "The state of this bed is suspicious, to say the least."

Stephen gave up trying to tuck in his shirt and just let it hang outside his trousers. He looked at me and said firmly, "It will be far less scandalous if we simply go ahead and get married, Annabelle."

It's you and me, Annabelle. Just you and me.

Once I had believed that to be true. If only I could believe it again!

"I'll think about it," I said.

He yawned so enormously that his eyes watered. "Do you think Giles would mind?"

I was sitting up in bed, watching him dress, and I answered, "I don't know, Stephen. Perhaps he would. Perhaps it would be wiser to wait."

A tear from the yawn was clinging to one of his long eyelashes. "I have to go into Brighton today to see Tom Clarkson, and when I get back we'll talk about it."

I folded my arms across my bare breasts. "We had plenty of opportunity to talk tonight."

He ran his fingers through his hair, pushing it away from his face, and the tear on his lash was dislodged. He said with a smile, "I had other things on my mind tonight."

My own voice held a distinct quaver. "Stephen, if you really think someone is trying to kill you, is it wise to go into Brighton?"

"I will be careful, Annabelle," he replied soothingly. "I promise." His hair had slipped back over his forehead, and the curve of his mouth as he looked at me was tender. But I knew my Stephen. Nothing I could say would keep him home.

"We'll talk after I come back from Brighton," he said. And with that promise I had to be content.

CHAPTER
twenty-one

When I saw Stephen at breakfast five hours after we had parted, I greeted him with the same degree of casual pleasantness with which I addressed Jasper and Nell. I proceeded to fill my plate, then took a seat and began to eat ravenously.

"You seem unusually hungry this morning," Stephen said from his place next to mine. I glanced at him and saw amusement in the faint narrowing of his eyes.

"I get a lot of exercise," I said, and his eyes narrowed a trifle more.

Jasper said, "I wonder where Jack is. He isn't in his room, because I looked in there before I came downstairs."

"He is in the nursery, having breakfast with Giles and Miss Stedham," Stephen said.

Damn, I thought. I had gone to check on Giles earlier, before the nursery breakfast was served, and at that time there had been no sign of Jack.

Jasper stared at Stephen. "And what were you doing in the nursery?"

"I just looked in to see Giles for a moment," Stephen replied. He stirred some cream into his coffee. "Being shot at is an unnerving experience."

"Yes," said Jasper, the Peninsula veteran. "I know."

I felt extremely encouraged by Jasper's obvious displeasure with Stephen. "My goodness," I said lightly, "Giles has become amazingly popular ever since he acquired such a beautiful governess."

Nell's eyes went immediately to Stephen, who was sipping his coffee calmly. I turned my own gaze on Jasper and found him looking grim.

I was delighted by this evidence that he was not indifferent to Miss Stedham's charms.

"I promised Giles and Miss Stedham that

they could accompany me on a ride to the Downs this morning," I said to Jasper. "Would you care to join us?"

Like magic, the harsh lines in Jasper's face transformed themselves into curves of pleasure. "I would enjoy that very much, Annabelle," he said.

"I'll join you, too, if I may," Stephen said.

Jasper's grim expression returned, and I had to repress a satisfied smile. My glee was short-lived, however, extinguished by Nell saying in an oddly hesitant voice, "I should enjoy a ride also, Annabelle, if you don't mind."

I shot her a quick look and found her stealing another glance at Stephen. "Of course I don't mind, Nell," I said pleasantly, but to myself I thought again, Damn.

It was beginning to look very much as if Aunt Fanny might be right about Nell having a *tendre* for Stephen. I turned to him and said, "You don't have time for a ride if you're going to the antislavery rally in Brighton today."

"I'm not leaving until noon. I have plenty of time for a ride this morning." His eyes met mine and he added gently, "It will be perfectly safe in so large a group, Annabelle."

I bit my lip.

"Safe?" Nell echoed in bewilderment.

I sighed. "Well, if you must come," I said to Stephen, "I have a horse I'd like you to ride."

Jasper put down his fork. "Which horse is that, Annabelle?"

I poured myself some more coffee and reached for the sugar bowl. It was empty. I turned my head and the footman stationed next to the sideboard came immediately and took away the bowl to refill it.

I answered Jasper, "One of the Thorough-breds I bought from Lord Carlton. His name is Magpie."

"An unusual name," Jasper murmured.

"Isn't Magpie the black horse with the white blaze, the one that threw the groom who was delivering him?" Nell asked.

"He is a trifle nervous," I conceded.

"A trifle nervous! I heard the groom talking to Grimes, Annabelle. That horse nearly put him under the wheels of a carriage three times!"

Nell was clearly upset by the thought of Stephen riding Magpie.

"He was probably afraid of the traffic on the road," Stephen said. "Thoroughbreds can be very skittish."

Jasper said, "Yes, but skittish horses do not make good hunters." He raised his eyebrows at me. "Why on earth did you buy such an animal, Annabelle?"

The footman returned the sugar bowl to the table. "Thank you, William," I said as I stirred a spoonful into my coffee. I looked at Jasper and explained, "Every once in a while I take a chance on a horse. This colt is extremely good-looking and extremely well bred."

"If he is such a wonderful horse, then why did Lord Carlton sell him?" Nell demanded.

I had to admit, "Because he is so skittish."

"He'll be fine," Stephen said, and got up to help himself to another plate of kippers.

Nell gave him a worried look.

Damn, I thought to myself once more.

An hour later, Jasper and I went down to the stables together.

"What did Stephen mean by being safe in a large group?" he asked me abruptly as we began to walk along the path that ran from the back door of the house directly to the stableyard half a mile away.

I couldn't see any reason for keeping my suspicions a secret from my cousin, so I replied, "It looks very much as if Stephen were shot at deliberately the other day, Jasper."

His long, purposeful stride faltered for a moment. "Nonsense." He looked down at me, his gray eyes hard. "Who could possibly want to shoot at Stephen?"

I told him everything Giles had told me about that walk in the woods. "Giles was convinced that the shooter had to know he was firing at a man and not an animal," I concluded.

"Good God," Jasper said. "If what you say is true, then we are not looking for a poacher, Annabelle. We are looking for a murderer!"

Murderer. The words sent shivers up and down my spine.

"I am sick with worry," I confessed.

We walked in silence for a few paces. Then Jasper said, "Do you think the shooting might have something to do with those smugglers Stephen got himself involved with all those years ago?"

"I have been wondering the very same thing myself!" I looked at him with gratitude, immensely relieved that someone besides me had thought of smugglers.

"They can be a pretty desperate lot, Annabelle," Jasper said gravely. "If they wanted Stephen out of their way, they wouldn't hesitate to shoot him. But why should they want Stephen out of their way?"

I said through lips that felt stiff with tension, "Jem Washburn is back in the valley, Jasper, and I know he was the one who got Stephen into all that trouble five years ago."

Jasper gave me a long, thoughtful stare. "But why would Jem want to harm Stephen? They were friends."

"I don't necessarily mean that Jem would want to shoot Stephen," I explained. "But with Jem's return, the smugglers may once again have started to use the path through the Ridge woods to transport illicit cargoes from the cove. I have been wondering if perhaps Stephen surprised someone who thought he was in danger of being caught in possession of the wrong goods."

Jasper's level brows now drew together in thought. I watched him, so intent upon his reaction that I neglected to watch the path. When I tripped over a branch, I lost my balance completely and would have fallen if Jasper had not grabbed me and held me up.

"Thank you," I gasped, grateful for his quickness. "I wasn't watching."

The arm that was holding me to his side was hard as steel. I tried to move away, but his arm didn't yield.

"I'm all right, Jasper," I assured him. "I shall have to tell the gardeners to be sure they clear this path. The storm seems to have brought down quite a few branches."

Very slowly his arm dropped away from me, and I stepped back. He bent, picked up the branch that had tripped me, and flung it into the surrounding trees.

We walked over the bridge in silence. Then I said, "I would appreciate it if you would keep a close eye on Stephen, Jasper. You know how careless he can be of his own safety."

Jasper kicked a stone off the path with his riding boot. Then he said carefully, "I must confess that this concern for Stephen rather surprises me, Annabelle. I was under the distinct impression that you and he had a falling-out before he left for Jamaica. Good God, during all those years that you maintained such a faithful correspondence with me, you never once even mentioned his name!"

Jasper's words took me by surprise. "It is true that I was… somewhat annoyed… with Stephen for getting himself packed off to Jamaica like that," I said at last. "But I certainly don't want anything to happen to him!"

"I see," Jasper replied quietly.

We had reached the stableyard by now, and my eyes ran over the people standing grouped in front of the big stable doors. Everyone was there whom I had expected to be there: Giles, Miss Stedham, Nell, and Stephen. My eyes stopped at the one face I had not expected to see. Jack.

The look I gave him was not welcoming.

"Anything wrong, Annabelle?" he asked amiably.

I could hardly blurt out that I suspected him of trying to seduce my son's governess. "Of course not," I snapped.

"Where are the dogs, Mama?" Giles asked.

At that moment one of the grooms came out of the stable, leading Magpie. Jack's eyebrows shot up. "You're not going to ride that Bedlamite up to the Downs, are you?" he said to me.

"No," I replied. "Stephen is." I turned to Giles and said, "I left the dogs home because I didn't want them to startle this horse, Giles."

"He is beautiful, Mama," Giles said with awe.

"Aye, that he is, my lord," Grimes said with an approving smile at my son.

We all fell into the reverent silence that the sight of Magpie always commanded.

He was an extraordinarily beautiful animal, a quintessential Thoroughbred, with long, slim, elegant legs that were perfectly formed and totally unblemished. His coat shone like ebony in the late summer sun, and his long, chiseled head had a perfect white blaze set dead in its center. He was stunning, but he really did not have enough bone to be a hunter.

"He's beautiful, but he looks nervous," Nell said.

As if to prove her right, Magpie snorted and threw his elegant head up and down.

"How old is he?" Stephen asked.

"Four," I replied.

Magpie pawed the ground with his right fore.

"He certainly looks as if he would be fast," Jasper said.

"Lord Carlton told me he could run like the wind," I replied cheerfully.

"Then why isn't he racing?" Jasper asked.

"The first race they put him in, he tossed his jockey, jumped the fence, and was loose on Newmarket Heath for hours," I said. "He did the same thing in his second and third races. He's fast enough to win everything, but he just won't stay on the track. Lord Carlton was happy to sell him to me before he hurt himself and became worthless."

"They probably jiggled his mouth," Stephen said.

I looked at the large number of people assembled around me and had second thoughts about the wisdom of taking Magpie.

"Perhaps it would be wiser to wait until it is just the two of us before you try him," I said to Stephen.

"He'll be fine," Stephen said again. He walked quietly up to Magpie and offered him a piece of carrot. Magpie's ears flicked back and forth when Stephen got into the saddle, but he stood fairly quietly while the rest of us mounted. The seven horses and riders moved out of the stableyard in an orderly procession.

When they are in a group, horses have a definite preference for being in the front or being behind. Magpie was one of those who liked to be in front, so Stephen and Nell led the way. Nell was riding one of my semiretired old hunters, and I knew I could count on Sentry to remain placid no matter what foolishness Magpie might get up to.

Magpie went like a lamb. There were perhaps half a dozen times when it looked as if he might startle and run, but Stephen always managed to reassure him before the event actually occurred.

If you are an intuitive enough rider, you can feel when a horse is about to be frightened. It's like a lightning flash interrupting the flow of communication through the reins. That's when you have to hold things together, before the horse himself realizes he's going to do something foolish.

Needless to say, there are not many riders who are capable of such sensitivity that they can catch the horse's flight signal in time to prevent it from activating. I can truthfully say that I myself knew of only four such horsemen, and I have ridden with the best that England has to offer.

"Magpie is being so good for Uncle Stephen!" Giles said with amazement.

I looked down at the small figure on the pony beside me. "Uncle Stephen can ride anything," I said.

"He doesn't ride as good as you, Mama," said my faithful son.

Jack's voice floated forward from behind us, where he was riding beside Miss Stedham. "No one can ride to hounds better than your mother, Giles. Absolutely no one."

Giles turned his head and said over his shoulder, "Not even Uncle Stephen?"

Jack said, "Uncle Stephen doesn't like to ride to hounds."

"Uncle Stephen doesn't like to hunt?" Giles's raised voice was clearly horrified.

I saw Stephen's head begin to turn.

"Not a word, Stephen," I warned loudly.

He looked at me and then he looked at Giles. "I'd fall off at the first fence," he said to his son, and then he turned back to Nell.

I let out my breath. The last thing I needed at the moment was one of Stephen's heart-wrenching dissertations on the fate of the poor fox.

We all had a good long gallop along the Downs, and Magpie behaved almost as placidly as Sentry on the walk home. I felt beautifully content as I watched Stephen's relaxed, easily following back in front of me and listened to Jasper and Giles talking across me. The sun shone through the overhanging trees and made designs of light and shadow on the soft dirt of the ride. For the first time I could smell a trace of autumn in the air. I noticed Magpie's black coat was wet with the normal sweat of exercise, not lathered with nervous foam.

It was then that I realized why I had bought the beautiful Thoroughbred. I had bought him for Stephen.

Stephen returned to the house only long enough to have a quick bowl of soup before the curricle was brought around to the front door for his trip into Brighton. I didn't want him to go because I was terrified that something might happen to him, but I knew nothing I could say would ever keep Stephen from what he perceived to be his duty. As soon as his carriage had disappeared down the drive, I excused myself from luncheon and went to lie down on my bed with a headache.

Marianne brought me cold cloths to put on my forehead, and I lay perfectly still for the rest of the afternoon, enduring the pounding in my skull and thinking gloomy thoughts about the tangle of romantic emotions that seemed to have invaded my household.

The worst of the headache passed in a few hours, but I sent a message to Aunt Fanny that I didn't feel well enough to eat dinner. Instead I went along to the nursery to share a light supper with Giles and his governess.

For once we were without Jack, who was in the dining room, enjoying one of Cook's delicious dinners. The main meal in the nursery was served at midday, and tonight's supper consisted of a semiwarm soup made from summer vegetables, cold roast beef, and bread.

In all my life I had never once had a hot meal in the Weston nursery. No matter how hot a dish might be when it left the kitchen, by the time it reached the third floor it was invariably lukewarm.

I sat at the old wooden table, with a bowl of vegetable soup in front of me, and regarded Miss Stedham with concern. I didn't like what I saw. She had the glow of a woman in love.

We talked about topics that Giles could understand: the horses we had ridden; the beauty of the Downs; the possibility of Giles being old enough to have one of Portia's puppies the next time I bred her.

When supper was finished and the dishes had been cleared away, I told Giles to take the dogs down to the kitchen for their supper. While he was gone, Miss Stedham and I sat across from each other at the scarred old table and talked.

I began as soon as the noise made by Giles and the spaniels had died away. "Eugenia," I said. "I hope you don't mind if I call you by your given name?"

"Of course I don't mind, Lady Weston," she replied.

"Please, won't you call me Annabelle? I have known you long enough now to know that I should like to be your friend as well as your employer. It would make me very happy to hear that you felt the same way about me."

"Why... thank you, Lady Weston," Eugenia said with obvious surprise.

"Annabelle," I corrected firmly.

She gave me an amazed look. "Well... if you desire it..."

"I do," I said. "If I have perhaps seemed a little... distant... to you, it was only because I'm not the sort of person who makes friends easily." I searched for words that would explain my caution. "I have to know people a long time before I feel perfectly comfortable with them," I finally said.

"I understand," she returned in a gentle voice. "Great beauty can often be as much a burden as it is a blessing, can it not?"

I stared at her, astonished by her perception. "Not many people understand that," I said at last. "Of course, you are very beautiful yourself."

"Thank you." She smiled faintly. "But my face is not the kind to launch a thousand ships. There is a difference."

We looked at each other in silence. The lines Marlowe had written about Helen of Troy rang in my brain: *Was this the face that launched a thousand ships / And burnt the topless towers of Ilium?*

I bit my lip in indecision, and then I told her something I had never told anyone else— not even Stephen. "I have this test I apply to people. I think: If I had smallpox, and my face became scarred, would this person's feelings toward me change?"

Eugenia said, still in that softly gentle voice, "And that is how you select your friends?"

"Yes. For example, I know that no matter what I looked like, Sir Matthew would still want to hunt with me, and Susan Fenton would still want to gossip with me, and..." I let my voice trail away. "Do you see what I mean?"

What I hadn't said was, "And Stephen would still love me." I kept that thought to myself.

"I see," she said. "And I have passed the test?"

I smiled at her. "Have you?"

"Yes, Annabelle," she said. "I believe I have."

I took a deep breath and said resolutely, "I am afraid you are not going to like what I have to say, Eugenia, but try to believe that I am speaking now as a friend and not as an employer."

Her face became instantly grave and faintly wary. "Yes?"

"I am extremely concerned by the attention my cousin Jack is paying to you," I said.

"Ah," she said, and her face closed completely.

"I distrust his intentions," I said.

Her beautiful, winged brows lifted slightly. "Oh?"

"Eugenia, I am afraid he is going to seduce you, which is just about the last thing you need right now, I should imagine."

She said in a tight little voice, "Is it so impossible to imagine that his intentions might be honorable?"

My reply was blunt. "Jack is impoverished, Eugenia. He needs a wife with money."

"I know he has no money. He told me that himself."

"Well then..." I spread my hands flat upon the table in front of me. "You see why I am concerned?"

"I can assure you, Lady Weston, that I have no intention of allowing myself to be seduced by Mr. Jack Grandville."

I said mournfully, "I see I've regressed to being Lady Weston again."

She didn't smile.

"You don't know what you look like when you're with him," I said. "You glow."

She bit her lip.

"It's a dangerous look," I said. "A woman who looks like that is capable of doing all kinds of foolish things."

"Are you saying that I look the way you look when you are with Mr. Stephen Grandville?" Eugenia asked politely.

I felt my lips twist into a wry smile. "Is it that obvious?" I asked.

"It is to me."

"Then you should know that I know what I am talking about," I said.

She looked a little bewildered by my syntax.

"I have done all kinds of foolish things in my time," I clarified. "I wouldn't recommend that you follow my example."

Eugenia didn't look at me but studiously traced a long scar in the tabletop with her forefinger. "What do you recommend for me, Annabelle?"

"You need a husband," I said frankly, "and Jack isn't going to come up to scratch."

"He wants to marry me," Eugenia said. Her eyes were still on the tabletop, and her face had gone very pale. "If he had a regular income, he would marry me."

"Has he said that?" I demanded.

"Yes."

"And you believe him?"

She looked up and met my eyes. "Yes, I do."

Her large brown eyes did not waver. I thought

306

that perhaps Jack *was* more serious than I had thought him to be.

"What about Jasper?" I asked. "He has a decent income, and if you made an effort, I think you could attach him."

"Oh, Annabelle," she said with a smile. "Jasper is in love with *you*."

I frowned. "Nonsense. Jasper and I have been friends forever. You have mistaken the nature of his affection."

"No, I have not."

Her words upset me. "You are mistaken," I repeated. "You must be."

"It is as clear as glass to everyone but you," she said. "Jack told me all about it. He said they were all in love with you when you were young, he and Jasper and Gerald, but that you never had a thought for anyone but Stephen. He said he didn't think that it had ever occurred to you that the rest of them were flesh and blood."

I stared at her, appalled. "I married Gerald," I said finally.

"And were you happy?" she asked.

We gazed into each other's eyes, two women who had quite suddenly and unexpectedly opened their hearts to each other. "No," I said. "I was not."

"Nor would I be happy, married to anyone but Jack. I love him. And what is more, I would be good for him."

I exhaled a long, carefully controlled breath and said in a steady voice, "Then we shall just have to find Jack some sort of regular income."

"I live in fear that he will try to win a stake at the gambling table," Eugenia confessed. "The

307

likelihood is far greater that he will lose Rudely altogether, and that would break him."

The scratching made by dog nails on the uncarpeted passage floor came distinctly to our ears, and then we heard the pounding of Giles's boots. A second later, boy and dogs erupted into the schoolroom.

"Merlin and Portia ate their supper, Mama!" he shouted. "And Cook gave me a piece of pie!"

"I am in the same room as you, Giles," I pointed out kindly. "There is no need to shout at me."

He moderated his voice. "I'm sorry, Mama. Will you play a game of spillikens with me?"

"I suppose so, darling," I said. "Why don't you set them out?"

Spillikens with Giles would help to keep at bay the terrible thought that had popped into my brain with Eugenia's confession.

Was Jack's love for Eugenia desperate enough to force him to resort to murder in order to attain the means he needed to marry her?

Surely not, I told myself as I watched Giles returning to the table with his hands full of small wooden counters. Surely Jack wouldn't want to be the next earl of Weston at such a terrible cost!

"Ready, Mama?" Giles asked.

I forced myself to focus on the game. "Ready, darling," I said, and we began to play.

CHAPTER
twenty-two

At twelve o'clock, when Stephen still had not returned to Weston, I gave up waiting for him and went to bed. I slept restlessly, my mind filled with terrible fears and suspicions, and I woke with a start to the sound of someone knocking imperatively on my bedroom door. I just caught myself in time from calling, "Stephen?" and substituted instead a weak, "Come in."

My son came catapulting into my bedroom. "Good morning, Mama!"

The dogs in the dressing room next door heard his voice and began to bark that they, too, wanted entrance into the inner sanctum. Giles went to open the connecting door, and Merlin and Portia thundered into the bedroom, woofing noisily. I sat up and stuffed a pillow behind my back.

"Good heavens, Giles," I yawned. "What are you doing out of the nursery?"

"Genie said I could have a holiday this morning, and we're going for a ride," he said. "I came to invite you to come with us, Mama." He gave me his most winning smile.

"Thank you, but I don't think I will, darling."

His face fell ludicrously. "Why not?"

I wanted to wait at the house to make certain that Stephen returned home safely, but I could hardly say that to Giles. "I just don't feel like it this morning," I said.

Giles hooted in disbelief. He clambered onto the bed and stared commandingly into my eyes. "You always feel like going for a ride, Mama."

I pushed my long braid off my shoulder. "Well, I don't this morning."

His forehead puckered. "Do you have a headache?"

"No." Then a nasty thought struck me. "Is anyone going with you and Genie?"

"Jack is going with us," Giles said.

"I'll come," I said.

Giles beamed at me. "I knew you'd want to come, Mama! I'll tell Genie and Jack to wait for you at the stable." He jumped off my bed. "It's no fun just going with the two of them," he confided. "They talk to each other all the time and not to me!" He headed for the door.

I supposed I should be happy that my son found Jack boring and not frightening.

I called after him, "Take the dogs with you, Giles, and tell one of the footmen to let them out."

"Yes, Mama." Giles called the dogs' names and the spaniels trotted after him, ready for their regular morning visit to the shrubbery.

Marianne helped me to get dressed, and she brushed my hair and replaited it as I drank a cup of coffee. I walked down to the stables with the dogs at my heels and found Jack and Eugenia and Giles standing horseless in the stableyard while Grimes talked to them. The head groom had a thunderous expression on his face, and I immediately wondered what catastrophe could have struck the stable overnight. As I approached, a groom came out from behind the carriage house leading Marlborough, one of my new hunters. His bright chestnut coat was patched with mud all down his right side. Grimes stopped the groom and ran an expert hand carefully down each of the horse's four slender legs.

"Seems fine," he grunted. "That's the last of 'em, then. Get him rubbed down and give him a bran mash."

The groom moved toward the stable, and I said sharply, "What on earth is going on here, Grimes?"

Giles opened his mouth as if he would answer, shot one quick glance at Grimes, then closed it again.

With great deliberation Grimes said, "You may well ask, Miss Annabelle."

I realized with relief that he was only put out and that none of the horses had been hurt. "What has happened?" I said in a more equable tone.

"His Lordship's pony escaped from his box this mornin'," Grimes said. He paused ominously.

"Cracker escaped?" My own voice was mild.

"Yes." Grimes folded his arms across his chest.

"That was very bad of him," I said.

Grimes gave me a jaundiced look. "Not bein' happy with just the one success, didn't Cracker set about openin' the boxes of all the rest of the horses on his side of the stable?"

My mouth dropped open. "He didn't!"

"He did, Mama," Giles said. His eyes were sparkling.

"The boxes' outside doors?" I asked Grimes.

"The boxes' outside doors, Miss Annabelle," came the grim reply.

All of the horse boxes had outside double doors that opened directly into the stableyard as well as the inside door that opened into the center aisle of the stable. In the summer, the top part of the outside door was always left open. If the pony had opened the latches that closed the bottom doors, all of the horses would have been able to walk out of their stalls into the freedom of the yard.

I glanced at the big wooden gate that at night was always swung closed across the arched entrance into the stableyard. "They couldn't have got far, Grimes. Wasn't the gate closed?"

Grimes said in an awful voice, "It was closed, Miss Annabelle, but Georgie forgot to latch it."

From the look on Grimes's face, things did not bode well for Georgie's future.

"The horses got out through the gate?" I asked.

"They got out." He relented enough to give me the good news. "We've got 'em all back, though, and it don't seem as if any of 'em took hurt."

"Well," I said. I glanced at Jack and Eugenia, but their faces were carefully expressionless. "Better do something about securing that pony more carefully, Grimes."

"Never you worry. I shall put him under lock and key, Miss Annabelle," Grimes assured me with awful calm.

As if on cue, a groom came out of the stable leading a bridled and saddled Cracker.

"You bad boy!" Giles said, and went up to pet his pony's neck.

Cracker rolled his eyes in the direction of Grimes, and I had to bite my lip to keep from laughing.

"He was in the rose garden, Annabelle, when they caught up with him," Jack said.

"You can smell them on his breath," Grimes said sternly.

I turned aside to cough.

The clicking sound of shod feet rang in the stableyard as three grooms brought out three horses for Jack and Eugenia and me to ride. I let Grimes give me a leg up onto Elf.

"Don't murder Georgie," I said to him as he stepped back from the mare. "Think of how difficult it will be for me to explain his demise to his mother."

"I'm not promising nothin'," Grimes replied with an awful frown.

Jack said, "Ready, Annabelle?"

I nodded and asked Elf to go forward. Giles brought Cracker up to my side, the dogs trotted in front of us, and Jack and Eugenia fell in behind.

We rode in silence until we were safely out of earshot of the stableyard. Then Giles said in a gleeful voice, "Mama, isn't Cracker *clever*?"

Jack said, "Can't you just picture that busy little pony going up and down the row of boxes, nosing back all the latches?"

We all started to laugh at the same time.

Cracker walked sedately along, looking like an angel.

I wiped my eyes when we reached the main drive and said to Jack, "Where were you planning to ride?"

"I thought we'd do the lake," he said, and I nodded and turned Elf in the proper direction.

When we reached the northern side of the lake, Giles thought he saw an unusual bird and we all dismounted and Eugenia went with him down to the shore to look for it. Jack and I sat side by side on a fallen tree trunk that flanked the ride, each of us holding two sets of horses' reins as we watched Giles and Eugenia make

313

their way through the undergrowth down to the shore of the lake.

When Jack finally spoke his voice was abrupt. "Eugenia told me she spoke to you about us."

I glanced at him out of the side of my eyes. "Yes. She did."

Jack's profile looked hard and bleak against the blue of the sky. "I realize you must think I have a nerve making up to a girl like Eugenia," he said. "I have nothing to offer her, I know that. I just want you to know that my intentions, laughable as they may be, are purely honorable."

I rubbed my gloved right thumb back and forth across Elf's leather rein. Giles looked back, saw me watching him, and waved. Eugenia looked around also and smiled.

"She really loves you, Jack," I said. "Do you really love her?"

"Yes." He paused, then added in a very different kind of voice, "I love her most damnably, Annabelle."

Eugenia and Giles had reached the place where Giles had thought he saw the bird. Jack and I sat in silence, our eyes on the governess's slender back and uncovered auburn hair. She was saying something to Giles, then they both sat on a rock and remained perfectly still.

"I hate to see her living this kind of life," Jack said fiercely. "It's not that you aren't good to her, Annabelle, but she should not be anyone's employee! She should have a house and children of her own!"

I turned a little so that I could watch him. "In order to have those things she needs a husband," I said. "And since she has informed me that the only husband she will accept is you,

Jack, I have come to the conclusion that we must find some way for you to be able to afford to marry her."

His mouth was set in a hard, straight line. "Do you deal in miracles, my dear Annabelle?"

"No, I deal in horses," I said, "and lately I have been thinking of expanding my business. You could help me with that if you wanted to."

Jack's fingers must have closed suddenly on the reins he was holding, because Sentry looked up inquiringly from the leaf he was eating. Jack said curtly, "What do you mean, Annabelle? Do you want me to school hunters for you full-time?"

I said, "No, I have something else in mind." I frowned a little, considering how best to broach my idea. Finally I said, "Have you ever thought, Jack, that no one actually breeds hunters in order to sell them?"

Out of the corner of my eye I saw his head turn, and he looked at me for the first time since we had begun this conversation. "What do you mean?"

I returned his gaze. "I mean that all of the big stud farms are devoted to breeding racing Thoroughbreds, yet many more people buy horses to hunt than buy horses to race."

Jack grunted. He was listening to me intently.

"I have built up a nice little business out of retraining Thoroughbred racehorses to hunt," I continued, "but lately I have been wondering if one might do even better by setting up a stud which had as its specific purpose the breeding of horses for hunting."

Jack's eyes were burning like light blue crystals in his hard, concentrated face. "A stud to breed hunters," he said slowly, almost reverently.

315

I nodded. "Most of the Thoroughbreds I look at aren't suitable to hunt. I have to shop very carefully to find ones with the proper size and disposition."

"You'd want to breed Thoroughbred crosses," Jack said. "Aim for foals that combine the speed and agility of the Thoroughbred with the bone and temperament of, let's say, the Irish horse."

I nodded again.

"It's a brilliant idea, Annabelle!" Jack said.

I smiled at his enthusiasm. "I think it has merit. I can't begin to supply the market that wants my retrained horses. If hunting people had good young stock available to them, I think they would buy, and what is more, I think they would pay a good price."

"I know they would," Jack said. His burning, crystallike gaze searched my face. "Are you implying that you will pay me to help you start such a stud?"

"No." I shook my head definitely. "What I want to do is advance you the money so that you can start it all by yourself."

The color drained from Jack's face. "You can't do that," he said thickly.

I mimed surprise. "I thought you just said you thought it was a brilliant idea!"

He shook his head as if to clear it. "I meant you can't advance me that kind of money."

I lifted my brows in an even more exaggerated gesture of surprise. "Why ever not?"

Jack said, "Well, for one thing, neither Adam nor Stephen will countenance your risking Giles's money on such a scheme." Two spots of hectic color had appeared on both of his cheekbones. "And they will be right, Annabelle."

"Neither Adam nor Stephen has anything to say about what I do with my own money," I replied. "I'll have you know that over the last few years I have made quite a tidy little profit from my hunters, and I propose to invest it in you."

The color in his cheeks was now a bright, burning red. "I can't let you do that."

I leaned toward him, willing him to believe me. "Why not? I promise you that I won't miss the money."

A muscle twitched in the corner of his mouth. "I can't take that kind of money from you, Annabelle," he said.

I looked at Elf, who was standing in front of me so patiently, waiting for me to decide to get back on her again, and tried to think of what I might say to overcome Jack's scruples.

"I would consider the advance to you an investment, Jack. I don't need the capital at the moment. In fact..." I hesitated, then decided to be frank. "I shall probably be getting married again one of these days, and I simply will not have the time to get into a new business. Nor will money ever be a problem for me, so you needn't worry that you'll be taking her sustenance from a poor widow. I shall be well provided for, believe me. Even if the hunter scheme fails, I won't be losing anything I can't well afford to do without."

There was a long silence.

"Stephen did receive a nice inheritance from his mother," Jack said.

I shot him a look out of the side of my eyes and didn't reply.

"I won't fail, Annabelle," Jack said.

I turned back to him and smiled. "I don't think you will, either." A leaf fluttered down from the sky and landed on the lap of my riding skirt. I picked it up and said, "Do you have enough room at Rudely to start a small stud?"

"I think so. The present stable will have to be enlarged, but that can be done easily enough. I haven't got the paddocks that you have here at Weston, of course, but they can be built, too."

The prospect of my marrying an extremely solvent Stephen had evidently relieved Jack of his scruples about taking my money.

I said, "Later, if you become a big success, you might have to buy a larger property, but it will be best for now if you can keep your costs as low as possible."

He laughed unsteadily. "Hold up, Annabelle! I have a long way to go before you can start talking about larger properties!"

"I will give you Aladdin to start your breeding program," I said. "Magpie is too slender to sire hunters, and besides, I want Magpie for Stephen."

Jack's breath caught and his eyes glittered brilliantly. I grinned at him. He was mad for Aladdin.

Giles and Eugenia had turned away from the lake and were beginning to come toward us.

"I don't know what to say to you, Annabelle," Jack said, speaking with obvious difficulty. "I don't know how to thank you."

I shook my head. "We're family, Jack. There is no need for you to say anything."

"I shall pay you back with interest," he said fiercely.

"That would be nice," I replied.

Giles and Eugenia arrived back at our log, and Jack stood up. "We couldn't find it, Mama," Giles reported.

Eugenia's eyes flicked from Jack to me and then back again to Jack. Obviously she saw from his face that something had happened between us. He gave her a quick grin, and her expression lightened.

My own heart felt lighter than it had in a while as I put my toe in the stirrup and swung up into my sidesaddle. I was relieved to have the problem of Jack's future resolved. I did care about him, and that feeling of affection had certainly been my main motive in helping him.

I tried not to think too overtly about my second motive.

Now that Jack knew he could make a future for himself, I wondered if the strange accidents that kept befalling Stephen and Giles would cease.

We had a delightful ride back to Weston. Jack had been the first one down to the stable this morning, and he gave us a hilariously funny description of the havoc Cracker had created with his escape maneuvers.

We arrived back in the stableyard to find it in a different kind of uproar. I watched a lathered Magpie being led into the stable and scowled down at Grimes, who had come trotting over to stand next to me.

"I thought you said you had caught all of the horses, Grimes," I said angrily. "Why is Magpie lathered like that?"

"Mr. Stephen came home not fifteen minutes after you'd left for your ride, Miss Annabelle, and he decided he'd try to catch up

319

with you. He rode after you on Magpie, and Magpie has just come back to the stableyard with his saddle under his belly and without a rider!"

CHAPTER
twenty-three

I could feel the color draining away from my face and my heart beginning to race with fear.

"Have you sent men out to look for Stephen?" I said to Grimes. My mouth was suddenly so dry that I had a difficult time getting the words out.

"I was just about t'do that, Miss Annabelle."

I tried to force my brain to work, though I felt almost paralyzed with terror. "He said he was going to look for us?"

"That is what he said, Miss Annabelle."

"Did you tell him we were going to the lake?"

Grimes shook his head. "You didn't say where you was going, Miss Annabelle. Mr. Stephen said he would look for you first on the Downs."

"All right," I said, beginning to turn Elf around. "I'll ride back that way immediately."

"I'll come with you, Annabelle," Jack offered. "You may need help if you find him and he's hurt."

"Do you want to take the dogs, Annabelle?" Eugenia asked calmly.

"Not yet," I said. "Go with Giles," I commanded the two spaniels.

Giles had dismounted, and now he came to kneel beside Portia and put his arms around her. "It's all right, Mama," he said. "They'll stay."

I nodded and urged Elf forward. She laid back her ears and dug in her heels, excessively put out that she was not going to be escorted into her nice box and given a rubdown and some hay. I smacked my long whip briskly against her side in the exact spot where my leg would be if I were riding astride, and she leaped forward. I rarely use my crop, but when I do my horses know I mean business.

As soon as I was clear of the stableyard I pushed Elf into full gallop. I knew Stephen was not on this particular section of ride because we had only just returned this way ourselves.

Jack was riding Topper, and he moved up alongside me and the two of us galloped all the way to the main drive. At the drive we picked up a different bridle path from the one we had taken to the lake, and Jack suggested we slow our horses to a trot.

"If he's gotten off the road and under the trees, we might miss him if we're going too fast," he said.

I knew that he was right, and even though my whole being wanted to gallop as fast as I could, I forced myself to slow down and search the right side of the path just as Jack was searching the left.

We reached the end of Weston Park, and still there was no sign of Stephen. In grim silence, Jack and I turned onto the public track that would take us up to the Downs. The dirt track led through woods for another mile or so before it reached the open turf of the Downs, and we had not gone above a quarter of a mile before we saw a horse approaching, led by two men on foot.

One of the men was shirtless and was obviously supporting the other man as they walked haltingly along.

The injured man was Stephen.

The relief that rocked through me when I saw him walking was so intense that it made me momentarily dizzy. It was only then that I realized I had been braced for the sight of his lifeless body stretched across the path.

The two men halted and waited as Jack and I trotted up to them. I didn't even glance at the second man until I was swinging down from the saddle.

It was Jem Washburn.

"*You!*" I said with loathing.

"Don't, Annabelle," Stephen said. "I don't know what I would have done if Jem hadn't come along when he did."

His voice sounded strangely thick and unsteady. His hair was hanging down, curtaining his forehead, and there was dirt on his right cheek and his chin.

"He hit his head," Jem said to Jack. "He was dead out in the midst of the road when I got to him. I stopped the blood best I could do it with my shirt whilst I waited for him to wake up."

By this time I was standing directly in front of Stephen, scanning his face intently.

"I'm all right," he said to me in that alarmingly thickened voice.

"You don't sound all right," I said. I pushed back the hanging curtain of hair with gentle fingers. The bullet graze wound on his temple had been beginning to scab over nicely, but it had been reopened by the fall and a nasty-looking bruise was forming all around it. The blood from the graze wound was minimal; certainly it was not enough to account for the blood that had soaked Stephen's hairline.

I felt Jack come up behind me. "What happened, Stephen?" he asked.

Stephen blinked twice and then looked over my shoulder in the direction of Jack. He was white as a ghost, and his eyes did not seem to be focusing properly. "Must've come off of Magpie," he said.

"That's what musta happened," Jem agreed. "I was coming along the opposite way when I heared the horse squealing and plunging. Then he come tearin' past me without a rider. Well, a booby woulda known somebody was in trouble, wouldn't he? So I gallop on up the road and find Stephen lyin' there like he was dead. By my reckonin', he was out for almost fifteen minutes. We just now begun to walk back."

"Why didn't you put him up on your horse?" I asked Jem angrily. "He's obviously in no condition to walk."

"Couldn't make it into the saddle," Stephen said. "My legs feel like rubber."

"I was feared he'd fall off t'other side and smack his head again, wasn't I?" Jem said, once more addressing himself to Jack.

"I think that between us we can probably put him up on Topper," Jack said. "Annabelle, you stand at Topper's head and Jem and I will get Stephen up."

It frightened me to see how wobbly Stephen was. Jack gave him a leg up, but if Jem had not done it for him, he would not have been able to throw his other leg over Topper's back.

"Can you hold yourself in the saddle, Stephen?" Jack said sharply.

"Yes," Stephen said. His face had gone from white to gray.

I said to Jack, "I'll lead Topper, and you and Jem walk on either side of Stephen in case he needs help."

The walk back through Weston Park seemed endless. Jack, who was walking beside Stephen and leading Elf, spoke only once, asking Jem if he had any idea of what might have startled Magpie.

"No," Jem answered briefly from Stephen's other side, where he was leading his own horse. "I didn't see nothing."

We were halfway home when we ran into Adam, who was also out looking for Stephen.

He looked relieved when he saw Stephen sitting on Topper.

"Ride back to the house and send for the doctor, Uncle Adam," I said. "Stephen hit his head and he most probably has a concussion."

Without another word, Adam turned and galloped back along the path in the direction from which he had come.

We brought Topper right to the back doorway of the house, and Jack and Jem made a seat with their hands and carried Stephen in through the door and up the stairs to his room. Aunt Fanny had come running as soon as she heard us.

"I have warm water waiting up in Stephen's room, Annabelle," she told me.

"We'll need ice, too," I said, and ordered one of the footmen to go to the kitchen and fetch some chipped ice.

Aunt Fanny followed the men upstairs, and I turned to Adam, who was hovering in the hallway, looking upset. "Did you send for the doctor?"

"Yes. Jasper rode to get him, Annabelle," Adam replied.

"Good," I said, and began to turn away to follow Aunt Fanny.

"Dear God, Annabelle," Adam said. "This is the second blow to his head that Stephen has sustained within the week!"

I knew that, of course, and I was terrified. I had seen head injuries before—anyone who hunts regularly has—and I knew how serious they could be.

I couldn't answer Adam; I simply nodded and ran up the stairs.

Inside Stephen's room I found him sitting in the same chair where he had had his last injury attended to, with Jem engaged in pulling off his boots. Aunt Fanny was standing next to him with a bowl of water in her hands, obviously waiting for her chance to get at the new wound.

Stephen's eyes met mine. His were so dilated that there was scarcely any blue showing, and the skin around the sockets looked bruised. I forced myself to smile. "There seems to be a conspiracy abroad to scramble your brains, Stephen," I said as I crossed the room to him.

"That's true," he replied. He sounded as if he were drunk.

Jem stood up with Stephen's two boots and went to put them against the wall. Aunt Fanny moved in with her bowl and her towel and began to explore the top of his head for the source of all the blood. I went to stand on Stephen's other side and gently tilted his head until my breast was supporting it.

"You're likely gonna need to shave some of his hair to get at that injury," Jem said. "There was a good-size branch lyin' crost the road right next to his head."

I felt a faint flicker of relief. A branch was not as bad as a rock.

I looked at Jem over the dark, bloodstained head I was cradling against my breast. No one had thought to offer him a shirt, and his well-muscled torso looked almost as brown as Stephen's in the light from the window. He was looking at Stephen with an extremely worried look in his deep-set eyes. "Do you remember what happened, Stephen?" he asked gruffly.

Stephen's head moved restlessly on my breast. "I remember hearing a sound in the woods, like a puppy crying," he said. "I got off, tied Magpie, and went to investigate. I didn't find anything. I remember getting back to Magpie and untying him, and after that I don't remember anything at all." Once more his head moved fretfully.

"It's all right," I said softly, and heedless of the watching eyes, I bent my head and touched my lips to his ear. "If you can't remember, don't worry about it."

"You gentlemen may leave now," Aunt Fanny said pleasantly.

"All right, we'll get out of your way," Jack replied. "Come along, Jem, and I'll lend you a shirt. All the local lasses will swoon if we allow them to catch a glimpse of those manly muscles."

The two men started for the door, and Aunt Fanny put down her bloodstained bowl and towel and picked up a pair of small embroidery scissors. Jem turned in the doorway and said abruptly, "Stephen, do you remember loosenin' your horse's girth afore you went lookin' for that puppy?"

"No," Stephen said. "I don't remember doing that."

Jem's lips folded together in a thin line. He turned to follow Jack out of the door, and Stephen lifted his head and called after him, "Why, Jem? Was Magpie's girth loose?"

"Will you please remain still, Stephen?" Aunt Fanny said sternly. "I don't want to stab you with these scissors."

I nodded to Jem to go and answered Stephen myself as I guided his head back to where it should be. "He came racing into the stableyard with the saddle hanging under his belly. Apparently the girth was too loose. The saddle must have slipped as you got on and panicked Magpie into a fit of bucking to try to get rid of it."

"I don't remember loosening the girth," Stephen said. "But perhaps I did."

I didn't think so. It was not something one would ordinarily do if one was planning to remount immediately. But I didn't want to worry him just now, so I said, "Perhaps."

By now Aunt Fanny had exposed the wound on Stephen's scalp. It had certainly bled a lot, but it didn't look too serious. What was serious, however, was the bruise on his temple and the evident shock his brain had suffered as the result of receiving two blows in such a short period of time.

Aunt Fanny and I decided to leave the wound unbandaged until the doctor arrived. The ice came up from the kitchen, and I wrapped it in a towel and applied it to Stephen's temple. He winced uncontrollably when I touched the sore area.

"Cold is good for the swelling," I said. I always stuck my horses' feet in a bucket of cold water if they came up lame.

Stephen's head grew heavier and heavier against my breast. Aunt Fanny and I decided to put him to bed and sent for his valet to come and undress him. Before Matthews arrived, however, Dr. Montrose came into the room, wheezing slightly from his climb up the stairs.

I said Stephen's name in his ear to wake him up.

"What are you trying to do to yourself, young feller?" Dr. Montrose said as he came over to stand in front of Stephen's chair.

Stephen tried to smile, but he couldn't quite manage it.

The doctor looked closely at the wound and said, "Very neat work, Fanny. You've got it cleaned up beautifully. I'll just put a plaster over it to hide the bald spot."

Aunt Fanny said, "I took off as little hair as I could."

"It's a good thing I'm not vain," Stephen said thickly.

His attempt at humor heartened me considerably. He had been so quiet and docile under our ministrations that I had begun to be seriously frightened.

Dr, Montrose looked at the ugly bruise on

Stephen's temple. "Same place as the last time," he said in a noncommittal tone.

"Yes," I said.

He tilted up Stephen's chin and looked into his eyes. "Hmm," he said. "Was he knocked unconscious at all, Annabelle?"

"Yes. Jem Washburn said he was unconscious for about fifteen minutes."

"How does your head feel, Stephen?" Dr. Montrose asked.

"It hurts like hell," Stephen said. "And I've got this ringing sound in my ears."

The doctor held up two fingers. "How many fingers am I holding up?"

Stephen squinted at them. "Four?" he said tentatively.

Dr. Montrose looked at me. "Definitely a concussion. Put him to bed, Annabelle, and keep him there for at least three days."

Stephen was outraged. "I can't go to bed for three days!"

"You can and you will," I replied firmly.

"How serious is a concussion, Martin?" Aunt Fanny asked.

"It's very serious if it is ignored," Dr. Montrose replied. "Ask Annabelle. She knows what happened to Henry Marfield."

"Who is Henry Marfield?" Aunt Fanny said to me.

"A friend of Sir Matthew's who used to hunt with us a few years ago," I replied. "He tried to jump a tree trunk in the woods, came off, hit his head on another tree when he landed, and was unconscious for a while. Just like Stephen. Dr. Montrose told him to go to bed,

329

but he wouldn't listen. He died while he was driving home from Stanhope two days later. Just dropped dead on the seat of his phaeton."

"Apoplexy of the brain," Dr. Montrose said.

"What an encouraging example," Stephen murmured.

"Yes, well, that is why you are going to stay in bed for three days," I said.

A voice from the doorway said deferentially, "Excuse me, my lady, but do you still need me?"

"We certainly do, Matthews," I said to Stephen's valet. "Come in. I want you to undress Mr. Stephen and put him to bed."

"Come and have a glass of port before you drive home, Martin," Aunt Fanny said.

"I can't, Fanny. I have a few other patients I must attend to before I can afford to relax with a glass of port."

"Some tea, then," Aunt Fanny said.

"Tea would be welcome," Dr. Montrose conceded.

The two of them began to walk toward the door, but before she went out, Aunt Fanny turned to me. "Will you join us, my dear Annabelle?"

"I will be with you shortly," I said. "Will you be in the morning room?"

"Yes," said Aunt Fanny, and she and Dr. Montrose went out and closed the door behind them.

"After you put Mr. Stephen to bed, I want you to stay in this room," I said to Matthews. "Under no circumstances are you to leave Mr. Stephen alone."

Matthews's prominent blue gray eyes bulged,

giving him the distinct look of a fish. "Yes, my lady," he said.

"I hardly think that is necessary, Annabelle," Stephen mumbled.

"I will be the judge of that," I returned.

He frowned. He looked so ill that all my fears came rushing back. I returned to his chair and cupped his face gently between my palms. "Will you please just rest?" I said. "Don't try to think about anything. Just rest."

His almost black eyes lifted to mine. He was still frowning.

"It will make me feel so much more comfortable if Matthews stays," I said. "Please, Stephen?"

His eyes drifted away from mine as if he couldn't keep them focused for any length of time. "All right," he said wearily.

I bent and touched my mouth to his. "I love you," I said, too softly to reach the ears of the waiting valet.

The corners of Stephen's mouth quirked as he tried to smile.

Downstairs, in the back passageway, I spied Jem Washburn, now garbed respectably in one of Jack's shirts. He was in the process of opening the back door when I called out his name. His hand fell away from the latch and he turned to face me, a distinctly wary expression on his bony face.

I stopped perhaps three feet away from where he stood in front of the door and surveyed the man from the top of his untidy black head to the tips of his decently polished boots. I crossed my arms. "I should like to know what you were doing on that particular path this morning, Jem," I said in a voice that I meant to sound pleasant but didn't come out that way.

Jem's mouth tightened. "I was by way of paying a visit to Marietta Adams." The hostility in his voice exactly matched the hostility in mine. "We are to be married, in case Your Ladyship has not heard."

"I heard," I returned. "I think it is wonderful, Jem, that you should have become so prosperous during the five years that Stephen spent in Jamaica. So prosperous, in fact, that George Adams finds you an acceptable suitor for his daughter's hand."

There was a slash of sunlight coming in through the small round window that was set over the back door, and it brightened the vestibule enough for me to see how white Jem had gone under his tan at my words.

"You blame me for Stephen's bein' sent to Jamaica, don't you, Miss Annabelle?" he said, reverting in the emotion of the moment to the name he had always called me.

I took a step closer to him. "Weren't you to blame?" I demanded.

He went, if possible, even paler. "Yes," he said in a choked-sounding voice. "I was."

"You were the one on the path that night, weren't you?" I said contemptuously. "Stephen was never involved with smugglers."

"Yes," he said again. "I was the one on the path." He tossed his head to get a lock of curly black hair off his forehead, and the gesture vividly brought back to me the boy he had been.

"He was your friend," I said passionately.

"Your only friend, Jem. How could you have taken advantage of him like that?"

Jem looked utterly wretched. "He made me," he said.

I snorted with disbelief.

" 'Tis true, Miss Annabelle. He may seem soft and mild, but you know what Stephen is like when he makes up his mind. A hundred horses couldn't move him."

I had to admit to myself that this was true.

Jem continued, the words spilling out of him as if they had been dammed up for a long time. "He knowed I was involved with the smugglers, and he learned that someone had informed on the shipment of brandy that was coming into the cove that night. He come to meet me in the Ridge woods and told me to get away home on foot, that he would take care of hiding the brandy. I didn't want to switch places with him, but he kept at me and at me and... well, I finally let him take my place."

I had always known that was what had happened.

"Noble of you," I said scornfully.

"It was a coward's trick. I don't need you to tell me that!" Jem flashed back. "But Stephen... he made it seem so *sensible* like. If I was caught, I would be transported—or even hung—whereas he, being the son of an earl an' all, would probably get off with nowt but a warning. That is what he said to me, Miss Annabelle, and that is what I believed when I let him take my place on that path. I was that shocked when I learned that he was bein' sent to Jamaica!"

I moved in closer to him, using my words like a knife. "Not too shocked to step forward and take responsibility for your own actions."

Jem ran his fingers through his tangled hair, and I noticed he had Stephen's blood caked under his nails. "You see," he said, "Stephen smuggled a message t'me by one of the footmen."

I stared at him in frozen silence. "He smuggled you a letter?" I finally said.

Jem nodded.

My heart felt scalded. Stephen had sent a message to Jem and not to me. "What did this message say?" I managed to croak.

"He said I was t'lie low and say nowt. If I tried to say I was the smuggler, Stephen would call me a liar. He would say I was only trying to help him out."

I had to make certain I was hearing correctly. "He sent you this message after he was locked into his room?"

Jem nodded his head.

Stephen had sent a message to Jem and not to me.

"He said they told him that he would only have to stay in Jamaica for one year," Jem said. His deep-set eyes bored into mine, and his voice took on an accusatory note. "The only reason he stayed away so long was because you went and married his brother."

I stared at him in horror. "What did you just say?"

"I said the only reason he—"

"No," I interrupted sharply. "I mean the part about Stephen's having to remain in Jamaica for only a year."

"That is what he wrote to me," Jem said.

"At least five years," my mother had told me.

In my heart, shock began to be replaced by rage.

Jem was hurling words at me. "How could you do it to him, Miss Annabelle? I was his friend, yes, but he loved you. I never seen two people what was as close as you and Stephen. How could you have done that to him, Miss Annabelle? How could you?"

"How could you have done this to me, Annabelle?" Stephen had said.

I backed up a few steps. I looked away from Jem's accusing eyes to the brass umbrella stand that stood beside the door and said unsteadily, "What is between Stephen and me is no business of yours."

In the ensuing silence I continued to stare at the umbrella stand as if it had a basilisk's eye and I could not look away.

Jem's voice said grimly, "You're not my business, but Stephen is. And I'll tell you now, Miss Annabelle, I think someone was hiding in them woods waiting for him."

The spell broke and my head snapped up. "Why do you say that?" I asked sharply.

Jem rubbed his hand up and down across his face. "For one thing," he said, "Stephen wouldna have loosened his girth. And for another thing, there weren't no puppy loose in them woods. I heard a noise all right when I was kneeling next to Stephen on the road, but the noise sounded to me suspicious like a bridle jingling as someone went away through the woods."

My hand flew to my throat. "I knew it," I breathed. "Oh God. Someone loosened Magpie's girth while Stephen was in the woods looking for that puppy."

"I'd bet on it," Jem said. "In fact, I have a

335

fearful notion that if I hadna come along just when I did, someone would've clapped Stephen on the head and finished the job altogether."

Jem's face suddenly went out of focus, and white spots danced in front of my eyes. I shook my head, blinked, then blinked again, trying to clear my vision. I felt an arm go around my shoulders, and I let it guide me to the oak Jacobean chair that had been provided for visitors whose lack of rank dictated they come in the back door. I sat gratefully and leaned forward to put my head down.

After a moment the blood came back into my head and my vision began to clear. I breathed deeply and slowly.

"Should I call for someone?" Jem asked me in a rough voice.

"No." Once more I filled my lungs with air, exhaled, then filled them again. I looked up at Jem, who was standing next to me. "I'm all right. It was just the shock of hearing that my worst fears were true after all."

"Jesus, Miss Annabelle," Jem said in the same rough voice as before, "who could want to kill Stephen? He ain't been back long enough to get anyone that angry at him!"

I straightened my shoulders. "I don't know who it is, but I can tell you this, Jem. I am damn well going to find out."

Jem's voice when he answered held a note of reluctant admiration. "You will," he said. "When you make up your mind, Miss Annabelle, you're every bit as stubborn as Stephen."

I sat back in the chair, not quite ready yet to trust my legs.

Jem said. "He shouldna be left alone, even in his own room in his own house. D'you want me to go and sit with him?"

"I told his valet not to leave him alone."

"That fancy man?" Jem snorted in derision. "If you want, I can go home, change my clothes, and come back here to keep a watch in Stephen's room."

I looked up into his hard face and admitted to myself that I needed Jem as an ally. He had been right when he had said that his presence on the path this morning had probably saved Stephen's life.

I realized further that the loosened girth meant the end of my cherished smuggling theory.

"You think it's someone in this house, don't you," I said in a low voice.

"It looks that way, don't it."

I wet my too dry lips with my tongue. "But Jem...

why?"

"Find that out and you'll find the villain," he returned.

I didn't want to find out. I didn't want to find out that someone in my own family...

I shut my eyes.

"D'you want me to come back?" Jem asked.

I opened my eyes. "Yes," I said. He had half opened the door when I added, "Jem?" His head turned toward me again. "Bring some clothes and plan to stay for a while."

He nodded once, decisively, and went out the door.

CHAPTER
twenty-four

Jem came back as he had promised and spent the afternoon sitting in Stephen's room, arms folded, eyes trained unblinkingly on the doorway. I looked in at about five and told him I had ordered his supper to be sent to the room I had allotted to him down the hall and that I would sit with Stephen while he ate.

"I can eat in here, Miss Annabelle," he protested.

I shook my head. "It's going to be a long night." Then, when he still seemed inclined to protest, I added softly, "I'd like to stay with him for a little while."

"All right," he said gruffly, and went.

The windows in Stephen's room were open, and the fragrance of newly cut grass floated in on the late summer air. Stephen lay perfectly still, and I stood beside his bed and stared down at him intently, watching him breathe.

It seemed to me that his breath was coming much too quickly and lightly, and a rush of panic sent the blood pounding through my veins. What if he wasn't sleeping normally at all? What if he couldn't wake up? What if he never woke up?

"*Stephen!*" I said urgently. "*Stephen, wake up!*"

He didn't move, but I thought I saw his lashes flutter slightly. I put my hand on his shoulder and shook him none too gently. "*You have to wake up!*"

This time I was certain that his lashes fluttered. I called his name again and his eyes opened. He squinted up at me through what I knew must be a thunder of pain in his head. "Annabelle?"

He sounded groggy, but he was awake and he knew me.

I bent until my face was close to his. "I'm sorry I woke you, Stephen. Everything's all right. Go back to sleep."

His lashes closed. My knees felt shaky, and after a moment I went to sit in the chair that Jem had pulled close to the bed. It was an exceedingly uncomfortable chair, with a carved lion protruding from its heavy oak back, and I made a mental note to have a more comfortable chair brought into the room.

I sat up straight, so that my back wasn't pressing against the hard bumps that were the lion, and let my mind contemplate the information that I had learned from Jem.

I thought with bitterness of how my mother had misinformed me about the length of Stephen's exile. Five years, she had said. Five years or else he would face prosecution as a smuggler.

Stephen's hand was lying palm up on the light blanket with which we had covered him, and I leaned forward and rested my lips against it. I turned my head so that my cheek was cradled by his warm palm and closed my eyes.

And once more I am seventeen years old and my mother has told me that I am pregnant.

It was the day after Stephen's ship had sailed, and I excused myself after a dinner I had hardly touched and went to my room. Mama presented herself at my door ten minutes later, and that was when she confronted me with the cataclysmic news of my probable condition.

I stared at her in absolute shock.

"Whose brat is it, Annabelle?" Mama demanded.

I couldn't answer her. I couldn't speak at all.

"Is it Gerald's?"

Dumbly I shook my head.

My mother's mouth pinched together in a way that quite spoiled her beauty. "No, I suppose that would be too much to hope for," she said bitterly. "It's Stephen's, isn't it?"

I felt so cold that goose bumps had come up on my arms and I hugged myself for warmth. "Y-yes," I stuttered. "It is Stephen's."

Mama had moved me out of the nursery when I turned sixteen, and we were standing now in front of the fireplace in my new bedroom, which was located halfway down the passage on the second floor. Its placement had been extremely inconvenient for Stephen and me, as I was forced to go past half the bedroom doors on the floor before I could reach either of the staircases that would take me to the relative safety of the third-floor nursery and Stephen.

Mama's eyes were as hard and as cold as emeralds. "We left you and Stephen alone for too many years, didn't we, Annabelle?" she said. Her perfectly chiseled nostrils were white with anger. "Weston and I always assumed that the two of you were like brother and sister. And that is precisely what you wanted us to think, isn't it?"

I wet my lips with my tongue. "Yes," I said.

Mama's hands were opening and closing, as if they itched to feel my neck between them. "When I looked at you across the dining room table tonight, and I saw that skin..."

She broke off, incapable for the moment of articulating her fury. She looked wildly around, and her convulsive fingers closed around a small china shepherdess that was perched on a table close by. She picked up the delicate figure and hurled it against the brick of the chimneypiece, smashing the fragile china into a hundred pieces.

I jumped.

"God," my mother said, able to speak now that she had vented some of her temper by an act of violence. "How could you be so *stupid*, Annabelle?"

I lifted my chin and said bravely, "I love Stephen, Mama, and he loves me."

"Oh yes," my mother said sarcastically. "He loves you so much that he got himself involved with smugglers and then sailed off to Jamaica to save his skin." She looked at me out of coldly calculating eyes. "Tell me, Annabelle, did he communicate with you before he left?"

I looked down at my feet so she couldn't see the expression on my face.

"He didn't."

There was a curious note of satisfaction in my mother's voice, and I looked up and said passionately, "You wouldn't let him see me! You locked him in his room and wouldn't let him talk to anyone!"

"That was the bargain Weston made with the authorities," Mama said. "They didn't want to take a chance that Stephen would communicate with his smuggling confederates."

"As if *I* were a smuggling confederate!" I cried.

"Stephen could have communicated with you if he had wanted to," my mother said scornfully. "If he was unable to see you in person, then he could have sent you a note." There was a pause as she scanned my face. "He didn't even do that, did he?"

I looked away.

My mother was ruthless in following up her advantage. "How do you defend that kind of behavior, Annabelle?"

How does one defend the indefensible?

I shook my head and didn't reply.

There were two wing-back chairs placed on either side of the fireplace in my room, and Mama walked around the table with its missing figurine and sat in one of them. She gestured for me to take the other, which I did gratefully. Both my legs and my stomach were feeling noticeably unsteady.

Mama regarded me across the deep blue Turkish rug upon which the chairs reposed. She said disdainfully, "This is a very pretty situation, I must say. My daughter is pregnant and the father of her child has been shipped off to Jamaica because he was about to be arrested as a smuggler."

"For how long must Stephen remain in Jamaica?" I asked in a voice that sounded far more vulnerable than I wanted it to.

Mama pushed a piece of broken china away from the chair with her foot. "God knows," she said. "The authorities said only that he would be arrested if he returned to England. I know that Weston feels that Stephen must remain in

Jamaica for at least five years before we can hope to bring him home safely."

"Five years!" Five years seems an eternity when one is seventeen.

"You will have to marry someone else," my mother said.

I stared at her in horror. "I can't do that!"

"Do you want your child to be a bastard?"

I pressed my hands to my temples, which had started to throb. "No, of course I don't want that."

My mother pressed on relentlessly. "Do you want us to put you on a ship for Jamaica? Can you face the thought of being seasick for two months, Annabelle? Of perhaps not surviving the journey at all? Does Stephen deserve such a sacrifice from you when he went off and left you without a word?"

I knew the answer to that last question without having to think about it at all. I dropped my hands, stiffened my back, and lifted my chin. "No, Mama," I said. "He does not."

"Then," my mother said, "you must marry someone else."

I moved my hands nervously on the tapestry arms of my chair. I chewed on my lower lip.

"Don't do that!" Mama said. "There is nothing so offputting to a man as chapped lips."

I stared at her in frightened bewilderment. "What do you mean that I must marry someone else?" I said. "Who will marry me when they learn that I am carrying Stephen's child?"

"There is no reason for your husband to ever know that the child you are carrying is not his," my mother said.

My head was throbbing with pain. "You aren't making any sense, Mama," I said wearily.

Mama had made an impatient noise. "Sometimes, Annabelle, I think that you are too stupid to live! Now pay attention to me and I will tell you what you are going to do."

Stephen's hand was warm under my cheek. I turned my head and dropped another soft kiss into his palm.

I should have followed you to Jamaica.

If Mama had not intervened, I thought, it would have been weeks, perhaps months, before I suspected that I was pregnant. By the time I did, it would have been too late for me to think of tricking anyone. I would have been forced to go to Stephen in Jamaica.

And all along she had known that Stephen's exile was for only one year!

If I had resented her interference before I learned this news, you might imagine how I felt about her now.

I raised my head and looked down into Stephen's sleeping face.

Why didn't you talk to me before you left? I thought, not in anger, but in pain. We would have been saved so much anguish if only you had talked to me.

His face gave me no answer.

Fifteen minutes later Jem returned, and I went downstairs to my dressing room to change for dinner.

Stephen slept for twenty-four hours straight. I was so afraid that he was dying that I woke him up every four or five hours just to make certain that he was able to be awakened and that he knew me.

Jem refused to relinquish his watchdog duty to Matthews for even a few hours, so I had a trundle bed set up in Stephen's room so Jem could get some sleep.

Nell was visibly upset by Stephen's injury and spent far too much time hovering around his room.

Aunt Fanny was upset by Nell's distress and actually became quite sharp with her daughter in her attempt to keep Nell away from Stephen.

Nell became hostile toward her mother.

The evening of the day after Stephen's accident, after Stephen had finally awakened and was able to sit up and eat something, Giles said to me in a small, frightened voice, "Mama, I think that someone is really trying to kill Uncle Stephen."

I was sitting in the big nursery rocker, reading a book to him. Giles was squashed in next to me, too big and too old to sit in my lap, yet young enough to still need the reassurance of feeling me close.

Slowly I looked up from *Robinson Crusoe*. Giles had not been paying much attention to the story, and now I understood why.

"Do you think so, Giles?" I asked carefully.

He ran his finger up and down the edge of the book's leather binding and wouldn't meet my eyes. "Yes," he said.

God, I thought, How did one go about telling one's five-year-old child that someone was trying to kill his uncle?

I began cautiously, "These accidents may seem suspicious, Giles, but..."

He tilted his head, looked up at me, and said angrily, "Don't lie to me, Mama. I'm not a baby."

I looked into the eyes that were so like mine, and I knew that if I lied to him now, he would lose all trust in me.

I sighed. "Well then, if you want the truth, it certainly does look as if someone is trying to kill Uncle Stephen, darling."

Now that he had the truth, he shivered and his firm little body pressed closer to mine. "I'm afraid, Mama. Who is going to take care of us if something happens to Uncle Stephen?"

I placed the book on the floor and put my arm around my son. "Nothing is going to happen to Uncle Stephen," I said. "And I will always be here to take care of you."

I rocked the chair gently back and forth.

Giles hid his face against my shoulder and said in a muffled voice, "Do you like Uncle Stephen, Mama?"

"Of course I like Uncle Stephen," I said, continuing to push the rocker with my foot.

"Do you like him *very much?*"

A warning bell went off in my brain. "Yes," I said calmly. "I like him very much."

"Do you like him better than me?"

I stared at the blue-and-white tile of the schoolroom fireplace and thought carefully about my answer. Stephen's whole future relationship with his son might depend upon what I said now.

I stopped rocking and said to Giles, "I will never like anyone better than you. I may like Uncle Stephen *as much* as I like you, but it is a completely different kind of liking. The love I have for you is very special and it belongs to you alone. No one else will ever have it."

"You look happy when you're with Uncle Stephen," Giles said in an almost but not quite accusatory tone.

I dropped a kiss on his sunny blond head. "I *am* happy to be with Uncle Stephen," I said. "We were best friends when we were children, and I have missed him very much."

Silence. The small body pressed against mine felt stiff, not relaxed. Clearly my words had not reassured him.

I said, "When you grow up, Giles, you will fall in love with a girl and you will marry. Will you love me any less because you have a wife?"

His head lifted from where it was buried in my shoulder. "Of course not, Mama!"

"We have a special place in each other's hearts, and that place can belong to no one else. Isn't that true?"

"I suppose so." His words were certainly not a ringing affirmation, but I felt the rigidity drain from his body and he became more cuddly.

But the filial inquisition was not yet over. "Are you going to marry Uncle Stephen, Mama?"

Good God! I thought. I haven't had time to prepare answers to these kinds of questions!

"Would you dislike it very much if I did?" I asked cautiously.

"I suppose you will have to marry someone," my son said regretfully, "and Uncle Stephen is probably the best. At least he listens to me. Not like Jack, who only listens to Genie!"

"We haven't decided anything, Giles," I said,

"so please do not go around telling everyone that Uncle Stephen and I are going to be married!"

"Everyone knows it already," Giles returned placidly.

It was my turn to stiffen. "Who is everyone, pray?"

"Mrs. Nordlem and Hodges and Cook, Mama. I heard them talking in the kitchen yesterday."

I was horrified.

Giles must have sensed my distress, for he hastened to assure me. "They were happy about it, Mama. They all like Uncle Stephen."

"I am relieved to hear that."

The irony passed right over Giles's head. "You can't marry Uncle Stephen if he is dead, Mama," he pointed out. "I think we should find the bad man who is trying to kill him."

"That is an excellent idea, darling." I began to rock the chair again.

"But how can we do that, Mama? Weston Park is so big! He could be hiding anywhere."

I realized that my son had no inkling that the enemy he sought might lie within the house and not without.

"I don't think any of us should go out until that man is caught," Giles said. His voice had lost its usual assertive timbre. "It isn't safe."

"You will be perfectly safe, darling, as long as you aren't with Uncle Stephen," I said.

"I don't *like* it that a bad man is after Uncle Stephen," Giles said.

"Nor do I, darling," I said. "Nor do I."

We rocked in silence for a few more minutes, and then I picked up *Robinson Crusoe* and began once more to read.

It was not until I was reflecting upon this conversation in the quiet of my own dressing room that it occurred to me how odd it was that Giles had never once expressed dismay that another man would be taking Gerald's place.

The house was very quiet for the two days after Stephen's accident. The refurbishing of the Dower House was nearing completion, and Aunt Fanny spent much of her time at her own home, supervising the finishing touches. She kept a reluctant Nell with her.

Adam was out about the estate for most of the day, and he took Jasper with him so that his soldier son could get some firsthand knowledge about how to administer his own property.

Jack and I spent hours in my office, making plans for the projected stud farm.

Stephen remained in bed under the eagle eye of Jem Washburn, who was still sleeping on a trundle bed in Stephen's room so he could be near his charge at night. Stephen protested mightily, but the fact that he allowed me to cajole him into remaining in bed was a testament to the fact that he still was not feeling very well.

I also thought that my story about Henry Marfield had had a salutory effect.

On the evening of the prescribed third day of rest, the ringing in Stephen's ears finally ceased. The following morning I found him at the breakfast table, fully dressed and eating steadily, if not heartily.

"That ringing was driving me mad," he confessed.

"What about the headache?"

"It's better."

"Is it gone?"

"Not quite. But it's considerably better."

He certainly looked better—if you discounted the ugly lump on his forehead and the bruises under his eyes. But his color was definitely improved, and his eyes were their usual shade of blue.

"It's a miracle you didn't break your nose again," I said.

"Believe me, I would have taken a broken nose to another pop on the forehead any day," he returned.

"That is true."

We were alone in the dining room except for the footman standing at the sideboard, which was loaded with silver dishes of eggs, bacon, kidneys, lamb chops, and muffins.

"James," I said, "will you bring us some more muffins?"

The silver basket standing not ten inches from James's arm was heaped with muffins.

"Certainly, my lady," James said in a wooden tone.

"Close the door on your way out," I said.

"Certainly, my lady," James said again.

As soon as the door was closed and we were private, Stephen said with amusement, "What was that all about?"

"I don't need any more gossiping among the servants," I said darkly.

"What do you mean?"

"Never mind. I didn't want to agitate you while you were feeling so poorly, but we simply cannot allow things to go on as they are,

Stephen! The next attempt on your life may be successful."

He sighed. "I realize that, Annabelle."

"Who is it, Stephen? Do you know?"

"Yes," he said, "I do."

"Tell me," I said steadily, and he did.

I didn't say anything when he had finished; I just shaded my eyes with my hands and stared at my coffee spoon.

"I kept hoping it wasn't true," Stephen said, "but the more I checked, the clearer his guilt became."

I nodded.

"When the man I sent to Northamptonshire came back, then I knew for certain."

I nodded again.

"Well... what do you want to do?"

"I know I should be feeling furious, Stephen," I said. "He tried to kill you, after all! But all I can feel right now is a terrible sorrow."

Stephen rubbed his forehead as if it hurt. "I know."

I bit my lip in indecision. "What do you think we should do?"

"I think we need to confront him."

I nodded. "And then?"

"Then... then we shall have to think of some way we can remove him permanently from Weston, Annabelle. I don't think you want to have him arrested?"

I shook my head.

"I'll talk to him," Stephen said. "You don't have to be there."

I straightened in my chair. "I have no intention of leaving you to face so unpleasant a task by yourself."

"Very well," Stephen said. The bruises under his eyes were looking darker. "We'll talk to him before he has a chance to leave the house this morning."

We heard a hesitant tap on the dining room door. Poor James didn't know if it was safe to come in or not.

"Come in!" I called.

James came in with a new basket of muffins, which he set next to the full basket that was already there.

"Your muffins, my lady."

I felt so sick to my stomach that I couldn't eat one of them.

I left a message with Hodges, and Stephen and I retired to the library. I told him about each of my new hunters, and he listened with apparent interest and exhibited the proper enthusiasm. But we were only marking time, and we knew it.

We had left the library door open, and our ears were so attuned that we heard the sound of the steps in the passageway at the same time.

We sat in tense silence, waiting. I was in the chair behind the desk, and Stephen was in the chair to my right. Two other chairs were grouped around the desk, one facing Stephen and the other facing me.

The steps stopped in front of the library, and then the partially open door opened all the way. A voice asked, "Did you wish to speak to me, Annabelle?"

"Yes," I said. "Come in, Uncle Adam, and shut the door behind you."

CHAPTER
twenty-five

He knew we knew. I could tell from his face as he came slowly into the library and took the big wing chair that faced the desk. He was ashen, but he tried to smile.

"It's good to see you out of bed, my boy," he said to Stephen.

The first flicker of anger licked through my veins. I looked at Stephen. His eyes were steady, his face was grave, and his voice when he spoke was very quiet. "I have been going through your books, Uncle Adam," he said. "And by my reckoning, during the past ten years you have embezzled at least forty thousand pounds from the Weston estate."

"Ah, Stephen," Adam said with regret. He looked old and very, very tired.

Stephen said, "It was the last big storm that made me suspicious. I went around to all of our tenants to check on the damage." Adam wasn't meeting Stephen's eyes; he was staring instead at the Turkish carpet at his feet. Stephen went steadily on, "The damage was extensive, Uncle Adam. Charlie Hutchinson's roof was leaking like a sieve, but according to the books, the Hutchinsons had received a new roof two years ago. Charlie told me that he had been asking you for a new roof for at least twice that long, but that you never authorized one. Yet our books identified a rather large amount of money that had supposedly gone for the Hutchinsons' roof."

Adam continued to stare at the rug, looking older and older with every word that Stephen spoke.

"You charged for a new well for the Martins and for new fences for the Thorpes, but neither of those improvements was ever done, were they, Uncle Adam?"

Slowly Adam removed his gaze from the carpet. "You know they weren't, my boy."

"The stream that flooded the Benningtons' house was never dredged, yet you charged the estate for the work."

"There is no need to detail all of my... subterfuges... Stephen," Adam said. "I do not deny that what you are saying is true."

I could hold in my feelings no longer. "How *could* you, Uncle Adam? We all trusted you! Relied on you! How could you betray us like that?"

He looked at me, and for the first time I saw a spark of life flare in his gray eyes. "I did it because I needed the money, Annabelle. Do you really think I could have afforded to buy Jasper a commission in the cavalry, or Nell a London Season, on the paltry salary that Gerald and his father paid to me?"

I blurted in surprise, "But you never seemed to be in need of money—"

My voice broke off, and I flushed. Stephen had just finished explaining precisely why Adam never seemed to need money.

Adam's lips curled in an ironic smile. He said, "I received a house to live in and a salary that kept us in food and clothing." The smile disappeared, and his lips pressed together to form a hard, straight line. "I did not want my children to end up like their father, a poor relation hanging on to the sleeve of his rich relative."

"Uncle Adam!" I was shocked. "No one ever thought of you that way!"

"Perhaps you did not, Annabelle," Adam said bitterly, "but Gerald and his father most certainly did."

I did not know how to answer him. I had always considered Adam to be a valued member of our family. Surely he was wrong!

Stephen's quiet voice filled the awkward silence. "Aunt Fanny's rich cousin never did exist, did he, Uncle Adam? You were the one who bought that property in Northamptonshire for Jasper."

"Yes," Adam said wearily. "I did."

Stephen went relentlessly onward. "You systematically charged the estate for materials that were never delivered. You regularly added large percentages to the bills for food purchased for the kitchen, and the additional amount went into your pocket."

I could feel my eyes growing larger and larger. "But I am the one who keeps the household accounts," I said to Stephen. "Surely I would have noticed if something were amiss!"

Adam gave me a crooked smile. "I was very careful to provide you with bills for all of my purchases, Annabelle."

Stephen said to me, "There is nothing wrong with your books, Annabelle. There is always a bill to back up an expenditure; everything is neatly recorded and balanced." He looked back to Adam. "It is only when one starts to make

355

inquiries about the veracity of the bills that things begin to come apart. I made a number of such inquiries in Brighton, Uncle Adam, at a few of the shops which supply food to Weston. Their records of the amounts they sold to us were considerably lower than the amounts recorded in Annabelle's books."

"The sugar!" I exclaimed suddenly. "I always wondered how we could consume so much sugar!"

"I regularly doubled the sugar bill," Adam said. At this point he was looking exhausted.

The sheer audacity of the scheme took my breath away.

Adam said slowly, "I can't help wondering, Stephen, what it was that put you on to me. It was clear as can be that from the moment you first picked up my books you were looking for something. What was it that raised your suspicion?"

"I told you; it was the storm," Stephen said.

But Adam shook his head. "You were looking for embezzlement before the storm hit, my boy."

Stephen picked up a silver letter opener from the desk and balanced the length of it between his fingers. "That is true," he admitted.

"Why?" Adam demanded. "As you yourself just said, by themselves the books are perfectly in balance."

Stephen's grave blue eyes regarded Adam from across the barrier he had made of the letter opener. "It just seemed so odd to me that Gerald would name me and not you to be Giles's guardian," he said quietly. "The only explanation I could imagine was that Gerald suspected something was wrong with the way you were handling the estate."

Adam's travesty of a laugh made me wince. "Now there's an irony worthy of a Greek dramatist," he said. "Is that really the reason you suspected my bookkeeping?"

Stephen lowered the letter opener until it hovered only a few inches above the top of the desk. "You must admit that Gerald and I were hardly the closest of brothers."

"Oh God," Adam said. He rested his gray blond head against the back of his chair and closed his eyes. "He didn't name me, Stephen, because it would never have occurred to Gerald to name his *agent* to be his son's guardian. That is all that was involved in that decision."

He looked so old, so tired, so... defeated. I heard myself saying, "I'm sorry, Uncle Adam." And, strangely enough, I was sorry. Sorry for what he had done and sorry that he had felt compelled to do it. Most of all, I was sorry for all the years of liking and trust that had been destroyed today by Stephen's disclosure.

But Uncle Adam's embezzlement was only the tip of the iceberg. The other person Stephen and I had summoned to meet us in the library today was infinitely more dangerous than poor Uncle Adam. The person we were awaiting now was not an embezzler, but a killer.

"What are you going to do with me?" Adam asked Stephen.

The library door began to open.

"Wait," said Stephen, "and see."

The door swung open all the way, and Jack stood upon the threshold. From Jack's place in the doorway, Uncle Adam would be completely hidden by the wing chair in which he was sitting.

"Annabelle," Jack said with pleasure, and began to advance into the room.

"What the devil are you doing here, Jack?" I said crossly.

He halted in surprise, but by now he was abreast of Adam's wing chair.

"Oh, I say, I'm sorry," he apologized. "I didn't see you, Adam. I was just going to talk to Annabelle about an idea I had for the new stud farm." He looked at me. "I'll see you later, shall I?"

He went quiet as he realized that both Stephen and I were staring past him at the next person who had appeared in the doorway.

"Come in, Jasper, and close the door behind you," Stephen said. He gestured to the chair on the opposite side of the desk from him. "We need to have a talk."

Jack backed slowly up to the wall, leaned his shoulders against, it, folded his arms, and prepared to stay.

"Jasper, my boy," Adam said heartily.

Jasper came forward, his bearing military straight. "Are we having a family conference?" he said lightly, but his gray eyes, so like his father's, looked wary.

When Stephen did not immediately reply, I said rashly, "We are gathered here to discover which one of us has been trying to kill Stephen."

The silence in the room was nerve-racking.

Adam broke it, saying quietly, "Are you saying that you have reason to believe it is one of us?"

"Yes, Uncle Adam," I said. "That is what I am saying."

Adam's eyes moved from my face, to Stephen's, to Jasper's, until they finally came to rest upon Jack. He said, "If someone in this room is truly guilty of such a terrible thing, Annabelle, it is Jack who has the most compelling motive."

Jack's face was impassive; he said nothing.

"If something happened to Stephen and Giles, he would be the next earl," Adam continued. "That is a powerful motive indeed. Especially for someone as purse-pinched as Jack is."

Stephen spoke quietly. "I do not think that the attacks have been directed against Giles. He was involved only because on two of those occasions he happened to be with me."

Jack spoke from his post along the wall. "Killing Stephen and not Giles wouldn't do me any good at all."

"How do you know the attacks weren't aimed at Giles?" Jasper asked suddenly. "Rigging the boat had to be aimed at him. Giles is the one who has been fishing all summer long."

Stephen carefully placed the letter opener he had been holding back on the polished mahogany wood of the desk. He said, "I know because when the shooter in the woods missed me, he didn't follow up his advantage by coming after me to try again. He didn't want to risk being seen by Giles because he didn't want to have to kill the child."

"He may not have come after you because he thought you had a gun," Jasper said.

"Everyone in this room knows very well that I never go out with a gun," Stephen returned.

Jasper shifted on his feet impatiently. "You say you can name this would-be killer, Stephen. Well, I for one would like to know how you plan to do this. Do you have any evidence that would point to a person in this room attempting premeditated murder, as opposed to some poacher taking an accidental shot at the wrong target?"

"Yes," Stephen said. "I do."

Someone's breath hissed audibly. Adam came to attention in his chair. "What is this evidence?" he asked crisply.

"Jem found it on the path near where I had left Magpie," Stephen said. "Someone dropped it while he was loosening the girth on Magpie's saddle. When Jem showed it to me I recognized it immediately." His blue eyes met the gray gaze that was waiting for him on the other side of the desk. "It was a cavalry glove, Jasper. One of a pair I've seen you wear many times."

Jasper's eyes narrowed. He opened his mouth to reply, but before he could say a word, Adam cut in.

"I was the one who loosened the horse's girth, Stephen. Jasper had left his gloves in the stable, and I picked them up there, intending to give them to him when next I saw him. One of them must have fallen out of my pocket."

"*Papa, stop talking!*" Jasper hissed furiously.

Adam looked at his son. "I am sorry to have embroiled you in this business, Jasper," he said. "But you see, Stephen has discovered that I have been embezzling from the estate. I knew he was on to me, and I wanted to stop him."

Jasper's face was a mask of white rage. "Papa, will you please just *stop talking!* There were no cavalry gloves near Magpie! Stephen is trying to trick you!"

Jack said in a measured tone, "How do you know that there were no cavalry gloves near Magpie, Jasper?"

Jasper gave him a hard stare and did not reply.

Jack went on, "Is it because you know that you were not wearing cavalry gloves that day?"

"Don't be ridiculous," Jasper said contemptuously. "What would I have to gain by killing Stephen?"

"You knew your father was embezzling from the estate," Stephen said. "You didn't believe that story about your mother's rich cousin any more than I did. You were afraid I was going to discover Adam's fraud, and that is why you tried to kill me."

"That is ridiculous," Jasper said. He looked at me. "Surely *you* don't believe this malicious fairy tale, Annabelle?"

I said, "It is extremely painful for me to believe such a thing, Jasper, but someone is most certainly trying to kill Stephen, and it has become increasingly clear that the person must be someone residing within this household."

"And you have come to the conclusion that this someone must be me." Jasper's voice was indescribably bitter.

Adam said, "Of course it is not you, Jasper. I have already said that I am the guilty party. I saw ruin staring me in the face, and I acted to prevent it." He looked at Stephen. "I am very sorry, my boy, but there it is."

"I am sorry, too, Uncle Adam," Stephen said.

Jasper said in a hard voice, "You know very

well that my father did not try to kill you, Stephen."

Stephen said, "He has just confessed."

Jasper looked at his father. "You should never have jumped at the bait of those cavalry gloves, Papa. Stephen tricked you. There is no proof." He turned back to Stephen. "Is there, Stephen?"

Stephen's face did not change expression, but I could see the muscles tense beneath his deeply tanned skin. "No," he said, "there is no proof."

"I am responsible, of course," Jasper said. "Once you started digging into Papa's books, I knew the game was up."

"Don't listen to him, Stephen—" Adam began.

"*Enough*, Papa," Jasper said. His eyes no longer looked contemptuous or even angry; instead they looked as cold and bleak as a winter sky.

Adam took one look at his son's face and fell silent.

I looked around the room, at the beloved faces I had known since childhood. I think it was then that the reality of what was happening finally registered in my brain.

Jasper had tried to kill Stephen.

"How could you, Jasper?" I whispered, staring at him in undisguised horror. "How could you even think of such a thing?"

The merciless face that looked back at me was the face of a stranger. It was the sort of face a man might carry into battle, I thought, and it came to me then that killing was not as foreign to Jasper as it was to the rest of us.

It was Jack's voice that broke the sudden silence. "I don't imagine it was just Adam's

362

peccadilloes that spurred you on, was it, Jasper?"

For the space of several charged seconds, the eyes of the two cousins met across half the width of the room.

"You poor, besotted devil," Jack said, and to my stunned amazement he sounded as if he truly meant it.

I said, "What on earth are you talking about, Jack? Jasper tried to kill Stephen!"

No one answered me, but Stephen got up and came around to stand behind my chair, as if he were getting into position to protect me.

Jack pushed his shoulders away from the wall. "It is really very simple, my dear Annabelle. If Stephen were to die, Jasper knew he could count on becoming your next husband."

I looked from Jack, to Jasper's hard, closed face, and then back again to Jack. "Why on earth would he think that?" I asked in bewilderment.

Jack ambled slowly toward Stephen's now empty chair. "Because he knows you, Annabelle—as I know you. You would inevitably marry again, if only for the reason that you would want more children. With Stephen and Gerald gone, that would leave Jasper and me as the only remaining candidates for your hand. And as I have found someone else, the road would be wide open for Jasper."

Jack lowered himself with loose-limbed ease into Stephen's empty chair.

"What would stop me from marrying some-one else altogether?" I demanded.

Very slowly Jack shook his head. "Not you, Annabelle," he said. "Not you."

It didn't take me long to recognize that Jack

was right. Under the circumstances he had just described, I would most probably have ended up married to Jasper.

Jack said, "You would want to marry someone who was connected to Stephen; and Jasper, poor bastard, would end up living the rest of his life in a losing competition with a ghost."

Jack's professed sympathy for Jasper was making me angry. "He would have had my money!" I retorted.

Jack gave me his attractive, crooked smile. "Annabelle, darling, I can assure you that no one in this room is interested in your money."

Stephen's thin, strong hands closed reassuringly on my shoulders. "That's enough, Jack," he said softly.

Jack picked up the paper knife that Stephen had discarded earlier. The light from the window fell slantingly onto his hair, giving him an almost uncanny resemblance to Gerald. He said to Stephen, "Gerald did love her, you know, but she never even noticed. She only married him to punish you."

Stephen must have felt the tension in my shoulders, for he said again, "That's enough, Jack." This time his voice was crisply authoritative, and Jack fell silent.

Stephen went on, "It is ridiculous to blame Annabelle for Jasper's murder attempts, and you know it. He is a grown man, and his decisions are his responsibility, no one else's."

I stared intently at the small Chinese vase filled with tiny white roses, which was set on the far side of the desk directly opposite my chair. Stephen's thumbs rested on the bare nape of my neck, and the rest of his fingers were spread out, fanwise, across my shoulders. He said to Jack, "If you must assign blame for Jasper's cold-bloodedness, then blame the war, not Annabelle."

My head came up as I heard him echo my own thought of a few moments before.

Jack looked up at the sharp letter opener he still held between his fingers. He said, "There is that, of course."

Jasper spoke at last, his voice hard and tight. "Are you going to have me arrested?"

With difficulty, I brought myself to look at him. "Did you sabotage that boat, Jasper?"

"No." His mouth twisted wryly. "But it was the boating accident that gave me the idea that I might resolve my problem by doing away with Stephen." For a fleeting moment his eyes held mine. "I never intended to harm Giles, Annabelle. Please believe me when I tell you that."

I nodded and dropped my eyes away from his.

"None of this is your fault," I heard his voice assuring me. "I never would have done it for you alone. I was primarily trying to save Papa. And myself, of course. I didn't want to lose all the good things Papa's embezzled money had brought me."

Adam gave a small sound indicative of the purest agony, and my heart wrenched.

I tilted my head back so I could look up at Stephen. "We don't want any arrests, do we, Stephen?"

"No," he said. "There will be no arrests."

Uncle Adam sagged in his chair, as if a hundred-pound weight had been lifted from his shoulders.

"Annabelle and I have talked," Stephen went on, "and we think it will be best, Adam, if you take Aunt Fanny and Nell and go to live upon the Northamptonshire estate you have purchased."

"You... you are going to allow me to keep it?" Adam said incredulously.

"That is what Annabelle wants," Stephen said.

"My dear, my dear," Adam said.

"I do not consider that you were well treated by your family, Uncle Adam," I said. "And I do not want to see Aunt Fanny or Nell hurt."

"And what... of Jasper?" his father asked fearfully.

Stephen said, "As part of my inheritance from my mother, I own a plantation in Virginia. I am prepared to deed it over to Jasper, together with an adequate sum of money to start a new life in America."

Jasper stared above my head into Stephen's face.

Stephen said to him, "I freed all of the slaves as soon as I came into the inheritance, and you must promise me that you will run the plantation using only hired labor. I am hoping that if other owners see that a plantation can be run profitably without slaves, they will be inclined to follow your lead."

Jasper's level brows rose a quarter of an inch. "You expect me to be successful, then?"

"I know you will be successful," Stephen returned.

The two men looked at each other for a

moment longer in silence. Then Jasper said soberly, "I will do my best, Stephen."

He lowered his gaze from Stephen's face to mine, and the plea for forgiveness that he could not voice was vividly present in his eyes.

"Annabelle?" he said softly.

I thought of all the happy childhood hours that we had shared. I thought of all the letters I had written to him while he was in Spain. I thought of all the prayers I had said for his safety.

His gray gaze begged me for forgiveness.

I thought that he had tried to kill Stephen.

"I never want to see you again," I said.

And I meant it.

CHAPTER
twenty-six

I left the library to the men and climbed the stairs to the nursery to tell Giles that we had found Stephen's enemy. I thought it was extremely important for my son to know that his world was safe once more.

Giles listened to me with wide-eyed attention. His first question after I had finished speaking was, "Did Jasper want to kill me too, Mama?"

I said firmly, "No, darling, he did not."

He sat for a few moments, drumming his heels against the bottom rung of his chair. Neither Eugenia nor I corrected him. "What about the boat, Mama?" he said at last. "And the time he shot at me in the woods?"

"It seems that the boat incident really was an accident, Giles," I assured him. "Jasper said he had nothing to do with that. And he didn't shoot at you; he shot at Uncle Stephen. The only reason he didn't shoot again that day in the woods was that he didn't want to risk hitting you."

Giles was actually silent. He looked as if he were thinking.

"Where is Captain Grandville now?" Eugenia asked quietly.

I turned to her. "Jack is going to take him to Southampton and book his passage on a ship to America. Stephen is allowing him to take over a Virginia plantation that once belonged to Stephen's mother's family." I sighed. "It is a solution that has the dual advantages of getting Jasper out of the country as well as saving the family from a scandal that nobody wants."

Eugenia nodded gravely.

We were all sitting around the table in the schoolroom with Giles's letter books spread out before us. I had interrupted Eugenia's lesson when I came in.

I looked at my son. "Did you hear that, Giles? Uncle Stephen is sending Jasper away to America, so there is no chance that he will try to hurt any of us again. There is no murderer hiding in Weston Park, darling. It is perfectly safe for you to go out."

"I heard you, Mama," Giles replied, but his brow was puckered and he did not look reassured. "Did Jasper say why he wanted to kill Uncle Stephen?"

My immediate impulse was not to tell Giles about Adam. I did not want my son to feel as if he couldn't trust any of the members of his own family. "He was jealous of Uncle Stephen, Giles."

"Why would he be jealous of Uncle Stephen?" Giles asked in amazement. "Jasper was a soldier, Mama! He fought in the war!"

Obviously, in Giles's eyes a soldier rated far above whatever it was he thought Stephen might be.

I bit my lip, not knowing how to answer him without involving Adam.

"Was Jasper jealous because you liked Uncle Stephen more than you liked him?" Giles asked.

I looked into his bright eyes. I hesitated.

"He was!" Giles said triumphantly.

"Perhaps a little," I said cautiously.

"Poor Mr. and Mrs. Grandville," Eugenia said. "How distressed they must have been to discover this dreadful thing about their son."

"Yes," I said, seizing on the opening she had given me. "They are so distressed, in fact, that they have decided they can no longer remain here at Weston. They are going to go to live upon Mr. Grandville's estate in Northamptonshire."

"I don't want Nell to go away from Weston," Giles said preemptorily. "I like Nell. She plays with me."

"Nell has to go with her mama and papa, Giles," I said. "They will need her very much now that Jasper is going away."

After a few more protests, Giles conceded reluctantly that this was so, and I was successfully able to introduce a new topic of conversation.

I took my lunch in the schoolroom with Eugenia and Giles and then went back downstairs, hoping to find Stephen. Hodges told me that he had gone out with Uncle Adam, so I repaired to the morning room with the dogs. The French doors had been opened to let in the morning sunlight, but the sky had grown more clouded as the day progressed and the room was growing a little chilly. I went to close the doors, and when I turned back into the room I saw Aunt Fanny coming in the door from the passageway.

For as long as I live I will never forget the look on her face that afternoon. She was white as a ghost, and her bones looked as if they were in danger of protruding through her skin. I had a sudden, horrible premonition that this was how she would look when she was dead.

Well, it had to have been a little death to her to have discovered the truth about her beloved husband and son.

I moved forward, lifting my hands, ready to take her in my arms and offer her comfort, but her face stopped me after I had taken just one step. I said, "I know this has been as much a shock to you as it has been to me, Aunt Fanny. Please believe that I will do anything I can to help you and Nell."

She answered in a cold, formal voice that didn't sound as if it belonged to Aunt Fanny at all. "Thank you, Annabelle. I was wondering if I might take a few pieces of bedroom furniture from the Dower House—just until we can get settled. Adam tells me that the house in Northamptonshire is very sparsely furnished. I will return them to you as soon as I have made my own purchases."

"You may take—and keep—anything you wish," I said.

"You are very kind." She turned to leave.

"Aunt Fanny!" I cried in bewilderment. "Why are you behaving like this? Surely you don't think I blame *you*."

She spun around to face me, and at the sight of her glittering eyes my voice died away. "*You* blame *me?*" she said. "I should think not. It is rather I who should blame you, Annabelle!"

I stared at her stupidly. "I d-don't understand you," I stuttered.

"Jasper would never, never have done such a thing if he hadn't been so desperately in love with you," Aunt Fanny said fiercely.

I was speechless.

She took a step in my direction, staring at me in the way I fancy Hecuba must have stared at Helen when they chanced to meet in one of the palace rooms at Troy. Truth to tell, it was rather frightening.

I gathered my wits and spoke up in my own defense. "I never encouraged Jasper to love me. I never regarded him as anything other than a good friend. Good God, Aunt Fanny, I was a married woman until six months ago!"

"It was Gerald's death that encouraged Jasper to think he might have a chance with you," she said. Her voice changed, hardened. "Then Stephen came home."

I felt as if I were talking to a stranger. "Aunt Fanny," I said, "do you realize that Jasper twice tried to murder Stephen?"

She said, "You and Stephen have ruined the lives of both my children."

I was appalled. "That's not true!"

She swept on as if I had not spoken. "The biggest mistake I ever made was allowing Adam to remain here at Weston for all those years.

371

Neither Weston nor Gerald ever appreciated him. They never gave a thought to the fact that the salary they paid to him was insufficient for a gentleman who had a wife and two children to provide for."

I said in a tone I tried to make reasonable. "Did Uncle Adam ever talk to Gerald or his father about increasing his salary?"

Aunt Fanny said, "They forced him to embezzle that money."

I wasn't quite prepared to agree with that conclusion, so I simply said, "I certainly do not wish to see him punished."

"That is charitable of you, my dear," Aunt Fanny said.

Her tone of voice was an insult. I could feel the color flame into my cheeks. I waited a moment until I had my temper under control, and then I said, "I am sorry you feel this way, Aunt Fanny. Is there anything else?"

"No." She turned her back on me and started out of the room.

I waited until she was opening the door, and then I said, "If ever you feel that you can forgive me, please don't hesitate to come to visit."

I saw her falter, as if she would turn around. But then she merely nodded, opened the door, and walked out into the passageway.

I sat down on the pretty flowered sofa and began to shake. The spaniels must have sensed my distress, because they came over to sit at my feet. Merlin nudged my hand, and I bent over to pet him. The feel of his silky black coat under my fingers was soothing, and my heart gradually began to slow its beat. The sun came back out from under the clouds that had been covering it and fell on my back with welcome warmth.

I was still sitting there, with the spaniels curled at my feet, when the door that Aunt Fanny had closed behind her opened again and Stephen came in. He saw my distress instantly.

"Is it just Jasper or has something else happened?" he asked as he sat beside me on the sofa. I felt his shoulder touch mine, but I didn't turn toward him. Instead I gripped my hands together in my lap and stared at them as I told him about my interview with Aunt Fanny.

"As you can see, it has rather overset me, Stephen," I concluded carefully, still not looking at him. "It is very painful to discover that someone whom you thought cared about you doesn't really like you at all."

"Aunt Fanny does care about you, Annabelle," he said firmly. "It is just that at the moment she is very upset about Adam and Jasper. She knows they were wrong, but she feels obliged to defend them. And the only way she can defend them is by pushing the blame off on someone else. In the case of Adam, the guilty parties are Gerald and my father. In the case of Jasper, the guilty party is you."

I continued to stare at my hands with mesmerized fascination. "Jack thinks it was my fault," I said.

Stephen's hands gripped mine, and he turned me so that I was forced to face him. "Annabelle, nothing that has happened here at Weston is your fault."

I shook my head and looked at his neckcloth, still evading his eyes, knowing that what he said was untrue.

"I think Aunt Fanny hates me," I said, and my voice cracked.

At that, Stephen gathered me into his arms. "She doesn't hate you, love," he said. I could feel his chin resting against the top of my head. "It is just that Fanny is a mother, and her children must always come first with her. Once she has reconciled herself to Jasper's departure she will be friends with you again. You'll see."

I had never come first with *my* mother, but I had never minded. I had always known I came first with Stephen.

It's you and me, Annabelle. Just you and me.

My whole life had been built on that foundation. When it had been taken away, I had crumbled.

My face was pressed against his neck, and I breathed in the familiar, beloved scent that was so unmistakably Stephen. I shut my eyes and said in a muffled voice, "Stephen, why did you send a note to Jem that night and not send one to me?"

I felt the shock that went through him at my question. He didn't ask me to clarify which night I meant. I lifted my head so that I might see his face.

He wouldn't look at me. "When did you learn that I sent a note to Jem?"

"The day that you were thrown from Magpie."

"Ah," he said, "I see." He drew a deep, uneven breath and tried to speak normally. "Well, if you have learned that I sent a note to Jem, then you must also have learned why I acted as I did."

I said, "Stephen, I have always known that

you took Jem's place that night. I never for one moment thought that you were involved with smugglers."

I saw a muscle jump in his cheek.

I went on relentlessly. "But what I have never known is why you left for Jamaica without one single word to me."

He ran a nervous hand through his hair. "They would have hung him, Annabelle," he said desperately. "Too many free traders were smuggling gold to France, and feeling in the government was running very high against them. Jem would have been just a small cog caught in the great machine of their so-called justice. I couldn't let that happen to him."

"I understand that, but that wasn't my question, Stephen," I said levelly. "My question was: Why did you send a note to Jem that night and not send one to me?"

"Oh God," he said. He bent forward, his elbows on his knees, and buried his face in his hands to hide it from my view. "I should have. I knew that I had made a mistake the moment I learned you had married Gerald. It was the worst decision I ever made, not to see you before I left."

I waited.

The anguished voice went on, "You see, I was in no doubt at all about what I had to do. I _knew_ I had to save Jem's life."

I continued to wait, wondering what he was trying to tell me.

The fingers that were buried in the smooth darkness of his unfashionably long hair were cramped, the knuckles white. He said in a choked-sounding voice, "I knew that if you begged me not to leave you, I wouldn't be able to hold out against you. I knew that the only way I could keep my resolve to do what I had to do was to go away without seeing you at all." He dropped his hands away from his head, and I stared in astonishment at his ravaged face.

"Christ, Annabelle, I never dreamed that I would force you into marrying someone else!"

I looked at him with a mixture of doubt and wonder. I had lived my entire life on the premise that nothing I could say would ever divert Stephen from what his conscience dictated that he must do.

He was going on in the same agonized voice, "I thought that I would write to you from Jamaica and explain what had happened. They weren't going to let us marry anyway. I thought that if they saw that we remained true to each other for the year that I was away, that maybe they would relent and let us have our way."

They, I thought. I hadn't heard the pronoun used with that particular intonation in years. Used as Stephen had just used it, it meant quite simply all the people in the world who weren't Annabelle or Stephen.

At last he turned to look at me. "I was a fool," he said bitterly. "A bloody, selfish, blind fool."

I said, "Everyone knows that when you make a decision, a herd of wild stallions couldn't change your mind."

"That may be true about the stallions," he said. "It's not true about you."

Our eyes met and held.

I thought about the seventeen-year-old girl I once had been.

"I might have asked you to give Jem up," I whispered. "I don't know. I might have."

His mouth was tense. He nodded.

"I didn't know about the baby," he said, "but I should have thought of that possibility. I should never have left you that way. You were right to blame me, Annabelle. I almost ruined both our lives. I can understand it if you say you will never forgive me."

A muscle jumped in his cheek once more.

I wrenched my eyes away from his, got to my feet, and walked behind the sofa to the closed French doors. The sun was once more hidden behind the clouds that had drifted in from the Channel. I looked out at the darkened day and said, almost wearily, "Don't blame yourself too much, Stephen. The fault was more mine than it was yours."

I heard him getting to his feet. "No, love, that's not true."

Overhead it was cloudy, but the sky along the top of the Ridge was almost all blue. The afternoon would be fine.

I said, "I should have gone to the earl and told him the truth. I should have demanded that he send me to join you in Jamaica."

His voice was soft. "You would have done that, Annabelle, if I hadn't hurt you so unbearably by leaving you without even a message."

I fixed my eyes on the line of blue sky, and for the first time I faced the truth about my own conflicted motives. I said, "Jack was right. I married Gerald to punish you."

Stephen said, "Annabelle, you had every right to feel that I had deserted you."

I shook my head. "I was jealous, Stephen. I was jealous that you had chosen Jem over me."

I felt Stephen move behind me, and I swung around to face him. "I have been blaming Mama for pressuring me and lying to me, but my marriage to Gerald wasn't Mama's doing at all. I knew that it had been Jem on that path, and I knew why you had taken the blame for him."

Stephen was standing on the other side of the sofa, and we looked at each other over its curved camel-back. I said, "I wronged Gerald by marrying him when I knew I loved another man. I wronged you, whom I did love. And most of all, I wronged Giles by cheating him out of his real father."

Silence fell between us. A ray of sunlight broke through the clouds, slanted through the French door, and fell on the carpet at my feet. Stephen walked around the sofa and said quietly, "You do come first with me, Annabelle. You always have and you always will. And that is precisely why I didn't have the nerve to talk to you before I was sent away."

He held out his arms and I ran into them, knowing that I had come home at last.

We held each other as if we meant never to let go.

I shut my eyes and thought about what would have happened if I had succeeded in convincing Stephen to relinquish his heroic protection of Jem and stay home with me.

"Perhaps it was all for the best," I said in a low voice, my lips moving against his neckcloth. "If something terrible had happened to Jem, you never would have forgiven yourself."

His arms tightened convulsively. "Annabelle," he said, and I lifted my face for his kiss.

"There you are, Mama," said an all-too-recognizable voice from the doorway.

Stephen's arms dropped like stones. I turned slowly to face the door.

"What are you doing downstairs, Giles?" I inquired dangerously.

"Genie is talking to Jack, so I thought I would come and find you," my son replied with a sunny smile.

Obviously it was time to replace Eugenia as Giles's governess.

"Were you just kissing Uncle Stephen?" Giles asked curiously.

As I considered a reply, Stephen came to my rescue. "Yes, she was, Giles. Your mama and I are going to be married."

Giles half ran, half skipped across the room to us. "Oh good," he said. "Luke will be so pleased."

"Luke?" Stephen said.

"One of the footmen," I told him. "He is a particular friend of Giles's."

"He betted that you would marry Uncle Stephen in September," Giles explained. "All the footmen have taken a month, and Luke's was September."

"Oh, my God," I said.

Stephen began to laugh.

"You are going to be married in September, aren't you, Mama?" Giles asked.

"Think of Luke, Annabelle," Stephen said. "You owe it to him."

I smiled. "All right," I said. "I know my duty. September it will be."

EPILOGUE

Giles's sixth birthday festival was a good deal larger and more elaborate than his fifth had been. The previous year we had entertained our own servants and laborers and tenants; this year we added the local townspeople and yeomanry to the list. This meant that on festival day Weston Hall was crowded with almost five hundred people, all of whom Stephen and I had to feed and entertain.

For some reason, Uncle Adam and his family were in my thoughts for the whole of the day. They had played so large a part in this festival, for so many years, that their absence made them vividly present in my mind.

From what we had heard from Stephen's legal correspondent in America, Jasper was doing well. He had made an immediate impact on the social scene and was engaged to be married to an American girl whose father was one of the largest planters in Virginia. I learned this last piece of information from the letter I had back from Aunt Fanny when I wrote to invite her, Uncle Adam, and Nell to attend Giles's birthday party. In the same letter she had given me the news that Nell also was shortly to become engaged to be married.

"It was kind of you to think of us, my dear," Aunt Fanny had written, "but I think it best if we do not renew a relationship that ended so sadly for the both of us."

The tone of her correspondence had sounded more like her old self, which had lightened my heart considerably. I also thought that she was probably right, and I determined to make no further attempts to reach out to her. There were some things that simply could not be undone.

The rest of my family were on hand, however, and everyone joined in to make the festival run smoothly. Eugenia organized and supervised the children's games. I had been hesitant to ask her to do this, as she was five months pregnant, but she had insisted. To my astonishment, Jack had said he would assist her, so I did not need to worry about her overdoing it. I knew he would watch her like a hawk.

Eugenia's brother, Tom Stedham, was at Jasper's old post at the lake. Tom had come home from Jamaica the previous November, and Stephen had given him Adam's old position as agent for Weston. He had also given Tom the Dower House and a very decent salary.

Stephen and Tom were close friends, and they had devoted a great deal of time during the past year attempting to organize an effective Society for the Abolition of Slavery.

I felt safe in putting Tom at the lake, as Tom could swim.

Giles's new governess, Miss Manders, was supervising in the gallery.

My mother and the duke were holding court on the terrace for the long-suffering rector, his wife, Stephen's uncle Francis, and any other poor soul whom Mama felt was socially elevated enough to deserve a conversation with the ducal pair. Uncle Francis met me at the food table late in the afternoon and told me that Mama had spent the entire afternoon deploring the lack of a gala house party of London friends such as she and the earl used to invite.

"Obviously the rector and I are not up to her standard," he said with a laugh.

"I am so sorry, Uncle Francis," I apologized. "I had to invite her, you know, and for some reason, she came."

"Oh, you know Regina, Annabelle," he replied carelessly. "She is secretly delighted that you fall so far short of her achievements as a hostess."

I stared into his pleasant, kind-looking face. His eyes were exactly the same shade as Stephen's. I said slowly, "You know, I never thought of that."

The dark blue eyes twinkled. "She comes to make certain that you don't outshine her," he said.

I laughed. "She will always be safe from me on that score, Uncle Francis. Still, it was wretched of me to stick you with her. I apologize, but I didn't know what else to do."

"Don't worry about me," Uncle Francis said cheerfully. "I am hopeful that the lord will count the hours I spend with Regina and Saye as penance for my sins. I asked the rector what he thought about my chances of this, and he said he thought they were very good."

We both laughed.

I hadn't seen Stephen for hours, as we had separated earlier in the afternoon in order to greet as many people as we possibly could. I had done my duty faithfully, speaking to hundreds of smiling faces, but at six o'clock fatigue struck me with a suddenness and a violence that would not be denied, and I made my way through the house and into the morning room, where I collapsed on the sofa with my head on a pillow and my legs up.

I had felt this kind of exhaustion only once before in my life, and I knew what it meant.

I was carrying a child.

I folded my hands on my still flat stomach, closed my eyes, and thought about how wonderful it would be to hold a baby in my arms once more. My eyes filled with tears of tenderness.

Another sign of my condition, I thought. Ordinarily I was not the weepy sort.

I thought about how the soft fuzz of the baby's head would feel under my lips, and the happy tears began to trickle down my face. I sniffed and wiped at my face with my fingers.

How happy Stephen would be, I thought. He had been cheated out of his firstborn, but this baby would be unequivocably his.

Although, over the course of this past year, Giles had certainly become excessively attached to "Uncle Stephen." A memory of the two of them, laughing themselves silly during a snowball fight in the Weston garden at Christmastime last year, got the tears going once more.

Then I thought of the four new hunter prospects sitting in my stables, and my tears dried up.

I rubbed my hand up and down my stomach, assessingly.

I had four Thoroughbreds who needed to be taught to hunt, and Jack was so involved with his own stud that I couldn't expect him to give me any time at all. Stephen had said he would help me during cubbing season, because Sir Matthew never actually found a fox, but I was the one who was going to have to get these horses out and over fences.

This baby is scarcely started, I thought. There is no reason why I cannot hunt until January.

We would be leaving Weston in January anyway, because that was when Parliament opened, and as expected, Stephen had been elected the previous year to his uncle Francis's seat. This was the reason I had cut back on the number of horses I had bought to retrain; I now had only half the season to make them into hunters.

Last year Sir Matthew had tried to convince me to let Stephen go up to London alone, but I had refused. Home for me was not a place but a person, and I would accompany Stephen to London this January as well.

The door to the morning room opened and Stephen's voice said, "Are you all right, Annabelle?"

I turned my head to look at him, but otherwise I didn't move.

"I'm fine. Just a little fatigued, that's all. How did you find me?"

"Hodges saw you coming in here."

"The all-seeing, all-knowing Hodges," I said. Stephen came over to the sofa, and I moved my legs aside to make room for him. He sat down facing me and picked up my hands.

"You're never fatigued," he said.

"I think I have as much right to be fatigued as anyone else," I said with feigned indignation.

"You have the energy of a lioness. Is something wrong?"

"Of course not," I replied.

"Your eyes are too big and your cheeks are too thin," came the inexorable response. "What's the matter, Annabelle? Are you with child?"

"Damn it, Stephen!" I yelled. I struggled to sit up. "You could at least have given me the chance to tell you!"

"But you weren't telling me," he said with a grin.

"I've only just suspected it myself."

I had managed to get myself upright, and now I stuffed a loose pillow behind my back. "You took all the fun out of it," I grumbled.

"I'm sorry, love, I didn't mean to." He didn't look at all repentant. "I was just so excited at the thought that I couldn't keep my mouth closed."

I turned my hands so that our palms faced and our fingers entwined. "*Are* you excited, Stephen?"

The grin came back. "I certainly am."

I said softly, "I have just been thinking that I cheated you out of your firstborn, but that this baby will truly be yours."

He reached one of his arms around my shoulders to pull me against his side. I relaxed against him, feeling myself draw energy and strength from his slim, hard body.

He said thoughtfully, "Do you know, I have this niggling little feeling, Annabelle, that young Lord Weston is not going to be overly pleased to find that he has a competitor."

"It will be good for him," I said. "Giles needs

to learn that the world does not revolve around him." I paused. "At least not all the time."

We laughed.

A little silence fell as we sat peacefully, our bodies pressed together, each of us thinking our own thoughts.

"What are you going to do about those new horses you bought?" Stephen asked suddenly.

"There is no reason why I cannot hunt until we leave for London, Stephen," I said. "I hunted while I was carrying Giles."

I felt his body stiffen. I remained very still and said nothing.

He said tensely, "What if you have a fall?"

"I'll be careful, Stephen. I won't fall."

The silence that fell between us this time was strained, not peaceful.

"Jesus, Annabelle," Stephen said in a low, taut voice. "I'm afraid."

I answered reasonably, "I'm not stupid, Stephen. If I don't feel well, I won't hunt. If I need to jump a fence I'm not certain my horse can get over, I won't attempt it. I want this baby very much, and I am not going to do anything to endanger it."

"I know that," he said. The arm that encircled me was absolutely rigid. "But it isn't just the baby who will be endangered if you have a fall."

I thought of all the times that I had held my tongue when Stephen planned to do something that I feared might bring him into danger. I didn't say anything.

The silence stretched on.

Then, gradually, I felt the tension begin to drain out of his body. He drew a deep breath and expelled it slowly, as if he were commanding himself to relax. He said, "You must do what you feel you must do, Annabelle. I know how much pride you take in your hunters. I won't ask you to stay on the ground."

My own shoulders relaxed as the stress that I hadn't even realized I was feeling melted away. "Thank you, Stephen," I said softly.

He looked down at me and said ruefully, "I have to admit to you, Annabelle, that I find I don't much like it when the shoe is on the other foot."

So I knew that his thoughts had run parallel to mine.

"Now you can appreciate how heroic I have been for all these years," I said lightly.

He gave me an unshadowed smile. "I have always known you were heroic."

The morning room door opened and Hodges appeared. Stephen didn't remove his arm from my shoulders; he just turned his head and asked pleasantly, "What is it, Hodges?"

"It is time to present the bouquet of flowers to Miss Annabelle, Mr. Stephen," Hodges said. "And the tenants have another presentation they wish to make to you."

Stephen sighed, removed his arm from my shoulder, got to his feet, and turned to assist me. "Tell them we will be there in a moment, Hodges," he said.

Arm in arm the two of us walked together to meet our guests.

If you have enjoyed reading this large print book and you would like more information on how to order a Wheeler Large Print book, please write to:

 Wheeler Publishing, Inc.
P.O. Box 531
Accord, MA 02018-0531